Romancing
the Goddess

Romancing the Goddess

Three Middle English Romances about Women

✧ Marijane Osborn

UNIVERSITY OF ILLINOIS PRESS ✧ URBANA AND CHICAGO

FRONTISPIECE: Sequanna, Goddess of the Source of the Seine. Bronze statue of the Romano-Celtic period. Courtesy of the Musée Archéologique of the Ville de Dijon.

OPPOSITE CONTENTS: Isis Using Her Sky-Cloak as a Sail. Relief from Delos. Courtesy of the École Française d'Athènes.

ORNAMENT: A Castaway Queen. Drawing by the author based on an unidentified block print, probably fifteenth century, in *Medieval Feminist Newsletter* 22 (Fall 1996): 14.

Library of Congress Cataloging-in-Publication Data
  Romancing the goddess : three Middle English romances about women /
  [translated and edited, and with critical commentary by Marijane Osborn].
      p.   cm.
  Includes bibliographical references and index.
  ISBN 0-252-02350-1 (alk. paper).—ISBN 0-252-06655-3 (pbk. : alk. paper)
  1. English literature—Middle English, 1100–1500—Modernized versions.
  2. Women—Crime against—Poetry. 3. Romances, English. 4. Castaways—
  Poetry. 5. Women—Mythology. 6. Tales, Medieval. 7. Queens—Poetry. 8. God-
  desses. I. Osborn, Marijane. II. Emare. English. III. Bone Florence of Rome.
  English. IV. Chaucer, Geoffrey, d. 1400. Man of law's tale. English.
          PR2064.R66   1998
          821'.1080352042—dc21   97-4702
                                                            CIP

For Desi

Contents

List of Illustrations   ✧   viii

Preface   ✧   ix

1. Three Tales of Castaway Queens   ✧   3

2. The Romances Rhymed in Modern English   ✧   51

     Emaré   ✧   51
     Le Bone Florence of Rome (Part II)   ✧   91
     Custance (Chaucer's *Man of Law's Tale*)   ✧   126

3. Backtracking the Goddess:
    Ancient Sources and Analogues   ✧   173

4. Goddess of the Human Dawn: Her Status Now   ✧   227

Notes   ✧   249

Works Cited   ✧   283

Index   ✧   297

Illustrations

Sequanna, Goddess of the Source of the Seine ✧ ii

Isis Using Her Sky-Cloak as a Sail ✧ vi

Map ✧ 5

FIGURE 1.   The Lover Recognizing His Danger ✧ 35

FIGURE 2.   The Madonna and Child on a Ship
Governed by Angels ✧ 184

FIGURE 3.   The Virgin Mary as Queen of Heaven
(Madonna and Child in a Rosary) ✧ 194

FIGURE 4.   The Virgin of Guadalupe as Public Art,
with Roses (Woodland, California) ✧ 196

FIGURE 5.   Our Lady of Solitude ✧ 197

FIGURE 6.   The Blessed Virgin
Rescuing a Floundering Ship ✧ 198

FIGURE 7.   The Hand of God Descending from a Cloud ✧ 206

FIGURE 8.   The Great Goddess
Demonstrating Her Control ✧ 211

FIGURE 9.   Three Shamans (identification uncertain) ✧ 215

FIGURE 10. Woman in a Boat ✧ 216

FIGURE 11. Sedna Angry ✧ 217

FIGURE 12. Alexandrine Isis Protecting a Ship ✧ 223

Preface

THIS STUDY BEGAN with the desire to make available to a general audience the woman-centered romances translated here, three medieval stories of women cast adrift that are still the book's central feature. But while working on these stories I became more interested in their mythic than in their relatively recent folkloric qualities, and especially in the apparent antiquity of the idea of the woman adrift in flight from incest and how it resonates both with modern experience and with that entity we call "the Goddess." I became interested in the way the woman adrift and the forces that aid her can function for modern women as a founding myth. Eldon Kenworthy explains that "founding myths often form when a nation [or other group] deals with what turn out to be recurring or traumatic situations. Myths form around experiences that demand explanation or expiation" (17). At the individual level, no experience is more confusing than being innocently parted from family and society (whether actually or metaphorically), and no abuse is more disorienting to all parties concerned than incest, though it is the victim, usually female, who finds herself most helplessly "adrift." All at sea, without friends in whom she dares confide and without parents whom she can trust or respect (hence emulate), how can she find herself again? This traumatic situation, particularly effective as a metaphor because of the real occurrence of incest in so many lives, calls for a miracle, or a myth—a saving hand.

The present book proceeds from two associated ideas: first, that the plot of the young woman who is cast adrift in her flight from incest and saved from the sea eventually to find power again, the underlying plot of these three Middle English romances, has mythic status. This plot is traceable back to the beginnings of our era, at least, and linked both to real-life casting adrift and to rituals celebrating a goddess of sea and fortune. The second, associated, idea is that this ancient plot, handed down alongside Christianity and accruing only surface contamination from it, may serve a modern audience as a charter myth, located within our culture, linking us to the protective and empowering Goddess to whom many are attracted today.

Romancing the Goddess is thus intended for a wider public than most books on medieval subjects, as it presents in modern English the three woman-centered narratives ranging from well known (Chaucer's *Man of Law's Tale* about Custance), to moderately known (*Emaré*), to scarcely known at all (*Le Bone Florence of Rome*), and sets them into a continuum reaching back much further than previous studies have ventured—back, in fact, to the earliest extant representations of "the Goddess," hence the book's title. The first chapter introduces the romances and sets them into the historical context of their late medieval composition, including some related social conditions such as incest and other gendered violence; this chapter is "straight" scholarship. The second chapter presents the romances themselves in metrical modernizations that attempt to be as faithful as possible to meaning while imitating the surface structures of the original. The third chapter links them back to the late classical narratives in Greek and Latin from which the stories they tell clearly derive, and beyond those narratives to Goddess-related concepts. While based on research, this chapter follows a clear agenda that has little to do with scholarship. It seeks origins significant only to a particular phenomenon—the modern idea of the ancient Goddess—that is contemporary and more or less localized within a Western feminist culture. It attempts to furnish that phenomenon with a teleology, a perspective in time that "authenticates" it. When I thought that with this essay the book was complete, a friend's grilling on whether I had really said what I felt was important about its implications alerted me to the fact that I had not. The fourth chapter attempts to rectify that lack by situating the subject within current discourse about the Goddess and revealing my own voice (or voices, they not being univocal or wholly engaged with a single attitude) behind the exposition. This chapter is more personal than the others.

A study of this kind accrues more debts than may be acknowledged or even remembered, beginning with the exemplary powerful women of my childhood and those who later taught me to think independently. This is an opportunity to acknowledge more specifically the young woman who first brought the subject of "the woman adrift" to my attention, Carolyn Hares-Stryker, who has since published accounts of this figure's place in medieval folklore and fiction, and the later students, particularly Denise MacLachlan and Margarita Jansen, who have become intrigued by the topic and added to my understanding of it in significant ways. Professor Jane Chance was the first to encourage me to publish this material, suggesting the arrangement of chapters that I have adopted. Dr. Patricia Hollahan, my editor at the University of Illinois Press, has been encouraging, tactful, and above all patient ever since she inherited my book proposal from a previous editor, and the manuscript editor, Louis Simon, was both thorough and friendly. My brother Remington Stone read my arguments with care and my nephew Remington Stone (his son) provided technical information for which I am grateful. Miriam Robbins Dexter offered good advice along with a number of pertinent sources that I would never have discovered on my own. Bibbi Lee presented me with the best image of "the goddess adrift" that I have seen, the bronze statue of Sequanna that is now the frontispiece of this book, and put me in touch with a helpful curator at the museum in Dijon where the statue is kept. I am grateful to Liv Mjelde and Richard Daly for going to great trouble in getting me a photograph of the Swedish rock carving of a woman dancing in a boat. Dominique Poulain and Jean Cristofol joined me in stimulating discussions about the Neolithic, took me to visit the village of Les Saintes Maries sur Mer in the Camargue, and continue to furnish firsthand accounts of rituals of the Virgin in the south of France. Tippi Schwabe communicated similar news from Portugal. Dolores Warwick Frese and her sister, Sr. Hélène de Jesu, arranged for me to visit a seaside chapel in Brittany. Peter Nicholson was generous with copies of his articles on the *Man of Law's Tale*, including prepublication copies. Sally Harvey Fed-exed me an article of which I was in dire need. Mary Judith Dunbar provided information about Renaissance echoes of the myth. Susan Utreras offered a series of valuable suggestions for improving the verse translations, and both Michael Steffes and Joseph Aimone also offered useful criticism. Dr. Robert Shelton, the vicechancellor for research at my university, was supportive in several ways for which I am grateful, as I am to the regents of the University of California, for continued support of my research over the years, and the College of Letters and Science, Division of Humanities, Arts, and Cultural Studies, for a subvention toward support of publication needs. On a more personal level, acknowledgment should go to Eldon Kenworthy for navigational assistance long ago, and to Laurie Hatch who, like the hand of Isis, guided this book to shore.

Romancing
the Goddess

1.

Three Tales of Castaway Queens

A Woman in a Boat

WHEN ONE IS DEEPLY focused upon a subject it may happen that random encounters seem to echo that subject as though drawn to the person thinking about it. This happened to me as I was thinking hard about the castaway queens, protagonists of the three Middle English romances translated here, and how they appeared to be related to certain manifestations of "the Goddess," as many like to call her, thus capitalized, today. The single most striking image in these and associated medieval stories in other languages is the woman adrift in a boat, in which dire situation she often appeals to the Virgin Mary for aid. Having already written the body of the book, I was debating how to begin it, when powerful modern images of a woman in a boat came at me, it seemed, from everywhere.

First a friend lent me Michael Ondaatje's novel *The English Patient*, set on the coast of Italy at the end of World War II. Midway through the novel, a young soldier on night patrol is warned that enemy movement has been spotted in the water, so he should be especially on his guard. Seeing a dark outline out there—"he raised the rifle and held the drifting shadow in his sights for a full minute. . . . He had the shadow in his sights when the halo was suddenly illuminated around the head of the Virgin Mary. She was coming out of the sea. She was standing in a boat" (78–79). A moment later he sees that she is a five-foot tall plaster statue being held steady by two men as two others row, her halo illuminated by small battery lights. As she is lifted from the boat and brought ashore, "the people of the town began to applaud from their dark and opened windows. . . . This was Gabicce Mare on May 29, 1944. Marine Festival of the Virgin Mary" (79). (In the film version the virgin in a boat is replaced by a hand copying a cave painting of a woman swimming.)

Shortly afterwards, urged by another friend, I read George Eliot's mid-nineteenth century novel *The Mill on the Floss* for the first time, my scalp prickling when I came upon this conclusion to her made-up legend of the local saint: "Yet it was witnessed in the floods of aftertime, that at the coming on of eventide, Ogg the son of Beorl was always seen with his boat upon the wide-spreading waters, and the Blessed Virgin sat in the prow, shedding a light around as of the moon in its brightness, so that the rowers in the gathering darkness took heart and pulled anew" (117). The legend of Ogg and his shining Virgin, whom Eliot associates with the moon, takes hold of the novel as Eliot presents her young heroine "adrift" in the world, "Borne Along by the Tide" in one metaphorical chapter title (457), and in the end cast upon the raging flood. About the same time that I was reading Eliot a visual representation of the mythic scene was offered me in the Italian art film *Il Postino*, in which a prayer boat is launched bearing a statue of the Virgin Mary surrounded by votive candles. This time she is quite alone. Later in the film we see the little candlelit boat bobbing upon the choppy waves at night, haunting, evocative,

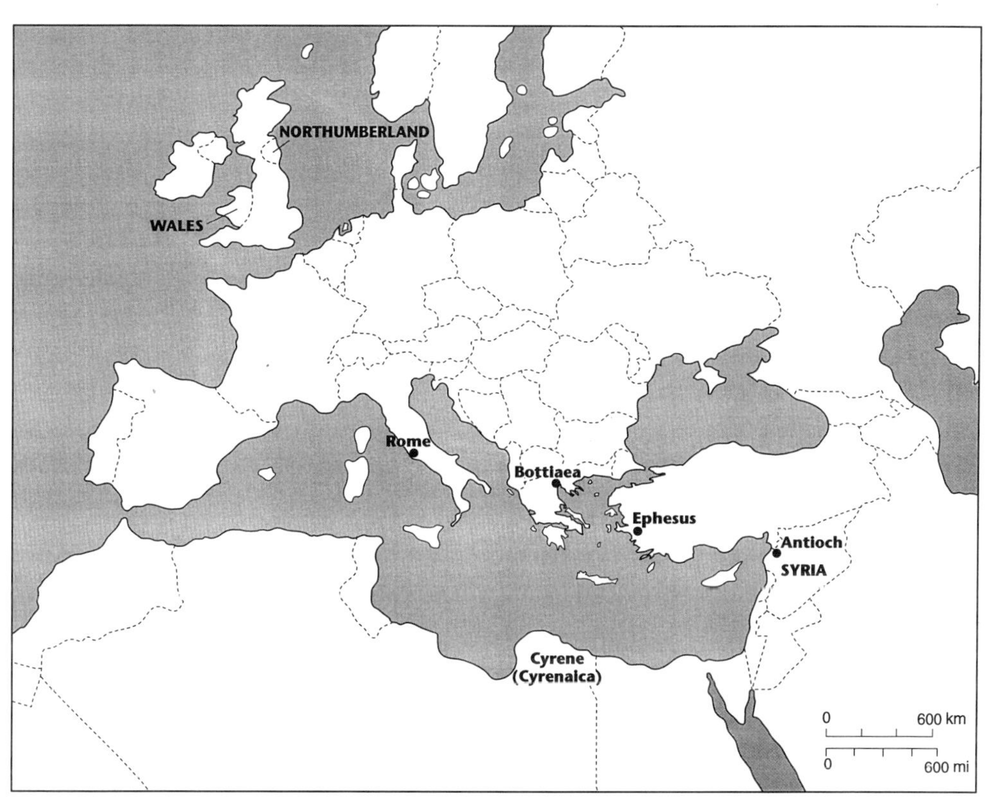

The Story Characters	*Major Associated Places*
The Wife of Apollonius of Tyre	Cyrene, Antioch, Ephesus
Emaré	Wales (or Galloway), Rome
Florence	Rome, Bottiaea
Custance	Rome, Syria, Northumberland

Map drawn by Ellen Guttadauro and used by permission of Creative Communication Services, University of California at Davis.

and having little to do with the plot. The Virgin does not appear in Skármeta's Chilean novella *The Postman* upon which the film is based; the director Michael Redford changed the locale to the Italian coast and added, among other details of local color, the candle-illuminated prayer boat.

What is the ubiquitous Virgin doing out there on the dark waters? This Virgin Mary of the floods and waves is no one we know from the Bible or accepted dogma. Yet she is often to be found among the ordinary folk of the Mediterranean, queen of the night and the sea, associated with the moon, and bearer of some mysterious, saving grace. *Romancing the Goddess* seeks to discover, if not the origin of this sea-virgin's power, at least the route by which her typically solitary figure has come to inspire English romance, and the connection of that figure with three more human women, Emaré, Custance, and Florence, as they too are seen adrift on the waves in their respective stories. While the Virgin adrift represents power, at the human level being cast adrift on the open sea has ambiguous connotations—of freedom from entanglements but also of helplessness in the currents of destiny.

Women's power, or the lack of it, is at issue in all three of these medieval romances. In each of them, events in the young woman's life initiated mainly by men (though wicked mothers-in-law also feature) disempower her, but her spirit and dignity never falter and she regains control at the end. The romances celebrate the woman's magnificent coping, even in that situation of utter helplessness of being at the mercy of the sea in a rudderless boat. As the good woman protagonist of these medieval tales thwarts the evil persons who attempt to subjugate, rape, or even slay her, her quest is to retain control over her body, and eventually she achieves a home and family with a man to whom she may be properly joined.

When the woman adrift receives supernatural aid in the quest to preserve her body or her life, that aid comes from the sources one expects in the Christian world of these medieval stories. But it appears that the plot of these stories was adapted from an earlier classical model in which the source of power was different and the woman herself became identified with the supernatural. While exploration of the Goddess aspect of the heroine is reserved for the final chapters of this book, it is important as one reads the translated romances in chapter 2 to be aware of the association of this wholly human medieval woman with her much more powerful mythic antecedents, since flashes of that former formidable power most interestingly, if sporadically, occur.

Those vestiges are a major attraction in the three romances as the heroine of each story defies male aggression of several kinds, usually beginning with the threat of incest that initially drives her into the wilderness of sea or forest. When a woman is set adrift in a medieval romance in connection with any form of incest, her story on the one hand reflects a genuine practice of medieval times (and earlier) in which the sea or another wilderness was called upon to arbitrate human judgments. In real life that arbitration was sought with particular frequency in the case of unauthorized sexuality and the issue thereof (for example, the children of incest, who were exposed). On the other hand the plot conforms to a particular and widely popular tradition of storytelling, a tale-type, as folklorists call it, that appears again and again. Literary critics, tending to disparage them, call these stories the Constance cycle or tales of accused queens.[1] Folklorists have named what they perceive as the controlling motif "The Calumniated Wife." But the calumny itself, the false accusation of the woman by an inlaw or rejected suitor, appears to be a medieval variant of an earlier plot in which the incest-threatened woman of royal blood is cast adrift on the sea, to be later washed ashore in an alien land where her integrity is further tested. Mindful of this earlier plot lacking calumny, I like to describe the woman protagonist as a Castaway Queen.

All three romances offer variations upon the basic medieval plot that begins with a good woman of high birth being cast adrift or sent overseas by or because of a close relative, usually her father. She comes ashore and perhaps marries, is set adrift again through the machinations (usually a false accusation) of a mother-in-law or else a rejected suitor who frames her for murder, but finally she arrives intact at a cult site where she is "adopted" and her dear ones eventually gather also. There she engineers a situation in which she reveals her identity, and a reconciliation scene concludes the story. Sometimes her hands are cut off and perhaps replaced by silver ones; when this mutilation occurs, a saint typically restores the hands before the tale ends.[2] A child may be born. In her moments of greatest distress, usually under direct attack, the woman receives the supernatural aid mentioned above. As a result of this aid she may be thought by her antagonist to possess supernatural powers herself.

In their own right the three medieval romances presented here are not great poems, or even, as critics measure poetry today, "good" poems—except for Chaucer's tale, and even it receives adverse criticism within the larger context of his work. They lack tautness, irony, and, again except for Chaucer's tale, figures of speech. (The intention of the heavily rhetorical telling of Chaucer's tale of Custance is a matter of much critical discussion.) But all three romances are interesting, fast-moving narratives. The pace may be attributed partly to the momentum provided by the verse form itself,[3] partly to the "perils of Pauline" plot that the three romances share. Both attributes place them in the tradition of popular culture rather than refined art, though they may have been considered courtly in their day.[4]

Like Shakespeare's *Pericles*, to which they are related, these romances have received bad press in this century. Although Schlauch speaks of their "warmth and charm" (114 and passim), Gibbs's remark that *Emaré* "illustrates the depths of ineptitude to which English medieval romance could sink" (37) is a more representative judgment. Edwards begins his article on "Critical Approaches to the *Man of Law's Tale*" by quoting a series of disparaging remarks ("Critical" 85–86). Concerning medieval romances in general, Richmond says that "the authors' carelessness about style, since their concern is exhaustive rather than elegant presentation, is certainly evident and the occasion for much hostility" (16). These works profit from fast rather than careful reading, which means that critics trained in the close analysis of highly wrought structures do not respond well to them. But there is entertainment and interest to be found here of a different kind. The time has come to reevaluate these lively romances and allow ordinary readers access to them.

The subject is unusual for medieval romance in that women are the main protagonists; they are active agents rather than mere quest-objects or courtly ladies to be honored by the male quest. Emaré, Florence, and Custance are heroic not because they slay monsters but because they survive alone against enormous odds, including sexual violence and literally being set adrift at sea. Survival was no small feat in times when in both real life and literature a woman without an obvious male guardian was considered fair prey. Thomas of Erceldoun, in the romance of that name, makes that attitude explicit when he speaks to a well-dressed lady met in the wilderness:

> If you, apparelled with such show,
> Come in your folly riding by,
> For love, lady, as you must know,
> You give me leave with you to lie.
>
> [If thou be parelde moste of prysse,
> And here rydis thus in thy folye,
> Of lufe, lady, als thou erte wysse,
> Thou gyffe me leve to lye thee bye.][5]

Such male assumptions[6] and the cliff-hanger plot in general of these three stories frequently leave us wondering how the heroine can possibly survive her trials, but the typically happy outcome of the romance genre reassures us that she will. At the most critical moments she also has the divine aid that may be a relic of her archaic origins. Finally, however, in the English romances if not in their Continental analogues, the woman finds power of her own. Though initially the helpless victim of family dysfunction, it is she who succeeds in orchestrating the joining together of generations at the end of the story.

✧ Sources, Provenance, Dialect, and Date of These Romances

The order in which the romances are presented in this book is not chronological but instead reflects my view of their complexity. I usually abbreviate their longer titles to the names of their stalwart heroines: *Emaré, Florence,* and *Custance.* No direct source is known for *Emaré,* and that of *Florence* is uncertain, though the growth of the story may be traced. Only *Custance* has a definite main source, the circa 1334 chronicle by Nicholas Trevet, to which, along with Gower's version of the story, Chaucer's work may be compared.[7]

Emaré, "a folktale in rhyme" (Kolve 480), was composed in East Yorkshire within fifty years of 1400 C.E. (Rickert edition xxviii). This romance conforms most closely of the three to the many other tales of similarly victimized women in that it concerns a young woman set adrift specifically as punishment for not meeting her father's sexual demands. It contains as well other identifying elements such as a magical love-garment, a wicked mother-in-law, forged letters, and the recognitions at the end. Adapted from an unknown French source related to Beaumanoir's *La Manekine* of circa 1270,[8] *Emaré* is identified in the last lines of the text as a "Breton lay," a short verse romance intended to be heard by an unlearned audience upon a single occasion. Marie de France, our chief medieval authority on the Breton lay, says at the end of *Guigemar* that such lays were sung to a harp (Hanning and Ferrante 54–55). Line three of the prologue to the Middle English romance about the harper-king Sir Orfeo seems to confirm this association with music, though the *Orfeo* poet refers specifically to reading as well:

> Written we find, and often read
> (As clerics teach us at our need),
> The stories that a harper sings
> About the most amazing things.

[We redyn ofte and finde i-write,
As clerkes don us to wite,
The layes that ben of harping
Ben i-founde of ferly thing.]
                    (Sisam 14, spelling modernized.)

I find that *Emaré* is most readable, whether in Middle English or
modern, if read as song, indulging in rather than fighting the sing-
song meter, and preferably aloud. Such an approach may even ease
much of what we now find silly in the narrative itself, such as the
tendency of everyone, especially otherwise stalwart males, to faint or
weep at the slightest provocation.

Le Bone Florence of Rome was composed in much the same area
of England as *Emaré* but possibly half a century later, in the early
fifteenth century. In this romance about a heroine named Florence,
the father's incestuous desire for his daughter that often instigates the
Castaway Queen plot is displaced onto a lecherous old man, the Greek
king Garcy (Ramsey 178; see also Hares-Stryker, *Sleeping* 214–16).
Florence's rejection of Garcy's advances starts a war that is the main
subject of the first, more chivalric, part of the romance, not included
in this book. During that war, two dispossessed brothers, Hungar-
ian noblemen named Miles and Emere (whose name in my version
rhymes with "m'dear"), come to aid Florence's father in defending
Rome. The father is slain though Rome is saved, and Florence weds
Emere. But she chooses to withhold her favors until Garcy has been
brought to her as a prisoner, so Emere goes off to war again, leaving
his brother Miles to look after Florence and Rome. That is a mistake.
Miles conceives a passion for Florence that, according to the legal
and moral codes of the time, is incestuous, like Gertrude's marriage
to her brother-in-law Claudius in *Hamlet*. The social constraints
upon incest unique to this period will be discussed below. Miles at-
tempts rape, which results in Florence's exile and wanderings.

In her careful study of the "Accused Queen" motif, Margaret
Schlauch aligns Florence's story with what she calls the "Crescen-

tia" cycle of romances, the earliest medieval form of which is a twelfth-century German romance about a heroine named Crescentia of Rome who is persecuted by her brother-in-law, and indeed the stories are very similar. For spurning her brother-in-law's love, Crescentia is thrown into the Tiber (the river running through Rome), rather than being abandoned in the forest or upon the sea. Surviving this ordeal, she is framed for murder by another spurned admirer, is granted the power to heal by St. Peter, heals her persecutors after they confess, and finally retires to a convent (Schlauch 108–13). Although this may be the earliest medieval version, there exists a third-century Greek narrative preserved as *The Clementine Recognitions* in which the protagonist similarly flees her brother-in-law's advances and also survives her ordeals with the aid of St. Peter, so I prefer to think of these brother-in-law incest stories not as a Crescentia cycle but as a "Clementine" cycle (technically pseudo-Clementine). They tend to follow a pattern related to but slightly different from those father-incest stories whose classical antecedent seems to be a story like the more famous *Apollonius of Tyre,* in which the queen bears a child midway through the narrative. In most Clementine-type romances the child, often a historical personage like Custance's Maurice, is born after events have calmed down at the end. These romances usually function as charter or founding myths, providing an interesting parentage for an emperor or prelate.

In its unabridged form, *Florence* is much longer and more complicated than *Emaré.* Unlike *Emaré,* however, *Florence* has an identifiable sister text, the French *Florence de Rome,* both versions probably deriving from a common source.[9] Over three times as long as the English story, the French romance (or the mutual source of both romances) appears in turn to have derived its last portion, the Castaway Queen material, from a briefer "miracle of the virgin" tale called "The Empress of Rome" or "The Chaste Empress," adding it on to the long first part about the war. One can get some idea of the earlier version of the story of Florence from Christine de Pisan's retelling in her easily available *Book of the City of Ladies* (1405), though Christine never presents her heroine adrift.[10] She claims to have obtained her version from one of the many collections of "Miracles of the Virgin" (176); her version is a "miracle" because Florence receives her healing power by dreaming that the Virgin Mary tells her of certain healing plants, which she discovers upon waking. One of the collectors of these tales, the Dominican preacher of Alais, Johannes Gobius, who completed his *Scala celi* around 1323–30 (Wilson 52), seems to acknowledge the source, or at least the family, of this Miracle story by locating it in his anthology immediately after a brief version of the Clementine romance mentioned above (Wilson 170). In the present translation I offer only the "tacked-on" last part of *Le Bone Florence of Rome* corresponding to the Miracle story, the part concerning Florence's own Clementine-type adventures. Beginning at stanza 106, the previous situation is summarized by a messenger and Sir Egravain, which suggests that the English romance-author acknowledges a two-part narrative, first a tale of war and chivalry, then a Castaway Queen story.

The third romance, Chaucer's *Man of Law's Tale*, which I here title *Custance*, is the most famous of these three stories about a woman set adrift, by virtue of its inclusion in the *Canterbury Tales*. Chaucer's story is the only one of the three that is not anonymous and for which we can trace the direct antecedents. He seems to have composed it sometime between 1390 and 1394–95 (Eberle 857), drawing on his friend Gower's retelling of the version found in Trevet's Anglo-Norman chronicle, as well as on Trevet directly (Nicholson 1991, and forthcoming). Trevet attaches the story to historical events, making his Constantia the mother of the emperor Mauricius who lived from approximately 539 to 602 C.E. and ruled in Byzantium, not in Rome as in the romance. Though Chaucer calls his heroine Custance, she is Constance in the sources and analogues. Following Trevet, Chaucer's romance combines themes from the other two story types; for example, Custance, like Florence, is implicated in a murder by a frustrated suitor, and like Emaré she bears a child during her travels.

Unlike both other romances, however, in Chaucer's story the heroine is sent overseas by her father to marry a newly converted

Syrian prince, obligation rather than incest thus provoking her initial journey. But then the prince's mother, after killing her own son on a religious pretext, sets Custance adrift and the usual adventures of family alienation follow, with Custance contriving reconciliation at the end.

✧ The Name and Nature of Romance

The word "romance," which today evokes the literary genre of women's thriller involving a love-attachment perhaps in a mysterious Gothic setting, originally was applied only to language. The term was coined in the early Middle Ages to designate a vernacular language "precisely in conscious contrast to the language of the learned, Latin" (Curtius 31–32). Later the term was used to designate a popular book in the vernacular, a tale of courtly adventure. In early medieval times the romance genre was especially associated with the courts of France, and the story was often Celtic or had major Celtic features, as in the romances of Chrétien de Troyes and Marie de France. Soon the genre spread to every part of Europe where the romance languages were spoken, and in due course it penetrated into other countries, including England. But the romance-language affinities of this genre are revealed at times even in English romance, for example in the Franco-Celtic name of the famous Arthurian forest, "Broceliade," in the Middle English Emaré's embroidering of her French name into other French meanings, and in the hybrid Anglo-French title "*Le Bone* Florence *of* Rome."

Like the classical myth in which the hero Perseus rescues the bound Andromeda from the sea-monster that comes to devour her, medieval romance is usually male-dominant, "a narrative about knightly prowess and adventure, in verse or in prose, intended primarily for the entertainment of a listening audience," says Helaine Newstead (11). Joerg O. Fichte rejects this as "much too vague to be a viable and useful definition" (150), but he, too, claims that "the intrinsic structure of verse romance derives its unity from the personality of the exemplary, knightly protagonist, whose actions in the form of knight errantry and quest, which determine the extrinsic structure of the romance narrative, are mostly accidental" (154). According to Northrop Frye, who has a particular interest in romance, the damsel in distress saved by a monster-slaying hero is the plot we most typically associate with the genre (*Harper Handbook* 402); this is the plot that Chaucer parodies in *Sir Thopas* and that Spenser elaborates in *The Faerie Queene*. Without specifying a male hero, W. R. J. Barron offers an obviously male-dominant pattern when he lists four motifs that he finds typical of medieval romance: "the mysterious challenge or summons to a mission, the lonely journey through hostile territory, the first sight of the beloved, the single combat against overwhelming odds or a monstrous opponent" (4–5). This list again recalls the classical hero who slays the monster to rescue the sacrificial maiden. Gender is also implied when Fichte, looking at the way the term was used at the time, finds that, with minor exceptions, "'romaunce' was used for works featuring an aristocratic protagonist in pursuit of adventure" (152).

By describing it differently, one can make the romance genre less gender-specific: a hero or heroine with whom we can identify has a series of thrilling adventures in strange places, reaching a happy and safe haven at the end. The exotic or wilderness location through which the romance protagonist travels, often alone, places life at the level of dreams, as Hermione says in *The Winter's Tale*; thereby the story becomes an analogy for the situation of all of us. A hair-raising alienation from normality, wild and thrilling encounters, and a return to a reassuring home place seems to be the essential formula for romance in any period. "Romance is about chance and change," says Rosalind Field, "and requires of its protagonists the youthful energy to deal with both" ("Rescuing Romance" 254).

The requirement that a romance should have a happy ending has recently been questioned, for example by Arlyn Diamond, and indeed the conclusion of the many-storied "romance" of King Arthur is one of the most heartrending scenes of literature. The designation of romance for that story, however, arouses disclaimers (as in the introduction to almost any edition of Malory's text or of the earlier Middle English Arthurian romances), because romance most typically belongs to the comic form, distinguishing it from tragedy. As Fichte (and others) point out, it is essentially conservative, "an affirmation of the existing class structure by the success and vindication of the alienated knightly protagonist" with whom the audience identifies (154). Thus romance and tragedy may be graphically expressed by the turning upward or downward of the wheel of fortune.[11] In the thirteenth century Vincent de Beauvais defines comedy, the form related to romance, as "a poem changing a sad beginning into a happy ending," and in the early fifteenth century Lydgate repeats this theme: "A Comedy hath in his gynnynge, a pryme face a manner complaynynge, and afterwarde endeth in gladnesse" (quoted by Coghill 259, 262). In his essay on Shakespeare's romance form, Nevill Coghill sums up the genre with a memorable formula: "a tale of trouble that turn[s] to joy" (259). It is this assumption about the romance genre that allows Fredric Jameson (among others) to associate the Marxian vision of history with the romance paradigm: "What is meant thereby is the salvational or redemptive perspective of some secure future" (103).

The exquisite "Breton lay" of *Sir Orfeo* (edited by Rumble 207–26 and translated by Tolkien) demonstrates just how radically Ovid's classical tale of Orpheus and Eurydice could be reformulated in order to make it satisfy the generic expectation of a happy outcome (though accommodation to Celtic sources, specifically the *aithed* form, was also involved). In the Greek myth Eurydice is bitten by a snake and dies, and her husband Orpheus, the greatest of mortal musicians, seeks her in the realm of the dead. There he plays his harp so magnificently that all torments briefly cease, and the king of Hades agrees to let Eurydice follow Orpheus back to the land of the living, on just one condition: if Orpheus should look back before reaching the boundary between the worlds, he will lose her forever. In Ovid's story he cannot restrain himself, and Eurydice is lost. As the medieval adventure begins, however, Eurydice (called Heurodis) does not die but is spirited away by the king of the fairies to his castle, and when the king releases her after Sir Orfeo's harp-playing, he does so without conditions. The Heurodis of romance is saved to live "happily ever after" with her devoted husband.

The medieval *Sir Orfeo* makes Heurodis the typical "damsel in distress"; her situation, like that of Andromeda chained to her rock, provides the knight with an opportunity to demonstrate his male prowess—or else persistence and skill, as in the case of Sir Orfeo. The romance heroine typically functions, like Heurodis, as a quest-object, or sometimes as a fairy-tale quest-reward (the knight having slain the dragon wins the princess), more rarely as a quest-helper (like the wise maiden who gives Percival advice), or as instigator or antagonist or observer. The woman taking a central and active role in medieval romance is an anomaly. Nanette McNiff Roberts finds in her dissertation that women are the protagonists or co-protagonists in only fourteen of the eighty-one Middle English romances that she examines, half of even these fourteen women primarily functioning as victims.[12] While it is true that the classic structure, the romance as male fantasy, requires an incapacitated sacrificial virgin whom the hero can save in the nick of time, the three romances gathered here present their woman protagonists in situations where they are a little better able to cope with their own fates and are left to do so. This variation upon the more usual Andromeda theme offers some surprising results.

✧ Woman as Hero in Middle English Romance

As observed above, the modern term "romance" brings to mind a genre of novel written specifically for women, in which love interest is paramount and the heroine, after being terrorized and perhaps solving a mystery, gets her man. These days in modern women's thrillers the heroine is less passive than she was even a few years ago, but marriage to her "prince" often remains her highest priority. The reader expects this closure. In intellectual circles such novels are considered vulgar and sentimental, and it is true that, written to formula, they rarely make demands on either author or reader, their main intention being to titillate then satisfy, to offer escapist daydreams in print, or, to phrase it less negatively, to offer time out, hope, and the good feelings that sustain us (Radway 86–118).

Janice A. Radway also finds, however, that "because the ideal romance symbolically represents real female needs within the story and then depicts their successful satisfaction, it ratifies or confirms the inevitability and desirability of the entire institutional structure within which those needs are created and addressed" (138). The same may be said of the medieval romances, though there is a difference. Upon casual reading the medieval romances about Florence, Emaré, and Custance seem of a similar escapist and conformist mold, with much repetition (especially in *Emaré*), generic or structural confusion (especially in *Florence*), and perhaps an overabundance of piety (especially in *Custance*). Although these stories share with the male romance the theme of a journey into the wilderness, there is no quest as such and no dragon to be slain. Instead, the heroine is buffeted by the whims of fate and the whims of any man along the way who is attracted to her. These features are an added count against the stories from either a literary or a feminist point of view. Nevertheless, despite countless critical assessments to the contrary, the heroines of the woman adrift romances may be read as far from merely passive in their trials (see Hares-Stryker, *Sleeping*, chapter 5). Strengthened by their optimism, faith, and staunch determination, these women who are victims of their male relatives in the beginning achieve control over their lives by the end; they become the authors of their own life stories. This "feminist" aspect of the medieval plot, not included in the two classical tales of Apollonius and Clement and curiously not observed by commentators before now, suggests the inadequacy of dismissing the story as mere escapism or propaganda about women conforming.

An implicit further level of meaning, however, takes these women's romances beyond gender. As Radway showed was the case among the modern readers she interviewed, as Northrop Frye has theorized on several occasions, and as Niklas Holzberg argues is the case even for the ancient novel (30), the romance genre provides a space for the psyche to move beyond everyday experience, how far beyond depending upon the reader. The romance of a woman's involuntary journey like that of the Castaway Queen, or of a woman's quest like that of the protagonist Psyche of Greek myth, asks to be read as an allegory for the human spirit—as is obvious when one recalls that the Greek word *psyche* means "soul." One may be further encouraged in such an allegorical reading of the woman's journey by the fact that in his most famous poem, "En una noche oscura," the sixteenth-century mystic San Juan de la Cruz presents his protagonist in terms of a woman slipping out into the night to encounter a lover. In this scene he combines the standard and accepted source for erotic love-mysticism, the biblical *Song of Songs,* with his own culture's popular *cantigas de mujer,* love-songs in the voice of a woman. In my imitative translation, limited here to the first three stanzas, I have given the impassioned (*inflamada*) speaker a dress to make up for the lack in English of the adjectival endings that in San Juan's Spanish at once identify her as female:

> Into the dark of night
> I went with longing flaming, amorous,—
>   O venture of delight—
>   Unnoticed in my dress,
> My house remaining now in quietness.
>
> Securely veiled from sight
> In darkness, down a secret stair I pressed—
>   O venture of delight!—
>   Disguised in my dark dress,
> My house remaining now in quietness.
>
> Into the blissful night
> I went so secretly that no one marked,
>   And I saw nothing, light

Or any guide, apart
From that which burned so brightly in my heart . . .

[En una noche obscura
Con ansias en amores inflamada,
    ¡Oh dichosa ventura!
    Salí sin ser notada,
Estando ya mi casa sosegada.

    A escuras, y segura,
Por la secreta escala disfrazada,
    ¡Oh dichosa ventura!
    A escuras, y en celada,
Estando ya me casa sosegada.

    In la noche dichosa
En secreto, que nadie me veía,
    Ni yo miraba cosa,
    Sin otra luz y guía,
Sino la que en el corazón ardía . . .]

The situation is pure romance and at some level would appeal to San Juan's listeners as such: a woman's nighttime assignation with her lover. But in the title *canciones del alma* ("songs of the soul") he identifies the woman protagonist as his own spiritual self. He has cleverly combined a popular genre with the ancient concept of the anima or soul represented as female, in order to dramatize an intense mystical experience, indeed an out-of-the-body experience, or, as San Juan himself says in his commentary, an escape from the house of the senses (122).

The woman's quest has been adapted since classical times to such spiritual and philosophical use. Writers from Apuleius to C. S. Lewis have adapted to this end the Cupid and Psyche story, mentioned above, and Boethius and King Alfred similarly appropriate the tragic figure of Eurydice. I do not think that *Emaré* can be regarded, without strain, as much more than a fairy tale, and the poet of *Florence*

seems to have had political matters in mind, but the more sophisti-
cated and literate Chaucer seems to be using Custance, as she comes
with Christianity first to pagan Syria then to pagan Northumbria, to
signify meanings beyond herself; Kolve elaborates this idea in his
chapter on the tale, finding more allegory than I am inclined to.[13]
Nevertheless, when God's voice thunders out in Alla's hall to iden-
tify her as "Daughter of Holy Church" (line 675), Custance is seen as
a woman of power in the realm of the spirit.

Within the physical world of the story, however, the women of
these medieval romances begin their adventures unmistakably as
victims of family violence. One of the principle differences between
romances with male heroes and those having heroines is the cause
behind the protagonist being in the wilderness, that "other space"
where transformations occur. In the male romance the man goes out
voluntarily to encounter his fate, venturing forth, confident and in
control of his adventure, or so it seems to him. "That the very es-
sence of the knight's ideal of manhood is called forth by adven-
ture . . . can be demonstrated on the basis of the courtly romance"
(Auerbach 135). The heroine of the usual woman's romance, on the
other hand, is thrust out involuntarily, having been exiled in some
way, as Dorothy is dropped by a whirlwind into Oz. In medieval
romance the woman may find herself adrift, the sea being the ar-
chetypal symbol of human impotence against fate; moreover, she
is often specifically deprived of any means of steering her craft, being
"up the creek without a paddle" in the modern idiom. But through
unwavering faith and heroic persistence she not only makes it home
unscathed but succeeds in uniting her family. In medieval romance
as well as in such later woman-centered novels as *Clarissa*, the
woman must additionally strive to retain her virginity or chastity
against great odds. "Behind all the 'fate worse than death' situations
that romance delights in, there runs the sense that a woman deprived
of her virginity, by any means except a marriage she has at least con-
sented to, is, to put it vulgarly, in an impossible bargaining position"
(Frye, *Scripture* 73).

The agendas of such well-known knightly heroes as Orfeo, Lancelot, and Gawain can provide a good standard by which to compare the aims of the woman protagonist of medieval romance. After the kidnapping of his wife Heurodis by the Fairy King, Sir Orfeo wanders for some time in the wilderness, but when he glimpses her on a fairy hunt (her spirit-form is out hunting with the fairies who hold her captive body in their otherworld hall), he voluntarily goes on a quest to save his damsel-in-distress. In Chretien de Troyes's tale of *The Knight of the Cart*, Lancelot goes out on a similar quest to rescue the kidnapped Guinevere. Later in the Arthurian romance-cycle, various knights of the Round Table go out from Camelot in quest of the Holy Grail, a spiritualized version of the treasure quest. *Sir Gawain and the Green Knight* offers an inversion of romance expectations that results in a feminizing of the role of the hero: instead of the knight achieving the passive, virtuous lady as a reward for valor, an aggressive lady seeks to seduce Gawain before his final confrontation with the Green Knight, and when Sir Gawain goes out to encounter his terrifying adversary, the monster-slaying quest is again inverted as the rules of the game allow the monster-knight to swing his axe at passive Gawain. Yet like other knights Gawain has ventured forth voluntarily. In *Sir Gawain and the Green Knight* he does so twice, in fact, leaving first the comfort of Arthur's court then that of Bercilak's court to go out in quest of his monster. In contrast, our three heroines, as they are thrust into the wilderness by sexual violence, politics, deceit, or false accusation, wish only to survive with their chastity intact and ultimately to get home.

It seems, then, that the male hero of romance engages in an identity quest of an essentially spiritual nature; he typically encounters a monstrous or god-like antagonist whom he must overcome with moral integrity, thereby winning a beautiful damsel or treasure as a visible token of his success. The woman hero, on the other hand, typically faces male violence against which she must preserve her honor as it is inscribed in the integrity of her body, her inviolate body itself being the hidden sign of her achievement. (It is offered as prize to a man in the end, but on *her* authority.) The genital implication is clear: the male finds his identity outwardly in heroic quest, whereas the female finds her identity inwardly in retaining her invisible "virtue." She succeeds in her quest by gaining physical authority over herself.

✧ Gendered Violence and Domestic Violence

Now that sexual integrity is no longer the measure of a woman's value and synonymous with her identity, as it was to some degree even a generation ago (I remember how "a bad girl" was one who had "gone all the way"), this passion about chastity for its own sake may strike the modern reader as obsessive. Northrop Frye points out, however, that "in the social conditions assumed, virginity is to a woman what honor is to a man, the symbol of *the fact that she is not a slave*" (*Scripture* 73, emphasis mine). Only a woman of high social status had any degree of control over her own body and of who might enter it, and even *her* virginity was often regarded as a commodity to be bartered by her menfolk. But at least it was thought to be worth something.

Some of the adverse social conditions that Frye mentions are vividly brought to our notice in a recent article by Jane Tibbetts Schulenberg. In "The Heroics of Virginity: Brides of Christ and Sacrificial Mutilation," Schulenberg shows how certain real-life women took the challenge of remaining chaste; under threat of assault they chose self-mutilation and death rather than enduring the identity-destroying humiliation of being raped, which might also endanger their access to Heaven. Schulenberg adduces grim details that lend a perspective to the fictionalized feelings of the women of romance. Beginning with the news that "the rather curious epigram 'to cut off your nose to spite your face' can be found for the first time in the sources of the twelfth century," where it is discovered to be more than a saying, Schulenberg offers background for "the aggressive defense of female saints when confronted with sexual assault during the early Middle Ages" (29). They were inspired to this defense mainly by the writings of certain fathers of the church, especially St. Jerome, who invokes the early Christian doctrine that "although God can do all things, He cannot raise up a virgin after she has fallen" (33). Jerome makes it clear that he considers *any* sexuality to reveal the woman's personal corruption, and in his *Commentary on Jonah* he goes so far as to endorse suicide "when one's chastity is jeopardized" (34). Ambrose also "justifies the practice of suicide in the preservation of virginity" (34). Augustine more moderately argues that "violation of chastity, without the will's consent, cannot pollute the character," and he recommends against suicide either before or after rape (35).

When they were bombarded by such didactic works, by preaching, and by hagiographic fictions centered on self-sacrifice, all laying emphasis upon total virginity of mind as well as body, it should be no surprise that religious women terrified by sexual threat might attempt to preserve their virginity by means of self-mutilation. Here is just one example of that strategy among those offered by Schulenberg. It is praised by Roger of Wendover in his early twelfth-century chronicle as "the admirable act of the holy Abbess Ebba," when her convent is threatened by a viking attack. Although Roger's chronicle is two centuries earlier than our romances and praises the acts of even earlier Anglo-Saxon nuns, his compelling story is useful for my purpose of illustration. I begin at the point after Ebba has exhorted her nuns to strength of purpose in preserving from the barbarians their virginity dedicated to Christ:

The whole assembly of virgins having promised implicit compliance with her maternal commands, the abbess, with an heroic spirit, affording to all the holy sisters an example of chastity profitable only to themselves, but to be embraced by all succeeding virgins for ever, took a razor, and with it cut off her nose, together with her upper lip unto the teeth, presenting herself a horrible spectacle to those who stood by. Filled with admiration at this admirable deed, the whole

assembly followed her maternal example, and severally did the like
to themselves. (quoted by Schulenberg 47–48)

The vikings do attack on the next day as expected and do indeed turn
away in disgust from these bloody and disfigured women, a rejection
confirming the partial success of their desperate strategy, but in their
anger at being thwarted sexually the vikings burn down the monas-
tery around the nuns. As Gravdal remarks of this period, "A woman
accedes to sanctity by prizing her chastity so highly that she dies for
it" (22). In Roger of Wendover's view their immolation enables Ebba
and her virgins to attain the glory of martyrdom. He makes it clear
in his chronicle that martyr was an honored status in that society;
rape-survivor was not.

Returning to the brighter world of woman-centered romance, we
do well to keep in mind this grim real-life dimension. In his "Letter
to Eustochium," she being a woman who has chosen to remain a vir-
gin for Christ, Jerome warns: "I do not wish pride to come upon you
by reason of your decision, but fear. If you walk laden with gold, you
must beware of a robber" (quoted by Schulenberg 32). This realistic
but dour advice recalls Thomas of Erceldoun's challenge to the well-
dressed fairy queen quoted above. The fact that our heroines are
family women rather than nuns (whose very attire marks them as a
challenge to the reprobate) is one factor that makes their survival, as
they enter the wilderness "laden with gold," even remotely credible.
Also, since they have God and the Virgin on their side and meet no
vikings, and above all since they are in a romance, their fate does
not hang so starkly in the balance between succumbing as a victim
or else dying to preserve their chastity, although from their perspec-
tive within the story it sometimes looks as though it must come
down to that.

In discussing the relation of Middle English romance to the func-
tioning of families, Stephen Knight considers several romances in
which women play a large role (referring to *Emaré, Lai le Freine,
The Erl of Tolous, Le Bone Florence of Rome,* and *Sir Triamour*):
"Although a general deference to the male is evident, the neurotic

control of feminine power found in the hero-based structure does not seem to be a feature here" (112). Perhaps it would be more accurate to say that the "neurotic control" is not absent so much as foiled, for instead of a "hero-based structure" in these romances, the usual feature of male desire for dominance is intensified and then reversed from successful male control to thwarted male violence. If the romance-quest of the male hero is to attack the outward monster and that of the female hero to defend her inward chastity, both heroic intentions may be said to parallel the "genital" urgings of their respective desires in romance—male outward-bound, female homeward-yearning—thereby evoking from the audience differently associated responses. (These "essentialist" responses to romance do not mean that such male and female desires are biologically bound in reality.) Our admiration is principally sought by the man's story, our emotive participation by the woman's story. Chaucer gets a lot of mileage out of playing to this latter response in his tale of Custance. But of course these responses are not mutually exclusive, since we are also asked to pity the hardships of the male journey (poor Sir Gawain, for example, sleeping in his icy armor), and to admire the resilient and resourceful woman in her exile.

Above all, the romance about a woman asks us to respect her accomplishments and valor, to admire the way she maintains faith in herself and her religion despite the most extraordinary hardships, and to applaud the drive and enterprise she demonstrates in improving her situation as soon as the opportunity arises. The arrangement of this book presents the story of Emaré first because that protagonist most closely corresponds to our expectation of the gentle medieval heroine, and the story of Florence second as her romance moves us further away from that expectation. Both protagonists belie the criticism that traditionally groups them with passively patient women like Griselda,[14] that describes them as primarily displaying "a meek Job-like faith" (Hornstein 120), or that dismisses their stories as merely "the passive endurance of abused women" (Barron 204).[15] Chaucer's tale of Custance comes last as a culmination of the story-type, which Chaucer escalates into real art while (along with his source Trevet) restoring to the heroine an overtly religious meaning like that found in her late-classical origins and submissive attitudes that will disturb many readers (see Schibanoff and the critics whose views she summarizes, 62–63). But as Jill Mann says, quoting Sheila Delany, "Constance's 'silent endurance' does not imply limpness or inertia" (137)—for example, in stanza 113 she successfully fights off a rapist. Mann argues further with Delany: "'Constance seems to exist in order to suffer,' [Delany] protests, with the confidence of one who is sure the answer to such questions can be found in an inadequate social-welfare programme or lack of a revolutionary commitment. The 'why' that Chaucer turns on the problem of suffering in the Man of Law's Tale is larger than that" (134). As often in Chaucer's work, the problem is of cosmic scope, one that may not be solved, though it may be eased, by human benevolence ("pitee"). Moreover, neither the suffering nor the benevolence it evokes are gender-specific, though the particular plot of the Castaway Queen story is.

✧ Analogues: A Tale of Incest, Family Rupture, Exile, and Return

This brings us to the next question one must ask: Why did their makers find it appropriate to present in the same romance genre stories that are so different from the male-centered or male-flattering metrical romances, and where do the shared elements of these stories come from? How did Emaré, Custance, and especially Florence find their way into and so radically transform a genre that usually calls for the distressed maiden to be as helpless as Andromeda in her chains? How did they escape the male fantasy?

Floating about in medieval European culture, chiefly in those countries bordering on the Mediterranean, were a pair of stories going something like this (to reprise the summary offered more briefly at the beginning of this introduction): A beautiful young woman, perhaps clad in a shimmering garment that may be magical, is approached by a lustful male, usually her father ("Apollonius" version) or, if she is married, her brother-in-law ("Clementine" version), whose sexual overtures she either does or does not succeed in spurning. As a result of disobedient rejection or instead because she has succumbed to the sin of incest (she is in the wrong either way), the woman flees to or is exposed in some wilderness, often the sea. Sometimes her elegant hands that may have provoked the male lust are cut off or disabled. (This feature is an important element in the *Gregorius* romance that will be mentioned again below, and occurs in the thirteenth-century *La Manekine*, to which *Emaré* is closely related.) The woman adrift arrives in another land where she is taken in or adopted by a good merchant or official, and perhaps meets and marries the king of that land, becoming pregnant by him. The king goes away to war, and a thwarted suitor (in *Custance* and *Florence*) contrives to accuse the heroine of murder, or the jealous mother-in-law (in *Custance* and *Emaré*) manages an exchange of letters that indicts her; Chaucer's story manages to include both. With her child, if she has one, she is again cast adrift, possibly to further adventures. In her absence the mother-in-law's plot is revealed and its perpetrator punished. Now she drifts to a sanctuary, often a holy site, where usually her talent in sewing or healing (both being women's occupations connected with the theme of "hands") enables her to survive while keeping her true identity a secret. In due course other characters important to her story also converge on her place of sanctuary. Cleverly bringing all parties together, and often (in the Clementine-type versions) encouraging confession from the villains (as St. Peter does in the *Clementine Recognitions*), the heroine then reveals her identity and history. After this revelation the villains may be punished, penitent family members forgiven, and the heroine succeeds in reintegrating her ruptured family. Chaucer's incest-suppressing source allows him to have the beloved husband die after a year of married bliss so that Custance may return to her benevolent and nurturing father, thereby closing the circle of the plot and bringing her completely "home."

The double journey plot in this story is traditional. First comes an outward journey impelled by family violence, with discovery of a shelter elsewhere that proves only temporary, then a second outward journey impelled by calumny and concluded by the protagonist finding sanctuary in Rome or its usually religious equivalent, where she manages to effect reunion and forgiveness. To describe this as either a Father-Incest story or a Calumniated Queen story misses the point that in the full version there are at least two sequential "castings out," both of them the result of violence by devious or more powerful members of the heroine's own family. Otto Rank sees this doubling as a mirror, with the first landfall enabling the incest to be carried out in the disguise of legitimate matrimony, and then punished by exposure as before (309, 315). I see the doubling as substitution, a proper man-wife relationship replacing an improper one, with the mother-in-law mirroring the wicked father and also providing the figure of the missing dysfunctional parent. The heroine's mother has died, the ultimate dysfunction. Perhaps it is relevant that in some versions the apparently innocent husband goes to Rome as a penitent specifically for putting his own mother to death. Even with the episode of the calumniating mother-in-law, this is a tale above all about family dysfunction expressed in violence and a brave woman's self-possessed effectiveness despite the violence. In every case, the innocent woman is set adrift as the result of a man's sexual desire, either itself a violating lust or one that instigates a displaced and perverted reaction in his mother. The latter is a doubling in terms of the plot, and in psychological terms it suggests incestuous desire of another kind.[16]

As Edith Rickert says in her introduction to *Emaré*, "The ramifications of this tale extend so far back and so widely" that the concerted efforts of numerous scholars "have by no means exhausted the subject" (*Emaré* xxxii–iii). Limiting her attention to the medieval romance, she classifies according to their date and place of origin twenty variants on the sketch above, as follows: three in England (twelfth to fifteenth centuries), four in France (thirteenth to fourteenth centuries), three in Germany (thirteenth to fifteenth centuries), seven in Italy (fourteenth to seventeenth centuries), and three in Spain (fourteenth to fifteenth centuries); Schlauch adds to Rickert's list, as do others.[17] Believing with antecedent scholars such as Gough that the tale in its medieval version originated in northern England, where several of the castaway heroines come to shore and eventually marry the local king, Rickert argues that it spread out from England across Europe. In this attractive but questionable theory of diffusion she gives a great deal of weight to the digression in *Beowulf* about the queen whom I shall call "Thryth" (many call her Modthryth). Rickert finds in this digression the same association between themes of murdered suitors and a father-instigated sea-crossing as in some of the stories under discussion. As we shall see, later documents confirm that the Anglo-Saxon story of Thryth is indeed connected with that of the Castaway Queen, whether or not directly.

In lines 1931–57 of *Beowulf* the poet has just praised the Geatish Queen Hygd's generosity to her people; he speaks now of a queen who began poorly, issuing arbitrary death sentences, but later became admirable in her giving. Scholars agree that comparison to Hygd seems to be the poet's point in introducing Thryth here, and most remark upon the suddenness of the intrusion—"a crude excrescence," says Sisam (49).[18] My alliterative translation of the complete digression follows Fred C. Robinson's attractive suggestion that in line 1931 Queen Hygd is comparing *herself* to Thryth.[19] I am persuaded to this view by the fact that earlier in the poem Queen Wealhtheow appears to be comparing her potential situation in Heorot to that of a character in a song she has just heard, the hapless Hildeburh at Finnsburg (lines 1159–91). Other such comparisons occur throughout *Beowulf*, though rarely made by the character herself as in the case of these two women. By taking into account this practice of finding models for behavior in stories, and by rereading the introductory lines, especially line 1931, as Robinson suggests, with Hygd instead of Thryth being "that good queen" (which makes better sense than other readings), one finds the digression both more coherent and less abrupt than previously thought. Hygd's private meditation upon Thryth also bears out the poet's description of her in lines 1926–27 as wise though young:

Hæreth's daughter Hygd was not empty-handed
1930   or sparing of gifts to the Geatish people;
that good queen weighed the arrogance
of Thryth, who committed a monstrous crime.
Not any among the men of her court,
except the great lord,[20] dared set his eyes
1935   openly on her—or he ought to expect
a death-noose ordained for him and a doughty
hand to twist it! Then hurriedly after
that fist, a sword was further appointed,
a damascened blade to do the rest,
1940   make certain of death. Such is no queenly
practice for a lady, though peerless she be,
a peace-weaver taking, because of pretended
affront, the life of a loving man!
But Hemming's kinsman cut that short.
1945   Drinkers at ale told a different story,
of how she committed the fewer crimes
against her people once she was given
as gold-adorned bride to a brave young warrior
of fine descent. She had sailed to Offa
1950   on the fallow flood on her father's advice,
sought his hall, and happier when
she took that throne was her reputation
for better using what life had brought her.
She held high love with the heroes' lord,
1955   with him who was, as I have heard,
of all between the two great seas,
of all immense humanity, best.

[Hæreþes dohtor—   næs hio hnah swa þeah,
1930   ne to gneað gifa   Geata leodum,
maþmgestreona.   Mod þryþo wæg
fremu folces cwen,   firen' ondrysne;
nænig þæt dorste   deor geneþan
swæsra gesiða,   nefne sinfrea,

1935 þæt hire an dæges   eagum starede;
     ac him wælbende   weotode tealde
     handgewriþene;   hraþe seoþðan wæs
     æfter mundgripe   mece geþinged,
     þæt hit sceadenmæl   scyran moste,
1940 cwealmbealu cyðan.   Ne bið swylc cwenlic þeaw
     idese to efnanne,   þeah ðe hio ænlicu sy,
     þætte freoðuwebbe   feores onsæce
     æfter ligetorne   leofne mannan.
     Huru þæt onhohsnod[e]   Hem*m*ings mæg:
1945 ealodrincende   oðer sædan,
     þæt hio leodbealewa   læs gefremede,
     inwitniða,   syððan ærest wearð
     gyfen goldhroden   geongum cempan,
     æðelum diore,   syððan hio Offa flet
1950 ofer fealone flod   be fæder lare
     siðe gesohte;   ðær hio syððan well
     in gumstole,   gode mære,
     lifgesceafta   lifigende breac,
     hiold heahlufan   wið hæleþa brego,
1955 ealles moncynnes   mine gefræge
     þone selestan   bi sæm tweonum,
     eormencynnes.]

In her 1904–5 article "The Old English Offa Saga," Edith Rickert offers the most complete study available of the relation of this digression to its later analogues.[21] She focuses on the twelfth-century *Vitae Duorum Offarum* ("Lives of the Two Offas"), that is, the lives of the probably semi-mythical continental King Offa and his historical descendent, the Offa who ruled the Anglo-Saxon kingdom of Mercia from 757 to 796 and was responsible for the building of Offa's Dike. The *Life* of Offa I refers clearly to incest and the tale of the queen accused through exchanged letters, and the Offa II *Life* presents the woman adrift on the sea. Taken together, they represent the earliest medieval version that we have of the story. In part 2 of her article

Rickert juxtaposes three items, *Emaré*, the Constance story from Trevet's *Chronicle,* and the story from the *Life of Offa I,* to demonstrate the similarities between them, which are persuasive (358–59). The Offa I story begins with "the Daughter of the king of York condemned to die for refusing the unnatural love of her father, but spared by her murderers and left to perish in the woods" (ibid. 358). Events then proceed as expected, with Offa finding the castaway young woman while hunting, marrying her, then going off to aid the king of Northumbria in battle. The queen's own previously thwarted father in York then intercepts and changes the letters, as the mother-in-law does in *Emaré* and most analogues; this is the earliest known example of the manipulated letters motif presented in connection with this story. On the pretext that she is a witch working against her husband, the father in his letter calls for the queen's and her children's hands and feet to be cut off and for them to be left in the forest to die. This is done, but they are rescued and healed by a hermit, and finally found by Offa. The family is thus reunited, though without the woman's direct and forceful agency. With such a plot, no one can doubt that at some point the stories of Offa and the Castaway Queen were connected.

The second *Life,* that of Offa II, gives us more. The name of Offa's queen, Drida in Latin, is cognate with Anglo-Saxon Thryth; in this account she is a kinswoman of Charlemagne, as are certain other Castaway Queens of later romance. In this historical connection, however, the relationship is believable, since in or around 789 Charlemagne proposed that his son Charles should marry one of Offa's daughters, probably Ælfflæd; it did not work out (Stenton 220). Drida's story begins with her being

> legally condemned to a disgraceful death because of some exceedingly evil deed which she had committed; yet, out of respect for the king's [Charlemagne's] honor, she was not condemned to die by fire or by the sword, but to be exposed to the winds and seas, with all their hazards, in a small boat lacking all gear, and equipped with very little food. After she had been long tossed to and fro by changeable storms,

she was driven, as luck would have it, on to the shores of Britain.
(Simpson translation 236)

She soon marries King Offa, but unlike Thryth in *Beowulf* she does
not reform, and indeed plots to kill her husband. The descriptions of
character in the two accounts are so strikingly different as to sug-
gest that the later writer had a political agenda accounting for his
changes.

What was the "exceedingly evil deed" with which Drida began
her career of crime? In the *Life* she explains to Offa that "she had
been condemned to this peril [of the sea] through the injustice of cer-
tain ignoble persons, whose offers of marriage she had spurned so as
not to bring dishonor on her race" (Simpson translation 237). There
is nobody present to contradict her story, which could have omitted
the information that she not only spurned her admirers but had them
slain, as Thryth did. Or perhaps the evil deed was incest itself, a com-
plicity that led her, like the daughter of Antiochus in *Apollonius of
Tyre*, to accept the murder of suitors in order to maintain the illicit
relationship. The passage in the *Life of Offa II* could be interpreted
thus, placing the guilt upon the young woman instead of the father,
whose incest then is transferred to the *Life of Offa I* and incorporated
with other familiar motifs. If incest is involved here, it could throw
light on the opening situation of the digression in *Beowulf*. There the
poet suggests—if the word *sinfrea* refers to the father as I believe it
must—that Thryth welcomes her father's attentions, he being the
only man who dares openly gaze at her (lines 1933–35). Figure 1
illustrates the opening scene of Gower's tale of Apollonius, showing
that young man's dawning and horrified realization of the situation
he has entered (Eberle 364). It could equally illustrate the Thryth
story in the scenario I have suggested, with the frightened young man
suddenly realizing his danger and in the story in *Beowulf* unable to
escape the rope and blade.

Nevertheless, the digression in *Beowulf* resists both Rickert's ef-
forts and mine to join Thryth firmly to the incest theme as we know
it in the romances.[22] Only our knowledge of the later Offa story and

The Lover Recognizing His Danger. Miniature from a manuscript of Gower's *Confessio Amantis*. Courtesy of the Pierpont Morgan Library, New York, M.126, f.187v. Photograph by David A. Loggie.

the slight possibility of a criticism or pun in the word *sinfrea* at line 1934 would lead us to imagine that the story in *Beowulf* suggests incest or that the father mentioned there has any but the best intentions toward his disturbing daughter.[23] Much as in the story of Custance, the sea voyage to which Thryth's father recommends her appears to have as its intention the encounter with a man of a stature making him worthy to marry her. All we can say is that at some point these themes and stories converge.

Whatever relation *Beowulf*'s mysteriously motivated Thryth may bear to the heroines of our romances, it is clear that the late classical romance *Apollonius of Tyre*, of which there exists a partial translation from the Latin into Old English, shares many features with the medieval versions of the generic Castaway Queen story. In fact, Rickert says that this "enormously popular" classical romance is "almost certainly" the source of the incest idea (Rickert, *Emaré* xliv). Schlauch, because she, like some others, wishes to locate the source of the story in England (see especially 64–65), denies this affinity (75 n.23), but stories that I will examine in chapter 3 lead me to agree in principle with Rickert's statement, while modifying it to suggest that *Apollonius of Tyre* may not have been the source but rather the channel of that incest-related theme, a theme that takes us much farther back than I wish to explore here.[24] It cannot be doubted that *Apollonius* had a strong influence upon many medieval and later stories, and perhaps even provided a literary source for Thryth's early hostility toward those suitors who threatened to displace her father. An extant partial prose translation of *Apollonius* into Old English shows that the story was known at least late in the Anglo-Saxon period, and by way of Gower the same romance became the model for Shakespeare's *Pericles, Prince of Tyre*, another branch of this proliferating tree.

It is time now to tell the tale of Apollonius. The original story has three main protagonists, Apollonius himself, his wife, and his daughter, each having their own set of adventures, whereas the three medieval romances of this book have only one protagonist, corresponding to the "wife." But enough other identifying features occur to posit this story of a family's separation and reunion as an important antecedent to the Castaway Queen romance. The Latin story, of which Gower's is a fairly close version, begins with a scene reminiscent of Thryth's wicked execution of her suitors, but the scene is replete with the necessary detail that the Thryth story omits. The hero Apollonius has fallen in love with the daughter of King Antiochus (eponymous ruler of Antioch) who has offered her hand to the suitor able to solve a certain riddle, whoever tries and fails to be slain. Interpreting the riddle correctly and seeing that it

reveals the king to be living with his daughter as his wife, Apollonius
recognizes his danger and flees. Soon shipwrecked upon an unknown
shore, he meets there another princess, unnamed in the original text
but called Arcestrate in the Old English version, a useful name that I
shall adopt here. Apollonius marries her, and together they sail off to
claim his inheritance in Tyre. Arcestrate appears to die in childbirth
at sea and receives honorable sea-burial in a casket, thus being cast
adrift. This version of the story has dissociated the incest and the sea-
exposure into two more or less unrelated plots joined only by the
figure of Apollonius, one plot concerning the incestuous couple and
the other concerning an apparently dead wife cast adrift.[25] The casket
floats to shore where Arcestrate revives and a kindly physician takes
her in. Finding herself near Ephesus, she goes to the temple of Diana,
takes vows, and becomes a priestess there. Meanwhile her daughter,
brought up in Tarsus, is persecuted by a jealous foster-mother (analo-
gous to the wicked mother-in-law in later stories), and as a result has
various adventures including surviving celibate in a brothel. She is
hired out to cheer up the recently arrived Apollonius, who luckily is
too depressed to be "in the mood," and as a result she talks to him
instead, circumventing unintentional incest and inadvertently re-
vealing her identity. In a dream soon afterward, Apollonius is di-
rected to go to Ephesus, and at the temple there all is revealed. If a
female agency appears in the recognition scene, it is that of the god-
dess Diana herself. Except for the incestuous king and his daughter,
who have previously been killed by a thunderbolt from heaven, all
villains are punished at this point, and Apollonius is united with his
lost wife and the grown-up daughter with whom he fortunately did
not have sex. (This summary is based on Perry, *Ancient Romances*,
Appendix 2).

As Northrop Frye observes, the opening incestuous episode of
Apollonius of Tyre is a "demonic parody of the end, and the action
takes place on two levels of experience" (*Scripture* 49). Frye finds
this "vertical perspective" to be typical of romance in general: "The
realist, with his sense of logical and horizontal continuity, leads us
to the end of his story; the romancer, scrambling over a series of

disconnected episodes, seems to be trying to get us to the top of it" (ibid. 50). Frye's assessment seems exactly right, the "top" that the romancer (or the impetus of the romance genre) is trying to achieve being the elevation of myth, but again this subject must be postponed for the later essay. Suffice it to say here that if one were to shift the focus found in *Apollonius of Tyre* by presenting the princess at the beginning as reluctant about incest (i.e., a "good" princess) and then fusing her with either a feminized Apollonius or his wife, thereby making her the central protagonist of what follows, one would discover the main outlines of the Castaway Queen romance of later times—and a much tighter narrative than the classical *Apollonius* offers. Both Otto Rank (307–8) and the classicist Ben Edwin Perry argue independently that the story on which the *Apollonius* author drew must have been something along just these lines.[26]

In the third-century Greek *Clementine Recognitions*, the second late classical work examined in this connection by Archibald (and before her, Schick), features of the generic story including the flight from incest, in this case from a brother-in-law's approach, and the mutilated hands are combined with a plot in which Christianity triumphs. St. Peter heals the woman's hands and brings the family together in the recognition scene celebrated by the title, then all are baptized.[27] Her son Clement later becomes Bishop of Rome. A tale presenting brother-sister incest as the fraught background of Gregory the Great (see Rank 285–89) was retold by Hartman von Awe in his *Gregorius* (ca. 1195) and twice adapted by Thomas Mann.[28] This background legend of incest aligns the famous churchman with the numerous incestuously begotten or connected heroes of myth examined by Otto Rank in *The Birth of the Hero*.

Another Christian legend about the conception (not incestuous) and childhood of a hero of the church, the Emperor Constantine the Great, bears specific resemblances to *Emaré*. According to this story, Constantine's mother Helena goes to Rome secretly or in disguise, and there her beauty attracts the Emperor Constantius. Unknown to him she bears his child, whom she supports by exquisite needlework. Years later the boy attracts the attention of his father, and Helena contrives recognition by means of a ring. The emperor then formally recognizes Constantine as his son, makes him his heir, and "according to some accounts" for the first time marries his mother (Rickert, *Emaré* xxxvi–vii). In his *History of the English Church and People* (completed before 731 C.E.), the Anglo-Saxon Bede refers to Constantine's mother Helena as a concubine (Book 1, chapter 8), which leads Rickert to propose that the story may already have been in circulation at that early date.

This legend surfaces again as a full-blown French romance in *La Belle Hélène de Constantinople*, reworked in prose by Jean Wauquelin in 1448 from an earlier metrical version. This Helena specifically flees her father's plan to marry her, has various sea-adventures, is falsely accused by her mother-in-law, and apparently becomes the mother of St. Martin of Tours. (The story is retold by Schlauch, 120– 21.) In other words, the legend of the persecuted woman set adrift attracted stories about real persons into its romance net and provided a series of legendary mothers for popes, saints, and emperors. Indeed, all three of our heroines become mothers of emperors. Florence gives birth to the (possibly Byzantine) emperor Otis, and Custance to the historical Byzantine emperor Mauricius Flavius Tiberius (ca. 539– 602), both stories relocating their capitols to Rome. Only Emaré produces the nonhistorical Roman emperor Segramor, but the Breton lay form of Emaré's story traditionally invites fantasy. Kolve emphasizes that in its chronicle context the romance of Constance was regarded as history in the Middle Ages, and he describes Chaucer's version as "the record of a poet's meditation on a story found in history and honored always, even in those moments when its images become most general in their significance, as being literally true" (Kolve 357). Bede's casual recognition of Helena's unusual youth assumes the story's historicity, and the poets of both *Florence* (stanza 182) and *Custance* (stanza 142) refer a reader to Roman chronicles for further information about their "historical" tale.

The antecedents of the Castaway Queen story suggest that the flight from incest and woman adrift themes are classical, whereas the accusations, whether by jealous mother-in-law or thwarted suitor, are medieval additions probably derived from folklore. Although Archibald supposes that "the popularity of Incestuous Father stories which focus on the vicissitudes of the daughter who flees her father seems to have begun only in the twelfth century, at least in Western European literature" (*Apollonius* 65 n.5), there is evidence that the story itself with its theme of sea-exposure pre-existed *Apollonius of Tyre,* whose author perhaps drew on it. The possible associations of Goddess-related rituals with this earlier story will be discussed in chapter 3.

✧ Incest and Marriage in the Real Medieval World

The twelfth-century chronicler Jocelyn de Brakelond's version of the *Life of St. Kentigern* has the pagan king of northern Britain cast his daughter Taneu adrift in a coracle when she becomes pregnant after being raped. Miraculously, "that little vessel, in which the pregnant girl was detained, ploughed the watery breakers and eddies of the waves towards the opposite shore more quickly than propelled by a wind that filled the sail, or by the effort of many boatmen" (Forbes translation 39). When she comes ashore in Fife she gives birth to the saint. The fusion of romance with historical reality that such stories demonstrate is in part the result of social unrest and anxiety. As we have already seen, the concerns recorded in this escapist literature, as in all escapist literature, can be very real in the life of the times. Quoting R. W. Southern, Hares-Stryker says: "Standing at the 'frontiers of knowledge,' the Middle Ages realized the great dangers that 'menaced the traditional harmonies of Christian thought.' Setting adrift proves a fit image of that mingling and of the period's growing sense of unease" ("Sleeping" 160). Hares-Stryker argues eloquently for one way of reading these romances, yet we can be much more specific about the "unease" they manifest by concentrating on social rather than spiritual or existential crises. Though also reflecting earlier custom and story, the two introductory motifs of the Castaway Queen tale, incest followed by setting adrift, reflect and to some degree may be explained by specific social concerns in the times in which the romances were composed.

Margaret Schlauch was convinced that the incest motif reflected the customs of a much earlier society, "a matriarchy, or that system of human society in which descent is reckoned through the mother" (41; today we would call this a *matriliny*; see Ehrenberg 64). In such a society the royal succession would come through the woman, resulting in a practice where "the successor to a king is often not his own son, but the husband of his daughter" (41). Thus to preserve his kingship the father had to prevent his daughter's marriage to another; one way of doing this, Schlauch observes, was to marry her himself. Although the three queens do become the mothers of emperors in these tales, and their sisters in similar tales become the mothers of popes and saints, Schlauch's argument on this subject is not fully convincing to us today, nor would a scholar now rely on her main sources (in 1927), Frazer and Hartland.

In any case, of more interest to the modern scholar is the question of why a particular motif, such as the incest motif, became popular at the time that it was given literary expression. Elizabeth Archibald, the most notable scholar writing on the subject, mentions that Alessandro d'Ancona suggested long ago (in 1869) "that the incest scandals of the twelfth century might have been responsible for the revival in a highly moral form of Greek myths about incest" ("Incest" 8). The beginning of the Castaway Queen story apparently reflects two main issues of contemporary uncertainty or unrest, the construction of incest itself (how, exactly, was it to be defined?) and individual as opposed to paternal control of marriage. Each issue will now be examined in turn, the second more briefly than the first, though both discussions must necessarily be schematic in this introduction.

In the early Middle English period, the theological doctrine of contritionism was being developed. As modern cases demonstrate, acknowledged incest provides an excellent catalyst for the self-scrutiny leading to contrition. But the concept of incest itself was being radically redefined and elaborated in the eleventh and twelfth centuries as the church campaigned to enforce consanguinity laws (Archibald, "Flight" 5), incidentally adding to its inherited assets by using this principle to restrict marriage. The Fourth Lateran Council of 1215 C.E. (so-named because it was held in the Lateran basilica in Rome) defined incest as "sexual intercourse between those related to the fourth degree" (Donavin 9). This was a modification of Peter Damian's 1063 C.E. definition of incest extending to the sixth degree "computed by the Germanic method of counting" (ibid.), that is, counting back from the self to the ancestor held in common with the prospective partner; the *third* degree would be, for example, a common great-grandfather (ibid. 96). "Since hardly anyone knew all their relations to the sixth degree without genealogical research"—and most people in a nonmigratory community, as well as most of the ruling classes of Europe, would be related at the sixth degree—"many couples committed incest unwittingly, and the Church commonly turned a blind eye toward marriages beyond the fourth degree, that is, marriages between fourth or more distant cousins" (ibid. 9). This difficulty about enforcement lay behind the council's decree; it was an attempt to bring ecclesiastical theory in line with practice.

Nevertheless, the degree of relationship within which one might not marry being still extreme, especially when property and other considerations entering into the marriage decision reduced the pool of appropriate partners among the elite, appeal to the pope and marriage under his special dispensation became more common. This is the historical background for the peculiar papal dispensation that allows Emaré's father to think he can legitimately marry his own daughter; the widowed king in *La Belle Hélène de Constantinople* and the king in the Swedish folktale "The King of Russia's Daughter" (among others) also receive sanction from the pope to marry their offspring. (In *Florence* the pope is incorporated in the narrative as author not of a dispensation but of the story itself.) The real-life incest scandals provoked by this overzealous doctrine of the church, along with the Lollards arguing for a reduction of the incest prohibitions to the second degree (Donavin 10), must certainly have helped to revive the interest in Greek romances and myths in which incest is an element, and to establish an atmosphere welcoming to the Castaway Queen romances.[29]

The concern in this same period about control over marriage and the woman's right to select her own husband more obviously raises questions about the audience of these romances. At what group of listeners were they directed? Recent work on readers' response to rape scenes in modern women's romance suggests that, contrary to the usual male interpretation, women readers are not titillated by this theme so much as practicing for contingencies: "Rape 'fantasies' may indeed enable women to contemplate sexual violence without fear of consequence . . . not because they wish to be victims of rape but rather because they can, in the safe space of imagination, explore violent conflicts between men and women and rehearse strategies for living with male aggression" (Gravdal 18). In this context wish-fulfillment may offer a picture of our romances' readership. The scene of Florence bashing in her attacker's teeth must have been as refreshing for women then as it is now (I am happy to say that today's men applaud the scene also). But when the sobering male vengeance follows, only the romance form consoles us: the genre demands that Florence must survive. Romance is a safe space where a woman may come ashore in alien lands, may return violence for violence—and may choose her own marriage partner without parental interference.

To whom would it appeal that the three queens could, eventually if not at first, choose their own husbands? In her article "Construction of Class, Family, and Gender in Some Middle English Popular Romances," Harriet E. Hudson focuses on four romances, *Sir Eglamour of Artois, Torrent of Portengale, Paris and Vienne,* and *The Squire of Low Degree,* in which men are the heroes but the doubled exile-and-return episodes and the calumniated queen motif play an important part. She shows how "concerns about gender, class, and family are brought to a crux in the romances' depiction of father-daughter conflict over control of marriage" (77). It was a period in which on the one hand the emerging gentry class displayed "an obsessive concern for the preservation and extension of property and the advancement of family through marriage" (81), and on the other hand an increased emphasis on an affective individualism was upheld by the law, which insisted on "the free consent of the couple and the equality of the sexes in constituting the union" (86). This social conflict bore literary results. As Hudson says of her four male-centered romances, "The constant in our romances' representations of family dynamics is the generational conflict over marriage" (85). The three woman-centered romances about Emaré, Florence, and Custance avoid this conflict by separating the marriageable woman protagonist from the sphere of parental domination. *Emaré* requires no comment here. Although Custance's father arranges her marriage in the manner usual among royalty, her wicked mother-in-law subverts the alliance by killing her own son (symbolizing the final degree of dysfunction in a family), and *then* Custance is set adrift, to make her own way and choose her own man. With her indulgent father's support, Florence rejects lustful but aged Garcy (an incestuous-father surrogate) in the earlier part of her story not translated here, then when her real father is slain in Garcy's military expedition to gain her by force, she chooses the hero Emere as her husband.[30] The incestuous father typically, as in *Emaré*, seeks to deprive the daughter of her choice of another man, but the plot of the romance gives that opportunity back to her.

Arguing that the poet John Gower's interest in the theme of incest governs the structure of his important and lengthy *Confessio Amantis*, Donavin points out that in lines 148–61 of that poem Gower "reminds us of Aquinas' warning that incest leads to sexual exploitation at home and a loss of social connections in the community" (11). She traces how that loss of connection is dramatized in the Arthurian romances. The theme of incest enters the Arthurian legend in the thirteenth century, perhaps in the *Mort Artu*, Mordred earlier being the son of Arthur's sister Anna and King Loth; in later tradition Mordred becomes Arthur's son by his sister Morgause, and in Arthur's absence he desires to wed the king's wife Guinevere, thus complicating the incest theme. Such complications and antisocial lusts for sex and power are among the factors leading to the demise of the Round Table and the death of Arthur at his evil son's hand. "These thirteenth-century Arthurian poems reflect the concern evident at the Fourth Lateran Council about incest and its moral and social implications" (Donavin 12). Our romances additionally incorporate the concern about control over marriage evident at the same historically significant council.

Archibald finds in stories of this period three new motifs not in the classical tales: the double incest motif (as in the Gregorius tale), incest as catalyst (as in our stories, where the father or father-substitute fades out of the narrative once he has launched the plot), and incest as a crime to be expiated (usually in saints' lives, again as in the tale of the "holy sinner" Gregorius). Sometimes, as in *Emaré*, the molesting father is sufficiently contrite to be incorporated back into the happy family at the end, always by the daughter's authority. This is not the case in *Apollonius of Tyre*, where the incestuous father is divinely punished (but that story gives us two fathers, the one who commits incest and the one who is tempted to but does not), nor is the lecherous and aged father-substitute Garcy in *Florence* forgiven and reincorporated; he dies.

✧ Setting Adrift as Legal Punishment

When the incestuous father or father-surrogate launches the usual plot by punishing the reluctant daughter, he sets her adrift upon the sea of fortune that enables her perilous adventures to take place. Though the setting adrift of the heroine in the story has the important allegorical significance of the soul adrift on the seas of this world, the theme is also connected with a real-life practice, or rather two related practices: the abandonment of unwanted children, particularly females, and the legal exposure of criminals and other undesirables. In "The Politics of Scarcity: Notes on the Sex Ratio in

Early Scandinavia," Carol Clover forcefully documents the practice and implications of the abandonment of baby girls, a practice that she calls "female infanticide," and John Boswell discusses the other side of the picture, the adoption of foundlings, in his disturbing book, *The Kindness of Strangers*. With all three of our heroines experiencing "the kindness of strangers," adoption is an important element in these romances. Both exposure and adoption were matters much discussed and legislated in the Middle Ages, but I know of no modern study discussing the medieval sheltering of fully grown females, and child exposure is not central to these romances. Therefore I will concentrate here on the other issue mentioned above, the setting adrift of unwanted persons in the community.

In his 1941 article, "Setting Adrift in Medieval Law and Literature," J. R. Reinhard conveniently compiles the evidence for medieval sea-exposure. The dates and content of some of Reinhard's fascinating array of examples reflect in an interesting way upon the theories of Archibald and Donavin about the renewed emphasis on incest during this period. According to Reinhard, there were three classes of persons who might be set adrift. First were the noncriminals like Odysseus or the Irish saints, persons lost at sea and thus in God's hand (or, as in Odysseus's case, in the hand of the goddess); second came innocent persons unwanted in the community, such as undesired children and persons possessing dangerous information or talents; third were criminals or presumed criminals, like murderers and witches. All three classes of victim demonstrate a belief that the sea will be a just arbiter of human destiny, thus guaranteeing that the innocent will be spared—which fulfils the demands of romance. Reinhard tells us specifically that appeal to the sea as legal arbiter (through trial by water) was "frequently made in the case of children born of incestuous relation" (37).

In *A Guide to Early Irish Law*, Fergus Kelly tells us more. A fragment of an Old Irish law text with its accompanying commentary refers specifically to children born of incest; they are to be placed in a "leather shrine" (i.e., a casket?) that is taken out to sea "as far as a white shield is visible" (221). If the little shrine is washed ashore, the child must be spared, but only to be a servant in the family. Citing the Middle English Gregorius legend, Reinhard explains that God "shall judge whether [the sea-exposed infant] shall live or die, and thereby judge also whether or not the sin may be forgiven" (38). A similar sentiment lay behind the exposure of criminals: "Setting adrift was a penalty assigned in those cases wherein the evidence of guilt was not or could not be conclusive in the eyes of a human judge, or which he was not wholly competent to weigh, or in which it was desirable to temper justice with mercy" (ibid. 47). The *Caín Adomnáin* describes the procedure, associating it specifically with a female offender: "She is put into a boat with one paddle and a vessel of gruel, and is set adrift on an offshore wind. Judgment is left to God" (*La Día brithimnacht furi ísin*) (Kelly 220).

Considerations of this kind are seen at work in *Emaré*, where the heroine is set adrift as a disobedient daughter at the beginning and as a possible witch later on. But in *Florence* and *Custance* the heroine is more in the nature of Reinhard's first category, the noncriminal who is placed in God's hands upon the open sea. Forest exposure was practiced upon much the same principle of trial by ordeal; the innocent must by their nature be immune to life-threatening dangers. Sexual abstinence, like that of hermits or our chaste heroines, provided additional protection. When the Lady is lost in the forest in Milton's *Comus* (lines 414–21), her elder brother expresses the theory well:

> Elder Brother:
>   My sister is not so defenceless left
>   As you imagine, she has a hidden strength
>   Which you remember not.
> 2 Brother: What hidden strength,
>   Unless the strength of Heav'n, if you mean that?
> Elder Brother:
>   I mean that too, but yet a hidden strength
>   Which if Heav'n gave it, may be term'd her own:
>   Tis chastity, my brother, chastity:
>   She has that, is clad in compleat steel . . .

Reinhard cautions that "setting adrift" does not include the intention to seek adventure or pursue a quest upon the sea in a well-provisioned boat, and that the legal purpose of the practice also excludes sea-burial (66), that is, the practice of casting overboard the bodies of persons who died at sea, in a coffin if they were suitably important. The story of Apollonius's queen shows, nevertheless, that *mistaken* sea-burial could have the same effect as a purposeful setting adrift, and in both cases it is assumed that the sea or its gods will send the vessel to an appropriate destination.[31] Reinhard concludes his argument by returning to the subject of romance:

> The marine adventures of Constance and her congeners have frequently been dismissed as unworthy of too much attention by the serious-minded because they were medieval and seemingly inexplicable. What happened to Prospero has been set down as another shabby trick from the same Gothic bag. But if there be any cogency in the illustrations and arguments which have here been set forth, it must now be clear that the manners and customs, the beliefs, superstitions, and even the laws of human societies form the forcing-bed out of which literature springs. (68)

Although Reinhard wrote his article half a century ago, he makes here a very contemporary observation about the part that social history plays in the literature of all periods. Certain troublesome doctrines of the church and legal practices of the day, reflected in and combining with the living anxieties of the people, perhaps particularly of women, have contributed to the remodeling of an ancient story into a medieval romance that speaks to its time.[32] Though the story is gender-specific in having the woman protagonist escape an incestuous embrace, find her own man without parental guidance (i.e., hindrance), and heal her dysfunctional family, it also has a broader appeal, in this period when the soul was regarded as female and the sea a place of trial, when we see the vulnerable but innocent protagonist unharmed by her ordeal. If certain problems of form and surface structure can be surmounted, the experience of reading about a "mere woman" (or a mere anyone) surviving the tossing billows of fate can be as interesting and as inspiring to us as it was to that audience of the Middle Ages—an audience that, perhaps perceiving the story "expanding into insights and experiences beyond itself . . . like a shell that contains the sound of the sea" (Frye, *Scripture* 59), demanded that it be told over and over, combining elements in different ways and with different emphases.

2.

The Romances Rhymed in Modern English

EMARÉ COMES FIRST IN this sequence of translations as the most typical example in English of the incest-instigated plot of the woman cast adrift that is found in many versions throughout Europe. *Le Bone Florence of Rome* (the second part only) is a lively variation on it, and Chaucer's *Man of Law's Tale* about Custance, the fourth of *The Canterbury Tales*, is a sophisticated version of the story. They are presented here in imitative translations that attempt to capture the liveliness of their verse forms.

✧ *Emaré*

Of all the similar stories, *Emaré* is the only one in the form of a Breton lay. This means that it may be meant to be sung and the stanzas should be read that way, like song lyrics.

The *Emaré* poet's dialect reveals north-east Midlands origins with a strong Northern element, "mid-Yorkshire," says Edith Rickert, who suggests a location specifically "between the Humber and Knaresborough" (edition xviii). The text is found in only one manuscript, British Library Cotton Caligula A ii. I have used Thomas C. Rumble's 1965 edition of *Emaré* in *The Breton Lays in Middle English*, checking this against Edith Rickert's edition of 1908.[1]

The protagonist's name "Emaré" rhymes with "lady gay," and is sometimes spelled "Emarye" with the same pronunciation. Her mother's name "Eranye" and her own alias "Egaré" (or "Egarye") are also pronounced as though the stressed final -ye were -ay, or yay with the first y only slightly sounded. In the name of her father, the emperor Artyus, every letter is pronounced: ART-ee-yus. His friend Sir Tergaunt, appearing in the eighth stanza, also sounds every letter of his name: TER-ga-unt. In the name of Emaré's nurse, Abró, the last vowel is stressed, as indicated, rhyming with "toe" and "sew." All the lovers pictured on the marvellous embroidered cloth described in stanzas 7–15 have names in which every letter is pronounced: Y-DO-y-ne, and so on. Other important characters, the King of Wales, his mother, and the burgess (city-dweller) of Rome who takes Emaré in, are not named in the story.

Although the poet uses the twelve-line "tail rhyme" stanza typical of English romance, rhyming aab-ccb-ddb-eeb with the "tail" (the shorter b-rhyming line) supposed to rhyme four times on the same sound, it should be observed that the original Middle English text of *Emaré* breaks this pattern frequently with both near rhymes and non-rhymes. In stanza 2, for example, the b rhymes are land, sand, among, and song. In the Middle English these are londe, sonde, amonge, and songe, which makes them closer sounding than in modern English because of the o followed by n throughout, but they are still not exact rhymes. This looser rhyming may reflect a French source or French influence, where assonance (rhyming the vowel-sounds only, as above) was more acceptable than in English. Sometimes I go along with this discrepancy (as again in stanza 6, where the original has bowre, flowre, honour, emperour), but when a better modern rhyme comes to mind I use it, believing that the romance-poet would have done so also. The point is to make the verses ripple along, their movement carrying the story enjoyably and singably.

The stanzas of all three romances are numbered, with line numbers appearing at the beginning of each stanza. Notes keyed to line and stanza will be found in the notes section at the end of the book.

1

1   *Jesus, king, on Heaven's throne,*
    Maker of the sun and moon
        And all that gives delight,
    Now grant us grace such deeds to do
    That someday we may dwell with you
        In bliss called "heaven-light."
    And Jesus' Mother, Mary, queen,
    Who's such a lovely go-between,
        Direct our praying right
    To thy good son, so one day we
    In Heaven above with Him may be —
        That lord of greatest might.

2

13   *Minstrels wandering to and fro,*
     Here and there, wherever they go
        In many a different land,
     Ought as they begin to sing
     To mention first the heavenly King
        Who made both sea and sand.
     Now if you'll listen for a time,

I'll tell you a delightful rhyme
    (Though sad notes be among
The lighter ones) of a lady gay.
The lady's name was Emaré,
    And here I sing her song.

3

25 Her sire, an emperor of power,
Held a castle and mighty tower.
    Sir Artyus was he.
And he had other halls and bowers,
Fields and forests fair with flowers;
    No greater lord could be.
The well-born lady that he wed
Was fair and lovely. Skin she had
    As white as ivory.
They called that empress Eranye;
No lady with a more loving way
    Was ever known than she.

4

37 Sir Artyus was the best of men
In all the world who was living then;
    A strong and valorous knight.
Courtly he was in every way
Both to old and to young and gay;
    He treated people right.
Just one child in all his life
Had he begotten of his wife,
    And she was fair and bright.
Forsooth, her name again I'll say:
They called that baby Emaré.
    She was a lovely sight.

5

49 When her dear mother gave her birth,
She was the fairest child on earth,
  Her fate a sad one, though:
The empress, who was fair and good,
Had died before her baby could
  Walk or talk, and so
The father sent his pretty baby
To be fostered by a lady
  Called Good Dame Abró.
She taught her courtesy and manners,
And how with gold on silken banners
  (With other maids) to sew.

6

61 Abró taught well that maiden small
How to comport herself in hall
  While she was yet in bower.
Courteous was small Emaré
Both to old and to young and gay,
  White as a lily flower,
And also skilled and quick of hand.
Everyone loved her in that land
  And wished to honor her.
Now let us leave the maiden there
With Dame Abró, so good and fair,
  And speak of the emperor.

7

73 This emperor of noble blood
Was a courteous lord, and good
  In every sort of way.

After the death of his dear wife,
He quietly led a widower's life
     Though much inclined to play.
So when the king of Sicily
Came to visit Artyus, he
     Was glad for him to stay.
A present the Sicilian brought,
A cloth that was most worthily wrought,
     Embroidered rich and gay.

8

85   Sir Tergaunt, the Sicilian knight,
Unrolled the gift and placed it right
     Across the emperor's knee.
The cloth that he presented him
With many a bright and precious gem,
     Was studded gleamingly.
Topazes, diamonds clear as ice,
And other stones of equal price
     Were beautiful to see.
Toadstones, rubies, agates fair,
Exquisitely were set out there.
     It's true as it can be!

9

97   They hung the cloth upon the wall,
But Artyus could not see at all
     The sight he looked upon.
The glare of many a precious gem
Into his eyes had blinded him.
     He said, "What's going on?"

And then he bellowed angrily,
"Is this a fairy trick on me
        Or such phenomenon?"
The King of Sicily calmly spoke:
"Of treasures owned by Christian folk,
        There's no comparison!"

10

109   The heathen daughter of an Emir
Designed this cloth, or so I hear,
        And wrought it all with pride,
Embroidering lovers and their ilk
In rich gold threads and azure silk
        And jewels on every side.
The story that we have in hand
Says precious stones from every land
        Were sought for far and wide.
For seven winters it was sewn
Before she felt it could be shown —
        'Twas not a thing to hide!

11

121   Embroidered in one corner was
Ydóyne with Amadas,
        Their love that was so true.
And they were shown, for honest love,
Entwined with a true-love flower of
        Gems of a brilliant hue:
With sapphire and with carbuncle,
Chalcedony and onyx, all
        Set into gold brand-new,

And diamonds, rubies, many a stone.
Singing troubadors were shown
    And all their instruments, too.

12

133   The second corner showed the pair
Sir Tristram and Isolde the fair,
    Most elegant to see.
Because the love was pure between
The two of them, with gems the scene
    Was thick as it might be:
Topazes, diamonds clear as ice
And other stones of equal price
    Shone there exquisitely.
Toadstones, rubies, agates fair,
All precious stones beyond compare
    Were set there carefully.

13

143   The third corner showed two lovers more,
Florys and Lady Blancheflor,
    Each to the other dear.
And they were shown, for honest love,
Entwined with a true-love flower of
    Jewels most bright and clear.
Many a senator and knight
Was also shown, in emeralds bright
    And faultless; and there were
Diamonds, corals pink and white,
Crystals, yellow chrysolite,
    And garnets everywhere.

14

157   The final corner showed the son
Of the Sultan of Babylon,
      And also, standing near
Was she who loved like life itself
This man for whom she made the cloth,
      The daughter of the Emir.
Before this maid, a unicorn
Lifted his solitary horn
      High into the air,
And birds and flowers on every side
Gleamed with gems found far and wide.
      Figures were everywhere.

15

169   And when at last the cloth was made
And to the sultan then conveyed,
      It was a lovely sight.
Sir Tergaunt said, "My father won
This cloth so elegantly spun
      With mastery and might.
To show his love he gave to me
What I to you affectionately
      Present now, rich and bright."
He gave that cloth to the emperor
Who courteously thanked him for
      The treasure, as was right.

16

181   The King of Sicily stayed there
Enjoying life with the emperor
      As long as he chose to stay.

In due course he decided, though,
Politely that he had to go,
　　And went upon his way.
And then the lonely emperor
Thought of his daughter, longing for
　　A word with Emaré,
So by a messenger he conveyed
His wishes to that gentle maid,
　　Bright as a summer's day.

17

173　His messengers made ready quickly,
Going with music through the city,
　　Through the throng and press,
By thoroughfare and alleyway,
Until they came to Emaré,
　　So pretty in her dress.
The Dame who cared for her, Abró,
Into the carriage stepped also.
　　The maiden with her nurse
Went to the emperor then, who
Came out himself a mile or two,
　　And good that meeting was!

18

205　The maiden, white as a lily flower,
Stepped down to meet the emperor;
　　Two knights were in the lead.
Her father, who with great renown
Bore on his head the kingdom's crown,
　　Alighted from his steed.

When they were both down on their feet,
He gently kissed his daughter sweet.
    They turned then to proceed
In joy, the maiden with her father,
And to the palace walked together,
    In story as we read.

19

217   Great lords had gathered there to eat.
They washed and sat down to their meat,
    And quickly they were plied
With food and drink. The maiden fair
Was led up to her father's chair
    And seated at his side.
The fairest woman of that day,
She smiled whenever he looked her way;
    He often looked and sighed.
And thus he fell in love — until
With her he thought to have his will
    And take her for his bride!

20

229   When after dinner he'd withdrawn
And to his royal chamber gone,
    He called his council there.
He said they must go on a mission
To get for him the pope's permission
    To wed that maiden fair.
Away the messengers then went,
Nor dared to question his intent,
    And earls went with them where

Quickly from the court of Rome
They brought that dispensation home
To wed his daugher fair.

21

241   *Then wasn't the emperor elated!*
He ordered a wedding robe created
Out of that cloth of gold.
When in that shining robe the woman
Dressed, she seemed no longer human,
Cast in the common mold.
And then the emperor, turning to
His daughter, said, "I'll marry you,
So lovely to behold."
That worthy maiden, in her gown,
Said, "Nay, sir! God in Heaven would frown
If we should be so bold.

22

253   *"If it befell that we were wed*
And played together in your bed,
Lost we both should be.
The news would spread out far and wide
Through all the world, on every side,
By rumor, endlessly.
You are a lord of reputation.
Let God guide you. To your nation
Don't bring such misery.
That to the altar I should go
To wed my father, I say no,
I never will agree!"

23

265 The emperor, swelling up with wrath,
Spoke in his rage a dreadful oath.
    He said that she should be
Slain, and ordered at once a boat
Prepared for setting his child afloat
    In that embroidery.
No money must be in her purse,
No food, no drink to slake her thirst
    When cast upon the sea.
Soon the lady was far from shore
Without an anchor or an oar,
    And pitiful was she!

24

277 There came a wind, I understand,
That blew the boat away from land,
    And swept her out of sight.
Now to the emperor came the thought
That possibly his deed had not
    Been absolutely right.
He stood there thinking with a frown
Then fainted suddenly, falling down.
    He was a sorry knight!
The noble lords who stood around
Caught up the emperor from the ground
    And comforted him all night.

25

289 When Artyus recovered, he
Cried out and said remorsefully,
    "Alas, my daughter dear!

Alas that I was made a man,
Oh, wretched lecher that I am!"
    He shed then many a tear.
"Against God's holy law I sought
To harm my daughter true of thought,
    And now she is not here!"
The tears poured out from both his eyes,
And all his lords heaved mighty sighs
    And also shed a tear.

26

301 Neither young nor old could keep
From tears, nor could they cease to weep
    For her with the golden hair.
So in their vessels fleet and fast
They looked for Emaré at last,
    So young and pale and fair.
Though over all the seas they sought her,
They could not find the emperor's daughter.
    And soon returned to where
The emperor waited, sad and grave.
Leave him, for of her on the wave
    I shall now declare.

27

313 The lady floated forth alone.
To God in Heaven she made her moan
    And to His mother, too.
Far was she driven by wind and rain
And mighty storms on the bounding main,
    Those seas so rarely blue.

I have heard minstrels sing the tale:
Far from home and land, her sail
    Over the ocean flew.
Driven rudderless deep to deep,
She hid her head and began to weep.
    Nothing else could she do.

28

325 Now Emaré was in this plight
A little over a seven-night.
    It must have been God's will.
Heart full of care and sighing sore,
She was ordained this fate of yore,
    So ever she lay still.
At last she was driven onto land
Through the great mercy of God's hand
    That all things may fulfil.
After days of constant danger,
She was nearly mad with hunger.
    Woe to the winds of ill!

29

337 She was driven onto a land
Called Galys (Wales, I understand).
    That was a pleasant shore.
The king's own steward dwelt nearby
In a castle proud and high;
    His name was Sir Kadore.
Each day he strolled upon the sand
Along with anyone on hand,
    A squire or two or more.

On one fair morning he went out
With two good knights and strolled about,
     When suddenly before . . .

                    30

349   Their very eyes at the surf's edge loomed
A boat, and something in it gleamed.
     They thought it must be fey,
But all went forward, nonetheless,
And found the lady in her dress
     Where in the boat she lay.
So long with no food had she been,
It made them ache, she was so thin,
     About to pass away.
Kadore asked her to say to him
Her name. She changed it on a whim,
     Said she was Egaré.

                    31

361   Then sorry for her, good Kadore
Led homeward from the wild shore
     That lady from the sea.
She had no food when under sail,
And thin, it seemed now, as a rail
     Under her dress was she.
Now to his castle they came apace,
And took her to a quiet place
     And fed her copiously
With every delicate kind of food
That anyone thought might do her good,
     That in that place might be.

32

373   When slowly Emaré the fair
With meat and drink was able there
    Her color to regain,
She taught the women how to sew
Embroidered hangings that would glow
    With silks from shining skein.
Courtly she was in every way
Both to the old and to young and gay,
    Adored by great and plain,
And able to sew up anything
To clothe an emperor or king,
    Or baron, earl, or swain.

33

385   Kadore then had an inspiration:
He planned a happy celebration
    For his lord the king.
He thus had many minstrels come
With trumpet, psaltry, horn and drum,
    Harp and fiddling.
The lady, regal now and slim,
Alone in the hall was serving them
    Before that noble king.
She wore the robe that shone so bright
It seemed like an unearthly light,
    And she no earthly thing.

34

397   The king of Wales who watched her there
Had never seen someone so fair
    That she his heart could hold.

So captivating was the sight
Of her, he could not eat a bite,
But wished only to behold.
She was so courtly in her manner,
The king's love settled firmly on her,
In story as it's told.
So when that dinnertime was done,
To his chamber he went anon,
And called his barons bold.

35

408   *He called for Sir Kadore to come*
With other barons to his room,
And waited there until
His dukes and nobles, wise of lore,
Had quickly come and bowed before
Their king, and asked his will.
The king of Wales, in rich array,
To Sir Kadore had this to say
In fair words, sitting still:
"Sir, explain, please, whence comes she
Who in the hall was serving me.
Tell, if it be your will."

36

421   *Then said Kadore, I understand,*
"She's an earl's daughter from a land
That I have never seen.
I sent for her. For many days
She's taught my children courtly ways;
Up in their rooms she's been.

And she does needlework with her hands,
The cleverest in Christian lands
    Of any I have seen."
Then said that ruler of great power,
"I'll have that maiden for my bower,
    And wed her as my queen."

37

433   The noble king, with this intent,
After his royal mother sent
    To hear what she would say.
And Emaré they brought there too,
The maiden lovely as a blue
    Sky on a summer's day.
The robe she walked in shone so bright
When she was in it, like a light
    On gentle Emaré,
That then the old queen, with a laugh,
Said, "Never saw I a woman half
    So shining and so gay."

38

445   And then she spoke these words unkind:
"My son, that robe . . . she is a fiend
    Whom you have thought to wed.
So if you want your mother's blessing,
May you never have this wedding.
    Nay, may God forbid!"
Then said that ruler of great power,
"Mother, I'll have her for my bower!"
    When by the hand he led

Fair Emaré, the aged queen
Said angrily, "I do not mean
    To stay to see you wed."

39

457   And so he married his lady fair,
And great the celebration there
    In Wales was, in that hall.
Noble lords were served all night,
Duke and baron, earl and knight,
    Persons both great and small.
So many came to that abode,
The castle nearly overflowed —
    It says so in the tale.
And there was every kind of thing
Proper to a king's wedding,
    And minstrels played for all.

40

469   When the wedding feast was done
And lords were leaving one by one,
    A seemly sight to see,
The king was left then with his queen,
And great the love there was between
    That couple, joyously.
She was so courteous and sweet,
I never heard of another yet
    So loving as was she.
Quite soon that lady meek and mild
Conceived, and she grew big with child
    As God willed it should be.

41

481   The King of France, around that time,
        Was in distress. Attacking him
                Was many a Saracen.
        He sent a message to his friend
        And other great lords who could lend
                A hand; his need was keen.
        The King of Wales prepared for war,
        Gathering men from near and far
                In armor bright and clean.
        Then said the king to Sir Kadore
        And other lords who stood before
                His throne, "Care for my queen!"

42

493   The King of France called everyone,
        His under-kings and, sparing none,
                His knights, and clerics too.
        Only the steward was left at home
        To serve the fair queen, pale as foam,
                For nothing of war he knew.
        As long as God's will let it be,
        Beneath her smock, quite prettily,
                The baby lay and grew,
        Until at last she bore a lad.
        A double royal mark he had,
                As kings' sons often do.

43

505   When the time for christening came,
        Upon that royal child the name
                Of Segramor was bestowed,

And then the steward, Sir Kadore,
Wrote a noble letter for
      The king, wrought all with gold.
He quickly wrote down many a word
And sent the letter to his lord.
      So good news might be told,
He sent a messenger in a hurry.
With the king's mother he stopped to tarry
      When past her castle he rode.

44

517   The messenger being cordially
Received, she asked him hastily
      What child the queen had had.
"Madam, she had a little boy,
A fair man-child and all her joy,
      And now she lies in bed."
She gave for the news he brought to her
Forty shillings and a cloak of fur,
      So he was richly clad.
She filled his cup with ale and wine,
And when she saw that it was time
      Upstairs she led the lad.

45

528   The moment he began to snore,
The queen came through his chamber door.
      Wicked was her desire!
She took the letter from his cloak
And sent it quickly up in smoke
      That rose from the bedroom fire.

And then she wrote an evil letter,
Saying the bride had borne a devil
    And no one dared come nigh her.
Three heads he had, she wrote, of bear,
Dragon, and lion — and too much hair!
    Thus was that queen a liar.

46

540   In the morning, when it was day,
The messenger went on his way
    By roads both low and high
(This tale is true!), arriving where
The good king and his armies were,
    Bearing his lord a lie.
The king took the letter in his hand
And read it there, I understand.
    A tear came to his eye,
And as he stood there reading it,
Down he fell in a fainting fit,
    So sad he thought he'd die.

47

553   But noble lords who stood around
Soon caught the king up from the ground.
    His heart was full of woe.
Sorely he wept and said, "Alas,
That ever born a man I was,
    That ever it should be so!
Alas, that I was made a king,
And then must wed the fairest thing
    That ever on earth did go!

Alas, that Jesus chose to send
A child who is a loathsome fiend
        To come between us so."

48

564   But seeing that grief made nothing better,
He sighed and wrote another letter,
        Sealing it with his seal.
This was the message of the king:
That they should help her in everything
        Till she was fully well,
And everyone should do their best
To carry out her least request
        Both in woe and weal.
The messenger took it from his hand
And rode by the same route over land
        Where the old queen liked to dwell.

49

577   Again he stayed there overnight.
Received so well and treated right,
        He let the old queen ply
The wine that stole away his reason,
But never did he think of treason
        As that long night went by.
When he was deep into his dreams,
The wicked queen began her schemes.
        She sought until her eye
Lit on that letter. She wrote another
Ordering that the fair young mother
        Be cast on the sea to die.

50

589 *She must be led down to the ocean,*
Her robe agleam with every motion,
  And with her little child.
No money might she have in purse,
No food, no drink to slake her thirst,
  When led into the wild.
"On penalty of your family,
And your own life, so fair and free,
  To pleas you must not yield."
The messenger, who knew no guile,
Went riding home for many a mile
  Past forest, farm, and field.

51

601 *And when that messenger came home,*
The steward, taking the letter from
  His hand, began to read.
Sorely he sighed and said, "Alas,
Something dreadful has come to pass!
  This is a doleful deed."
And as he stood there reading it,
He suddenly fell in a fainting fit.
  His heart began to bleed.
Then no one young or old, not one,
Failed to weep at what was done
  To Emaré in her need.

52

613 *That lady, hearing in the hall*
Such lamentation, went to call
  The steward: "What can be

The trouble here? What's gone amiss?
Tell me exactly what it is,
     And don't go sparing me."
Then mournfully the steward said,
"Here is the letter I just read,
     And therefore, woe is me!"
She took the letter in her hand
And read therein the cruel command
     To cast her out to sea.

53

625   But then, "Be calm, good sir," said she.
"You do not have to mourn for me,
     And you must not ignore,
To your own peril, the king's command
Here in this letter in my hand,
     That there's some reason for.
Perhaps he thinks he wedded poorly
Marrying me, a simple lady,
     And feels some shame therefore.
Give greeting to my lord from me,
For nobler bred there shall not be
     A babe whom lady bore."

54

637   Much was the sorrow, much the woe
When Emaré to her ship must go,
     With everyone wringing their hands.
The lady fair, so meek and mild,
Bore in her arms the little child
     And took her leave of land.
When she went floating out to sea

In that bright robe so rich to see,
Grown men fell on the sand.
Sorely they wept and said, "Alas,
That such an evil should come to pass!
Woe to this command!"

55

649 The lady and the little child
Floated away on the waters wild.
His luck was not the best.
Across her face the collar wide
Of that bright robe she pulled to hide
The churning ocean, lest
Of the sight she be too afraid,
And down upon the deck she laid
Herself, and to her breast
Clutched the child, as from below
Great waves smote them blow on blow
With many an awful crest.

56

661 And when the child began to weep,
She sang him sorrowfully back to sleep,
His mouth upon her breast,
Then said, "If from these waves that roar
So high, I could only get to shore,
Whether to east or west,
Then well ought I to curse thee, sea,
When I am guiltless, for beating me."
Sorely she sighed, distressed,
But then sat up and said a prayer
To Jesus and His mother dear,
The way that she knew best.

57

673   *Now the lady was in this plight*
       A little over a seven-night.
          It must have been God's will.
       With heart full of care and sighing sore,
       She knew a sorrow ordained of yore,
          So ever she lay still.
       At last the waves drove her to Rome
       Through grace of God on Heaven's throne
          Who all things may fulfil.
       After days of constant danger,
       She was nearly mad with hunger.
          Woe to luck gone ill!

58

685   *There in that capital city, Rome,*
       A wealthy merchant made his home,
          Jordan by name, and he
       Had plenty of wealth in gold and treasure,
       And often liked to take his pleasure
          Walking by the sea.
       When he went out on this occasion
       To take a walk beside the ocean,
          Wishing alone to be,
       He found a boat cast up on shore
       And in it a lady weeping sore,
          For woebegone was she.

59

697   *But what she was wearing shone so bright*
       That he was startled by the light
          That glowing garment shed,

And in his heart he was afraid
That she was not an earthly maid.
          Nevertheless, he said,
"What is your name, my lady, pray?"
"Lord," she said, "I'm Egarye,
          Lying here in dread."
Then up he took that lady fair,
And homeward with her baby there
          The wealthy merchant led.

60

709   He brought her to his house in Rome
And welcomed kindly to his home
          That lady fair and bright.
He bade his wife bring right away
Some food for hungry Egarye,
          And feed the lady right.
"Whatever it is that she may crave,
Whatever she desires to have,
          Give it to her tonight.
So long has she been lacking food
That you must be especially good.
          Give comfort with all your might!"

61

721   Now Emaré stayed there with them,
And any food for which her whim
          Prompted, she had at will.
Courtly she was in every way
Both to old and to young and gay,
          To lowly and notable.
Her son began to grow and thrive,

And soon was the prettiest child alive,
Fair as a flower on hill.
She sewed bright silken tapestries
And taught her small son courtesies,
But ever was mournful still.

62

733   When Segramor was seven years old,
Growing up both wise and bold,
Well formed of flesh and bone,
His clothing showed his mother's pride.
Well could he mount a steed and ride.
More courtly child was none.
Both in the hall and ladies' bower,
Wherever he went, young Segramor
Was loved by everyone.
Now let us leave them there in Rome,
And go to Spain where the king turns home
His seige and battles done.

63

745   As soon as the siege was broken, he
Set out for Wales quite happily,
Glad with a victor's pride.
His dukes and earls of rich estate,
Barons and knights both noble and great,
Were riding by his side,
And Sir Kadore, his steward, then
Rode up to him with his best men,
As fast as he could ride.
Of all that had happened, everything
In hall or bower, he told the king,
Events both far and wide.

64

757 The king interrupted, "In God's name,
Good Sir Kadore, you are much to blame
    For not telling me at first
What you're just now beginning to say
Befell my lady Egaré,
    Her whom I love the most!"
The steward's heart nearly broke with woe.
He said, "My lord, why say you so?
    Of kings are you not the best?
Look here at the letter you sent to me.
As you yourself may clearly see,
    I carried out your behest."

65

769 The king took up that letter to read,
And when he saw the wicked deed
    He went all pale and wan.
Sorely he wept and cried, "Alas,
That ever conceived and born I was,
    Or ever made a man!
Good Sir Kadore, I swear to thee,
This letter was never written by me
    Or sealed by my hand."
Then both men wept and thought it ill,
"Alas, though this be God's own will!" —
    And fainted on the sand.

66

781 The great lords who around them stood
Caught up their king, and then the good
    Kadore, with sympathy.

When both came to, the weeping king
Showed him the letter numbering
       His baby's heads as three.
"Oh, lord," Kadore said, "this I swear,
I never said that anywhere!
       Alas, how may this be?"
Then for the messenger they sent.
The king asked him which way he went
       To make delivery.

67

793   "Right past your mother's house," said he.
"Alas," said the king, "that there could be
       A woman so unkind.
For treason she shall be burnt! I give
This judgment, that she may not live,
       And that is my command!"
The great lords modified between
Themselves this judgment on the queen
       Who wickedly purloined
The letters. They sent her from her nation
And seized all her accumulation
       Of castle, tower, and land.

68

805   When she had fled across the foam,
The noble king remained at home
       And heavy was his air.
Heart full of sorrow and sighing sore,
Many a moan he uttered for
       His Egarye the fair.
And seeing any child at play,

He wept and said then, "Wellaway,
          My little son so dear!"
So sad he was that no one could
Cheer up at all that king so good,
          Until the seventh year.

69

817   Then the idea to him came,
Of how his lady white as foam
          Had drowned to save his soul.
"Through grace of God who is our hope,
I'll go to Rome to see the pope
          With penance as my goal!"
He ordered ships then, filling them
With worldly wealth up to the brim,
          Good presents to cajole
His men, and many alms he gave,
Intending thus his soul to save
          And make his spirit whole.

70

829   The sailors, worthy men at sea,
Dressing their tackle expertly
          In an experienced way,
Drew up the sail and laid out oar,
Blessing their luck for the weather, for
          The wind blew right that day.
They sailed over the salty foam
By grace of God on Heaven's throne
          Who holds, over all, the sway.
In the great city when they came,
They lodged in a burgess's house, the same
          In which lodged Emarye.

71

841 Observing this, she called her son
   From boyish play to quickly come,
     For now approached his test.
   She said, "My darling son, today
   Please do exactly as I say,
     And you shall be most blest.
   For now the finest cloth you shall
   Wear to serve the king in the hall,
     Fulfilling his least request
   So courteously that none can see
   Any way that you can be
     Challenged for being best.

72

853 "When serving the after-dinner sweet,
   Kneel down quickly at his feet
     And take his hand in thine.
   After this take his goblet up
   And pour into that golden cup
     A draught of honey-wine.
   And what he then shall say to thee,
   Come back at once and tell to me,
     To gain God's blessing and mine!"
   The child went then into the hall
   Where gathered were those rich lords all
     Clad in their robes so fine.

73

865 Those noble lords both great and good
   Washed and sat down for their food,
     Minstrels presiding o'er.

The first course came, the child served
So well, all loved him who observed;
    They praised him more and more.
Then all those said, who looked upon
The child, that never had they seen one
    Who plates more gracefully bore.
The king then asked him, just for fun,
"What is your name, my little son?"
    He answered, "Segramor."

74

877   The King of Wales gave such a sigh
And was so sad, he thought he'd die,
    For *his* son was called so.
Truly I say, I tell no lies,
The tears came pouring from his eyes.
    At heart he knew great woe.
But quietly he began to eat,
While looking upon the child so sweet.
    Greatly he loved him, though.
He asked the burgess somewhat later,
"Is this your son? Are you the father?"
    The burgess said, "That's so."

75

889   The noble lords then, good and great,
Washing again after they ate,
    Now waited eagerly.
The child, whose manner so appealed,
Brought the king dessert, and kneeled
    And served him courteously.
The king then to the burgess said,

"Sir, let me have this little lad,
If thy will it should be.
I'll make him lord of town and tower,
Of many a mighty hall and bower.
I love him especially."

76

901 When he had served the king so well,
Segramor went to his mother to tell
All he could understand.
"My son, when to his chamber he goes
(Your father, but nothing of this he knows),
Go up and take his hand.
Bid him come speak to Emaré
Who changed her name to Egaré
In Wales, his own dear land."
The child again went to the hall
Among those great lords, one and all,
And served in the manner grand.

77

913 When they were well replete at last
After that generous repast
Of bread and meat and wine,
The king stood up and turned to go
Into his chamber. He met there, though,
The child who led him in,
And said, "Sir if your will it be,
Take my hand and come with me,
For I am of your kin.
Come and speak with Emaré
Who changed her name to Egaré,
Lady so fair of skin."

78

925 The King of Wales became so sad
   With heartache when young Segramor had
     Mentioned by name his queen,
   He said, "My son, why say you so?
   Why thus upbraid me for my woe,
     The saddest I've ever been?"
   Nevertheless he went on down
   And then saw coming, bright in her gown,
     The fairest ever seen.
   His lady in his arms he wound,
   And both of them fainted to the ground
     For joy and love so keen.

79

937 Catching them up from the chamber floor,
   Lord, how glad was Sir Kadore
     At seeing the good king fold
   His lady in his arms so tight!
   Other lords also thought that sight
     Delightful to behold.
   And thus the queen they'd cast to sea,
   Through grace of God in Trinity,
     Recovered from cares so cold.
   Let's leave her there and speak now further
   Of Artyus, her royal father
     Of whom this tale first told.

80

949 He of whom this tale first told
   By now was growing rather old
     And thought about his sin

THE ROMANCES RHYMED IN MODERN ENGLISH ♦ 87

Against his daughter Emaré
Whom he had ordered cast away
    At sea, so fair of skin.
He planned a pilgrimage to the pope,
An act of penance, with the hope
    That Heaven he still might win,
So he sent messengers from home
Who soon thereafter came to Rome
    To find their lord an inn.

81

961   On seeing them, fair Emaré
Went to her husband. "Lord, please stay
    And meet this man, for me,
And dearest sir, in everything
Acquaint yourself with this other king.
    An honor it will be."
The king replied then to his queen,
"In Christian lands there's never been
    A greater lord than he."
"And now," she said, "whatever betide,
To meet that great lord go to ride,
    And take thy knights with thee."

82

973   Then Emaré said to her son
Just how everything should be done
    And how he should behave:
"My son, you must show even more
Courtesy now to the emperor.
    Be gentle and somewhat grave.
When he kisses thy father, see

Whether he also kisses thee,
  And bow to him, and crave
That he come speak to Emaré
The daughter that he cast away;
  Himself the order gave."

83

985 Now Artyus comes to the Church's home.
Now see the Welsh king leaving Rome
  And toward him proudly ride!
The child now is a prince indeed,
Trotting along on a noble steed
  Beside his father in pride.
And now the emperor, when they meet,
Casts back his hood to kiss the sweet
  Child at the stranger's side.
The other great lords also bend
To kiss young Segramor, their friend.
  Their hearts they do not hide.

84

997 The emperor was liking greatly
This child riding close and stately,
  His face so young and fair.
He saw him holding back his steed
And saw the Welsh king taking heed
  And others who were there,
So he could speak to him alone:
"Sir, for the honor of your throne,
  My words you now must hear.
Come now to speak with Emaré
Who changed her name to Egaré
  And is your daughter dear."

85

1009   The emperor grew quite pale, and said,
"Why thus upbraid me? She is dead.
    There's nothing to be done."
"Sir, if you will, I'll bring you where
My mother waits for you, so fair
    A face to look upon."
And so the emperor went with him
And saw approach that lady slim
    Walking all alone.
Then off his steed the emperor leapt,
And into his two arms he swept
    Her whom he'd thought was gone.

86

1021   Joyful was that meeting for
The king, the noble emperor,
    And lovely Emaré,
And also for Sir Segramor
Who later was the emperor
    And suitably held sway.
And great was the feast that they held then
For all the loyal noblemen,
    As those who tell this say.
For this is one of the Breton lays
They used to tell in the olden days,
    Called "The Lament of Garye."

87

1033   Here ends the story.
Jesus, on thy throne above,

Grant us to live with thee in love
In thy perpetual glory!

Amen.

Explicit Emaré. (Emaré ends.)

✧ *Le Bone Florence of Rome*

The romance of *Le Bone Florence of Rome* contains a lively version of another branch of the Castaway Queen story. It appears to have been translated into Middle English verse from a French source (probably a different text from the *Florence de Rome* preserved in a fourteenth-century manuscript in the Bibliothèque Nationale: Nouv. acq. franc. 4192). The English romance is found, like *Emaré,* in only one manuscript, Cambridge University Library Ff 2.38, written down around 1500 in a northern dialect and possibly copied, suggests its most recent editor Carol Falvo Heffernan, from "a manuscript written about fifty years earlier in the north-east Midlands" (41).

The long first part of the romance, not given here because it is not part of the traditional Castaway Queen story, is mainly chivalric. It tells of the aged Greek king Garcy's mad lust for beautiful Florence, how he attacks Rome when her refusal of him is backed by her father the emperor, and how two dispossessed Hungarian noblemen, the brothers Emere and Miles, come to the defense of Rome against the Greeks. Miles turns out to be a coward and a traitor, though where we pick up the story noble Emere does not know this. Florence's father is slain in battle (stanza 66). Garcy's Greeks capture Emere, but Garcy lets him go because Emere's father once befriended him in need (stanza 80). On his return Florence "weds" (pledges herself to) Emere, who is crowned emperor, but she makes a vow not to consummate the marriage until he brings Garcy, her father's slayer, to her as a prisoner (stanza 84). So she remains a virgin for now as Emere sets out on his quest; the situation makes it clear that her virginity is to be his reward. On his way back, victorious in battle, Emere decides to reconquer Hungary, their father's kingdom, for his brother Miles to rule (stanza 105).

Emere has left Miles in Rome to look after Florence in his absence, but Miles shows his true colors in misdeeds (which Sir Egravaine later reports to Emere in stanzas 112–16), and Florence has him imprisoned. The part of the romance given in the following pages tells of the subsequent adventures of Florence, determined to preserve her chastity for Emere. The incest theme that is the plot's traditional impetus interestingly reduplicates in this story, with aged Garcy, whom the lady rejects, standing in for the incestuous father figure in the first part of the romance, then the brother-in-law Miles stepping into that role in this second part. As the reader may remember from *Hamlet,* a sexual relationship between brother- and sister-in-law was considered incestuous at this time, and then as now incest was considered far worse than adultery.

Christine de Pisan, one of the two most famous woman storytellers of the European Middle Ages (Marie de France being the other), includes the story of Florence in her *Book of the City of Ladies,* abbreviating it and beginning where the following text does. Differences in Christine's version include Sir Terry's daughter being a child and Miles being her murderer, the Virgin sending Florence the vision of a healing plant with which she works her cures, and Florence soothing her emperor-husband at the end, deflecting the further violence that occurs in our version. Above all, Christine recounts no sea voyages. There may not have been one in the version she knew. If that were the case, *Florence* would be an example of how readily the story of an isolated woman undergoing hardships could conform to the tale of "the woman adrift."

The following translation of the story begins at stanza 106 with Emere returning victorious from the war against Garcy, and good but naive Florence releasing Miles from prison to greet his brother. "They" at the beginning of stanza 106 refers to Emere and his army, now bound for Hungary, but pausing en route to send Florence a message.

As in *Emaré*, the poet uses the twelve-line stanza typical of English romance, rhyming aab-ccb-ddb-eeb, though this poet is more adept, or at least more conventional, in the rhyming than the *Emaré* poet. I have based my translation on Heffernan's edition. Notes to *Florence* are keyed to line and stanza, like those for *Emaré*, and will be found in the notes to this chapter at the end of the book.

106

1258 *They put ashore a loyal man*
   Who sometimes rode and sometimes ran
    Until he got to Rome,
   And lovely Florence then he told
   How Sir Emere, her champion bold,
    To Sir Garcy had come
   And conquered all his empire there
   And soon would bring his prisoner
    To kneel to her at home.
   The joyful lady in delight
   At those glad tidings made the knight
    The gift of a barondom.

107

1270 *Oh, Lord who is both God and man,*
   If only Emere had known of then
    The treason of his brother,
   What he had done in our hero's absence
   To Sampson and the Lady Florence,
    To Egravaine for another!
   But after the greeting her husband sent,

Good Florence and her ladies went
     Together to the tower
And brought down Miles, that wily thief
Who later would cause further grief.
     Never was prophesy truer!

108

1282   The lady prayed to Egravaine
And other knights that they refrain
     From raking up the past.
"For all that Miles has done to me
Forgiven now please let it be,
     For God's love. That is best."
She gave him then a gallant horse
And set him out upon his course
     To Emere and all the rest.
But as he rode thus toward the sea,
A desperate, wicked calumny
     Was swelling in his breast.

109

1294   Sir Egravaine leapt on his steed
And galloped after at great speed,
     Doubting that all was well.
When Miles had met the emperor, he
Directly went down on one knee
     From the back of his stallion tall.
Emere said, "Miles, what troubles you?"
He answered, "Florence has been untrue.
     When I said I would tell
I saw her and Egravaine in bed" —
And thus he lied — "she had me led
     Away to a prison cell!"

110

1306 Emere reeled back then, deeply shaken,
All the joy that he had taken
  In Florence swept away.
He felt the bitterness of this wrest
The pleasure of his lengthy quest
  From him, and sorrow lay
Upon his heart. But then the lords
Around him offered consoling words,
  And one came forth to say,
"Grieve not, until we learn the truth
From scholars old and humble youth.
  We'll ask without delay."

111

1318 This gladdened him. But Egravaine
Came spurring through with might and main.
  The truth he would have told,
But Miles, before he could say a word,
Came at him with a flashing sword.
  He barely had time to fold
A cloak several times around his arm,
Thus protecting himself from harm,
  For hardy he was and bold.
The emperor ordered them to be parted,
Saying, "The one of you who started
  This fight shall pay in gold."

112

1330 Sir Egravaine said, "Sir, I'll tell
A tale or two if you listen well.
  When you went over the sea,
You left behind a hundred men

Armed in iron and steel, and then
    Over them placed us three
To guard your queen till you came again.
Because of this my brother was slain,
    Sampson, tragically.

113

1339   "Your sail was scarcely lost to view
When Miles, lying, claimed that you
    Were now forever gone.
He named himself the emperor
And planned to wed your lady fair,
    Her whom you call your own.
The hundred men at his command
He promised rents and granted land;
    He hewed Sir Sampson down
And on a litter brought him here,
And said that *you* lay on that bier,
    And made poor Florence moan.

114

1351   "But when he would have made her wed
At his command, she quickly fled
    And nearly got away,
Except that he had twelve armed knights
Guarding her chamber, days and nights,
    Who close about her lay.
I had to swear loyalty or I,
Like my poor brother, would also die.
    This is the truth I say.
I went to the pope, explained my oath,
And he absolved me, nothing loath,
    Without the least delay.

115

1363   "Then he ordered a hundred clerks,
Men brave and wise in moral works,
    To arm, and led them where
They fought your hundred till at last
Those traitors were overcome and cast
    In prison; they still are there.
But Florence ordered Miles' release
So he could come and make his peace.
    This is the truth, I swear.
I offer as witness Pope Symond
Who never for a thousand pound
    Would lie or be unfair.

116

1375   "You should come home tomorrow, sir,
By breakfast time, to be with her
    Who longs for you alone."
The emperor lunged then to attack
His brother Miles. They held him back,
    So he shouted out, "Begone!
Traitor, I order you to flee
And nevermore to look on me,
    For the false things you have done!"
Then Miles fled away from there
Straight to Rome. In dreadful fear
    He galloped on and on . . .

117

1387   Until he fell at Florence's feet,
And thus he lied to that lady sweet:
    "Emere says, do not fail

To come to meet him in the morning."
The maiden then was blithe and singing,
   For she believed the tale.
She called that night for the pope and said
That he should come too, clad in red,
   With many a cardinal.
And then she gathered her retinue,
And with that traitor so untrue
   Rode out over hill and dale.

118

1399   As soon as they had left the city
Miles began, "Dear gracious lady,
   We two must ride on fast,
Leaving the pope and his retinue
To follow on behind us two,
   For here's the plan I've cast:
You must have time to greet your lord
And wicked Garcy, get in a word
   Before your chance is past.
For later on there is no hope,
For once Emere has met the pope,
   Their talk will last and last."

119

1411   "Oh, Miles," she said, "May God forgive
All your offenses while you live.
   I'll see my lord today!"
Eastward lay the proper path,
But Miles soon had twisted south,
   Leading her astray.
At last they came to a deep crevasse.

"This road," she said, "is so rough, alas,
We must have missed the way.
I think that we should ride back up
And wait there for my lord the pope."
Then Miles said to her, "Nay . . .

120

1423　"You'll never see Emere again!"
The lady sighed, but all in vain.
When she began to sway
And fall, he beat her with his sword.
She uttered many a piteous word
And cried out, "Wellaway,
And shall I never see him more?"
"No, by Christ who died of yore!"
Was all that man would say.
He helped her mount and on they pressed,
Pausing for neither food nor rest
All that long summer's day.

121

1435　When darkness came the road had led
Into thick woods. Miles built a shed
Beneath an ample tree,
Intending there to rape the maid,
But fervently to God she prayed,
And Mary fair and free:
"Do not let this false villain shame
Either my body or my name,
Oh, Thou in majesty!"
At once his lust quite withered away.
Then morning came. When it was day,
He saddled up speedily.

122

1447 Up he set her and forth they rode
   Through a forest long and broad,
     With greenery dappled o'er.
   And soon another sorrow weighed
   Upon the spirits of that maid.
     Hunger within her tore.
   She felt that she would rather hold
   A loaf of bread than all the gold
     She'd ever seen before.
   So when at last, as darkness fell,
   Far off they heard a tinkling bell,
     Florence rejoiced therefore.

123

1459 A hermit in his hut of sod
   Dwelt there, fearing the wrath of God
     And eager to obey.
   They asked him for a bite of food.
   "Dear damsel, yours shall be as good
     As mine," he said. Away
   He hastened and brought back barley bread
   And good spring water, on which she fed,
     Remembering to pray,
   And when she bent her head to eat,
   She thought she'd tasted nothing so sweet
     Ever, by night or day.

124

1471 Miles was eating the same as she,
   But found it stuck in his throat. Said he,
     "I cannot get this down.

So churl, unless you want to die,
Bring us your better bread of rye,
        Or I shall crack your crown!"
"By God," said the hermit, "who bought me dear,
I've had no better this seven year."
        Then Miles grabbed his gown
And villainously beat him through
His doorway, setting fire to
        The poor man far from town.

125

1483   He burnt the holy hermit there,
Leaving his well-built dwelling bare,
        Pretty though it might be.
Then the lady began to weep,
"May Satan in fire forever keep
        Your soul when doom you see!"
So Miles then made the lady swear
To tell no person anywhere
        In all the world what she
Was called, her lineage, or whence she came.
"And if you breathe," he said, "my name,
        You'll burn as well as he!"

126

1495   She promised under such threat, of course,
But when he thought to take her by force,
        She prayed God be her shield.
When he was ready for the assay,
He found his lust had withered away,
        Through might of Mary mild.
The sun came up, so did his hopes.

He led her through a pretty copse
    And into the wasteland wild.
At midday he alighted by
A chestnut tree that was arching high,
    The fairest in the field.

127

1507   He said then, "You have cast a spell
To hinder me from performing well.
    Undo it or pay the price!"
She answered him with dignity,
"Through him who died upon the tree,
    False traitor, you shall not rise."
So by her hair then brutally
He hanged her on the chestnut tree
    And trimmed to a handy size
A birchen rod. He set upon
And beat her till his wrath was gone,
    Ignoring all her cries.

128

1519   Nearby a lord, Terry by name,
Was dwelling, and by chance he came
    Upon that very day
Into the woods with hawk and hound
To do some hunting. When he was bound
    Into the greenwood gay,
Riding with all his company there,
He heard the cries of the lady fair
    And went by the quickest way.
As soon as Miles their galloping heard,
He leapt on his horse and away he spurred.
    He dared no longer stay.

1531   *He left the best of the horses there*
And Florence hanging by her hair,
    Bright in her silken gown.
Her saddle and bridle also shown,
Set with many a precious stone
    And gleaming in the sun.
But she herself was the fairest glory,
White as a lily, says the story
    (To be read by anyone).
Her face was shining fair and bright.
The strangers toward this wondrous sight
    Urged their horses to run.

1543   *They loosened then her lovely locks,*
Yellow as newmade candlewax
    Touched with hints of red.
She could not speak, our poet states.
By litter to the castle gates
    They took her, almost dead.
In water sweet with herbs and flowers
They bathed and stroked her skin for hours,
    Then they gently fed
Poor Florence with the daintiest food,
With everything that would do her good,
    Serving her in her bed.

1555   *Sir Terry ordered everyone*
To ask no questions, truly none,
    About her being there.

They stabled her horse and gave him water,
And brought her things to her. A daughter
    Terry had, good and fair.
Her name was Beatrice, and her face
Was bright with gentleness and grace.
    She was to be his heir.
To put fair Florence at ease again
With other folk, both women and men,
    The two slept as a pair.

132

1568   They slept together for, in truth,
Florence, though in the flower of youth,
    Now watched men fearfully.
If one addressed her, she'd reply
So briefly that he would not try
    Further gallantry.
She prayed to God who had brought her here
To keep her pure for Sir Emere
    Who won her honestly.
As for Emere, now back in Rome,
It seemed a sad arrival home
    Not knowing where she could be.

133

1579   Of Garcy let us speak some more,
Of him who caused her grief so sore
    And her father to be slain.
Emere avenged those deeds for her,
Bringing Garcy as prisoner
    Back to Rome again.

He liked it little, pined away.
The truth cannot be hid, they say:
    He died, to make it plain.
So Florence would never more behold
That wicked ruler grey and old
    Who caused her so much pain.

134

1591 Now let us turn to her again.
With Terry lived Machary, a man
    As strong, they said, as a bear.
He wanted Florence, so he lay
In wait and watched her every day,
    Filling her with despair.
At last he saw that she had gone
Into her chamber all alone.
    He followed her, and there
He forced her down upon the bed.
The lady weeping, cold with dread,
    Saw no help anywhere.

135

1603 But near her bed there lay a stone
That she could get her hand upon.
    She hit him in the mouth
So hard he spat out all front teeth,
Both those above and those beneath
    That lay in her weapon's path.
Blood bursting from his mouth, his nose,
Quickly Sir Machary rose
    To flee that lady's wrath.

136

1612 When to his room he took his flight,
He stayed there hidden a full fortnight.
On coming out, he went
To tell his lord how he'd been struck
In a bad moment, out of luck,
In a great tournament.
"The truth cannot be hid," he said;
"My teeth were knocked out of my head.
My sorrow is evident.
Except for revenge, I'd rather be dead."
Did she but know, how Florence would dread
The force of that intent!

137

1624 That night a sharpened knife he brought
Of iron and steel finely wrought,
That bitterly would bite,
And stole to her room and took his stand
Behind a curtain, knife in hand
To complicate her plight.
When certain they were both asleep,
Toward Beatrice he began to creep
And raised his knife, and quite
Severed her throat! And then he laid
That red, incriminating blade
By Florence, a woeful sight.

138

1636 Forth from the chamber door he crept
While Beatrice bled and Florence slept
With all her cares erased.

Just then Sir Terry in a dream
Saw his daughter try to scream
    As lightning flashes raced
And thundered around her. Terry woke,
His own cry echoing, snatched his cloak,
    And trembling in his haste,
He lit a candle in a lamp,
And through the hallways dim and damp
    To the maidens' room he raced.

139

1648   He found his daughter Beatrice dead,
Her crimson blood upon the bed,
    A knife in Florence's hand.
He called his lady Eglantine
And others quickly to the scene,
    A wondering, weeping band.
There, as the noblewomen wept,
Good Florence innocently slept,
    No fairer to be found.
But roused and dazed by the hideous din,
As sad a waking she had then
    As any in all the land.

140

1660   They pressed about her like a thicket,
Knights and ladies and the wicked
    Traitor, who then betrayed
Her further. "Sir, I'll set a stake
Outside the town," he said, "and make
    A fire for this young maid.
From her fine clothing you can see

She's no mere mortal enemy.
Behind that fair parade,
She is a devil in disguise
Come hither for your child's demise.
The penalty must be paid!"

141

1672 They dressed her then in plain attire
And led her forward to the fire.
Great was the crowd. She said,
"Father, Son, and Holy Ghost,
Oh, Thou on high who knowest most,
I never wished her dead.
If I be without guilt in this,
Bring my soul to heavenly bliss
Today by thy Godhead."
The people watching her at prayer
Wrung their hands in pity there,
Behaving like folk gone mad.

142

1684 To Terry his dear daughter's death
Was painful, but he caught his breath,
A teardrop in his eye.
"Florence," he said, "I cannot bear
For all the world to put you there
Upon the pyre to die."
Back to her room he had her led.
When her own clothes she donned, he said
To all there, "I defy
Those who think burning her no sin.
Now let her journey hence begin,
For here we say goodbye."

143

1696 He put the bridle in her hand
And led her to the borderland
  Where mighty chestnuts grow.
He blessed her, bidding her good day
About to see her on her way.
  One thing concerned her, though.
She said, "Sir, for your charity,
Let no man follow after me
  To cause me further woe."
"None," he said, "shall be so bold
For nine times nine your weight in gold."
  He turned his horse to go.

144

1708 As through the forest the lady rode,
Everything around her glowed,
  Branch and bole and leaf,
Until she saw a gallows high
With people milling about nearby
  Intending to hang a thief.
She went to them and hailed them kindly.
They said, "Who are you, dressed so finely,
  Yet betraying grief?"
She answered them, "Know only this:
A woman mistreated with no redress
  For remedy or relief.

145

1720 "Thus no protection do I have —
So will you give me yonder knave
  You plan to punish here?

God grant he'll more obedient be
If I have saved from the gallows-tree
    The life that he holds dear."
On taking council together, they
Decided they could not say her nay,
    She was so young and fair.
They gave him to her willingly,
But warned her of his larceny.
    She thanked them for their care.

146

1732   She asked him, "Will you serve me true?
You shall be paid for all you do."
    He said, "To answer no
Would show I was a stupid fool
Fit only for drowning in a pool
    When you have saved me so."
She thought if she could cross the sea,
Then at Jerusalem she would be,
    A place she ought to go
To try to get some news of Rome
And whether her lord had yet come home.
    But now came further woe.

147

1744   A burgess, receiver of stolen goods,
Encountered them coming from the woods
    As they came over a hill.
"Clarebold! I thought they'd hang you high!"
The other villain winked his eye,
    Meaning by this, "Be still."
He said aloud, "She came to save

Me just in time, if I behave,
     To serve her at her will."
Later he whispered in his ear,
"I promise you, her wealth and gear
     Will make your coffers full!"

148

1756   Clarebold then guided her to town
And at the burgess's helped her down,
     That to be where she stayed.
At dinner to a seat he led her;
With meat and good red wine he fed her.
     The table was amply laid.
The wife of the burgess welcomed her
And said with kind and gentle cheer,
     "Be at your ease, young maid."
But maddened by cupidity,
The men beheld her finery
     And laughed until they brayed.

149

1768   The wife knew well their evil thought
And said, "Indeed, you'll do it not,
     If I have any say!"
She took the girl with her that night
Into her room and locked it tight,
     And safe in her bed they lay.
Next morning Florence called her knave
And said, "There's an errand that I have
     For you to run today.
Find out which of the ships is bound
Out to Jerusalem. Come around
     And tell me right away."

150

1780   Clarebold sought his friend in crime:
"Thwarted we've been, but still there's time
To plan another wile."
So they went down to the port and sold
The lady to a mariner bold.
It took just a little while.
"I promise," Clarebold said, "she's pretty
As any you've seen in field or city."
Broad was the captain's smile.
He promised them gold that would outweigh
The beautiful Florence, as their pay.
On each side there was guile.

151

1792   He said, "I'll put the gold in a sack
And hang it here upon a rack
Right at the cabin-end.
When you have brought that maiden fair,
Put up your hand and take it there."
Smug with success, the men
Came back and told her, "We have found
A ship that is Jerusalem bound."
She said, "Then this will mend
My fortunes." She gave her horse and saddle
To the good woman, with its rich bridle,
And kissed her as a friend.

152

1804   She stopped at a church before she went,
To take the holy sacrament
And pray God for His grace.

She prayed to go to the land above
That evermore was ruled by love
Before His holy face,
And prayed, before she died, to see
Emere, who by now ought to be
In Rome, that royal place.
And then they went down to the harbor.
Where Clarebold handed to the sailor
The lady under lace.

153

1816   *They took the moneybag of gold*
And carried it home to their treasure-hold
And found it filled with lead.
The burgess was furious at Clarebold.
"A sorrowful business to have sold
Your lady thus," he said.
"May God give you the shameful end
You've earned, beguiling such a friend
And selling her maidenhead!"
Down to the ship they rushed, but fast
Had sail been raised upon the mast,
And away the vessel sped.

154

1828   *Each of the many men who sailed*
With Florence tried, but none prevailed
In making her his own.
Through God they failed in what they sought,
For shielding her was He who wrought
The shining sun and moon.
But when she called Clarebold, her lad,

The captain laughed and said, "You're mad,"
And told her what he'd done.
She prayed God would forgive that crime,
But no one sadder at that time
Lived under heaven's throne.

155

1840 *Onto his bed the captain threw*
The lady, brought to grief anew.
The ship leapt on the wave.
He told her, "Damsel, I have paid
Dearly for you, a pretty maid
Worthy for me to wive."
She said, "Nay, that shall never be,
Through aid of Him in Trinity
Who suffered the woundings five."
He came at her his will to take.
She thought that all her ribs would break
As they began to strive.

156

1852 *Struggling, she called on Virgin Mary,*
"Now, if ever, show me mercy.
Always you've brought me aid.
Oh, hear me, as you only may;
Protect me from being shamed today,
And keep me still a maid."
Just then a mighty storm blew up
That threatened harm to men and ship.
The captain was dismayed.
Quickly he climbed up on the mast.
They took in sail, but in the blast
Rope after rope was frayed.

157

1864   "Unless this storm at once calms down,"
He said, "all those aboard will drown."
    Then Florence sighed with relief,
Much preferring to be dead
Than made to lose her maidenhead.
    The man's embrace was brief;
The ship broke suddenly asunder
And most upon it soon went under,
    Drowning with cries of grief.
But not the woman. She floated free,
And away from the wallowing vessel's lee
    Was cast ashore on a reef.

158

1876   The captain to an oar held tight,
But neither knew of the other's plight;
    Each thought the other drowned.
Florence, washed up on a skerry
Near the convent Beuerfayre
    (Owning a plot of ground
On Lake Bottiaea, an inlet of
The Aegean), saw a spire above
    And, looking about her, found
A roadway, relatively dry.
Thanking God, she thought she'd try
    To follow where it wound.

159

1888   Sir Lucius Ibarnius
Founded the house of nuns; that was
    A fair and noble band.

The twentieth after Yule they pray
To their Saint Hilary, on his day.
        Helped by no human hand,
The bells rang out through holy grace
As Florence was drawing nigh that place.
        When at the bells' command
The nuns came, they saw no one there
Except a lady, bright and fair,
        Who came inside to stand.

160

1900   The gentle abbess came and took
Her hand and led her, says the book
        (Her strength was nearly done),
To kneel and pray before the cross.
She praiséd God in a quiet voice
        For the help she'd come upon.
They asked her if she was afraid.
"Of no one living," said that maid,
        "Underneath the sun."
A home she asked, of their charity.
They gave her a habit too, and she
        That day became a nun.

161

1912   The lovely lady then lived there
Within the convent Beuerfayre.
        She praiséd God for her luck,
And Blesséd Mary who came to save
Her flesh from rape and a deep-sea grave
        By casting her on the rock.
It happened a nun of the house grew ill

From gout and other things, until
   She could not speak or walk.
So Florence came to her and healed
Her pain. "But it must not be revealed,"
   She urged her; "please don't talk."

162

1924   *The nuns, though, simply had to tell*
Others about their miracle,
   And they rejoiced to say
How none who saw her, sick or sore,
Could feel their illness any more
   After they went away.
Through every land and every home
The good news spread — as far as Rome
   Where poor Emere now lay
With pain so evil in his head
That from his heart all joy was fled
   Both by night and day.

163

1936   *That pain resulted from his war*
Against the king of Apulia, for
   When he attacked again,
And paused a moment to remove
His helmet, an arrow ripped a groove
   Direct through bone and brain.
The doctor tried to pull it tight,
But still it festered. Day and night
   Emere was in such pain
That all his gold he would have given
Just to be buried and go to Heaven,
   Or simply to be slain.

THE ROMANCES RHYMED IN MODERN ENGLISH ✧ 117

164

1948   He called for good Sir Egravaine
And asked him, "What can stop this pain?
    It is destroying me!"
"Sir, a nun is said to dwell
At Beuerfayre who makes folk well,
    Somewhere across the sea —
But we can find the place." They took
Chests full of gold, so says the book,
    And set out quietly.
Long was the time to Beuerfayre,
Though nowhere did they stop to tarry,
    And traveled hastily.

165

1960   At last arriving, Sir Emere
Chose to stay in a dwelling near
    The convent of his goal.
By chance his brother Miles had come,
A leper now, to make his home
    With one Gyllam of Pole.
He too heard of that lady meek
Who healed, and made his way to seek
    Her comfort. True as my soul
My story is. Reclusively
They dwelt now, so that none could see
    His face, no longer whole.

166

1972   And Sir Machary came as well,
He who had been so quick to tell
    Those lies concerning who

Had slain the girl; he had accused
The lady. Now he was abused
    By pain bending him in two.
Hoping to save his warrior's life,
Terry came with him, and his wife
    Called Eglantine came too.
They'd come to ask the lady there
To heal Machary, unaware
    Of what, for her pain, was due.

167

1984 Terry, the gracious governor,
Had found a house near the emperor;
    They lived almost next door.
And then the captain, who had thought
To make a slave of her he'd bought
    And drifted on an oar,
Arrived there too, his skin in patches,
Hobbling like the devil on crutches
    With many an open sore.
And Clarebold, too, the rescued thief,
Came with a pain that caused him grief.
    To Beuerfayre came all four.

168

1996 The emperor, thinking praying might
Perhaps relieve his painful plight,
    Went to the altar to kneel.
When mass was over, the abbess came
To where he was and welcomed him,
    Inviting him to a meal.
He thanked her graciously and said,

"This time I've come to see the maid
    They say knows how to heal.
A wound in my head has festered so
That all my bliss has turned to woe.
    To her I make appeal."

169

2008   Florence, dutifully at prayer,
Observed that her own lord was there.
    She knew him well, although
If he knew her, he did not say.
As in the cloister they walked that day
    He told her of his woe.
Florence saw there the other four
Who once had tormented her so sore.
    When testing she thought to go
Near them, they knew her not a bit.
She thanked the King of Heaven for it
    With laughter sweet and low.

170

2020   Leprosy foully ate away
At Miles, who'd led her so astray,
    With pustules black as soot.
Machary, who'd hoped to see her slain,
Stood wracked and creaking in great pain,
    Shaking where he was put.
The captain who had thought of rape
Had each eye bulging like a grape
    And limbs falling off with rot.
His friends pushed Clarebold through the narrow
Streets, doubled up in a wheelbarrow,
    For he had lost each foot.

2032 To each she said, "If you wish to be
Healthy and free from misery,
  You must confess your sin
In public, in front of everyone,
All these people. It must be done
  In a full voice from within."
Such a thing they were loath to do.
But then said Miles, "If we have to,
  I'll be the one to begin.
My lust has failed me day and night
Since I first led a lady bright
  Away from kith and kin."

2044 Then all the story he revealed,
Of how he meant to make Florence yield,
  Confessing each detail:
He said he'd wished to be emperor
And wed that lady white as a flower.
  And therefore, down a trail
That innocent maiden he had led
Astray to take her maidenhead,
  But never could prevail.
"Against her firm defense," he said,
"I never got the girl in bed;
  Her purity did not fail."

2056 He told them of the barley bread,
And how he'd burnt the hermit dead,
  And hung her by the hair.

"But seeing men and hounds appear,
I fled into the woods in fear."
        Sir Terry took it there:
"Yes. I came and cut her down
And brought her with me into town,
        Entirely unaware
That deed would bring me such distress.
She slew my daughter Beatrice
        Who should have been my heir.

174

2068   "And yet, since she was bright as gold
And so delightful to behold,
        I chose to let her go."
Machary spoke then, his turn next:
"She did me evil, too. She vexed
        Me with a mighty blow.
I merely wished to share her bed;
She battered my front teeth from my head,
        Beginning all my woe.
So I slew Beatrice with a knife
And set up Florence to lose her life.
        Truly, it was so."

175

2080   While Terry raged like a man gone mad,
"Traitor, how could you be so bad?"
        His wife began to speak:
"Alas that we befriended one
Who caused such evil to be done.
        Yet now my heart may break
Rather more for the fair and good

Maiden banished to the wood
    When innocent and weak."
Clarebold spoke up, then. "She rode by
When I stood under a gallows high,
    A rope around my neck.

176

2092 "When from that hanging she rescued me,
I promised her that I would be
    Her servant along the way.
We were together a single night,
And then I sold that lady bright
    Upon the second day."
Then spoke the captain who had bought
The maiden fair: "I only sought
    To marry her, but nay.
She broke my ship with a mighty tempest
Then floated south and I northwest.
    I've not seen her to this day.

177

2104 "I came to land upon an oar,
A melancholic ever more
    Without a chance to heal.
Looking around this dismal sight,
I think that each man in this plight
    Hampered that lady's will."
Florence then touched them with her hand
And they were well, I understand,
    Like others who had been ill.
She touched her own lord at the end.
The venom gone, he began to mend,
    And thus she did with all.

178

2116 The venom bursting from his ear,
"It was a plot!" exclaimed Emere.
His rage leapt, bright and strong.
He told his men to make a pyre
And cast in the four in full attire.
Florence thought this was wrong.
But then he took Dame Eglantine,
Sir Terry and his own fair queen,
And with this little throng
Went to the church. They knelt and prayed,
Praising God they had found the maid
Who'd been away so long.

179

2128 Then there was a celebration
Never equaled in that nation!
To every nun they gave
Such gifts that they almost did not
Keep any back, almost forgot,
For traveling home, to save.
They thanked the nuns with courtesy.
Said Florence: "Terry rescued me.
For him a boon I crave."
The city Florence Emere bestowed
Upon Sir Terry for what he owed
With thanks, and they took their leave.

180

2140 Terry to his own land went home.
Emere to his rich city, Rome,
Set forth that very day.

The Pope Symond heard they were coming
And went to meet them, quickly donning
    His very best array.
The cardinals, summoned each by name,
Sang the Te Deum as they came
    (It is the truth I say).
All praised God without restraint
For bringing home without a taint
    Their lady, long away.

181

2152   They then put on a wedding there
Never equaled anywhere.
    Never has there been
Its like for cheer and minstrelsy.
And gifts! Such gold and finery
    The guests had never seen.
At last, upon the fourteenth day,
They all began to drift away,
    Thanking the king and queen
And praising God with might and main
That Florence had come home again
    In safety, chaste and clean.

182

2164   The son begotten on that night
Whom they named Otis, became a knight,
    A noble man and fair
(The book says), and a warrior bold
Who after his father, we are told,
    Became the emperor there.
But first Emere and his faithful wife

Had joy and bliss for all their life;
They were a noble pair.
I, Pope Symond, wrote this story
In the chronicle of Rome's glory.
Who looks will find it there.

183

2176 The moral is, men and women, too,
Before they're false, should think things through,
It makes so foul an end.
However slyly it be cast
It shames the liar at the last,
Wherever he may wend.
Example take of the fickle four
Who harmed fair Florence, more and more,
The truest known to men.
Thus ends this good romance. May He
Who bought us on the gallows-tree
Bring us to bliss.

Amen.

Here ends *Le Bone Florence of Rome.*

✧ Chaucer's *Man of Law's Tale* of Custance

Chaucer departs from the traditional Castaway Queen tale in
many ways as he remakes it in iambic pentameter for his pilgrim-
age storytelling. Apart from the meter and his own stanza form, the
most radical of his departures are the emotional and credulous nar-
rator (including all that narrator's references to the stars), the asso-
ciation of the heroine's wanderings with the Ship of the Church (see

Kolve's persuasive argument for this reading), and, following Trevet and Gower, his omission of incest at the beginning of the story. Chaucer draws attention to this omission in the Man of Law's Introduction when he has that invented character assess Chaucer's real poetry. In the following conclusion of this assessment (lines 77–89), "he" is Chaucer and the vehement speaker is the Man of Law:

> Certainly, not a single word wrote he
> Of that example, wicked Canacee
> Who wrongly loved her brother—such tales I
> Consider cursed, and on them I say fie!—
> Or else of Tyre's king, Apollonius,
> How that accursed king Antiochus
> Bereft his daughter of her maidenhead
> (A tale as horrible as I have read),
> And threw her down upon the tiled floor.
> Chaucer has chosen not to write, therefore,
> Anywhere, after due consideration,
> Of such unnatural abomination,
> And nor shall I relate it.

Many commentators have taken this digression as an implicit criticism of Gower, who did include in his *Confessio Amantis* the stories mentioned here, but it could equally reflect an ongoing discussion between the two poets, a conversation that perhaps included or entertained their audience (see Nicholson, forthcoming). In any case, it was their mutual source Trevet who introduced the episode near the beginning about the sultan and his mother, thereby substituting a murderous mother for an incestuous father as the perpetrator of family violence resulting in the heroine's being set adrift.

It is obviously useful whenever possible when reading to have some sense of who is telling a story. Some have suggested that Chaucer may originally have meant this tale for a different teller (see Nicholson, forthcoming), and one can easily imagine, for example, a storyteller like the romantic yet devout Prioress, who might well be inclined to use the sentimental rhetoric, to consider incest an unspeakable abomination, and to give a traditional tale an allegorical nuance. Scheps has pointed out, however, that recourse to conventionally emotive rhetoric is a typical courtroom ploy, thus suitable to Chaucer's Man of Law.

The narrator's rhetoric reinforces the victim status of Custance and associates her tale with those of martyred saints, thereby making her seem more passive than the inherited plot suggests she is. Chaucer "creates more sympathy for her than admiration," says Nicholson; "with the lessening of her own responsibility for the action, there is a corresponding increase in the importance of Fortune, Providence, Satan, and the protective intercession of God" (forthcoming). On the other hand, Robert B. Dawson claims that if one examines Custance's own speeches, they appear as strong illocutionary acts belying the storyteller's presentation of her as *truly* "a passive and helpless victim" (294). For purposes of her own she presents herself that way, especially to her parents, yet according to Dawson her "rhetoric of victimization with her father," for example, "reverses the actual power-structure of their reunion. Custance completely orchestrates and dominates the scene, which occurs at the time, place, and condition of her choosing" (299). It is my view that Chaucer invites a very close look indeed at the ambiguities of power structure in this particular story, as well as the layers of narrative competence and commitment: What is the storyteller's agenda concerning Custance? What is Chaucer's agenda and how does the story fit his pilgrimage scheme? (Sometimes Chaucer seems to take an amused joy in his own excesses; see lines 1070–71.)

My translation of *Custance* is based on Patricia J. Eberle's edition of the *Man of Law's Tale* in *The Riverside Chaucer*. Much of my understanding of Chaucer's purpose and technique in the tale is indebted to V. A. Kolve's chapter on the romance subtitled "The Rudderless Ship and the Sea" in *Chaucer and the Imagery of Narrative*. The line numbers preceding each stanza correspond to the numbers in *The Riverside Chaucer*, where the numbering begins with the Man of Law's Introduction and Prologue, not included here.

1

134 In Syria once there dwelt a company
Of wealthy merchants, steady men and true.
They sent their spices far across the sea
With cloth of gold and satins rich of hue
And other goods so useful, bright and new,
That everyone enjoyed their purchasings
And selling them in turn their own good things.

2

141 It happened that the masters of that band
Decided to sell in Rome — I don't know whether
For work or recreation — and they planned
To travel to that city all together,
Instead of sending agents. With good weather,
They got there safe, and chose, in the location
That seemed most suitable, their habitation.

3

148 And when these men had sojourned in that town,
Taking their pleasure, for a month or more,
It happened that the excellent renown
Of Custance, daughter of the emperor,
By gossip was, as these things were of yore,
Reported to each Syrian merchant's ear
Day after day, in words you now shall hear.

4

155 For this was everybody's common view:
"Our Emperor of Rome, God give him bliss,

A daughter has, and since the world was new
There never was another maid like this
In terms of beauty and sheer worthiness."
"I pray that God sustain her honorably.
I wish that Queen of Europe she could be!"

5

162   "Hers is a flawless beauty without pride,
Youth without greenness or frivolity."
"In all her actions virtue is her guide,
Humility displacing cruelty."
"She is a paragon of courtesy,
A home of holiness that heart of hers,
Her hand most generous of ministers."

6

169   And all these words were true as God is true.
But to the merchants let us now return.
With goods they loaded up their ships anew
And, after seeing Custance to discern
The truth of hearsay, they began to yearn
For home. They sailed, and sold extremely well
Their merchandise. There is no more to tell.

7

176   Arriving home, high in the sultan's grace
Those merchants stood, for it befell that he,
When they came from a far, exotic place,
Would often, of his royal courtesy,
Entertain them, asking eagerly
For news of sundry lands, for he was keen
To hear what wonders they had heard or seen.

8

183   Along with other news, these merchants gave
The sultan a minute evaluation
Of all the charms of Custance, young and grave.
He asked them more, until with fascination
He harbored her in his imagination,
And then his only goal was loving her
So long as life and reason might endure.

9

190   Perhaps in that large book they call the sky
Was written in the stars what came to pass —
Was known before his birth that he would die
From complications due to love, alas!
For in the stars is written, clear as glass,
For anyone to see, God knows, who can
Decipher it, the death of every man.

10

197   For in the stars were written, long before
They died, the deaths of Pompey, Hercules,
Sampson, and Julius Caesar, many more,
Achilles, Hector, those who fell at Thebes,
The deaths of Turnus and of Socrates.
But in the end our reason is so dull
That nobody can read it very well.

11

204   Then for his councillors the sultan sent
And briefly put his case. To them he said
That having Custance was his firm intent,

Because, unless he very shortly led
The Roman emperor's daughter to his bed,
He'd surely die. He said they urgently,
To save him, must contrive a remedy.

12

211 Various men had this and that to say
When casting up and down for some solution.
Many a subtle argument that day
They gave, proposing magic and illusion.
But at the last, to come to a conclusion,
Seeing no further reason they should tarry,
They said he had no recourse but to marry.

13

218 But in this plan a hitch they could foresee.
To put it plainly, trouble came to mind,
Because there was so much disparity
Between their countries' customs. They opined:
"A Christian prince would hardly be inclined
To marry off his one and only daughter
Into the faith that our Mohammed taught here."

14

225 "Well, rather," said the sultan then, "than lose
My Custance, I would be christened, for unless
I'm hers, I'll die. None other can I choose.
So pray contain your arguments, and press
Onward with plans to ease my great distress.
She holds my life in thrall, and lacking her
Is torment that I cannot long endure."

15

232   *What need is there for more elaboration?*
I say, by treaties and diplomacy,
And by the pope's own mighty mediation,
And since the church and all nobility
Had vowed destruction of idolatry
And spreading of the Christian faith and creed,
As you shall hear forthwith, they soon agreed.

16

239   *Hear how the sultan and his noble band*
And those who followed them now wished to be
Christened, so that he thereby won the hand
Of Custance, and all her gold (what quantity
I do not know), and with this surety
Equal accord was sworn on either side.
And now, fair Custance, may God be thy guide!

17

246   *I think you probably anticipate*
That of the emperor's foresight I will tell —
Of how he, such a noble potentate,
Provided for her. But, as you know well,
Arrangements meant thus greatly to excel
Cannot be told in just a simple sentence,
When he prepared a match of such importance.

18

253   *Many did he appoint to go with her:*
Great lords and ladies, knights of high renown,
Bishops and other people. Soon there were

Proclamations made throughout the town
That all who lived in Rome should kneel down
And pray that Christ bestow upon this marriage
His favor, and make fortunate the voyage.

19

260 And now, I'm forced to tell you, came the day
When she must leave. The woeful time had come
When there could be no longer a delay.
The band had gathered to depart from Rome.
So rising, though in tears at leaving home,
Fair Custance dressed and soon prepared to sail,
Knowing that nothing else might now avail.

20

267 Alas, what wonder was it that she wept? —
Soon to be sent to strangers on a mission
Far from the friends who loved her, to be swept
Into dependence in her new position
On someone with an unknown disposition . . .
But husbands are good! They always were of yore
As all wives know, and I dare say no more.

21

274 And yet that maiden murmured to her father,
"I'm so unhappy!" Then in the gentle way
She had been raised, she added to her mother:
"Most dear to me except for Christ, I pray
That in the grace of both of you I may
Remain, for soon to Syria I'll be gone,
Never again for you to look upon.

22

281   "Alas, for to a strange and barbarous nation
I now must go because it is your will.
May Christ our Lord, who died for our salvation,
Give me the strength his teachings to fulfil.
It's not important if those heathens kill
A girl like me. Women in misery
And under men's control are born to be."

23

288   Never was heard — when Pirrus broke the wall
And Troy was burnt, or when at Thebes, that free
City was lost, or later when Hannibal
Vanquished the Romans not one time but three —
Such weeping as expressed the misery
That Custance felt about her voyaging.
But go she must, whether she weep or sing.

24

295   Oh, you First Moving, cruel firmament,
Who with your dismal always-crowding sway
Go hurling all from east to occident
That naturally would pursue another way —
Your crowding set the skies in such array
That at the very outset of her voyage
Already had cruel Mars destroyed this marriage.

25

302   Infortunate ascendant tortuous
Of which has fallen the helpless lord, alas,
Out of his angle into the darkest house!

Oh, Mars, oh, atazir, placed to harass
The feeble Moon! Moon, by degrees you pass
Onward to where you are not well received.
Where you were welcome, why did you have to leave?

26

309   Imprudent Emperor of Rome, alas!
Did you have no astrologer about?
Is one hour like the next? Can one not cast
A suitable time to choose one's setting out?
When natal horoscope is not in doubt,
Have we no choice electing when to go?
Alas, we are too ignorant or too slow!

27

316   When woeful Custance to the ship was led
Most solemnly, with pomp and circumstance,
"Now Jesus Christ be with you all," she said,
And they could only say, "Farewell, Custance!"
With effort she composed her countenance,
And thus I now shall let her sail away
And turn to other things I have to say.

28

323   The sultan's mother, very pit of vices,
Observing that her son was quite intent
On giving up his heathen sacrifices,
A summons to her privy council sent.
Quickly they came to find out what it meant,
And when she had assembled all her folk,
She sat, and as you now shall hear, she spoke.

29

330   "My lords," she said, "you each know, every man,
How my own son is ready to abjure
The holy teachings of the Al-Koran
Brought by Mohammed, God's own messenger.
My life, I swear to God above, as sure
As I stand here, shall from my body part
Before I cast Mohammed from my heart!

30

337   "For what does this new teaching promise us
But corporal servitude and misery
And afterwards in Hellmouth to be thrust
Because we left Mohammed slavishly?
My lords, will you assure me you'll agree
To all I say, and swear obedience for
The sake of being safe forever more?"

31

344   They promised and assented, every one,
To stand with her and die, until the end,
And each, whatever way it could be done,
Must amplify her army with a friend.
Then she to all the details would attend.
She plotted with her followers this way
About which you shall next hear what I say.

32

351   "Christened, first, we must pretend to be
(Some chilly water will not hurt a mite),
Then I shall plan a feast — such revelry!

I swear the sultan I shall so requite
That though his wife be christened ever so white,
To wash away the red she will require
More water than a font-full to be by her!"

33

358   *Oh, sultaness, you root of iniquity!*
Virago, second Samiramis! Snake
Arrayed in guise of femininity
So like that serpent bound in the hellish lake!
Oh, counterfeit of woman, you unmake
All innocence and grace! Malignity,
You nest of every vice, is bred in thee!

34

365   *Oh, Satan, envious from the fatal day*
That you were exiled from our heritage,
Well known to women in the ancient way,
Seducing Eve to cause our vassalage,
This Christian mating now you sabotage.
Thus you manipulate — alas the while! —
To be your tool, woman, whom you beguile.

35

372   *This sultaness whom thus I curse and blame*
Convinced her folk to look at things her way.
But why should I prolong this tale of shame?
Riding to see the sultan one fine day,
She told him she was ready to put away
Mohammed for Christ, ashamed of being wrong
And choosing to be heathen for so long.

36

379   She begged him then to let her have the pleasure
Of entertaining as her honored guest
Each and every Christian. "Every measure
I'll take to please them that you can suggest."
He knelt and thanked her for her kind request.
So glad he was, he knew not what to say.
She kissed her son, and homeward took her way.

End of the First Part

Part II

37

386   Now when these Christians landed on the shore
Of Syria with a large, imposing band,
The sultan for his mother sent, before
Announcing that event throughout the land.
His wife-to-be, he told her, and her grand
Entourage had arrived. Would she please ride
To meet her, and sustain his kingdom's pride?

38

393   Great was the crowd and rich was the array
When those of Rome and Syria came together.
The mother of the sultan, rich and gay,
Saluted Custance sweetly — as a mother
Might with affection greet her darling daughter.
Then to the city standing by the sea
They rode an easy pace, with dignity.

39

400 I don't think the triumphant ride of Caesar
   That Lucan tells of in such boasting style
   Was royaller or more designed for pleasure
   Than this procession was — and all the while
   The sultaness, this scorpion, this most vile
   Of wicked souls despite her flattering,
   Planned underneath, most mortally, to sting.

40

407 The sultan came himself soon after this,
   His elegance a miracle to say.
   He welcomed Custance with great joy and bliss,
   And thus in mirth and joy I'll let them stay
   While I get to the point. Too soon the day
   Drew to a close, and people thought it best
   That revels cease and all retire to rest.

41

414 The time came when this sultaness decreed
   The celebration feast of which I've told,
   To which her guests began now to proceed.
   All of the Christians came there, young and old,
   Where they could sit for feasting and behold
   Both food and folk most royally arrayed.
   But all too dear, before they rose, they paid.

42

421 Oh, sudden woe that always, bitter neighbor,
   Follows close upon our worldly bliss
   And ends the joy of all our worldly labor!

Sorrow concludes our every happiness.
So pay attention, for your health, to this:
On every happy day keep well in mind
That unexpected woe comes close behind.

43

428 To make the story brief as I am able,
Except for Lady Custance, her alone,
The sultan and the Christians at the table
Were hacked and hewn apart through flesh and bone.
This ancient sultaness, that curséd crone,
Had joined with friends to do, with her own hand,
The curséd deed, wanting to rule the land.

44

435 And every Syrian who had been converted
Was hacked to bits before he could, in fear,
Leap up to flee. Then hot-foot they escorted
Custance to a ship that had, I hear,
No rudder giving her the means to steer.
They said she'd better learn how, rapidly,
To sail now, if she yearned for Italy.

45

442 To Syria she had brought a certain treasure;
They let her take it now, and, truthfully,
They gave her clothes and food in ample measure
When forth she sailed upon the salty sea.
Oh, Custance, full of sweet benignity,
Oh, Roman emperor's daughter fair, my dear,
Now may the Lord of Fortune help you steer!

46

449 She crossed herself and with a mournful voice
   Addressed the Cross of Christ, and thus spoke she:
   "Oh, glorious blessed altar, holy cross
   Red with the Lamb's blood, that pure clemency
   That washes all the world's iniquity —
   Safe from the fiend's infernal clutches keep
   Your servant, me, when drowned upon the deep.

47

456 "Victorious tree, protector of the true,
   Alone of tree-kind worthy of the dear
   Ruler of Heaven when his wounds were new,
   The snow-white Lamb they wounded with a spear,
   Oh, Cross, expelling fiends from all who rear
   Themselves upon your branches to extend
   Their souls — allow me strength my life to mend."

48

463 Now Custance floated forth for days and years
   Upon the sea of Greece, till wind and fate
   Blew her out past Gibraltar. Drenched in tears,
   Many a sorry dinner now she ate,
   And frequently for death would sit and wait,
   Until the wild waves chanced at last to drive
   Her ship where she was destined to arrive.

49

470 One might well ask why Custance did not die
   With all the others. Who chose to defend
   Her body? With a question I reply:

Who guarded Daniel in the lion's den
When the cruel beast had eaten, lord and men,
All of the rest before they could depart?
No one but God, whom he bore in his heart.

50

477   How by His providence He often works
Great miracles was what God wished to show
Here, too. By certain means, as known to clerks,
Christ, who is antidote for every woe,
Does certain things for ends we cannot know.
The presence of his mighty foresight we
Cannot, within our human limits, see.

51

484   And then, when Custance managed to survive
That feast, who kept her safe upon the sea?
Well, who kept Jonah in the whale alive
Until on Nineveh it spewed him free?
We all know that it was no man, but He
Who kept the Hebrew people from the grave,
With dry feet passing through the Red Sea wave!

52

491   Who bids the angels of the wind to rest,
Those four with power to ravage land and sea?
Who said, "From north and south and east and west,
Do harm to neither ocean, land, nor tree"?
He who gave orders for that peace was He
Who also from the violent tempest kept
This woman, both awake and when she slept.

53

494 The meat and drink that Custance had — who gave
 Her food for more than three years spent aboard?
 Who fed Egyptian Mary in her cave
 Or in the desert? None but Christ our Lord.
 Five loaves and just two fish to feed a horde
 Of five thousand folk was far more great a deed.
 God sent His plenty when He saw their need.

54

505 Thus driven north into our seas she came
 Upon the mighty waves, until at last
 Beneath a castle that I cannot name
 In far Northumberland was Custance cast,
 And in the sand her ship was stuck so fast
 It could not be dislodged by wind or tide.
 There, by the will of Christ, she must abide.

55

512 The constable of the castle came to check
 The ship and carefully through that vessel sought
 Until he came on Custance in the wreck
 Beside the treasure chest that she had brought.
 Speaking in her own language, she besought
 His help, by slaying her body, to release
 Her soul from woe and let her die in peace.

56

519 Although her Latin was corrupt, her speech
 Was not too difficult to understand,
 And tired of scavaging, back to the beach

The constable brought the lady. Once on land,
She knelt and thanked God for his saving hand.
But who she was she uttered not a breath,
For good or ill, even on pain of death.

57

526   She claimed to be bewildered by the ocean
And therefore to have lost her memory.
This caused the constable so much emotion,
And his wife too, they wept in sympathy.
So helpful and considerate was she
In waiting on the people in that place,
That all looked fondly on her lovely face.

58

533   This constable and Hermengild his wife
Were pagans, like most others living there.
But Hermengild loved Custance more than life,
And Custance, spending many hours in prayer,
Persuaded her with patient, tender care,
Until the lady constable of that place,
Hermengild, was saved by Jesus' grace.

59

540   Christians dared not assemble in that land.
Most had long ago been forced to flee
By pagans who invaded, tribe and band,
Those northern regions both by land and sea.
Withdrawn to Wales were the majority
Of British Christians dwelling on this isle,
But Custance sheltered there a little while.

60

547   Some Christians, though, who in the neighborhood
       Remained in exile, worshiped privately.
       Gathered in little groups, they often would
       Beguile the heathens, praying. Of these, three
       Dwelt near the castle. One could only see
       With that most subtle inner eye of mind
       That people sometimes see with when they're blind.

61

554   Bright was the sun upon one summer's day
       When with his wife the constable thought to go
       Walking with Custance. They had made their way
       Along the beach a quarter mile or so,
       Taking their pleasure, walking to and fro,
       When in their walk it happened that they passed
       This bent old blind man, both his eyes shut fast.

62

561   "In name of Christ," the blind old Briton prayed,
       "Dame Hermengild, restore my sight again!"
       At this request the lady was afraid;
       Her husband, the most dutiful of men,
       Seeing her love for Christ, might have her slain.
       But Custance boldly prompted her to work
       The will of God, as daughter of the church.

63

568   The constable, perplexed about the sight,
       Asked them the meaning of this strange affair,
       And Custance answered, "Sir, it is the might

Of Christ, who helps folk out of Satan's snare."
Then our religion she presented there.
To faith in Jesus, long before day faded,
By her was that good constable persuaded.

64

575 The constable was not the master of
The castle where they dwelt, or of the land.
He held it strongly many a year for love
Of noble Alla, King of Northumberland,
A prudent king who ruled with iron hand
Against the Scots who came to raid and burn.
But now again to Custance I return.

65

582 Satan is always quick to lead astray
Us mortals. Seeing Custance's perfection,
He promptly cast about how to betray,
And caused a knight who had a predilection
For lust to love her with such foul affection,
It seemed to him that he would die unless
He just one time could pierce her holiness.

66

589 He courted her, but that did not avail,
So finding that with him she would not lie
By choice, he sought by vengeance to prevail,
Hoping to shame her first, then make her die.
The constable was gone. He thought he'd try
In through the door that very night to creep
Where Hermengild and Custance were asleep.

67

596 *They were exhausted from their lengthy prayers*
  And sleeping soundly (innocent people do),
  When he whom Satan tempted came upstairs.
  They slept in bed together, as he knew.
  He cut the throat of Hermengild clean through
  And next to Custance laid the bloody knife.
  May God give him calamity for life!

68

603 *That night the constable came home again*
  Along with Alla, ruler of the land,
  And went upstairs and found his dear wife slain
  And there beside the other woman's hand
  The bloody knife, exactly as was planned.
  With evidence like that what could she say?
  Alas, her mind entirely slipped away.

69

610 *To Alla this disaster was made known,*
  And also where and how and on what day
  The lady in her vessel had been blown
  Upon his shore, as you have heard me say.
  The king's heart leapt in pity at the way
  A woman seeming so benign as she
  Had suffered so much cruel adversity.

70

617 *For as the snow-white lamb is led to slaughter*
  She stood in innocence before the king,
  And when the knight who to this point had brought her

Affirmed that she had truly done this thing,
Among the people was great sorrowing,
For they could not, despite the evidence,
Believe her capable of such offense.

71

624 Always, they had seen her virtuous
And loving Hermengild like her own life.
Of this all those who dwelt within that house
Bore witness but for him that had the knife.
The king then thought the murder of that wife
Grew so suspicious as he testified
That by a fight it should be verified.

72

631 But Custance, you don't have upon your side
Champion to prove you true, or warrior's skill —
Except for Him who to redeem us died
And bound old Satan where he's lying still.
May Christ then save you with a miracle,
For He must by a miracle make plain
The truth, or guiltless, Custance, you'll be slain.

73

638 She set herself upon her knees and prayed:
"Immortal God who rescued sweet Susanna
From false accusal; thou, too, blissful maid,
Mary, I mean, the daughter of Saint Anna,
Before whose child the angels sang Hosanna,
If I be guiltless of this felony,
Help me, or executed I shall be!"

74

645   Have you not seen sometime the pallid face,
       Among a crowd, of someone being led
       To death because he has received no grace? —
       Just such a color in his face he had
       That one could recognize whose luck was bad
       Amid all other faces in the press.
       Thus appeared Custance, standing in distress.

75

652   Oh, queens who live in such prosperity,
       Duchesses, ladies, on your couch or throne,
       Pity poor Custance in adversity!
       An emperor's daughter standing all alone,
       She has no friend to listen to her moan.
       Oh, royal child, in terror, far indeed
       Are all your friends in this your hour of need!

76

659   So much compassion had King Alla, though,
       As filled with pity noble heart may be.
       He had to brush away a tear or so.
       "Now quickly fetch a Holy Book," said he,
       "And if this knight swears then that it was she
       Who murdered Hermengild, we will decide
       Whom to appoint to have the lady tried."

77

666   They brought a British Gospel book, and then
       The knight took oath on it in somber tone
       That she was guilty. He'd barely finished when

A hand struck on his neck against the bone,
And down he fell directly, like a stone,
Both of his eyes protruding from his face
In sight of everybody in that place.

78

674 And all those listening heard a mighty voice:
"You slanderers of the innocent and good
Daughter of Holy Church, I hold my peace,
Though in my sight you've done what no one should!"
Then those who saw this miracle all stood
Aghast and stunned, afraid of holy vengeance —
Every one of them except for Custance.

79

680 Great was the fear and also the repentance
Of those who had maintained a wrong suspicion
Of this poor innocent, the Lady Custance.
So, to conclude, this holy apparition,
Supported by the lady's own petition,
Convinced the king and others in that place
To be converted, thanks to Christian grace.

80

687 The lying knight, by Alla's just decree,
Though Custance pitied him for being bad,
Was executed for his perjury,
And then Lord Jesus, in his mercy, had
King Alla wed the maiden, once so sad,
Yet young and beautiful, who now was seen
As holy, too. Thus Christ made Custance queen.

81

694 But who was furious when she came to see
   The royal wedding? Donegild, that's who,
   King Alla's mother, full of tyranny.
   Alla, she thought, would break her heart in two
   By doing what she did not want him to.
   It seemed to her a shame he should decide
   To take an unknown woman as his bride.

82

701 It pleases me to make the chaff and straw
   Less lengthy in the telling than the corn.
   Why say what royalty the feasters saw
   Or what fine courses first to them were borne,
   Or who blew on a trumpet, who a horn?
   The fruit of story one should simply state:
   They drank and danced and sang and played and ate!

83

708 Then Custance and King Alla, as was right,
   Went off to bed. Though wives are holy things,
   They must accept with patience, in the night,
   Necessities that passion's pleasure brings
   To husbands who have married them with rings.
   To lay a bit of holiness aside
   Just briefly is the business of the bride.

84

715 A child upon his wife the king begot.
   Bishop and constable, while she was weak,
   He asked to care for her. Wars must be fought

In Scotland; he had enemies to seek.
Now Custance, who so humble was and meek,
Soon grew so big with child that she lay still
Within her room, awaiting there God's will.

85

722 Her time came and she bore a little boy.
They named him at the font Mauricius.
Appointing a bearer to convey the joy,
The constable wrote the king in furious
Haste about how fine the baby was,
And other news that he could quickly write.
The bearer took it, riding forth by night.

86

729 But lured by what advancement he might get,
He paused en route at Alla's mother's door.
With formal greeting, in his dialect,
"Madam, a hundred thousand times or more,"
He said, "you may rejoice and thank God, for
Custance the queen has borne a little boy,
And all the realm is going mad with joy.

87

736 "Look at the sealed letters I must run
To give the king with all the haste I may!
If you should wish to send your royal son
A message, I'm your servant, night or day."
Donegild answered, "At the moment, nay.
But if you could but rest here for the night,
By morning I shall think of what to write."

88

743 Both ale and wine he drank, in cups so big
   That from his box the old queen secretly
   Stole letters while he snored there like a pig.
   Another letter, very cleverly
   She substituted, that purportedly
   The constable had penned directly to
   King Alla, which I'll now report to you.

89

750 This letter said the queen had been delivered
   Of so deformed a fiend, so foul and queer,
   That everybody in the castle shivered
   At the very thought of coming near.
   The mother was an elf, it would appear,
   Who came to them by charm or sorcery,
   And everybody loathed her company.

90

757 Distraught the king was when he saw this letter.
   He told his sorrow, though, to no one there,
   But in his own hand wrote another, better:
   "Welcome the messengers of Christ, who care
   To make me know what suffering I can bear.
   Welcome, oh, Lord, your every wish and will.
   I have vowed faith in you and have it still.

91

764 "Constable, guard this little baby's life,
   Whether it's fair or foul, till I am there,
   And Custance too, for Christ may send my wife

A child more to my liking as my heir."
Weeping, he wrote this letter out with care
And sealed it. To the bearer it was sent,
Who then (what more to say?) took it, and went.

92

771 Oh, messenger defiled by drunkenness,
Your stinking breath and faltering limbs betray
Your vice, as do the secrets you confess.
Your mind is gone, you chatter like a jay,
Your face distorted in a rare display.
Where drunkenness can reign over age or youth,
There is no secret kept — that is the truth.

93

778 Oh, Donegild, I have no English fit
For telling your malicious tyranny,
Therefore I'll let the devil attend to it;
Let him describe your foul iniquity!
Fie, unfeminine, fie! Or rather, he,
The fiend, should be reviled, for I can tell,
Though you walk here, your spirit walks in Hell!

94

785 The messenger, returning from the king,
Alighted at the royal mother's court.
She greeted him, which he found flattering,
And tempted him with food of every sort.
He drank until his belt had firm support,
And then he slept and snorted through his nose
The whole night through, until the sun arose.

95

792   Again she stole his letters, forging one
Of crucial consequence, with this reply:
"In his good judgment, Alla commands anon
His constable, on pain of hanging high,
That he should not allow the queen to try
To tarry longer in his land than for
Three days and just one quarter hour more.

96

799   "Into the ship where, beached upon the sand,
He found her, with her son and all their gear
He now must put her, cast her from this land,
And tell her never again to venture here."
Alas, my Custance, now well should you fear,
And sound asleep, well might you have bad dreams,
When Donegild invents such wicked schemes!

97

806   The bearer in the morning when he woke
Back to the castle quickly made his way
And to the constable this message took.
On seeing what the letter had to say,
The latter shouted out, "Alas the day! —
Lord Christ!" he cried, "how may this world progress
When people are so full of wickedness?

98

812   "If this is your true will though, God on high,
Being a righteous judge, how can it be
That you allow these innocents to die

And wicked folk to have prosperity?
Custance, good soul, alas and woe is me:
I must torment you if I am to live,
Or shamefully die. There's no alternative."

99

820   Hearing the curséd letter Alla sent,
Everyone burst out weeping in that place.
On the fourth day, down to the seaside went
Poor Custance with a deadly pale face.
Accepting nonetheless with perfect grace
The will of Christ, she knelt upon the sand
And said, "I always welcome His command!

100

827   "He who has saved me from that false knight's blame
While I dwelt here upon the land can now
Protect me also from abuse and shame
Upon the ocean, though I see not how,
For he is strong as ever. I avow
My faith in Christ and Mary will not fail,
For they shall be my rudder and my sail."

101

834   Her little child lay weeping on her arm,
And kneeling, tenderly to him she said,
"Peace, little son. I'll do thee no harm."
With that she plucked the kerchief from her head
And laid it on his little eyes instead,
And in her arms she lulled him while he slept,
And cast her eyes to Heaven, though she wept.

102

841   "Mary," she prayed, "maiden bright and mother,
True it is through feminine affliction
Mankind was lost and damned to die forever,
For which your dear son suffered crucifixion.
Your blessed eyes watched over his transfixion,
And there is no comparison between
Your woe and any woman may sustain.

103

848   "Your child was killed before your very eyes,
Yet my child lives, and soon will sail afar.
Lady to whom the woeful sufferer cries,
Glory of womanhood, fair maid, you are
A haven of refuge and the day's bright star!
I pray to your compassion for distress:
Take pity on my child in gentleness.

104

855   "Oh, little child, alas, what is your guilt
Who never managed sin as yet, pardee?
Why does your cruel father want you killed?
Have mercy on us, constable," said she,
"And let my little child stay here with thee.
But if you cannot save him, fearing blame,
Just kiss him once more in his father's name!"

105

862   But then, with one more glance around the land,
"Farewell," she said, "my ruthless husband proud!"
Then up she rose and walked along the strand
And to her vessel, followed by the crowd.

Praying her baby would not weep too loud,
She said goodbye and, with devout intent,
She crossed herself and into the ship she went.

106

869   Fear not, it was a well-provisioned ship,
Having abundant cargo for the space
Of years, if need be. Food for the longest trip
She had in plenty, praise be to the grace
Of God. Now may His wind and weather race
To bring her home again, that's all I say!
Once more upon the sea she sails away.

End of the Second Part

Part III

107

876   Alla the king returned soon after this.
He came back to his home of which I've told
And sought the wife and baby whom he missed.
He asked for them. The constable's blood ran cold.
Then he began the business to unfold
As you have heard, nor can I tell it better.
He showed the king his royal seal and letter.

108

883   He said, "My lord, all you commanded me
Under the threat of death, I carried out."
The messenger was tortured then, till he
Confessed it all, and told them all about
Where he had slept in his nocturnal route.
And thus by subtle questioning they came
To guess and understand whom they should blame.

109

890   *They found by whom the letter had been forged*
And all the venom of her cursèd deed.
What means they used to do so, whom they scourged,
I know not, but what follows one can read:
Alla his mother's guilt, then death, decreed.
She owed him loyalty, but nearly killed,
And was a traitor. Thus ended Donegild!

110

897   *The sorrow Alla felt by night and day*
For his lost wife and for his baby too
No tongue of storyteller could convey.
But now to Custance I return with you.
She sailed with nothing but the sea in view,
As Christ in wisdom pleased, five years and more
Before her ship approached another shore.

111

904   *Under a heathen castle at the last*
(No name in my old manuscript I find)
Dame Custance and her little child were cast.
Oh, God Almighty, helper of mankind,
Keep Custance and her little child in mind,
For now she falls to heathen hands again,
Once more upon the verge of being slain!

112

911   *Down from the castle people came to view*
The ship and Custance with astonishment.
But shortly came the master's steward — who

Had previously renounced our Testament,
God curse him! Now with criminal intent
He boarded her ship at night and said he thought
To have her, whether she wanted it or not.

113

918   In misery was this wretched woman then.
Her baby cried; she too wept pitifully.
But blesséd Mary hastened to help her when
She struggled with that villain vigorously.
He stumbled overboard quite suddenly,
And in the sea for sin he drowned and vanished.
By Christ himself was Custance kept unblemished.

114

925   See what you lead to, lust of lechery! —
Not mere effemination of the mind.
The body itself you damage, verily.
The end result of passion going blind
With wicked lust is woe. Does one not find
Many who not for deeds but mere intent
Find death or bodily disablement?

115

932   Where did this fragile woman find defiant
Strength enough to save her body from
That renegade? And you, old wicked giant,
Goliath, how did David overcome
Your might, when armorless yet mettlesome
He dared to look upon your fearsome face?
One may well understand it was God's grace.

116

939   And who to Judith strength and courage gave
       To slay old Holofernes in his tent
       And out of all their wretchedness to save
       God's people? Pressing home my argument,
       I say, that very spirit of vigor sent
       To save them from their great adversity
       Custance received in her necessity.

117

946   Her ship returning through the narrow mouth
       Of Septe and Gibraltar sailed away
       Sometimes west and sometimes north and south
       And sometimes east, for many a weary day,
       Until Christ's mother (blessed is she, I say!)
       Through her unbounded mercy chose to bring
       An end to Custance's long voyaging.

118

953   Now let us leave Dame Custance for a while
       And find what course her father has begun.
       He heard, by news from Syria, of the vile
       Slaughter of Christians and dishonor done
       To his own daughter by that lying one —
       I mean the curséd wicked sultaness
       Who slew the feasters out of spitefulness.

119

960   Revenge in mind, the emperor then sent
       His senators a royal mandate. They
       And other lords (God knows how many) went

To Syria, there to pillage, burn, and slay.
They slaughtered enemies for many a day.
But finally the war came to an end,
And back to Rome they all prepared to wend.

120

967   One senator who with a victor's glory
Had started out for Rome across the sea
Encountered out there drifting, says the story,
The ship that Custance sat in mournfully.
Her name or from what country she might be,
Or why she sat there in such disarray,
Even on pain of death she would not say.

121

974   He brought her home and gave her to his wife
Along with her young son, to serve her, so
With that good senator she led her life.
Thus did Our Lady rescue her from woe,
As she will always help us all to go.
For some years then dwelt Custance in that place
Performing holy works, as was her grace.

122

980   The senator's wife, it happened, was her aunt,
Who did not recognize her any more.
I will not linger with them, for I want
To get back to King Alla, as before
Missing his wife and child, and sighing sore.
Let us move on then, leaving Custance there
Under the senator and his wife's good care.

123

988   *Upon this king, who angrily had slain*
His mother, came one day a deep remorse,
So that, if I may tell it short and plain,
To Rome he came in penance, and of course
Submitted to the pope in all, perforce
Obedient, and he prayed that Mary's son
Forgive the wicked things that he had done.

124

995   *Throughout all Rome the news, without delay,*
Was borne by heralds who had gone before,
Announcing the royal pilgrim on his way.
As noble custom was, the senator
Rode out with all his lords and many more,
As much to flaunt his own magnificence
As to display appropriate reverence.

125

1002   *Cordially did this noble senator*
Give Alla greeting. He in kind replied,
Each honoring the other. When three or four
Days passed, the Roman happened to decide
That it would be a pleasant thing to ride
To Alla's inn for feasting. With him was
The son of Custance, young Mauricius.

126

1009   *Some say that Custance's petitioning*
Had made him take her son to that repast —
But I can't vouch for every single thing!

Be as it may, the boy was there at last,
And this I know is true: that she had asked
That during all the banquet he should stand
In front of Alla, ready and near at hand.

127

1016   Gazing upon the boy made Alla wonder,
And to the senator he said anon,
"Whose is the handsome child that's standing yonder?"
"I know not," said the other, "by Saint John!
Mother he has, but father he has none
That I know of," and in a moment he
Had told the king of finding them at sea.

128

1022   "And yet God knows," he added, "that boy's mother
So virtuous is in all parts of her life,
That I have never heard of any other
Such woman on this earth, unwed or wife.
I dare say she would rather have a knife
Thrust in her breast than be a wicked woman.
She cannot be seduced by any human."

129

1030   The child was now the image of his mother
As closely as a son could ever be.
Alla recalled that same face on another
So dear to him, and wondered inwardly
Whether the child's mother could be she
Who was his wife. Then privately he sighed
And hurried from the feast before he cried.

130

1037   "Goodness," he thought, "such ghosts are in my head!
Perfectly well I know and must consent
To realizing that my wife is dead."
But shortly he contrived this argument:
"What if Christ again has hither bent
Her course by sea, just as he had her come
The first time from wherever she floated from?"

131

1044   To look upon the lady that afternoon
He went with the senator, who cordially
Welcomed him to his home, and Alla soon
Was hinting at the sight he came to see.
Believe me, though, she did not dance for glee
When she knew what the summons was about.
Barely could she stagger, coming out.

132

1051   Observing her, his wife, he greeted her
And wept so hard that it was sad to see,
For at the first glance Alla set on her
He knew with certainty that it was she.
But Custance stood there silent as a tree,
Her heart in her distress closed to the king,
His treatment all too well remembering.

133

1058   As twice she sighed and fainted in his sight,
He begged forgiveness, then began to cry:
"I swear by God and all His angels bright,

Their mercy shining on my soul from high,
Guiltless of harming you I swear am I
As Maurice my son, his face so like your face —
Or may the devil snatch me from this place!"

134

1065   Long was the sobbing and the bitter pain
Before their hearts could find surcease from woe.
And it was tragic hearing them explain.
Their very trying made their sorrows grow.
I pray you, people, from this let me go.
Release me, please, at least until tomorrow.
I'm so exhausted, telling of such sorrow!

135

1072   But when she finally understood the gist,
That he was really guiltless of her woe,
I think a hundred times they must have kissed.
Such joy between them then began to grow
That, but for the joy of Heaven we hope to know,
It was among us humans unsurpassed
By any joy so long as the world may last.

136

1079   She asked her husband gently if he might
"Relieve a long and sorrowful pain of mine"
By visiting her father, to invite
His majesty, if he would so incline,
To vouchsafe someday soon with him to dine.
She also asked that not in any way
A word to him about her should he say.

137

1086   *Some would avow it was the child Maurice*
Who took this message to the emperor.
But Alla, I think, would never be so foolish
As send a child to be ambassador
To someone of such rank, indeed before
The highest of Christian rulers. I expect
He went as well, to be more circumspect.

138

1093   *Most graciously the emperor agreed*
When Alla asked him to, to come and dine.
But while they spoke, intently (as I read)
He watched young Maurice, thinking, "How like mine."
Back at his inn, King Alla chose the wine
And making first arrangements for the table,
Began what preparations he was able.

139

1100   *The day came. Custance and the king arrayed*
Themselves with care and elegance to meet
The emperor, and in a fine parade
They rode up to her father in the street,
And she alighted, falling at his feet.
"Father," she said, "your only child, I see,
Is gone entirely from your memory!"

140

1107   *"I am your daughter Custance," then said she,*
Whom once you sent to Syria. It is I
Who long ago upon the salty sea

Was cast alone, expected there to die;
And now, good father, mercy to you I cry!
Send me no more to lands of heathen blindness,
But thank the senator for all his kindness."

141

1114   Who can relate the affecting joy of friend
Rejoined by friend when three have met this way?
But of this tale I now shall make an end.
The day goes fast; I wish no more delay.
I leave them sitting at the banquet, gay
With food and talk and laughter, safe and well,
A thousand times more pleased than I can tell.

142

1121   Young Maurice was in time made emperor,
Crowned years later by the pope's own hand.
Though honoring the church, he gets no more
Story from me because this tale is planned
As Custance's alone, you understand.
In ancient Roman histories one may find
That emperor's life. I bear it not in mind.

143

1128   King Alla, when he saw the proper day,
Homeward to England with his lady went,
With Custance, sweet and holy, there to stay,
And there in peace and joy their lives were spent.
But joy of this world, I promise you, is lent
For little time, and time will not abide.
From day to night joy changes, like the tide.

1135   But who has ever lived in pure delight
     Unmoved by conscience for a single day,
     Unmoved by anger, fear, or appetite,
     Or free from envy, pride, or passion's sway?
     Only to make this point here do I say:
     Such happiness is brief in this short life
     As Alla shared with Custance, his dear wife.

145

1142   For death, who claims his toll from high and low,
     In just about a year or even less
     Forced Alla from this brittle world to go,
     And sank his lady into heaviness.
     Now may God bless him. May He also bless
     Good Custance too, as I conclude my tale
     And on a final voyage let her sail.

146

1149   That holy woman, coming back to Rome,
     Found all her former friends there whole and sound.
     Surviving misadventures, she came home
     And there again her royal father found,
     And once again she knelt upon the ground
     Weeping for tenderness, with heart upraised,
     A hundred thousand times her God she praised.

147

1156   In virtue and in deeds of generous heart
     They lived till death divided them, these two,
     Father and daughter, never again apart.
     And now, farewell, my friends, for I am through.

May Christ, who of His might all things can do,
Turn woe to joy and keep us in His grace
And hold us safe who sojourn in this place.

Amen.

Here ends the tale of the Man of Law

Myth is a discourse of some complexity "constructed from a se-
miological chain which existed before it."
>—Eldon Kenworthy quoting Barthes,
>*America/Américas*

In its second phase, religious feminist criticism is marked by the
theme of quest. Most notably, the search for lost voices, for
myths and symbols excluded from patriarchal tradition, mani-
fests itself as a "quest for the goddess."
>—Dawne McCance, in Hurtado

3.

Backtracking the Goddess: Ancient Sources and Analogues

Romancing the Goddess

THE WOMEN ADRIFT in the three Middle English romances of this book, despite their helplessness as they wander the seas and forests, present icons[1] of female power that startle and sometimes frighten those who encounter them. Our response to the handed-down theme of the woman adrift, our narration of a story about her, does not mean that we understand this evocative icon in the same way as did the authors of these romances or their medieval audiences. Even within the individual stories themselves, people interpret the heroine in different ways. Moreover, once one moves beyond the documentation of written texts to go deeper into the past, dependable verification of meanings and connections is in most instances impossible.[2] Therefore, after the first two introductory sections of this chapter, the discussion of how the romance heroine leads us to "the Goddess" will be partly scholarly and partly intuitive; with intuition necessarily increasing the farther back and farther afield the story goes, the last two parts are especially speculative. The first two sections address issues importantly related to the ensuing exploration: the question of reliability of sources, and how mythic narrative may be adapted to new ends. Both issues remind us that the story and its central icon are human, hence malleable, constructs.

The specific image itself of the solitary woman on the open seas, which serves as such a powerful iconographic focus for the three Middle English romances of this study, has a history that may be traced back as far as texts and archaeology can take us. This history may be traced clearly to connections with cults of late classical times (approximately from the time of Christ to the end of the Western Roman Empire in 476 C.E.), and intriguingly though with less certainty to connections with ancient "Goddess" statues, much farther back. Although opinions on these statues range widely, for the purpose of this chapter it will be assumed, following Gerda Lerner's assertion that "the Mother Goddess is virtually universal as the dominant figure in the most ancient stories" (148), that the many Neolithic female statues that have been discovered in possibly religious contexts in eastern Europe represent, in some sense, a single generalized "Goddess." (This assumption itself will be examined in chapter 4.) In "The New Cults of the Goddess," Mary R. Lefkowitz presents succinctly the argument that the Goddess, as we of the modern day view her, is a modern construct. She sees "the natural world of the Goddess" as "more likely to be informative about the present than any time in the past" (263). Indeed, those who seek roots in the past do well to remember that all *living* trees are rooted in the present. Because finding ancient roots is a romance in itself, and because the discovery that those roots may greatly empower women corresponds to my desire and that of many of my expected readers, I have warily titled this book "Romancing the Goddess," a title that evokes the idea of a quest, as for the precious stone in the popular movie, and also the idea of a fiction. While this chapter associates the three Middle English romances with the modern Goddess quest, the book's title leaves up to the reader the question of authenticity and its attendant anxieties: How much are the identities we find here the product of a desire to see them, and how much does an uncertainty about their historical authenticity disturb us? The degree to which the hitherto unrecognized pattern recovered here of myths, legends, and stories appears to exist objectively, as opposed to being a construct established like other similar patterns through a particular choice of examples, hence being itself a "romance," will depend to some extent on the reader's own investment in a quest for the Goddess. Although I admit, then, that the argument in the "deep antiquity" portion of this chapter may itself be moving into myth, the following two sections trace what I believe to be a clear connection between the Christian romances and a pagan past.

✦ Redeploying Myth

The first link back, the late classical associations of the basic plot, has already been made in chapter 1. To summarize: The medieval romances translated in this book reflect two distinct but related literary plots instigated by a young woman's flight from incest, one plot exploiting the threat of a father's incestuous desire for his daughter and the other exploiting the incest-threat from a near relative, usually a brother or a brother-in-law. As Elizabeth Archibald has demonstrated, this basic "flight from incest" story adapted to the two forms of incest may be found in two late classical sources, the Latin *Apollonius of Tyre* and the Greek *Clementine Recognitions*. *Apollonius* opens with father-daughter incest, though it is the daughter's suitor who escapes the situation (the woman he later marries becoming "the woman adrift"); and in *The Clementine Recognitions* the mother of the Clement referred to in the title flees sexual pressures from her brother-in-law, pressures construed as sibling incest,[3] and later symbolically loses the use of her hands. Apollonius's "dead" wife comes to shore at a cult site dedicated to Diana, where she is revived and later rejoined to her lost family through the goddess. A similar role is played in *The Clementine Recognitions* by St. Peter as he brings together Clement's family and cures the mother's hands, the Christian story typically assigning the supernatural agency to a male. Neither of these classical works focuses upon the woman in the story. In later times the plot is centered on the woman, who then becomes a much more autonomous protagonist, and it is enhanced by folklore, most notably by the addition of the accusation theme that multiplies the journey sequences. (This folkloric accusation theme is not relevant to our present examination other than its becoming firmly attached to the medieval plot. As her title suggests, it is the main topic of Margaret Schlauch's fine study, *Constance and the Accused Queens*.) Similar stories of women set adrift were transmitted orally, but our three medieval romances all appear to be derived specifically from written texts.

This plot's literary association with the earlier Greek and Latin texts should be emphasized, since it suggests a conscious adaptation and reworking of the older pagan story. When B. P. Reardon includes the Latin *Apollonius of Tyre* in his anthology of *Collected Ancient Greek Novels*, he argues in the introduction that the fifth or sixth century C.E. Latin work probably derives from a third century C.E. Greek original (4), and he mentions the Greek *Clementine Recognitions* as a "fringe novel" related to the form (3). This is how Reardon describes the "ideal" Greek romance in general: "Hero and heroine are always young, wellborn, and handsome; their marriage is disrupted or temporarily prevented by separation, travel in distant parts, and a series of misfortunes, usually spectacular. Virginity or chastity, at least in the female, is of crucial importance, and fidelity to one's partner, together often with trust in the gods, will ultimately guarantee a happy ending" (2). Thwarted incest and a woman's exposure at sea are the two themes marking the Castaway Queen story as a subset of this Greek romance form (or a story incorporated into this form, as I suggest below), with her survival and reconciliation with her family at the end because it is a romance. The reconciliation is aided by a holy figure or located at a sacred site because the fiction contains a cult association. The incest theme with which the woman-adrift romance often begins reflects male control, or a male urge for control, over women's bodies, as does the theme of maiden sacrifice to the sea, the setting adrift theme itself that goes with incest in this plot. Although the sea is associated with death by the person launching the victim, it is revealed as a site that refines and proves rather than destroying the protagonist, much as the young knight of courtly romance discovers his identity by proving himself in encounters in the magical forest. In the classical and medieval versions of the Castaway Queen romance, the sea represents not death but escape from the danger of male control (among other things), and the end of the romance provides a balance to this control when the sea-sacrificed woman survives to become associated with female control figured as a goddess of abundance and destiny, as does the wife of Apollonius of Tyre on landing at Ephesus. When Apollonius and his daughter encounter her at last, "she radiated so much glittering beauty that they thought she was the goddess Diana" (Reardon, Sandys translation 770). Though Florence is not deified, the situation at the end of her romance is very similar, her sanctity even disguising her identity from those who have previously known her.

This plot presenting the woman first as victim then as goddess has usually been attached to some particular historical situation.[4] In the Middle English romances the historical interest is essentially etiological (concerned with tracing or establishing a source or cause), with *Florence* and *Custance* showing this concern more than *Emaré*. In the *Clementine Recognitions* (though not in *Apollonius of Tyre*), the family aspect of the medieval story conforms to a genealogical plot in which the heroine survives the incest threat to become the properly mated mother of an important male historical figure. In other words, this genealogical concern turns the woman's quest into her son's birth story. As Spong says in *Born of a Woman:* "Birth traditions do not develop around all people. When they do develop, they constitute a powerful commentary not on the birth of the subject, as people suppose, but on the adult significance of the life whose birth is being described. They reflect the human need to understand the origins of greatness in the person who has so affected and shaped human history" (26). Thus legends of the life of the Virgin Mary herself were developed from her brief biblical appearance in the birth story of Jesus and her shadowy scriptural presence later; these few hints were woven eventually into a lengthy apocryphal narrative on the principle that the mother of someone so important must have her own story.[5] The Virgin Mary's story becomes complex, as will be seen very shortly. In the case of Clement (of the *Recognitions*), who became Bishop of Rome, the mother story chosen for his life was that of the woman adrift, and Trevet (writing in the 1330s) likewise adds the similar story about Constance to enhance his historical account of her son, the emperor Mauricius.[6] He fits the tale of Constance into the particular "Mauricius" slot in his *Chronicle* from which Chaucer and Gower individually extract it later. Custance's reintegrated family reveals, or mythically constructs within a familiar paradigm, a birth story for the historical emperor Mauricius. The contemporary audience of this medieval story, as V. A. Kolve points out, probably perceived it as history rather than fiction (298).

The three Middle English romances reflect a double etiological function, however. In addition to providing genealogical interest for a male figure in the manner of a hagiography (defined by Reardon as "ideologically directed biography," 3), the story appropriates and Christianizes a historically documented ritual in which a goddess (or her substitute, a symbolic object or a priestess) is set adrift in a curious sort of sacrifice of the divinity herself, to placate the waters and bring good luck to the practitioners of the rite. In certain legends such a "priestess adrift" miraculously comes ashore where she founds a new temple or resanctifies an earlier foundation (like Mary Magdalen, the friend of Jesus in the Gospels, in a legend recounted below). In other words, at the religious level the story plot, like ritual, may be designed to be commemorative. It dramatizes the miraculous powers of the numinous female,[7] while at the same time establishing the credentials of an institutionalized locus of her power.

Narrative becomes a crucial instrument here. As Eldon Kenworthy observes, "At first cut myth can be understood as a story that constructs meaning by mobilizing associations *already extant* in the culture and *redeploying* them toward new objects . . . that then acquire the authority of those older meanings" (14, his emphasis). The association of the Virgin Mary with the sea provides a perfect example of such redeployment of myth. Originally undertaken, perhaps, to "tame" an earlier sea-goddess worshiped by the laity by subsuming her in the person of Mary meek and mild, this taming got out of hand and the opposite result occurred: Mary became independent and goddess-like. No longer required to resort to what one critic has described as "pillow talk" with God the Father (Spong 221) in order to intercede for those who pray to her, she is able to take action on her own. Mary's medieval meaning is mainly built, then, using the words of Barthes quoted at the beginning of this chapter, upon *two* "semiological chain[s] which existed before [her]." One comes from the young Hebrew virgin who gave birth to Christ, producing Mary-meek-and-mild, and the other comes from the powerful Mediterranean goddess who rules both the sea and the fortunes of those humans who live beside it. The combination produces a figure that an anonymous seventh-century hymnist hailed as *stella maris*, "star of the sea."[8] We may call this version of Mary "Mary Pelagia" (meaning "Mary of the Sea") to distinguish her from her meeker counterpart or identity. In the redeployment of the classical woman adrift plot as a medieval Castaway Queen story, Mary Pelagia, who typically aids the protagonist, has received the powers and perhaps even the sites of worship associated with an earlier goddess. In the three medieval romances she improves the status, at least in the mythic sphere, of her own "priestess" or devotee (Emaré, Florence, Custance), who in a limited sense represents her. Thus, like the mother-of-the-hero aspect of the Castaway Queen story, this religious aspect also explains or celebrates origins, or attempts to do so, though the origins are of an institutional rather than a genealogical nature. Such origins, again, would be assumed by the audience of the romance to be historical.

To cite Kenworthy once more: "History is a narrative about the past that possesses credibility with the relevant audience. A founding myth is a history (thus a narrative) that has acquired the additional authority of a paradigm" (17–18). In the case of these founding stories where the woman adrift becomes a famous man's mother or her landing place a cult site, the legendary paradigm has been spliced into the historical account, becoming part of it, subsumed in the patriarchal record and enhancing its authority. As Kenworthy says, adding to the passage just quoted above, "Such authority is in the eyes of the beholders. Thus the reproduction of myth is a *political* process" (18, his emphasis). It is political in the sense of being concerned with power relationships. Even as the medieval patriarchy redeployed the woman-centered myth to enhance its own authority, we now disentangle the myth from that context for our contemporary purposes, to enable women to enhance their autonomy through such myths. As we backtrack the Castaway Queen story through its various historical contexts in an effort to discover the Goddess who may loom behind those contexts, it is well to remember that this quest is itself a reproduction of myth, and political.

Roland Barthes asserts that "the fundamental character of the mythical concept is to be *appropriated*" (119, his emphasis), and ours is certainly a story that lends itself to appropriation, partly because it has that paradigmatic quality of which Kenworthy speaks. The examples assembled below show one line of development, pertinent to our romances, by which a previous Near Eastern agricultural mother goddess becomes connected with the Mediterranean. Possibly through assimilation with a sacrificed victim-intermediary-goddess figure of subsistence fishing communities (discussed further below), this mother goddess becomes a universal saviour figure, who in turn becomes Mary Pelagia, quasi-Christian mistress of the seas and protector of those who sail. Tracing this figure backwards in time and distant in culture, several medieval, classical, and archaic divine women will be examined in relation to the motif of the Castaway Queen. These are the "other" Marys (or Maries) who floated to Provence in their rudderless boat and the Virgin Mary herself (a plethora of Marys that confused even those medieval storytellers who told their legends), Sequanna of Burgundy, Pagan Artemis, Venus (called in Greek Aphrodite), Isis as she is imported from Egypt to Rome, Inuit Sedna, and the purported Great Goddess of prehistory. Then a discussion will follow concerning the sacrificial maiden of attested ritual. Other maidens and goddesses could be fitted into the scheme,[9] but each of the figures listed provides an intriguing link back to the next in line—a trail winding back truly to "the depths of time"—and each has something to do with the narrative provided by our three romances and certain stories and motifs closely associated with them. To confirm the persuasive power of this protean myth and argue for its usefulness for the current feminist agenda, for its truth as a potentializing agent while avoiding any truth-claims in the more conventional sense, will be the goal of the final chapter.

✧ Connecting the Woman Afloat with the Goddess Adrift

As we have already seen, the evidence shows that certain typifying elements in our romances appear in texts and practices of the late classical era. Joining these elements in a composite paraphrase allows us to imagine a plot that conforms to the three parts of the hero tale defined by Campbell as "separation—initiation—return" (30), modified for a woman protagonist. First the woman is separated from friends and family, under duress or, as in the case of Florence, through treachery; then she is initiated in a journey through wilderness or upon the sea; and finally she is reunited with loved ones, perhaps with an apotheosis, that is, her elevation to divine or holy status.

The transmission of a story such as this from classical times to become the medieval Castaway Queen romance confirms a view put forward by the German scholar Schick. He was writing in 1929 in opposition to those earlier scholars (Gough and Rickert) who wished to find the medieval story's source in Britain, Britain being a location frequently associated with the accusation scene. Since that scene does not occur in the classical analogues, the accusations along with their British location seem to represent a later folkloric addition to the story. Thus Schick is probably right when he says that, despite their frequent landfall in medieval times upon Welsh or Northumbrian shores, the women of the "Offa-Constance Saga" first wandered solely in the Mediterranean. (His title for the story connects the Middle English romance with the two Latin lives of the early medieval kings named Offa, introduced in chapter 1.) According to him, these women were drifting on the great central sea when Britain was still on the edge of the map. As evidence that the earlier story was available in Anglo-Saxon England, hence a possible influence on the stories of Offa and maybe Thryth (whose story is examined in detail in chapter 1), Schick observes that the Anglo-Saxon scholars Aldhelm (ca. 640–709) and Bede (ca. 673–735) both allude to the fifth-century Greek *Clementine Recognitions* (35). His unsupported avowal is confirmed by Ogilvy (116). Nor is Schick convinced of the East Indian source that some have proposed for this material, despite the similar folktales apparently deriving from that culture (34). He concludes his argument:

> The Offa-Constance-Saga probably does not derive from England and probably is not Indian either. Rather, it is of Hellenic Greek origin and derives from Christian legend. The soil on which it most likely grew seems to have been the Holy Land or Syria. It is a thousand years older than the Life of Offa I or any similar or probably related Indian narrative, and, with its sister legend of Cresentia, has as its ultimate root the novel-like part of the *Clementine Recognitions*.

> [Die Offa-Konstanze-Sage entstammt sicher nicht England und wohl auch nicht Indien; sie ist vielmehr hellenistisch-griechischen

Ursprungs und entstammt der christlichen Legende; der Boden, auf
dem sie am ehesten gewachsen ist, dürfte wohl das Heilige Land oder
Syrien sein; sie ist tausend Jahre älter als die Vita Offae I. oder irgen-
deine ähnliche, sicher verwandte indische Erzählung und hat mit
ihrer Schwesterlegende von der Kreszentia ihre Grundwurzel in dem
romanhaften Teile der klementischen Rekognitionen.] (56)

Since the Hellenic Greeks preceded Christianity, Schick's chro-
nology is confusing here in terms of origin and derivation. It cannot
be true that an originally Hellenic story "derives from Christian leg-
end"; rather it must have been transmitted by Christian legends.
Strong evidence, moreover, will be noted below for a classical plot,
woman-centered and very like the plot of the romances presented in
this book, that antedates the stories of Apollonius and of Clement.
That story might therefore have been familiar in the Hellenic Greece
of which Schick speaks.

But at this point our journey into the past is only beginning. A
comment by Edith Rickert launched it. In the final footnote of her
introduction to *Emaré*, she presents the following interesting idea,
referring to two different Saint Marys ("Maries" in French) whose
legendary voyage, supposed to have taken place soon after the cru-
cifixion, is famous in Provence, where they came ashore. These
Marys are the mothers of St. James the greater and St. James the less.
Rickert says:

I believe that the Provençal legend of the two Maries . . . which tells
how they were driven from Palestine by the Jews, put out to sea in an
open boat without sail or rudder or provision, and under divine guid-
ance drifted to the village now called *Les-Saintes-Maries-sur-Mer*,
has exerted some appreciable influence, at least, upon the popularity
of the [Constance] cycle, but at present my facts are too disconnected
to be presented in an orderly manner here. The Provençal legend
seems to be connected with some worship of *Notre Dame de la Mer*.
An interesting suggestion of this is offered by a bas-relief, taken from
a sixteenth-century house in Lyons (now in the museum of that city).
It shows the Madonna and Child alone in a little ship, which is being

governed by two angels. [See figure 2.] The inquiry is worth pursuing. (Rickert xlviii)

I have, in a minimal way, pursued Rickert's suggestion, arriving by chance to see a friend in Marseille just as the Gypsies were gathering for their Maytime devotion to "St. Sara" in the Camargue village of *Les-Saintes-Maries-sur-Mer,* which we visited. The two "Saint Maries" whom Rickert mentions (Warner explains who they are in more detail, 344–45) are usually represented as drifting alone in their boat. The mysterious Sara, supposedly the servant who drifted to France with them, is today the patron saint of the Romany race (the Gypsies). She is called "the Egyptian" and her statue is black, hence she features in recent books about the 450 surviving figures of Black Madonnas (Begg, Birnbaum). On May 24, in a ritual condemned by the church (Birnbaum 14), the thousands of gathered

FIGURE 2.

The Madonna and Child on a Ship Governed by Angels.
Sixteenth-century bas-relief from Lyon. Courtesy of the Cliché Basset for the
Musée Historique de Lyon.

Romanies parade their saint through the town and down to the shores of the sea. I will allow others to describe the statue and her pageant:

> Most church crypts are cool and refreshing and even more meditatively silent than the churches themselves. And yet this one in Les-Saintes-Maries-de-la-Mer pulsates hotly, like some living human organ, or the molten core of the earth. The room fairly crackles with the light and heat of votive candles. And then there is Sara, the coal at the heart of the fire, her silly raiments shimmering in the fervent, jittery glow of those countless waxen tributes. Oh, she doesn't make sense, this one. Saint Sara? Who has heard of Saint Sara? Yet her fine eyes slam you; they nail you to the wall. . . .
>
> What's Sara's story, really? Her secret? We know the Christian legend. But history also tells us that Egyptian deities (remember her epithet, "the Egyptian") were fervently worshipped in this region as long ago as the fourth century B.C.E., their rites and religions having been carried to these shores by Egyptian sailors. The town now known as Les-Saintes-Maries-de-la-Mer was originally called Ratis, or Ra, in honor of the Egyptian sun god. Isis, too, counted this strange swampy region among the many places where she was known and loved. The Christian legend says that the Maries established their church on the debris of an old pagan temple. The legend neglects to mention to whom that temple was dedicated. (Rufus and Lawson 60–61)

Though these enthusiastic witnesses do not document their story (provoking some questions, for example about the name Ratis or Ra), the scholarly consensus seems to be that the Black Madonnas do in fact have some association with ancient goddess figures, a number of writers specifying Isis (Dexter, *Whence* 27).

Several other founding myths of specific churches and chapels reveal or suggest a similar story. Marina Warner tells us of the Black Madonna at Tindari in Sicily, who is said to have been "found washed up like sea-born Aphrodite on the shore in a casket during the Iconoclast heresy in the east" (267), and of another Black Madonna at Crotone, overlooking the gulf of Taranto, where on the second Sunday in

May the statue "is carried from the cathedral at Crotone to the church on the headland and then, by night, brought back over the sea to the town in a torchlight procession of fishing boats whose masters hope to secure the Virgin's protection" (267). At the Chapelle de la Rotonde in Boulogne-sur-mer there is another such virgin. Baring and Cashford provide a photograph of a carving of Mary and the Christ Child in that church, both crowned, in a boat (558). The woman and child statue they show could be adopted to represent either Custance or Emaré with the baby, the Middle English romances even offering an explanation for the crowns since both these women are queens. There are other references to Boat-Virgins, including the church in Rome called Santa Maria della Navicella, "Saint Mary of the Little Boat," which Baring and Cashford suggest may be connected with the Roman cult of Isis (558), and Notre-Dame de Confession Parée in Marseille. Today at a nearby bakery advertising itself as "la plus ancienne boulangerie de Marseille" one can buy delicious "navettes," six-inch-long cookies in the shape of little boats, representing the boat in which this uniquely green-robed Black Virgin is said to have drifted ashore; the brochure from the bakery recounts the myth, dating it to the thirteenth century. These days, believers begin their celebration of this virgin's festival "des gens de la mer" (of seamen) at the church of Saint-Victor before dawn on February 2. My Marseille friend, remarking that she is the virgin's neighbor, tells me that with a feast of light having notably green candles they bring her out of the church to look down upon the Vieux Port, blessing the sea and those who venture upon it (personal letter from Dominique Poulain). The ceremony was made official by the Abbé Isarn around 1020 C.E. Like the torchlight parade described at Crotone, the Romany ritual of parading St. Sara from the church down to the sea and back, a similar ceremony on the Portuguese coast of which I have even more recently been informed (personal letter from G. T. Schwabe), and no doubt others, the annual Marseille ceremony of the green-robed virgin with her honorary "navettes" recalls a rite in Alexandria and Roman Italy, amply documented, connected with Isis.

In the ancient Egyptian city of Alexandria, Greek inscriptions dating back to the fourth century B.C.E. refer to a festival in honor of Isis that opened the shipping year. Isis is known best to moderns as the "principal Egyptian goddess; sister-wife of Osiris; goddess of fertility" (Zimmerman 140). At Alexandria this agricultural deity derived from the goddess Hathor her association with navigation (Griffiths, *Apuleius* 45) to become Isis Pelagia, "Isis of the sea." In texts of the Ptolemaic era of Egypt (323–180 B.C.E.) appears a liturgy in which Isis greets Hathor "as a deity embodied in the barque of Sokar" (ibid. 36); the goddess is herself the ship (see Neumann, plate 118). Perhaps because the image of a boat was important in her cult, Isis was honored as the patroness of mariners, apparently as an easy extension of the idea of her journey by boat to recover the body of her beloved Osiris from the Nile. That boat was "transformed into a symbol of her as Mistress of the Sea" (Kee 119); it is notable that she was also goddess of the flooding Nile. The festival in honor of Isis was transferred to Rome in the time of Sulla to become the Navigium Isidis, celebrated on March fifth (Bonnefoy 1:125), and it lasted at least into the middle of the first century C.E. Apparently a figure or attribute (symbolic object) of the goddess was launched in a ceremonial boat and set adrift upon the waves, or else the boat itself represented Isis, or else as in the rite described by Apuleius (retold below) a prayership of Isis was launched upon the sea, the images of Isis and other gods being returned to the temple afterwards. Variants on this ancient ritual of the sea goddess have been reenacted throughout the centuries and, as we have seen, continue even today with figures of "St. Sara" and the Virgin Mary. This ritual informs, I believe, the Mediterranean tale of the Castaway Queen.

A vivid legacy of the ritual may also be found in the legend of Mary Magdalen, the first of all the disciples to see the risen Jesus (Mark 16:9–11). Her body was dramatically discovered in 1259 C.E. under the high altar of the crypt of Vézelay, where it had "long been" (Haskins 124); purported relics of the Magdalen rest there still, behind a little grated window. Susan Haskins, who takes a dim view of the timely discovery of these relics in Vézelay and recounts the probable politics behind it, retells the myth in terms with which we are now familiar:

> The most famous account is that of Mary Magdalen crossing the sea in a rudderless boat with Martha and Lazarus, and the three Marys [Salomé, Jacobé, and the mother of Jesus], and disembarking at Marseille. She is also variously accompanied by her servant Sarah the Egyptian and [others]. . . . In the *Golden Legend* we are told the purpose of the journey: of how, after Christ's death and the martyrdom of St. Stephen, the disciples "went into the divers countries, and preached the word of God." However, the "heathens" had set Mary Magdalen and her companions . . . adrift on the perilous sea of life, prey to storms and the tossing of the waves, in a boat "without any tackle or rudder . . . for to be drowned." (Haskins 222–23)

The plate accompanying Haskins's text (223) shows a late fourteenth-century diptych of a tremendously overcrowded little boat, being cast adrift by the heathens in the left-hand frame and then arriving at Marseille on the right, miraculously not having capsized. There Mary Magdalen "preaches to the pagan prince and his people" (223). The childless prince promises to cease his persecution of Christians if she will ask her God to give him an heir. "This unlikely arrangement, with its wonderfully naïve concept of the ways of the divine, results in Mary Magdalen's first miracle, the conception of that child. (It has also been seen to associate her with fertility powers, linking her back to the ancient figures of Ishtar and Cybele)" (224). The story continues with motifs that, though altered, are recognizable as similar to motifs in the Apollonius story recounted in chapter 1. The prince of Marseille and his wife go on pilgrimage to Rome, she is drowned in a shipwreck, and he leaves her body with the living baby on a rock until he can come back to bury her. Arriving back two years later, he finds the child still alive and healthy, having been suckling at his dead mother's breasts, which continued to give milk. "The prince's thanks to Mary Magdalen for keeping his child alive have the effect of restoring the princess to life. The couple return to Marseille where they are baptized, and the Christianization of Gaul is achieved" (224). In a late fifteenth-century variant of the story "probably written and illuminated for the instruction of the infant Philip the Fair" (224), the royal couple are the king and queen not of Marseille but of nearby Burgundy. "In this version, the child too is resuscitated, together with his mother, to become the second legendary king of Burgundy, whose true ducal rulers seem to have appropriated the Provençal legend to their own purposes, to add lustre to the house of Burgundy, within whose territories of course Vézelay lay" (224–25).

Yet the story is perhaps not so completely cut from the whole cloth as Haskins supposes. That is, it may owe something, as such legends often do, to a previous local legend of a goddess associated with the waters. When I went to Burgundy en route to visit my friend in Marseille, I had previously mentioned to the owner of the chateau where I was to stay my hope of finding traces of "a goddess in a boat." Upon my arrival she presented to me, with a justifiably triumphant air, a pamphlet from the Archaeological Museum of nearby Dijon. Its cover was graced with a photograph of Sequanna in her little duck-billed boat of bronze, the most elegantly represented "woman adrift" that I know; with the museum's permission I have used the photograph for the frontispiece of this book. Sequanna is the goddess representing the source of the river Seine, and her temple has yielded innumerable ex voto representations of body parts that identify her as a healer. But so far as I know, she was not a prosyletizer like the Magdalen, and like Chaucer's Custance.

In connection with Chaucer's tale about Custance carrying her faith to foreign shores, Kolve presents pictures of the ship of Mary Magdalen arriving at Marseille with her followers (312) and of the Virgin Mary and Child Jesus in a ship guarded by angels (313)—a little ship divinely governed as in the bas-relief presented in figure 2, which Rickert mentions. The "appreciable influence" that Rickert suggests the Provençal legend exerted upon the "Constance cycle" is much broader than she imagines. When she invited a future researcher to trace backwards from the medieval romance the narrative image of the *divine* woman afloat, it is clear that she did not imagine a source more remote than the early Christian era, and in fact she assumes a Christian source, which might be expected since variants of the story occur in collections of "miracles of the Virgin," stories typically recounting occasions when the Virgin Mary helps out someone in a crisis. Rickert would have been surprised to discover that following the particular lead she offers takes us back beyond Christian beginnings, to various goddesses associated with specific shrines, with protection, sometimes with healing, and above all with the sea. We may start this further descent into the deep past of myth at Florence's convent.

After her exhausting series of adventures, Florence comes to shore and finds refuge in the convent at Beuerfayre. The name corresponds to the "Bel-Repaire" of the French romance (Heffernan 148). But whereas in the French *Florence de Rome* the convent, built by Julius Caesar (line 5502), is vaguely situated "on some location on the east coast of central Italy" [en quelque endroit de la côte orientale de l'Italie centrale] (Wallensköld 1:47), the English romancer, more concerned with establishing a believable time and exact locale, reassigns the building of the convent to Lucius Ibarnius, the British king Lucius, who according to the Venerable Bede became a Christian in 156 C.E. (Bede 42), and situates the convent very precisely on "the water of Botayre" that runs into "the Greek sea," the Aegean (stanza 158). The English romancer has relocated the convent from Italy to Macedonia. Its spire rises in the woods by Lake Loudias (formerly called Lake Volvi or Bolbe, and once a bay) in ancient Bottiaea, hence "the water of Botayre." This places the convent near Pella and Nea Apollonia on the Via Ignatia, the main southern route by land to Constantinople and Jerusalem, which was taken especially by those who feared shipwreck. Though the author of the English romance may be associating Florence's convent with an English sister house that he (and perhaps his audience) knows something about, it is also the case that this stretch of the *Via* is dotted with recuperative stopping places associated with divine healers such as Isis.[10] But even more significantly, perhaps, the lake itself "was named after Bolbe, the mother of Olynthos by Herakles," and as goddess of the lake she "will send the people ample food [i.e., fish] if they honor her dead son with sacrifice" (Burkert, *Homo Necans* 209, citing Hegesandros).[11] One would very much like to know what personal contact or commitment prompted the English romance writer to move the convent from somewhere in Italy to this precise location having, no doubt by coincidence, a sacrificial ritual and goddess legend.

Centuries before Florence's romance-journey ended at the Bottiaean convent, the sea-borne wife of Apollonius arrived at the world-famous healing temple of Artemis the Virgin (called Diana in Latin) at Ephesus. In medieval times this Mediterranean city was important to Christians as the site where the Virgin Mary, in that legendary version of her life where she does not sail on to Provence, supposedly spent her last years and was buried.[12] In another version, official only since Pope Pius XII proclaimed the bodily assumption of the Virgin in 1950, it was from Ephesus that Mary was assumed into Heaven (Warner 87, 250). Thus the city was importantly connected with "the Virgin" in both her Christian and pagan aspects. This dual connection is not a coincidence, because as Mary became more queenly, the affinity between her and Artemis became more pronounced.

One might even say that Ephesus was an inevitable magnet for the Virgin Mary as she gained mythic status, since it had been the location of a virgin goddess cult for centuries. Excavation of the pagan Artemis's temple there shows several stages. The Greek traveler Pausanias, writing around 180 C.E., claimed that the first temple was built by the Amazons; its ruins date from the late seventh century B.C.E. If it is true that the temple was oriented on the star Spica (Allen 468), the brightest star of the constellation Virgo ("The Maiden"), this celestial orientation confirms with archaeological evidence that a virgin-goddess cult existed on the site very long ago, with the orientation on Virgo's Spica honoring the virgin goddess worshiped there. The celestial orientation and goddess worship could also account for the temple's association with the (legendary) Amazons as reported by Pausanius. In any case, this temple was replaced in the mid-sixth century by a much larger temple. In 356 B.C.E. this larger temple was burnt down by Herostratus, and it was replaced in the time of Alexander the Great by a huge temple that came to be counted as one of the Seven Wonders of the ancient world (Ferguson 42). This final magnificent temple is the famous "Artemisium" that Arcestrate (and her *Apollonius of Tyre* author) would have known. Today it has almost vanished, so meager are its remains.

Who is this goddess Artemis who was honored at Ephesus, later passing her honors to the Virgin Mary? She is defined "neither by relationship to a lover (Aphrodite), nor to a child (Demeter or Mary, Mother of Jesus), nor to a father (Athena), nor to a husband (Hera)," rather she is "represented in the absolute" (Ginette Paris 109). From the earliest myths of which we have record it appears that Artemis was a goddess of the wilderness in all its forms: springs, mountains, wild animals. Later she came to be seen as "the goddess who brings the mariner to the place where he would be," perhaps "through a natural extension of the notion and functions of a water goddess, or . . . from her relations with Apollo [her brother], or from her association with the Oriental goddess of Phoenicia, Asia Minor, and Cyprus, whose maritime character was recognized" (Farnell 2:430–31). Most importantly for this discussion, Artemis could move the seas in her anger, or cause them to be still. It is in her nature as a maritime goddess that Artemis demands that Agamemnon sacrifice his daughter Iphigeneia. She is pathetically slain in Æschylus' *Agamemnon* (105):

> Her father blessed her; told his ministers
> To go and take her as she cowered huddled
> In her tunic,
> And boldly lift her like a goat above the altar.
> (Trans. Roche 39)

The speaker of antistrophe six that follows says that he did not see and cannot tell what happened next; but clearly her throat was cut, for Agamemnon has previously lamented having to "bloody my hands in that virgin flood" (Roche 38). In the version by Sophocles

Artemis allows the last moment substitution of a doe: "This she prefers to the maiden / so that she not stain her altar / with the murder of a noblewoman" (*Iphigeneia at Aulis*, lines 1593–95; Dexter, *Whence* 117). In another Greek play, *Iphigeneia in Tauris* by Euripides, Iphigeneia becomes a priestess of Artemis, consecrating the goddess's human sacrifices (lines 34–41; Dexter, *Whence* 117).

The Romans assimilated Artemis to Diana, not only the huntress-goddess of the wilderness most familiar in myth, but also goddess of the moon that moves the waters. Diana was identified with the virgin goddess of Ephesus by Saint Paul himself, who preached against her there on the occasion when the statue-makers rebelled, shouting "Great is Diana of the Ephesians!" (Acts 19). Those artisans were making their living by producing images, probably tourist reproductions of the famous statue of the so-called many-breasted Diana. Some scholars have recently argued that those many objects hanging about her upper torso are not breasts but bulls' testicles,[13] appropriate for this goddess having control over generation. Others associate Diana's "breasts" with other objects, such as clusters of fruit appropriate to her role as a vegetation goddess.[14] As mistress of generation she also facilitated childbirth. Doubtless this odd joining of the virgin goddess with childbirth made it easy, despite St. Paul's trouble in Ephesus, for the Christians to assign many attributes of the virgin goddess Artemis to the virgin mother Mary, adding to the latter's power as Mary the Queen and separating her even further from the young Hebrew girl who married a carpenter.

As Queen of Heaven the Virgin Mary appears in many representations as a sky-goddess in a starry robe standing upon the crescent moon, an image that does not so closely correspond to the description of the "woman clothed in the sun" of Revelation as some would have us believe. In figure 3 a Renaissance Madonna stands upon the crescent moon holding her baby Jesus in her arms, unlike the Mediterranean virgin goddess but perhaps like the young mother-queen Emaré clad in her sparkling Asian love-robe and adrift in a little open boat. Lacking a child, these representations of the Virgin Mary would resemble the virginal Florence, or the river goddess Sequanna (see the

FIGURE 3.

The Virgin Mary as Queen of Heaven
(*The Madonna and Child in a Rosary*).
French woodcut, anonymous, ca. 1490. Rosenwald Collection.
©Board of Trustees, National Gallery of Art, Washington, D.C.

frontispiece), or some other Mediterranean virgin goddess. Indeed occasionally, as in the beautiful and familiar Mexican image of Our Lady of Guadalupe, the Virgin does stand alone on the moon in her robe of stars, the position of her hand and other emblems indicating her pregnancy. (Figure 4 is a careful but culturally nuanced copy on the side of a building near a housing project in Woodland, California; votive roses for the Virgin hang upon the barbed wire protecting this and surrounding public artwork.) Other images, like Duccio's various Madonnas with Child, show the Virgin Mary with the traditional single star gleaming on the shoulder of her blue robe (as worn by other Italian Madonnas of the period) and another on its hood. Goodman identifies that second star in Duccio's paintings as Spica, the star in the constellation Virgo marking the spike of wheat that for Christians may stand for Christ as the Bread of Life (87). Yet other representations show the Madonna holding the sheaf of wheat that Spica marks, or clad in a robe decorated with sheaves (see Neumann 264, figure 59). These ornaments of star and sheaf identify Mary with the Mediterranean vegetation goddess, as well as with the sky goddess riding her moon-boat. The slim, star-crowned maiden of figure 5, said to represent Our Lady of Solitude, is clearly related to the sky goddess. From the protective moon-associated sky-goddess, Mary receives her function as Our Lady of the Ocean (Notre Dame de la Mer), the Mary Pelagia to whom sailors sing their mariner's hymn: "O hear us when we cry to thee / For those in peril on the sea."[15]

In honor of Mary Pelagia (Mary of the Sea) innumerable ex voto paintings and ship models continue to be executed even today by those grateful to her for being rescued. Figure 6 represents one such ex voto (votive offering) delicately portraying Mary on her moon-boat. These extraordinary creations of naive art hang in seaside churches throughout the Christian Mediterranean countries. The great church dedicated to Notre Dame de la Mer that dominates Marseille contains a fascinating ship museum composed of ex voto models of particular ships that the donors believed were rescued by the Virgin herself. Yet tracking back in time this still-living and astonishingly potent legend of Mary as a saviour sea-goddess brings us, surprisingly not to

FIGURE 4.

The Virgin of Guadalupe as Public Art, with Roses
(Woodland, California). Photograph by Laurie Hatch.

FIGURE 5.

Our Lady of Solitude.
San Luis Valley Style II carving, 24 1/4" high,
late nineteenth century. Courtesy of the
Taylor Museum of Southwestern Studies of the
Colorado Springs Fine Arts Center.

FIGURE 6.

The Blessed Virgin Rescuing a Floundering Ship.
Ex voto painting on wood, dated 1770. Courtesy of the
Musée de la Marine, Paris.

Venus Anadyomene as one might expect (though she contributes to
the image), but again to Isis. The Roman poet Juvenal proposes in his
Satire 12 (composed ca. 125 C.E.) to make to this Isis "a thank-offer-
ing for the escape from a storm at sea of his friend Catullus" (Rudd
and Barr xxvi). He evokes the storm in detail and suggests a similarity
between his verse-tempest and those storms at sea painted "on vo-

tive tablets in countless shrines. / As everyone knows, it is Isis who saves our painters from starving" (lines 26–27, Rudd translation 108). Barr's note explains that "Isis was the goddess who protected mariners in time of danger. Those saved by her aid employed artists to paint the scene on votive tablets for the temples (l. 27), and also on boards to display when begging" (Rudd and Barr 217). Juvenal is presenting his Satire 12 as a mock ex voto in verse.

✧ How Isis Comes to Be Afloat

When one first begins exploring the idea that the woman adrift might have a divine counterpart antedating the Virgin Mary, the goddess who most naturally comes to mind is not Isis but Aphrodite, or Venus Anadyomene ("rising," as from the sea), that goddess whom the Italian painter Botticelli shows poised upon a delicate but apparently seaworthy scallop shell in his most famous picture. The equivalent shell in the ancient Pompeiian version of the same scene is large enough for the goddess to recline upon it as on a Roman couch. Aphrodite's presence at sea is associated with the mythologized family violence and mutilation of the Near-Eastern Kingship in Heaven myth as recounted by Hesiod in his *Theogony:* she is born of the seafoam (*aphros,* which Hesiod associates with her name) that arises when the testicles of Ouranos, cut off by his son Kronos, meet the waves (*Poems* 176–200). Yet Aphrodite is a goddess of love and generation, not of virginity, nor does one normally think of her as a rescuer (although in one of the ancient romances, Chariton's *Chaereas and Callirhoe,* it is she who rescues the lovers). The goddess of the Eastern Mediterranean who evolves to combine aspects of virgin moon goddess and generative sea goddess with rescuer is the Egyptian goddess Isis as adopted by the Romans from her temple at Alexandria.

The earliest recorded reference to Isis, in the *Memphite Theology* of 3100 B.C.E., has Isis and her sister rescue Osiris from "drowning" after being urged to do so by Horus, who revives him. Isis plays a relatively minor role here, but it expands until Diodorus Siculus in his *Bibliotheca Historica* (completed around 21 B.C.E.) has Osiris gain the Egyptian kingship through Isis, and eventually turn over to her his power as ruler (Kee 114–15). Her story evolves until she becomes famous as the sister-wife who seeks the mutilated body of her beloved Osiris throughout the world, much as Demeter seeks Persephone and as Psyche seeks Eros in other myths of the quest for the beloved. As she moves west, Isis assimilates the functions of every goddess she encounters and occasionally the role of a god, finally becoming a saviour goddess (Bleeker 11–15), a goddess who, among other things, aids mariners as Isis Pelagia.

In this maritime context, the star-adorned robe of the goddess takes on an added significance. The star Spica in the constellation Virgo, which we have already seen to be goddess-related, lies on the ecliptic (the apparent path of the sun and planets across the sky) and hence is useful to sailors navigating by night; it rises in the evening in early March and moves slowly across the night sky until dawn, an excellent, vivid guiding star for those knowing how to use it. Isis was more traditionally associated with Sirius, another navigational star of early summer (though not on the ecliptic), as the Virgin Mary was sometimes associated with the North Star and the planet Venus (named for that Roman love goddess who "rises from the sea" as does the planet when viewed from the eastward-facing shores of the Mediterranean). The guiding stars and planets that appear in the sky and upon the goddesses' garments symbolize their power as well as their majesty, so one might think that when both Florence's antagonist Macary and Emaré's reluctant mother-in-law regard these two women's glittering robes as supernatural, perhaps they have a point. In any case, the ease with which Isis can be assimilated to the story behind the woman-centered romances is demonstrated by the fourteenth-century Italian Boccaccio's euhemerized account of that goddess: "There are some who say that this virgin was seduced by Jupiter. Then, spurred by the sin she had committed and afraid of her father, she and some of her friends boarded a ship which had a cow as an emblem. Endowed with great talents and spurred on by desire to rule, she crossed to Egypt with favorable winds" (Boccaccio 18). Boccaccio's linking of Isis to the cow-goddess may be traced back to the *Bibliotheca Historica* (1 : 1 – 4) of the first century B.C.E. Greek historian Diodorus Siculus, and beyond, and it displays her assimilation of that famous Egyptian cow-goddess, Hathor (Solmsen 56 – 57).

The Greek historian Plutarch tells the story of this goddess in *De Isidis* around the end of the first century C.E. In this account he joins three major themes associated in many later Castaway Queen romances: an incestuous relationship, with her brother Osiris who is also her husband; severed limbs, though of Osiris not herself; and the resulting woman's journey across the sea, though it is a voluntary quest to gather up Osiris's parts so that he may be revived, not a casting adrift. The motif of difficulties within the family (a family that we in modern times would define as dysfunctional) shows up in this Egyptian context as fraternal jealousy. As mentioned earlier, the incestuous sibling mating of Isis and Osiris is not condemned within this culture, indeed it is even imitated by the rulers of the Ptolemaic dynasty of Egypt when they wished to associate themselves with the power of Isis (Kee 117). In Plutarch's retelling of the Egyptian story, the intact body of the dead Osiris is first cast adrift in a coffin by Typhon, who takes Set's place in Plutarch's version and achieves this disposal of his rival through trickery (Plutarch 139). Later when Isis has found Osiris's body and hidden it, Typhon discovers the hiding place and this time scatters the body in fourteen parts. "When she heard of this, Isis searched for them in a papyrus boat, sailing through the marshes" (Plutarch 145).

The icon of goddess with boat accompanied Isis as she took on the roles of many other goddesses, moving north from Egypt. Lucian of Samostrata, writing in the second century C.E., calls Isis *Merionyma*, the "Thousand-Named," and emphasizes her variety of forms in his book *The Syrian Goddess*. Around the same time, Apuleius, a Roman writer of African birth, presents Isis as a pivotal character in s novel *Metamorphoses,* more popularly known as *The Golden ..ss.* In that novel Isis claims that every goddess, by whatever name, may be perceived as an aspect of herself.

In Apuleius's many-faceted novel Isis is indeed the Great Goddess, and a boat appears in both her representation and her worship. The protagonist, Lucius enchanted in the form of an ass, is in desperate straits when he encounters her. In the famous Book Eleven (called "the Isis-Book") he is suddenly awakened by fear at the first watch of the night to see a full moon rising from the waves, and he has a vision of the goddess under whom "the bodies of earth, sea, and sky now increased at her waxing, and now diminished in deference to her waning" (218). In this book, the most famous description of Isis known, the relationship between all the mothers of the sky is revealed, for Lucius prays to Isis by the names of many goddesses, including among others "heavenly Venus . . . venerated at the wave-lapped shrine at Paphos" and "Phoebus' sister [Artemis] . . . worshipped in the famed shrines of Ephesus" (218–19), invocations that reveal Apuleius's politics of sychresis (the combination of elements from different cultures) as well as his character Lucius's devotion. The goddess tells him that her true name is Isis, and the being that he sees in his vision is in Egyptian costume, as described below. Though Griffiths includes a facing-page translation in the volume he dedicates entirely to Apuleius's Book Eleven, I offer Walsh's 1994 translation as minimally more suited to the present context. For the "ears of corn" in this British translation, however, an American should visualize "sheaves of wheat" to gain the proper effect:

> To begin with, she had a full head of hair which hung down, gradually curling as it spread loosely and flowed gently over her divine neck. Her lofty head was encircled by a garland interwoven with diverse blossoms, at the centre of which above her brow was a flat disk resembling a mirror, or rather the orb of the moon, which emitted a glittering light. The crown was held in place by coils of rearing snakes on right and left, and it was adorned above with waving ears of corn. She wore a multicoloured dress woven from fine linen. . . . But what

riveted my eyes above all else was her jet-black cloak, which gleamed
with a dark sheen as it enveloped her. . . . Stars glittered here and
there along its woven border and on its flat surface, and in their midst
a full moon exhaled fiery flames. . . . In her right hand she carried a
bronze rattle. . . . From her left hand dangled a boat-shaped vessel.
(Walsh translation 220)

When Isis speaks, after again naming many goddesses and claiming
all of them to be herself, she assures Lucius, "I am here out of pity
for your misfortunes" (221). Mary assumes the same mantle of starry
consolation when she replaces Isis as Queen of Heaven. The star-
garment itself, continually redesigned according to the fashion of
time and place, once covered the body of Isis's sky-goddess mother
Nut (as seen in any illustrated book of Egyptian myths) and is inher-
ited from her.

For all her Egyptian costume and parentage, Isis appears as a clas-
sic saviour goddess in Apuleius's *Metamorphoses*. Thus she appears
also in the Greek "novel" *Ephesiaca* by Xenophon of Ephesus, a ro-
mance that Apuleius might have known (Solmsen 149), and in other
romances of this Greek romance genre, a genre that "seems to have
emerged in the second century B.C., perhaps even in association with
the Isis cult of that era" (Kee 193). Cult devotions to Isis included
accounts of "deliverances of the faithful through trials on land and
sea, works of healing performed by her in response to petitioners,
and other extraordinary manifestations of her sovereignty" (Kee 193,
and cp. 132–34). Like Florence in her convent at Beuerfayre, Isis even
demands confession "as a prerequisite for healing" (Burkert, *Cults*
16). The concluding thesis of Kee's immensely useful book, a thesis
that he asserts several times in various connections, is that the early
romance in general, both pagan and Christian, "functions primarily
as propaganda, either for a cult or for a philosophical view, or both"
(253). Isian propaganda is as obvious in Apuleius's story as Marian
propaganda is evident in the medieval romances, and such prose-
lytizing (in other classical romances on behalf of other deities as
well) helps to explain the supernaturally guided movement of the ro-

mance heroine's ship toward a cult destination, whether Ephesus, Beuerfayre, or Rome.

Kee further observes that the classical romance writer typically fosters devotion "by describing the experiences of the main characters in ways that mirror or even reenact the experiences of the god, as told in the mythical stories of divine struggles and triumph" (194). Such narration of cult practice into story is one of the features that makes our three medieval romances about Castaway Queens different from either saints' lives or "miracles of the Virgin" tales (although the "miracles" genre has obvious affinities with the earlier classical romances). Actual cult practice may account in part for their visual and dramatic qualities also. Cumont reports that in connection with "the stirring and most suggestive" celebration of the "Finding of Osiris" there existed "a sacred performance similar to the mysteries of our Middle Ages" (98); the fourth-century Christian writer Fermicus Maternus describes such a performance in *The Error of the Pagan Religions* (see Meyer 159). Most pertinent to our story, however, is the ceremony that Apuleius has Lucius observe in Book Eleven of his *Metamorphoses*. It occurs immediately after his dramatic disenchantment from the form of an ass (upon eating the roses of Isis), when everyone is rejoicing. One of the priests chants to him, "Join the procession of the saviour goddess with triumphal step!" (Walsh translation 227), and Lucius recounts the experience that follows his joining in that procession:

> Amid the din of joyous prayers we edged our way slowly forward and drew near to the sea-shore, at that very place where as Lucius-turned-ass I had bivouacked the previous day. There the gods' statues were duly set in place, and the chief priest named and consecrated to the goddess a ship which had been built with splendid craftsmanship, and which was adorned on all its timbers with wonderful Egyptian pictures. Holding a flaming torch, he first pronounced most solemn prayers from his chaste lips, and then with an egg and sulphur he performed over it an elaborate ceremony of purification. The bright sail

of this blessed craft carried upon it woven letters in gold, bearing those same petitions for trouble-free sailing on its first journeys. The mast was of rounded pine, gloriously tall and easily recognized with its striking masthead. The stern was carved in the shape of a goose, and gleamed with its covering of gold leaf. In fact the whole ship shone, polished as it was in clear citrus-wood.

Then the entire population, devotees and uninitiated alike, vied in piling the ship high with baskets laden with spices and similar offerings, and they poured on the waves libations of meal soaked in milk. Eventually the ship, filled with generous gifts and propitious offerings, was loosed from its anchor-ropes and launched on the sea before a friendly, specially appointed breeze. Once its progress had caused it to fade from our sight, the bearers of the sacred objects took up again those which each had brought, and they made their eager way back to the temple, following in tidy order the same detail of procession as before. (Walsh translation 228–29)

Though the context is fiction, scholars agree that in parts of Book Eleven Apuleius is offering a guarded description of secret initiations and ceremonies that actually took place in the worship of Isis. The March festival of the Navigium Isidis, however, which most scholars assume is being described here, was a more public ceremony than the rest (Kee 127).

Yet however much their stories may distantly reflect a myth or ceremonial rite, the heroines of the Middle English romances are not divine or holy. The image of Emaré clad in brightness on her little boat may associate her distantly with the sky goddess Isis-Artemis-Mary, and the lovers embroidered on her cloak connect her also with Aphrodite, who would probably have been known as Inanna-Ishtar to the pagan "daughter of the Emir," embroiderer of the cloth in the romance. But Emaré is essentially a nice young woman wearing a magical cloak that makes her *seem* "no earthly thing" (stanza 33). Her potency as perceived by others lies mainly in her iridescent garment.

Florence's more substantial strength, on the other hand, lies in

FIGURE 7.

The Hand of God
Descending from a Cloud.
Drawing by the author based on
"Nebuchadnezzar" in the *Sacra
Parallela*, Parisinus Graecus 923,
fol. 259v, Bibliothèque Nationale,
Paris. (Reproduced in Blanch and
Wasserman, 78.)

herself and her faith, and Custance's lies wholly in her faith. Whereas Emaré in her bright robe may recall the goddess visually, the power that the others possess and the powers upon which they call connect Florence and Custance more directly with Edith Rickert's *Notre Dame de la Mer*. Much as Isis, Queen of the Ocean, is invoked by Philip of Thessaloniki in the first century C.E. to aid a friend at sea (Witt 123), Mary Pelagia is invoked by fourteenth-century Florence. That protectress performs a "miracle of the Virgin," raising a storm swiftly and effectively in the maiden's defence when the mariner throws her on his bed to rape her (stanza 156). When Custance is in dire straits at the trial, however, the hand of God the Father descends into the picture to smack down her perjuring accuser (stanzas 77–78). Medieval artists often represent the image of God's hand, defining the source of divine power, descending from a stylized cloud as in figure 7. (Blanch and Wasserman devote much of their chapter 4 to the image, including one picture in which God's hand smites the wicked city Gomorrah.) Even though Custance calls on the Virgin as a kindred spirit in stanzas 102–3, and that Lady does respond with aid in stanza 113, the stanza analogous to *Florence* stanza 156, Chaucer makes it abundantly clear that God is Custance's principal helper at sea (stanzas 49–54 and 106). Following the lead of Trevet and

Gower, Chaucer has taken firm masculine control over his character. It is the other two romances and other traditional versions of the story that reveal the Castaway Queen story's relationship to Isis by way of Mary as Stella Maris (star of the sea) and protector of mariners.

Many goddesses and heroines, as well as occasional males, share the maritime associations of these women, as Hares-Stryker so well demonstrates in her article "Adrift on the Seven Seas." But the medieval romance plot specifically of the young woman adrift in a boat that is cast ashore at a holy site is a particular case of such drifting. The plot about her recalls the earlier romances promoting certain late classical cults, particularly those showing Isis as rescuer. The power of Isis, guardian of the sea-lanes, is emphasized both in these cults and in the early romances. But perhaps most significant of all for this study, Isis is associated specifically with the ceremonial setting adrift of a boat in the Navigium Isidis, the rite celebrated chiefly at Alexandria and Rome.

So far as the plot itself of the woman adrift romance goes, the earliest reference to it that I have found is an allusion in chapter 141 of the *Life of Aesop* (the version designated Vita G). In this *Life*, probably written around the first century B.C.E. (see below), Isis is again celebrated, though not centrally. According to his fictive biography, Aesop was an excessively ugly mute Phrygian slave who had a clever ability to get himself out of trouble even though unable to speak. When Isis cured his disability as a reward for a spontaneous act of kindness, Aesop's verbal wit became unsurpassed. From that point on, most of the *Life* consists of a series of amusing anecdotes in which Aesop improves his situation by telling clever, pointed stories, but instead of offering explicit morals as in the fables we know, he allows the listener to figure out the meaning, as a sort of riddle. Aesop looks after the interests of his master Xanthus (though on occasion humiliating him for his stupidity) and continues to prosper in his reputation for wit and wisdom until he becomes a famous teacher. Eventually he saves an entire nation by capping a would-be invader's riddles. His *Life* is a lively, amusing, frequently sexy story.

But the conclusion of the story is tragic. Because someone has framed him by hiding a golden cup from the temple in his baggage (using the same technique by which Joseph in the Bible places a cup in Benjamin's pack, "framing" him to alert his father), the people of Delphi among whom Aesop is then living elect to put him to death for sacrilege by hurling him over a cliff. He tries to show them the error of their ways by offering a fable in his usual manner (that of the Eagle and the Beetle), but this time his listeners do not accept the fable's implications. So in a final attempt to save his life Aesop offers something quite different, not an innovative fable but an allusive reference to an apparently well-known story:

> "A man fell in love with his own daughter, and suffering from this wound, he sent his wife off to the country and forced himself upon his daughter. She said: 'Father, this is an unholy thing you are doing. I would rather have submitted to a hundred men than to you.'"

This time Aesop makes the application specific:

> "This is the way I feel toward you, men of Delphi. I would rather drag my way through Syria, Phoenicia, and Judaea than die at your hands here, where one would least expect it." (Daly translation 90)

As Perry says, "It is not difficult to imagine that the story which Aesop told the Delphians on this occasion related to some young woman who had wandered about in voluntary exile suffering many hardships in order to avoid the incestuous advances of her own father at home" (*Studies* 35). The parallel that Aesop is drawing with his own distressful situation is the shock and grief of such an attack coming from someone to whom one looks for love and protection, as to a father. Much as Chaucer does later, this brilliant storyteller is making full use of the tale's inherent pathos. But again the Delphians refuse to relent, so rather than being thrown ignominiously off the cliff, Aesop retains his autonomy and the courage that makes him such a sympathetic character, and leaps to his own death.

Because of the important role assigned in it to Isis, Perry suggests that the *Life of Aesop* as we have it "can hardly be older than the first century B.C." (*Studies* 25). But when the Greek playwright Aristophanes (ca. 448–399 B.C.E.) mentions the Delphians' accusation that Aesop stole a temple vessel and that he told the fable of the Eagle and the Beetle at this time, "this and similar early allusions [e.g., by Herodotus and Heraclides Ponticus] do not prove that a book about Aesop existed in the fifth century [B.C.E.], yet they render it likely" (Perry, *Studies* 25). Whether the final tale told by Aesop was added to the *Life* in the first century B.C.E. or had been included already four centuries earlier, of particular interest to us are its early linking of father-daughter incest to the theme of a Mediterranean journey, apparently in flight from that abuse, and the way the author of the *Life* assumes that both his own and Aesop's original audience would be familiar with the story.

We have seen that some twentieth-century scholars wish to locate the source for the setting-adrift theme in Britain, because scenes of the earliest medieval version, the *Life of Offa I,* are set there, and several of the later romances, including Continental ones, contain a landfall there in connection with the accusation episode. These scholars were unaware of the parallel themes and emphases to be found in the earlier classical romances set wholly in the Mediterranean.[16] But what Great Britain has lost, women, perhaps, have gained, as it is seen that the Castaway Queen motif of English romance provides a "missing link" back to Isis and beyond. This link through popular cult and ancient romance to an earlier goddess figure exists alongside but separate from the long-recognized and authorized appropriation of certain Isian features to dignify the Virgin Mary. In other words, this line of development lies outside the purview of the sanctioned institutions that attempted to incorporate and tame the Goddess by turning her into the human mother "Mary meek and mild." "Mary Pelagia" escapes this appropriation chiefly because those ordinary people who continue to need her, while willing to rename her, display a steadfast reluctance to give up their saviour-goddess.

✧ The Archaic Goddess of Generation and Bounty

It seems likely that the plot of the Castaway Queen story bears a relationship of some kind to an ancient goddess cult associated with the Mediterranean. We have seen that the woman's sea-exposure bears some similarity to a ritual of Isis put to sea in her boat, and the cult site at which she finally arrives appears to have its antecedent in classical narrative and later popular legend. But we can speculate on further goddess-related features that appear in these romances. Two features in particular seem rooted in a far more archaic, or at least savage, past than encountered so far: Florence's control of the threatening penis, and the mutilation of hands in, for example, the Latin *Life of Offa I* (written in England) and the French *La Manekine*, the latter closely related to *Emaré*. Though absent from the Middle English romances, this motif of the severed hands recurs often enough in related tales to justify considering it here. Also, there is a curious connection with a darker cult of Isis, Isis as Magician. But first let us consider the penis.

Earlier in Florence's story, before the Virgin Mary's stormy solution of the problem with the lustful mariner, that protectress has aided the maiden with a more direct control of male lust. We are told that when he attempted to rape Florence, Miles's "lyking vanysched all away / Thorow the myght of Mary mylde" (stanzas 121 and 126). If the storm is reminiscent of the powers of Isis as sea-protectress, Miles's detumescence suggests the interest of the goddess Cybele, to whom were sacrificed, according to Gimbutas (who refers to her as Artemis), "mutilated beasts, from which a member was cut off" and to whom were consecrated "the shorn genitals of her priests" (*Goddesses and Gods* 199). Gimbutas's account calls to mind the remarkable poem by the first-century C.E. Roman poet Catullus (no. 63) in which that poet tells how ecstasy leads Attis to sacrifice his own testicles to Cybele. Thus he becomes feminized, a "false woman" (line 27) destined to live out his (her) life in the wilderness, having gone mad with regret.[17] Gimbutas labels Artemis (Cybele) a "sur-

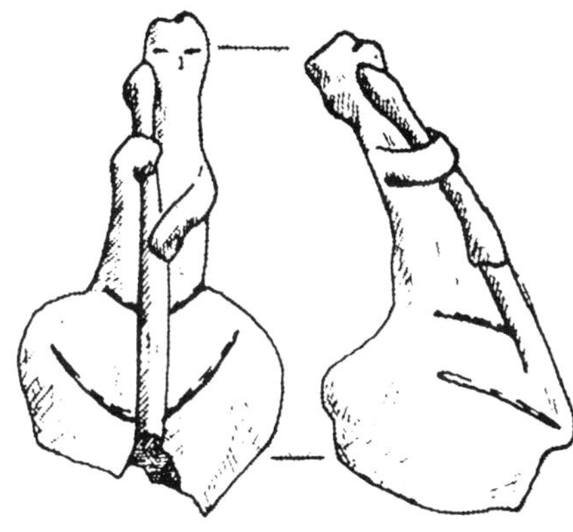

vival of the Old European Great Goddess" (196), which she has so amply documented and (with considerable imagination) discussed, and she says, "It is no mere coincidence that the venerated goddess of the sixth and fifth centuries in ancient Greece resembles the Goddess of Life and Death of the sixth and fifth millenia B.C. Mythical images last for many millenia" (ibid. 199). In a sentence Dr. Gimbutas plunges us back to prehistory.

The ancient Great Goddess is rarely represented as directly connected with the sea, though Gimbutas finds some Scandinavian and Aegean representations of the goddess of generation aboard what she labels "the ship of renewal" (*Language*, chapter 22). That ship functions as a metaphor, however, whereas this goddess is usually shown more directly. In the famous so-called Venus figures she is typically expressed as a faceless, armless being with massive buttocks and vagina, seeming to be associated with reproduction—though of course we cannot know that for certain or even what further implications such an association might have had. The clay figure of circa 5000 B.C.E. represented in figure 8 shows one of these women, herself rather resembling a penis, clutching either "a baby snake or a phallus" (Gimbutas, *Goddesses and Gods* 73). In the present context I prefer to regard it as the latter, as my title for this figure indicates. In stanza 127 Miles accuses Florence of exercising similar control over him, demanding that she release him from such bewitching. Though she evokes Christ in her reply, Florence again shows her power over the penis when she says, "False traitur, thou shalt lye!" (i.e., remain flaccid). If the devotees of the Goddess had such power as this, or were imagined to, no wonder the frightened patriarchy sought to tame her by subordinating her to the male pantheon!

Although various scenarios are offered for the way this taming of the Goddess took place and the degree of violence involved,[18] the result for our quest is the same. A once autonomous fertility figure—that is, an icon representing an elemental being requiring (or capable of) no explanation, She Who Is—was appropriated to the patriarchal hierarchy by giving her a name and a birth story, thus socializing her to the culture now dominant. The birth stories of Athena and Aphrodite provide examples of this social control. Apparently developed from a previous goddess who simply "was," in Greek myth Athena rises fully armed from her father's head in a version of androgenesis (birth from a male, without participation of a mother), which so far as I know is unique. The birth-story of Aphrodite echoes those of Iranian Armaiti and Indic Sarasvati when she is reinvented as the daughter specifically of a male god. Miriam Robbins Dexter explains how this works: "Androgenetic births may take place in a subtle manner. The Greek Aphrodite grew out of the foam formed from the severed genitals of Uranos, when he was castrated by his son Kronos. Thus she, too, according to the male mythopoets, was not born of woman. All of these goddesses were thus assimilated to their Indo-European cultures, and subordinated to the male deities of their respective Indo-European pantheons" (Dexter, *Whence* 162). Whether or not we believe that the subordination was intentional and contrived, a conspiracy, it is true that these myths of the goddesses' births authorized male control over procreation and thus over sex. Therefore, when Florence seems to assume such control, Miles accuses her of "witching" him (stanza 127), in other words, of using methods unauthorized by the patriarchy to prevent him from raping her.

Perhaps it is not necessary to invoke the Great Goddess in this matter, because there is an emphasis in both the classical and medieval romances upon just such sexual control. The story of how Isis performs the antithesis of Florence's "witching" can serve as an introduction to the discussion. I find it amusing. When Osiris was dismembered and strewn across the world by Typhon (in Plutarch's version of the story), and Isis sought all his parts to assemble them again in order to revive him, the single part she failed to locate was his penis, which had been devoured by several fish. So she fabricated one of gold, attached it to his body, and descended upon him, in the form of a bird in some representations, to conceive Horus. If that act of mythical necrophilia amuses me, it appalls me to discover (again from Plutarch) that Isis and Osiris fell in love and first mated in their mother's womb (137). The point is often made, however, that Isis herself was never free with her favors like Venus, and the Isiac romances place great emphasis on chastity (Kee 255–56). In that respect, the early Christian Fathers even hold up the cult of Isis as a model for members of their own congregations (Heyob 123–26).[19] The Romanized Isis and the Virgin Mary both urge chastity upon their devotees, and so it is natural that the Goddess should respond when called upon in romances in a crisis of this particular kind. It was at such a moment that even lusty Lucius-in-the-shape-of-an-ass called upon Isis. She can facilitate generation and childirth, but she can also subdue lust.

The hands that arc mutilated after incest or attempted incest may be another matter, deriving from truly ancient mythic and ritual sources. Folktale analogues for this profoundly disturbing element that occurs in numerous Castaway Queen romances suggest either a deep-seated psychological basis for it, or a source so ancient that its reflexes are nearly universal. (The two are not mutually exclusive.) In the *Clementine Recognitions* the woman loses control of her hands after her brother-in-law has made an attempt on her virtue and she flees him in a boat. The romancer rationalizes her incapacity by explaining that she gnawed on her hands in mourning for her lost husband. In several medieval romances in various languages, *La Manekine, La Historia del Rey de Hungria, Alixandre, La Figlia del Re di Dacia,* and others, the king falls in love specifically with his daughter's hands. She therefore cuts them off in remorse (or disgust) and in some cases sends them to him. Schlauch believes that this "prominence of the girl's hands as a love-inducing feature" is a folk-tale element introduced late into the romances and arising from the need to produce the severed hands as evidence that the woman has been put to death as her persecutor demanded (71n). This seems like the sort of rationalization found in the tales themselves, where the hands may be severed as a punishment—for example for the woman's supposed infanticide (Schlauch 13), or to prevent her from crossing herself as protection from the devil (ibid. 28), or in order to provide a token to be recognized (in the romance of *La Belle Hélène de Constantinople*). The romances mentioned above associate loss of the hands in every case specifically with male sexual aggression and violence. This motif has the effect of reducing the majestic, hieratic woman in a boat to the status of a helpless maiden.

The hand separated from the body appears, however, in a mysterious, powerful connection with Isis herself, in a context quite distinct from the narrative of her quest for Osiris that makes her a saviour goddess. This Isian appearance places a somewhat different construction upon the "severed hands" motif. The context is a curious formula of constraint preserved in *Papyri Graecae Magicae* (no. 57). As a result of this ritual constraining Isis to give a sign that she has heard the petitioner's prayer, the magician explains that the goddess will detach *her hand* to send it flying toward the adept, who will experience it exploding within "in such a way that you will be possessed by the goddess" (Bonnefoy 1 : 130).[20] One is reminded of the Iron Age Scandinavian rock carvings in which the uplifted hands of the possibly shamanic figures are hugely emphasized, seeming to indicate a power surging from them. In one fine carving three figures of ambiguous gender stand in a boat with powerful hands upraised (figure 9). Another carving, depicting a woman[21] in a boat, perhaps dancing, and waving her hands, perhaps magically (figure 10), recalls a comment made by Tacitus in chapter 9 of his *Germania*, where he describes the Germanic gods in the terms he knows. He says that some of the tribes "sacrifice also to Isis," whom he recognizes because of "the goddess's emblem, being made in the form of a light

FIGURE 9.

Three Shamans (identification uncertain).
Rock carving from Böhuslän, Sweden. Courtesy of J. M. Coles,
from his book *Images of the Past*.

warship" (108–9). Yet other rock carvings feature detached human hands (Coles figure 14). Whereas the living but detached hand of Isis has separate power, like that Hand of God that strikes down Custance's accuser, the motif of the hands cruelly severed may originate specifically in an attempt to quench such shamanic power.

In the context of shamanism, an attempt to control spiritual power, or even a mutilation of hands with no thought of such control, may backfire. In a culture much farther from the Mediterranean even than Scandinavia, the most famous and widespread of all Inuit stories provides an interesting analogue to the pattern of sexual violation, mutilation, and sea-voyage, with the magical severed hand very much alive, like the hand of Isis, and with the woman becoming a goddess of the sea. The story's wide range of distribution, across Inuit territory from Siberia to Eastern Greenland, suggests the antiquity of this myth; though there are variations, the essential ele-

ments remain the same throughout the culture. This goddess, along with the less storied mermaid figure Taleelayu, is currently a popular, often stunning, subject of Cape Dorset Inuit women's art (Leroux 128, 129, 175, 231, 232). My version of Sedna's story is an amalgam based on different retellings by the early twentieth-century anthropologists Franz Boas and Knud Rasmussen of the version from Baffinland best known to folklorists. A young woman named Sedna has a

Sedna Angry.
"Eskimo Print" type drawing by the author.

forbidden relationship with a man of another tribe, and her father goes after her. As he is taking her back home in his boat, an enormous storm comes up, and he realizes that with two in the boat neither of them will survive. So he throws his daughter out. She surfaces and grabs hold of the side of the boat. He chops off the tips of her fingers. She grasps for safety again, and again, and he chops away until the whole of both hands is gone. Then she sinks down into the sea. The severed parts of her hands become separately alive, her fingernails becoming shellfish, the next joints small fish such as herring, her palms becoming whales, and so forth, and Sedna is mistress of these sea creatures who are actually parts of herself. But she has no hands, so when her hair becomes tangled and dirty, she sulks. In her frustrated anger Sedna directs the fish away from the fishermen, and the people go hungry. (Figure 11 is my own interpretation of her anger after the style of an Eskimo print.) Then it becomes necessary for the shaman of the tribe to dive down, in trance and ritual reenactment, to comb out her tangled hair, making her beautiful and happy again so that she will release the bounty of the sea.[22]

The Sedna story uses the myth of paternal possessiveness followed by mutilation of the daughter's hands and sea-sacrifice to explain through story the changing aspects of the sea and the creation and divine control of its animals, so essential to Inuit surivival, perhaps adding narration to an earlier concept of a moody and autonomous sea goddess. In any case, the motifs of father-daughter conflict, exposure to the sea, and severed hands, followed by the victim's apotheosis (becoming a deity), give this story an intriguing similarity to the pattern observed in the European romances and fairytales. The Inuit are relatively new to the American Arctic, having begun to arrive some six thousand years ago (Whitehouse and Whitehouse 236), and some Inuit still live in northeastern Siberia, so accounting for the similarity by diffusion is not too far-fetched; it places in a distant past the origins of the story of a father-daughter conflict that engenders numinous power. If one prefers to attribute the geographical range of the father-abuse story of the woman adrift to similarity of psychological response, the implications may be equally intriguing, if more distressing. I am told by a practicing psychologist that when her women patients dream of severed hands, this motif seems to be associated with childhood experiences of ritualized sexual abuse, rather than with the father-daughter incest that I had anticipated. In either case the child is helpless while those who should be protective abuse her.

In the medieval romances the mutilation of hands (in the Continental versions only) and being put to sea in a boat without a rudder (a detail frequently present) have a single major effect in common: they both render the romance-protagonist absolutely helpless at the mercy of the seas. Her situation suggests an allegorical interpretation and at the same time evokes our shocked sympathy. Since she is in a romance, however, and a good woman, we know it will turn out all right. Even the horrible mutilation can be healed by her divine protector.[23]

✧ Maiden Sacrifice

But what if the supernatural being were not benign but hungry for sacrifice? What if the woman cast adrift were not a fiction? The thought sounds too bizarre to be taken seriously until one learns about the frequency of maiden-sacrifice in the real world. "Ethnology has shown that maiden-sacrifice occurred with disconcerting frequency from Mexico to Polynesia," Burkert declares, and he then points out how animals were explicitly substituted for maidens in Greek ritual (*Homo Necans* 65).[24] As we have seen in the discussion above, a doe was substituted for Iphigeneia in Sophocles' version of the Agamemnon story, much as the ram caught in the thicket was explicitly substituted for Isaac in the Genesis story (22:13). As documented by Burkert and others, daughter-sacrifices like that of Iphigeneia occurred in real life, especially in certain traditional cultures dependent upon fishing for their sustenance. Young girls (being less useful, perhaps, than boys, thus disposable) were actually set out, purportedly as a propitiation sacrifice for the deity in control of the desired catch or quarry, perhaps mythically as the bride of the quarry (*Homo Necans* 64), but essentially as bait for that quarry. Burkert himself uses the word "bait" in connection with the setting out of Andromeda in the Perseus story (ibid. 211). If the sacrifice was accepted it would prove that the gods were satisfied, and obviously the feeding quarry would then be present to be taken in turn, to feed the tribe. Since she represented an emotional and painful sacrifice on the part of the parents or the tribe, the maiden would be regarded as ritually more powerful than a young animal; Jehovah's command to Abraham to sacrifice as a burnt offering "thine only son Isaac, whom thou lovest" (Genesis 22:2) offers an example of such an excessive demand from the deity, though in Abraham's case the demand was only a test of his devotion. Jephthah's daughter did not get off so easily (Judges 11). But as the ritual became more symbolic an animal might be substituted for the maiden-sacrifice, as Burkert points out.

Burkert places the barbaric practice in direct association with our story when he relates maiden sacrifice to the myth of Sedna, "a sacrificed maiden" who becomes "Mother of Seals" (*Homo Necans* 79 n. 27), and later claims that among coastal inhabitants around the Mediterranean "maiden-sacrifices are documented in fishing cultures: a girl would be thrown into the sea at the start of the season" (ibid. 207 and n. 24, p. 64). I propose that this sacrificial "girl thrown into the sea" is a direct and brutal (not necessarily early because it may be atavistic) form of the more civilized Isian and Marian ritual in which a boat is launched upon the Mediterranean laden with prayers in the form of inscriptions or candles and bearing a statue or attribute of the maiden goddess. This figure of the goddess adrift functions as a substitute for the maiden sacrificed to the sea who is afterwards honored as a goddess of the waters or as her companion. Much as the animal replaces the child sacrifice, this boat ritual substitutes for the girl-as-bait. A relic of the animal sacrifice substituted for the child appears in Christian ritual in the title "Lamb of God" for Christ, the son allowed by his father to be sacrificed, and the girl or daughter-as-bait receives a medieval narration in the plot of the Castaway Queen romance.

I wish to spin out this speculation further. The boat with its "maiden" (a representation of some kind) was apparently launched in rituals of propitiation, sacrifice, and prayer, in hopes of calm seas and the bounty thereof. Since the structure of this ritual with its accompanying belief about the victim's spiritual voyage is similar to the pattern proposed earlier in this chapter for the woman-centered romances—the maiden departs (under duress) on an initiatory journey (thrown into the sea) to be an intermediary with the goddess of the waters and their yield or to become the goddess herself (apotheosis)—the ritual is essentially narratable. Therefore it inevitably engendered stories, like that of Sedna and others, in which the maiden becomes the saviour goddess.

Many chapters after George Eliot has established the vision of the Virgin shining in her boat in the passage in *The Mill on the Floss* quoted above in chapter 1 ("the Blessed Virgin sat in the prow shedding a light around as of the moon in its brightness, so that the rowers in the gathering darkness took heart and pulled anew" [Eliot, *Mill* 117]), she has her protagonist Maggie at one moment appear like, and the next moment *become*, the saviour goddess herself (516, 520). But in the end, this novel not being a comforting romance, the dark flood sweeps down, drowning Maggie and her brother in an embrace of "unconscious incestuous passion" (*Mill* xv, Haight's introduction). In Maggie's realistic Victorian England, unlike the earlier world of legend, there is no benign force protecting the innocent woman adrift and carrying her to the protected haven of the cult site. The metaphor of the river representing life was recognized by the very first recorded reviewer (anonymous, quoted in Carroll 112–13), but in this novel no shining goddess directs life's flow, only Eliot's relentless and overwhelming Fate. The medieval romances differ in that their protagonist is saved from the sea for a period of autonomy and active "work" before she, by her own choice and maneuvers, rejoins her man and the society in which she is his adjunct. The fiction must always in some way respond to current social realities.

It is curious that critics do little more than mention the mythic image that Eliot evokes and then weaves so importantly into her novel. Even though the death by drowning of Maggie Tulliver has become a significant item in current feminist discourse, apparently nobody has bothered to trace where Eliot might have found her inspiration for the supposedly native St. Ogg and his Virgin, vividly reminding one of Mediterranean legend. Published in 1860, however, the writing of *The Mill on the Floss* precedes Eliot's Italian journey of 1860 that produced her historical novel *Romola*, published in 1862–63. This later novel presents a protagonist-saviour in some ways similar to Maggie, but successful in her role. In chapter 61, "Drifting Away," the despairing Romola, clad in a nun's garb, is inspired by Boccaccio's story of Gostanza (the *Decameron*'s tale two of day five) to cast herself adrift in a little boat. But she does not die, she merely sleeps, and in chapter 68 she awakes upon an unknown shore where she becomes a healer. At this point Eliot is clearly working with a story akin to ours. The chapter concludes: "Many legends were afterwards told in that valley about the blessed Lady who came over the sea, but they were legends by which all who heard might know that in times gone by a woman had done beautiful loving deeds there, rescuing those who were ready to perish" (*Romola* 649).

Legends take hold of us as much as we of them. Given either an image or a myth from another culture, those who receive it narrate it in terms of their own culture, explaining in their own way what seems peculiar. They restructure the story to fit the needs both of comprehensibility and genre, and also to suit their current social condition. Always the requirements of the period itself are a factor, and so overwhelming that sometimes the teller may not even be aware of remolding the tale to suit that need. Another factor is what the storyteller perceives as the desire of his or her patrons. Some have suggested that the promotion of Isian worship by the Flavian emperors was a considered political move, and Heyob offers a history of the series of promotions and suppressions of the Isis cult in Rome (10–35). Whether establishment of the cult in Rome was a considered political move by the emperors or not, Roman women responded to Isis with particular enthusiasm, dressing in Isian attire, gathering at her temples, and so forth; their attitude suggests that the time was ripe for the cult. The early romances growing out of this and related cults both confirmed the need and advertized the cult. Kee's summary of the conclusion of Apuleius's *Metamorphoses* is suggestive about the nature of the need, which emerging Christianity also addressed in this period of awakening and social flux: "Released from the cruel domination of a blind Fortune, under whose control he had fallen as a consequence of his 'ill-starred curiosity,' Lucius is now the servant of the Fortune who can see, 'and who illumines the other gods with the radiance of her light' (11:15). He passed through three stages of initiation, and, after taking up residence for a period in her temple (11:19), he resumed his career as rhetor and lawyer" (Kee 139). The personified, unblindfolded Lady Fortune who now takes direction over Lucius's life is obviously Isis herself, the shining saviour goddess whom George Eliot did not allow to show herself to Maggie as Mary Pelagia, Mistress of the Waters. Sometimes Isis is

associated in art with the wheel-bearing goddess Fortuna and de-picted with a wheel upon the open sea (of life), and at other times she appears with a cornucopia in one hand and a rudder in the other (Glueck 229). These latter two symbols emphasize her control over harvest and waves, and the wheel expresses the mutability of for-tune—which Isis-Fortuna can control as easily as she can the crops or the sea. Figure 12, my representative drawing of a twelfth-century ivory, shows her with a ship in her hand.

The European renewal of the romance genre in the eleventh to fifteenth centuries suggests an awakening of desires similar to those that stimulated the classical narratives and the Isis cult. Thus the medieval authors of the Castaway Queen tales, influenced as they are by the earlier stories, really are "romancing the Goddess," though surely unaware that it is a goddess they are romancing. They attribute all supernatural aid to God, Christ, and the Virgin Mary, where in their culture such aid is naturalized.

But still today, in pockets of tradition around the Mediterranean, the boat is launched with its surrogate maiden sacrifice, who represents a plea for divine aid. As Burkert says of another ritual, "The actors are interchangeable; the ritual remains" (*Homo Necans* 58). Living ritual and contemporary ex voto offerings give evidence that many believers, most of them humble in terms of their culture and life-style, can still experience the Goddess on the waters, shining in the storm, lending a hand.

In other words, the symbol is continuously acquiring fresh
significance, while older ones, no longer considered apt or fully
up-to-date, are permitted to slough off and fade away.
          —Keith H. Basso, *Portraits of "The Whiteman"*

What images return
O my daughter . . .
What is this face, less clear and clearer . . .
Given or lent? More distant than stars
and nearer than the eye.
          —T. S. Eliot, from *Marina*

4.

Goddess of the Human Dawn: Her Status Now

AT A SITE IN SIBERIA near Lake Baikal was discovered a series of those strange female statues that many are eager to associate with the Goddess.[1] According to Joseph Campbell, the sculptures date from the Paleolithic (Old Stone Age), which places them "a full twenty thousand years or so before their Neolithic counterparts" (165), "tentatively" 24,000 B.C.E. says Gimbutas (*Language* 4). Although others consider such an extremely early date extravagant (see Baring and Cashford 24), these figures of women are nevertheless both ancient and evocative, so it seems odd that until recently they have rarely been mentioned, and then most often obliquely or in passing (attention being fixed on the far richer relics of Near Eastern cultures). The Baikal women are accompanied by six representations of geese in full flight with extended wings, and all are carved, it appears, from mammoth ivory.[2] The very suggestion of mammoth ivory emphasizes the extreme antiquity of these figures of women and offers a dawn-world landscape to our imagination, a world radiant and "auroral."

Their being accompanied by geese recalls the shape-shifting women of Northern European myth who put on feather-coats to become birds, often geese or swans, and embark on their journeys thus transformed (see Leavy). The myth transcends cultures. According to one seventh-century B.C.E. text, Isis journeyed to Egypt in the form of a goose (Dexter, *Whence* 26), and other bird-women are discovered worldwide, some less attractive than others. Mediz Bolio's man-entrapping Yucatecan bird-goddess, Xtabay, comes to mind (298–301). Campbell associates the Siberian ivory carvings of geese in flight with shamanism in particular (166–67) and with the quest of the spirit in general, as the title of his book on folklore, *The Flight of the Wild Gander,* indicates. Despite his evocation of the Baikal women and their geese, he does not trace this quest back to ancient times so directly as does the modern French epistemologist Jean Cristofol. Arguing that the "goddess" figures represent a turning point in human consciousness, Cristofol refers to Jacques Cauvin's thesis in his 1994 *Naissance des divinités, naissance de l'agriculture* that evolving religious ideas, marked by an interest in representing human beings, especially women, in sculpted forms, were a major factor leading to the sedentary culture that produced agriculture and eventually, through complex waves of influence, migration, and increasing population, produced western civilization.[3] Cauvin's idea reverses our usual assumptions about such processes, rather as does Burkert's theory that first comes the ritual then the articulated beliefs that arise to sanction that ritual. The sequence "theophany (manifestation of a deity), ritual, theology" is a truism in studies of the evolution of religion (see Townsend 95), and Cauvin is proposing that a similar sequence applies to the development of social structures. If Cauvin's thesis is correct, we might owe the very manner in which we think, in part, to Neolithic desires that once lay behind the expression in quasi-abstract form of the human, the feminine, perhaps the divine in early intuitions of "the Goddess." If "She" has accompanied us since so long ago, does this mean that she must be regarded as real? Does she have to be real in order to be worshiped—or to be effective? In some sense she clearly does; we cannot engage significantly with a concept we do not believe in. But how do we define "belief" or "real" when some understand those concepts more broadly than others?[4] Without attempting to answer the more slippery questions, this chapter will approach the issue of authenticity and suggest how the narration of Elementary Ideas, as Adolph Bastian called them (Campbell 44), including such ideas as the divinely protected journey, can function decisively in our lives even today.

The Castaway Queen romances of this book have themselves drawn me to discussion of the Goddess. In this chapter I engage directly with the question of why she might be relevant or important. I speak here as a scholar who is also a particular woman engaged in living, and I look at the romances from this person-centered cultural perspective. I have found a heady pleasure in looking down the long track of the Goddess to a distant past, and I am interested in examining the source of this pleasure. It clearly has much to do with the way the track stretches out *from where I stand*, marked by personal perception, desire, and selective readings of myth. I make no pretense, therefore, of disinterested scholarship in this chapter, and some readers may prefer to stop here.

Carol P. Christ speaks for a person-centered point of view when she says, "Whatever God the Mother and the Goddess may have meant in ancient cultures, today God the Mother and the Goddess symbolize the emerging power of women, the celebration of the powers of the female body, and an acceptance of humankind's rooting in nature and finitude" ("Symbols" 249). She adopts the ancient symbol of the Goddess for a present feminist purpose. In another context she severely criticizes the androcentric attitudes displayed by the historian of religion Mircea Eliade as typifying an "unacknowledged, but classical, Western bias against the physical" ("Mircea Eliade" 78), that is, against, as she phrases it, "humankind's rooting in nature and finitude." She criticizes Eliade and with him Western religion for valorizing transcendence over "the chaotic and dangerous flux of things" (81, using his words), and she associates this flux with the images of goddesses that "celebrate change in the form of birth, death, and transformation" (82). To Eliade's "generally androcentric theories" (87) she offers as a corrective her own picture of early human religion, which provides a good summary of the current view in general of many feminists:

> In the Neolithic the Goddess rules over a religion centered around birth, death, rebirth: the mysteries of the female body including the awesome power to give birth become universal symbols of the birth and growth of the crops; male power is also recognized in the symbol of the bull and the young male god; both the seed and the human corpse are returned to the mother in order to be reborn; the center of the world is the womb or navel of the Goddess; the earliest temples are symbols of her body. (Christ, "Eliade" 87)

This vision of the Neolithic has been called into question and even severely criticized by some (as by Townsend 183–98 and Biehl 29–56). The criticism is valid in that over the vast stretch of time and geography encompassed by the general term Neolithic there certainly existed many individual and different "Neolithics." Moreover, such hierarchical ideas as that of an all-controlling deity would be unlikely to develop in a society of small tribes where authority tended to be consensual.[5] Though the social structures of early societies make a paramount deity unlikely, there could nevertheless have been other ways of regarding a "goddess" of which we know nothing. Moreover, we could not know now what the "goddess" figures meant to people then, even if we could be certain that they represented a goddess: "The form of an artifact . . . may be similar or identical through several cultures, regions, and time periods; nevertheless, the meaning of the artifact to the people and its use by those people may differ completely from one society to another" (Townsend 187). Townsend gives as an example those female figurines holding their breasts, which "are sometimes indicative of fertility concepts. The Pyramid texts of ancient Egypt, however, indicate that holding the breasts was an accepted way to depict mourning in that society" (187).

Despite the cautions of Townsend and others about its historicity and their doubts concerning its usefulness, the feminist vision of "the" Neolithic is in my view a valuable construct, a myth that gives shape to a worthy idea and evokes a society toward which we would do well actively to aspire. As Mary Jo Weaver says: "Because Goddess feminists have interpreted the advent of patriarchy as a defeat of a women-centered world, they have drawn attention to ancient history and have argued that patriarchy, from its beginnings in human history, is a cultural construction rather than a God-given reality. Because of their questions and assertions, one may imagine alternatives" (93). They are mythologizing (or adapting myths masked as scholarship in order to create) a past that "explains" the present social situation that is in need of revision. Their myth is not so much about the past as about the present and the future. It is Utopian. Christ's Neolithic, even with its cosmologically and architecturally gynocentric aspects, is egalitarian in its social structure.

Carol P. Christ reveals Mircea Eliade's vision, by contrast, to be not only androcentric, investing authority in masculine gods and the males of the society, but also dualistic, partly because of Eliade's emphasis on transcendence and the resulting division between body and spirit.[6] But when, basing her association between transcendence and dualism on a long tradition of Western thought, Christ rejects both together, this double rejection gives me pause. "Transcendence" is in fact a red flag word to postmodern theorists, from those who reject "the transcendental signifier" on a philosophical basis to others like Patrick D. Murphy who reject the idea of transcendence on political grounds: "To my mind, it is fundamentally anti-feminist, non-dialogical, and contrary to the inhabitation that we need to learn for an environmentally ethical life practice" (97). Within our complex and hierarchically organized culture, however, the very idea of deity evokes transcendence; but the etymological association of that word with climbing as of mountains, which Murphy himself evokes, can shift the metaphor to make it more acceptable. As soon as one applies the term "Supreme Being" (as Christ does, 84) to a deity of either gender, even if that being is thought of as a divine immanence within ourselves, there is an enlargement or "heightening" both of self and the projected deity. This sense of amplitude is an essential element of the religious experience; it lies behind the iconicity of such figures as the woman in the boat, for example, as well as my own urge to backtrack that iconic woman to classical antiquity and beyond. That tracking involves a mental journey from a familiar now to a mysterious then that functions against the feeling that "then" is alien and inaccessible.

Apparently what Christ and others mainly find objectionable about the idea of transcendence (especially as expressed in a "God above") is the way it cuts us off, in Western religious and philosophic traditions, from "that rooting in nature and finitude" of which she speaks. It need not do so if deity is thought of as an organic extension, expressed with the appropriate language and imagery. Etymologically, *trans-cendere* means "to beyond-pass," with the *-cendere* element related to the idea of "leaping" or "springing" as in Sanskrit *skándoti*. All the early *Oxford English Dictionary* entries for "transcend" suggest passing a limit, and in his *Oxford Dictionary of English Etymology* C. T. Onions explains that "transcendental" (with its implications of a mind-centered, non-experiential understanding of the world, which has affected our understanding of the word "transcend"), is "in current use due to Kantian philosophy" (936). Many who are using the word today seem to wish to go back to the word's earlier meaning and "root" their transcendence "in nature and finitude."

An excellent image to express such rootedness is the World Tree, which in some cultures is closely related to the idea of the Goddess;[7] it allows for a transcendence that avoids Eliade's platonic and androcentric dualism. From roots firmly locked in the earth, the Goddess-Tree may be imagined to "spring" (cp. *skándoti*) upwards and outwards, verdantly alive, to embrace all creation, while at the same time providing a shamanic means of traversing that creation, of transcending the body to explore elsewhere. In northern Eurasia the Tree functions as a link between worlds, the Siberian shaman climbing it like a ladder to the heavens (Eliade, *Shamanism* 269), and the Norse mythographers similarly envisioned a tree as unifying the cosmos (Davidson, *Lost Beliefs* 69). In shamanism the primacy of the physical body is always respected, however; if anything happens to the body while the spirit wanders, the shaman is doomed.

As the biblical Eden demonstrates, the Tree at the center of creation may also be taken to symbolize the auroral world itself, an existence of peace, gender equality, and harmony with nature that Carol P. Christ and others like to believe preceded the violent rise of patriarchy. Rosemary R. Ruether remarks, "Unquestionably this story [of a once peaceful, gynocentric, agrarian world] has powerful mythic appeal for people in the late twentieth century, deeply concerned by ecological and militaristic threats to the earth; but is it really history?" (151). I would argue that the feminist "Neolithic" is more appropriately viewed as revisionist cosmology. This story about beginnings is increasingly receiving acceptance as an alternative to that other story in which the woman in the garden is forbidden by the Sky Father to partake of the Tree (the body of the Goddess whose fruit was ritually consumed, suggests Merlin Stone in *When God Was a Woman* 214–15). In the Bible the woman partakes anyway; she plucks and tastes, for which act humankind has been punished ever since and women in particular reviled. The effects of that now-subverted story remind us that cosmological fictions are far more powerful than factually based history in the way they influence thought and culture. "In the Beginning" is the most powerful story of all. It roots us.

Irrespective of its historicity, or in this case its lack of it, I am drawn by the feminist vision of the Neolithic as an uncorrupted culture of which the Goddess figures, as we interpret them, offer powerful talismans for our time. A "nostalgia," as Eliade calls it, "to immerse oneself in the auroral world" (*Cultural* 20)—a dawn-world both of nature and finitude and of numinous beginnings—informs my quest for the Goddess and also the spiritualized readings that the journey of the Castaway Queen evokes. As chapter 1 attempted to indicate by showing some social conditions that contributed to its medieval retellings, the story of that journey is not in itself a particularly spiritual one. Nevertheless, like the Oedipus story that is similarly marked by incest, it contains a quality of uncanniness that calls for understanding at a deeper level, a level that must be half-created or projected before it is "understood." But does that projection not vitiate the authenticity of the story?

In his book *Totem and Taboo* published near the beginning of this century (1913), Freud rationalizes God on the basis of his understanding of primitive sacrifice in connection with the Oedipus story, his own founding myth. Eliade summarizes Freud's story:

> In the beginning, the father kept all the women for himself and would drive his sons off as they became old enough to evoke his jealousy. One day, the expelled sons killed their father, ate him, and appropriated his females. "The totemic banquet," writes Freud, "perhaps the first feast mankind ever celebrated, was the repetition, the festival of remembrance, of this noteworthy criminal deed." Consequently, Freud holds that God is nothing other than the sublimated physical father; hence in the totemic sacrifice it is God himself who is killed and sacrificed. "This slaying of the father-god is mankind's original sin. This blood-guilt is atoned for by the bloody death of Christ." (Eliade, quoting both Freud and commentators upon him, *Cultural* 4)

Freud's idea is ridiculous and its ethnological basis faulty. As Eliade says, "In vain the ethnologists of his time . . . demonstrated the absurdity of such a primordial 'totemic banquet.' In vain they pointed out that totemism is not found at the beginnings of religion, that it is not universal . . . that of the many hundred totemic tribes only *four* knew a rite approximating the ceremonial killing and eating of the 'totem-god' (a rite assumed by Freud to be an invariable feature of totemism) . . . that [among pre-totemic peoples] patricide would be a 'sheer impossibility, psychologically, sociologically, and ethically'" (*Cultural* 4–5), and so forth. Yet, "Freud was not in the least troubled by such objections, and this wild 'gothic novel,' *Totem and Taboo,* has since become one of the minor gospels" (5). Despite the objections of those better informed, with his Oedipal myth Freud has made a far greater impact upon the twentieth-century mentalité than did any of his more reasonable detractors. What he had to say, despite its external "untruth," resonated with certain needs of our culture at the time, or at least with the needs of certain opinion-makers of our culture. Authenticity was not a factor. John E. Toews, regarding Freud's Oedipal theory itself as a mythic text on a par with versions of the myth both earlier and later (for instance that by Melanie Klein), explains that this theory:

> constitutes a narrative account, a story, in terms of both personal and collective history, of the primal genesis and universal structures of human experience as nature remade in culture. The verification of the truth of this story ultimately remains dependent not on the marshaling of empirical data or on logical incontrovertibility, but on the act of mutual recognition whereby one person discovers an adequate symbolization of his or her life story in the story of another. (Toews 289)

Ernest Jones gives evidence that early in his career Freud had discovered such an "adequate symbolization" for his own life story in the Oedipal myth as dramatized by Sophocles, invoking that myth when he first committed himself to his vocation (Toews 291).

The bird-woman's journey has a similarly early meaning for me. As a twelve-year-old I wrote a poem (preserved by my mother) in which I identified with that figure and her effortless mode of travel to faraway places. Perhaps that is one reason I find those ancient Siberian carvings so haunting. A child of four, a little boy, was buried with all those ivory goddesses and their geese. Were they there to help him journey somewhere else? I like to think so. How much is that "an adequate symbolization" of my own desire for his life-and-death story and hence questionable in terms of fact?[8] As Eliade has shown, myths and shamanism of the northern world substantiate that understanding of the Baikal bird figures, but even without that authority the juxtaposition of the child's bones and the birds would have personal meaning for me. Similarly, as Weaver says, "If Goddess feminism is perceived as a quest motivated by religious experience, then it has a right to be valued as authentic, at least *as a religious experience*" (92).

Many have remarked on the need for an adequate symbol, or icon as I have been calling it, to represent the modern woman's strength in crisis, remarking also on the need "of contemporary religious individuals . . . to experience the goddess as part of their own personal biography" (Olson 1). This strongly felt need to associate oneself with the heroic or divine, to imagine oneself largely, "transcendentally," is not unique to our culture. For example, Johannes Eingartner has assembled an extraordinary number of monuments from Imperial Rome displaying women clad in Isian attire and assuming the powerful pose of Isis, even when standing in effigy beside representations of their more conventionally clad husbands (Eingartner plates 62–75). These monuments attest to the empowerment those women found in relating to that caring but strong goddess. Today as well, the story of Isis venturing out upon the waters (originally of the Nile) to seek her dismembered beloved will be recognized by many women as congruent to their own roles as wives, lovers, sisters, and daughters—perhaps above all as mothers.

That being the case, some will ask, "Why not use as a focus the Mater Dolorosa, the Blessed Virgin, as Western women have been doing for centuries?" To many the Virgin remains inspiring, especially when she slightly transcends her orthodox maternal role (Rodriguez is particularly eloquent on this matter), but others find her narrative debilitating. *Stabat* Mater: she is standing still, fixed within the patriarchy. Perhaps imagining her rather as Mary Pelagia, the active, forceful mistress of the high seas that surround us, or as Mary Queen of Heaven, can offer a more inspiring view. Others will wish simply to seek beyond her for an icon of the Goddess, a focus for their personal biography, which is less inscribed in certain aspects of our culture.[9]

For me the combination of a quest story with a protective Goddess of those "in peril on the sea," a figure like Mary Pelagia, is moving and powerful, but especially so when a more ancient mystery is admitted to add depth to the picture, to give it amplitude. Whether or not I believe in the Great Goddess intellectually, I am moved by the notion that "her personal biography is an ancient story that begins before the dawn of history" (Olson 6). Antiquity itself confers romance and esteem. Families take pride in documenting an ancient heritage, as do nations, and many claim authority from such heritage. The genealogy of certain early English kings, going back to the native god Woden and beyond him to Noah and Adam, authorized those kings as appropriate hereditary Germanic rulers for a Christian country. But a mysterious source half-hidden in the depths of time— a myth—may provide an even more potent "chartering" than claims based on historical or pseudo-historical documentation, especially if it may be connected to more modern times as by the links suggested in chapter 3. So far as myth-making goes, those links do not have to be authentic, merely viable.

Two stories from my own life, both stories incorporating themes associated with the woman adrift, show how a myth can have a viability transcending that of its sources. Some time ago I was married to a very personable, extremely bright and verbally adroit man in another country. Suddenly his personality changed radically and he began "battering" me with words, against which I had no defence. He could talk circles around me, and did: hedges, barbed wire. His control of the language was far greater than my own. So I learned to retreat inside my head, where I discovered, of all things, a quiet garden. As the pressure became greater, I was forced to retreat there more often, and I began recognizing a presence in that garden. At first I thought it might be a statue hidden in the undergrowth, but I found nothing. Once I saw blue footprints in the grass, where the grass had been pressed down in the dew to reveal the tiny flowers of speedwell (the "luck" plant) growing beneath. But those footprints could have marked my own passing. In any case, even when part of me believed I was making it up, that garden with its presence sustained me through a terrible time that I was determined to wait out, trusting that my dear husband would return to his kinder self.

Years later I recognized the main source from which that presence in the garden came to fill my need, and I remember blushing in the moment of recognition, it struck me as so banal. The source was a sentimental hymn that I had loved as a child: "I walk in the garden alone," and someone "walks with me, and he talks with me, and he tells me I am his own."[10] Yet the garden was "really" there—a psychic reality—and so was that comforting presence, helping me to survive a very dark time.

The second anecdote, also from that time, involves hands, again an important element in the woman adrift story. Despite my determination to weather the marital storm, I couldn't stick it out after all. I found myself in shock, penniless, and homeless except for the kindness of friends. Remarkably like the Castaway Queen, I had even landed on another shore, to be given shelter there by someone I scarcely knew in a "castle" (a luxurious house) by the sea. I didn't know what to do; I couldn't live on the bounty of others forever. Finally one night in a particularly vivid dream I remembered the advice of Carlos Castaneda's teacher Don Juan, that if you can look at the palms of your hands in a dream your life will be transformed. With terrible, straining effort (it seems that I was sleeping with my arms behind my back) I pulled my hands to the front in my dream and slowly turned them over to look at the palms; the moment was so vivid I can still remember the very lines in my palms as I gazed down at them. In my dream landscape I was standing on the outer steps of a huge building with bolted doors. As I gazed at my palms, the doors sprang open, and nothing was the same after that. Yes, reader, I divorced him. I left behind the Gothic romance I had been living in Yorkshire and took control of my own separate life, as he went off to join a Bhagwan community in the south of England and wear orange clothing.

In that dream, with the help of Don Juan, I freed myself to act out my own life-story instead of being an adjunct, and at that time a burden, in someone else's story. I freed my incapacitated hands and took control. Even though everyone knows that Don Juan is a fiction that Castaneda constructed to convey his ideas about shamanism—I even knew that at the time—his advice worked. In fact I feel that in great part I owe my present situation to that calm presence in my garden and Don Juan's advice. In terms of the Castaway Queen story, the presence may be described as a nourishing saviour god and the advice as from the "saint" who restored my hands.[11] Thus I have been twice sustained by myth, even when later recognizing that myth as fabrication. So how does this affect the question of authenticity?

I have a personal problem with much of the Goddess rhetoric that demands uncritical or untenable belief, such statements as "Goddess religion is unimaginably old" (Starhawk 50; in what sense is it unimaginably old?), and "All of the myriad varieties of patriarchal oppression—co-opting and replacing the Goddess [et cetera] . . .—*all* of these acts are motivated by one desperate drive: to prevent women from experiencing her power" (Spretnak xii, her emphasis). Such rhetoric alienates me in much the same way that pentecostal Christianity does. Also, as a scholar, I am disturbed by the way that some of the more radical Goddess advocates flout, mock, or ignore the contrary evidence, much like those Creationists who, wishing to take literally the biblical story of the creation, oppose the teaching of evolution in the schools. These particular Goddess feminists will state as uncontrovertible fact that a Mother Goddess religion persisted continuously for 30,000 years (an assertion discussed by Townsend 194), or that a female deity ensured high status for women (discussed by Townsend 194–95 and by Biehl 40–41). In many ways an admirer of Marija Gimbutas, who has built up and provided visual resources for our image of the archaic Goddess, I am yet in sympathy when Bernard Wailes, a professor of anthropology at the University of Pennsylvania, first praises then criticizes her. Speaking on behalf of many in his profession, he finds Gimbutas "immensely knowledgable but not very good at critical analysis. She amasses all the data and then leaps from it to conclusions without any intervening argument" (Steinfells C12). In her beautifully presented books I have found both fascinating information and food for thought, but Gimbutas's casual attitude toward interpretation of the facts troubles me much as it does Steinfells. I need to be persuaded that the data actually lead to her conclusion that a "civilization of the Goddess" existed in prehistoric times or that "Kurgan hordes" raged down from the north to destroy it.[12] Gimbutas's storytelling does not trouble me so much, however, as the suggestion (or assertion) of such considerably less scholarly but widely popular writers as Merlin Stone and Charlene Spretnak that a worldwide male conspiracy actively suppressed Goddess-worship and even now suppresses the evidence for it.[13] Also dramatic but somewhat better fitting the archaeological evidence is Gloria Feman Orenstein's spinning of the Gimbutas theory into a Holocaust-level "ravishment of our prepatriarchal Goddess cultures by invading hordes of Indo-Europeans, who brought sky gods and war to more peaceable and earth-revering matristic cultures" (5). ("Matristic" as distinct from "matriarchal" refers to egalitarian cultures in which men and women live in harmony.) But even this construction of the facts is highly debatable (as summarized by Townsend 193–94; in more detail but still briefly, Renfrew), and in Orenstein's case I would ask to whom *our* Goddess cultures" refers, most of us being Semitic or else descendants of those same ravishing Indo-Europeans.

But what the critics of modern Goddess culture, whose skepticism I have been imitating here, fail to take into account is the heuristic or experimental nature of much of this too-assertive speculation, including that of Gimbutas. Janet Biehl is particularly disturbed by the fact that the Goddess discussion is incoherent (2–3 and especially 85). Feminists of the Witchcraft movement would reply, So what? Wicca, a British and American movement that seeks to reconceptualize religion mainly by regendering and politicizing the concept of God, endorses the theory of invading hordes elaborated by Orenstein without particular concern for its historicity. Before beginning this study I assumed that the Wicca movement partook of the irresponsible scholarship and paranoia represented by the male-conspiracy theorists, and until I read Naomi Goldenberg's respectful defense of feminist Witches, I categorized them with right-wing Christian groups as a movement from which I preferred to keep my distance. As it is, their rituals do not attract me, and unfortunate associations with Satanism, though emphatically repudiated by most modern witches, remain a tarnishing factor.[14] But Goldenberg's account at least has

made me look at the movement with greater interest and less preju-
dice. What she says of one of their main principles allows me to see
their "fluid" response to facts in a new light, as it endorses both my
understanding of my own life-enhancing myths and the usefulness
of the present book's backtracking of the Goddess through medieval
romances to the classical world and before. Objective truth, like the
dependability of my personal myth-sources or the verified ancient
worship of a benevolent Goddess in a matristic society, is not the
point so much as having "an adequate symbolization" in story form.
Goldenberg explains:

> Witchcraft is the first modern theistic religion to conceive of its deity
> mainly as an internal set of images and attitudes. Although Witches
> do often speak of the times of the matriarchies, most are more con-
> cerned with that concept as a psychological and poetic force than as
> an historical verity. . . . Witches consider any thought or fantasy real
> to the degree that it influences actions in the present. In this sense
> a remembered fact and an invented fantasy have identical psycholog-
> ical value. The matriarchies, i.e., the times when no woman was a
> slave of any man, create visions of the pride and power women are
> working to have in their present lives. Thus matriarchies are func-
> tioning in modern covens and in modern Witches' dreams whether
> or not societies ruled by females ever existed in past history. (Golden-
> berg 213)

According to Goldenberg, historical "reality" for the Witches is con-
tingent upon its present effectiveness. Similarly I argue that tracking
the Goddess, finding her imprint on a sequence of cultures extending
backwards from our age to "the Neolithic," allows us more readily to
make her a part of our own life stories now.

We are vastly different from one another in the ways that we need
to consolidate our beliefs. When I first heard that Castaneda had
probably invented his Don Juan, I was chiefly amused: what a feat!
But when I mentioned the discovery to an old friend of high academic
standing, someone I admired greatly whom I knew to enjoy Casta-
neda's writings, he was appalled. He wanted Don Juan to be real; I

didn't really care. He was annoyed (as were many) that Castaneda had perpetrated a hoax (as indeed he had); I was more intrigued by Castaneda's creativity and what seemed viable in principle in his writings. What *did* shock me, however, was my friend's need to believe in the academically verifiable truth of Castaneda's stories. That never seemed to me what those books were about. Indeed, the stance of the notebook-bearing investigator seeking facts was an attitude that Don Juan actively mocked. In my own life, when the comfort of that imaginary presence in my garden is with me still, remaining useful long after my need, it seems that questioning its value in terms of objective fact would subvert the authenticity of the experience.[15]

But even appreciating the myth in terms of its usefulness loses much of its point, and here I approach the finitude or transcendence problem again. Amplitude is the key. To be effective for me, a myth must seem to extend beyond the immediate situation, into the absolute or at least the archetypal.[16] While my memory of the mythic experience with the friend in the garden was undercut by a later recollection of the childhood hymn, I realize now that even that hymn was only one way of speaking (or singing) about something more profound.

I do not know how to speak of that profundity; perhaps no one does, though some can speak *to* it. My brother is an astronomer and a "hard" scientist, with little time for the naive beliefs of laymen. Yet when he lectures about deep space, and shows his slides of the magnificence of the universe, he uses numbers like poetry. He talks of the multiplicity of universes far beyond unaided human vision, and of distances and times and galaxies huge beyond anything we can humanly understand. Some of those who listen have said that they feel overwhelmed by their own insignificance, while others are amazed and thrilled at being part of that vast web of creation. I am of the latter group, finding in my brother's science-based evocation of the modern astronomical universe a spiritual refreshment seldom met elsewhere. He "roots" me in hard data while allowing me to transcend my home-world, the solar system, even this galaxy in my reaching imagination. Those of us who do not share his foundation in science and facility with numbers must invent or adopt myth to help us comprehend the void, or else simply ignore it. Yet being told a story of the cosmos rooted in fact makes the inexplicable void all the more profound because it is presented as something real, not imagined or contrived by the creative or magic-seeking mind. This makes the cosmos appear even more astounding. On the other hand my skeptical self finds it intriguing that my astronomer brother believes firmly that there must be other planets, somewhere, with living beings on them. However he defends that belief with numbers, I find it to be an essentially spiritual affirmation of life, obviously unverifiable at least at this moment of our history.[17] His slide lecture becomes a song about profundity, about a "goddishness" (of which he never speaks) that goes beyond gender or race, or even anything human, into mystery. He is a poet using numbers as his language of myth, a shaman climbing us all to the top of the Tree.

My private spirit-helpers described earlier were clearly masculine also, though the presence in the garden was as nurturing as any mother and the advice about hands could have come just as well from a woman. Their gender was a function merely of their source. That it never even occurred to me to question their gender reveals the endemic patriarchy that surrounds us. The one manifestation I have experienced of a power figure in itself—a figure, that is, not formed so far as I know by an antecedent textual experience—was female, and more forceful and fierce than any other figure I have encountered in life or art. She was also, more than anything else, inscrutable. The experience occurred at the beginning of the dissolution of our marriage, when my husband, grasping for his personal renewal, wanted to experiment with drugs, simple ones in those drug-innocent days. He had gotten a friend to give him a little bag of dried mushrooms, and insisted that I accompany him on his experimental "trip." I was glad to go along on that one, as intrigued by the experience as he was. He set up a cozy situation in front of the fireplace, and, having forgotten to ask about the dose, gave each of us a heaping teaspoon of the black powder. For all I naively knew it could have killed us, but it didn't. (An acquaintance who is an authority on psychotropic drugs assures me that it would have taken four pounds of the powder for its chemistry to be fatal; he estimates that a sandwich bag full of ground, dried mushroom powder would weigh about an ounce.) Enormous thirst hit us, and then we "wept" from every orifice, and I saw his nose start to ramble all over his face. When he turned into the Devil, which was hilariously funny to us both as I told him what I was seeing, that metamorphosis did not seem at all threatening or frightening. I was clearly "all at sea," without a clue about what was happening in my life, or in my mind.

Then, sitting there together by the fire, we each went into our own world, as one must always, eventually, do. Campbell says, alluding to the legend of Percival, "There is, in fact, in quiet places, a great deal of deep spiritual quest and finding now in progress in this world . . . [where people] in small groups, here and there, and more often, more typically . . . by ones and twos, [enter] the forest at those points which they themselves have chosen, where they see it to be most dark, and there is no beaten way or path" (226). Suddenly I found myself in a spacious, open field on the other side of the forest, and someone was coming toward me. The vision haunted me. Later on I incorporated it into the following poem (Osborn 1986), having somehow connected my vision of the hieratic female with a Mexican Indian woman who in real life saved my grandfather from bandits. In a similar way the peon Juan Diego of Tepeyac, famous for his vision of the Virgin of Guadalupe, perceived that Lady as both the holy virgin and an actual girl, as a miraculous woman who named herself Tlecuauhtlacupeuh, "she who comes flying from the region of light like an eagle of fire" (Rodriguez 45–46), and as the young woman of his own race represented in the famous painting (copied as public art in figure 4).[18] The 1531 record continues, "And he saw how the rainbow clothed the land so that the cactus and other things that grew there seemed like celestial plants, their leaves and thorns shining like gold in her presence" (Warner 303). My Goddess figure, also moving through a golden landscape, was a powerful presence whose warning—and implicit offer of aid—I might better have heeded at the time. I offer her image with reverence now.

Through shining fields she
comes in her
dull-purple
veils flowing bust
deep through the unfolding
wheat nothing else
moves her face
is hidden

My grandfather
as a youth was
captured by bandits
and held for ransom in
the high Sierra. An Indian
woman came at him in
the dark with a knife
gleaming cut his
bonds and led him
to safety.

Who is she? Why does she
veil her face and
come when the wind

has died? I am empty
and quite still nothing else
moves and her shape comes
closer over the
sharp wheat

Modern astronomical cosmologists Primack and Abrams offer the following useful description of myth: "In common parlance, 'myth' has come to connote the opposite of reality, or the simplistic fare of the hopelessly backward or quaint. But myths, as they function in human societies, actually are explanations of the highest order: the stories a culture communally uses in order to connect with and give meaning to its universe." Since their concern is with cosmology, they go on to discuss specifically cosmological myths: "Every traditional culture known to anthropology has had a cosmology—a story of how the world began and how human beings took their place within it. A functional cosmology grounds people's everyday expectations of each other in the larger patterns of the universe. Such a shared cosmology may be essential to successful human community and even to individual sanity." But no description is ever totally accurate, they say, pointing out that the map is not the terrain. "What we humanly need is to know the truest story of our time" (70).

I observe that I could have written this chapter as a dialogue between two voices, one expressing a will to believe, the other a compulsion to doubt. Both attitudes are my own, and both can be equally extreme. I do not regard either as being sex-typed, the one attitude more feminine and the other more masculine. Each is part of me. But the first voice is more concerned with "what we humanly need," so suppressing skepticism about the actual terrain, I return now to the map, the story behind this study, and where reading it takes me.

Drifting across the waves, through the seas, through wheat in my mushroom-induced vision, crossing over many a border, the icon of the woman afloat transcends cultures and has acquired different meanings within cultures, adapting to different cosmologies or world views. Becoming legendary when she mothers popes and emperors, she is essentially a primary myth, and one matter that she frequently expresses, scarcely touched on in this book, except in the case of Isis absorbing many goddesses into herself, is cultural syncretism (assimilation of one culture's forms by another). When cast not adrift but ashore, this sea-borne woman is an image of the non-oppressive meeting of cultures, a myth about ideas brought by the winds or destiny, sheltered because they are perceived by the community as intrinsically good ones—and violently rejected by some because they are "not ours" or because they threaten the particular rejector's status.

Whether or not she is indeed, as I like to believe, associated with a Goddess worshiped long ago and still powerful for many, a great and mysterious Being who exercises control over generation, abundance, and the fate of mortals in the world, the iconic image of the Castaway Queen of late classical and medieval story does not lend itself to the usual forms of colonial exploitation. This is because, though radiating personal power and beauty, she is only perceived as a threat by those who themselves exploit. She is always represented as a good person, devout, living as well as she can by the standards she knows, nourishing when the opportunity arises, while retaining her personal integrity with all the power at her disposal. Only in these three Middle English romance versions of the story, however, does her autonomy clearly prevail, so that her own efforts bring about the final healing. Transcending the abuse that launched her journey, through persistence and example she changes her world and that of others, bringing a new cosmology, what she believes is "the truest story of [her] time," and quietly bringing order out of moral chaos. Hers is a story to cherish.

The woman adrift in these stories, however, is not a goddess but a human protagonist. Within and beyond her the mystery remains, brooding with significance, like the archaic statues of distant Lake Baikal whose antiquity is part of their power. Like Marina in T. S. Eliot's poem, another woman adrift, her face is "more distant than the stars" and yet incredibly near. Anne L. Barstow says in her essay on "The Prehistoric Goddess" that although "drawn to the ancient female figurines as expressions of female power, I could not appropriate them as meaningful symbols in my own religious life because they were from cultures totally alien to my own" (8). To her these figures seem cut off historically from modern Western society. I have tried to develop in this book a continuity that allows us to reach back along the route of the woman adrift to discover a distant past that does after all lie within the past of our own culture, to "root" our "transcendence," so that the ancient Goddess who shows herself in many forms no longer seems so inaccessible. But one does not wish to domesticate her. Her power, like that of any conception of deity, lies partly in what cannot be appropriated or tamed. It is that very wildness or alienness, the element of the unfathomable, that makes her numinous.

Here is an example of what I mean by the unfathomable. When I was a young girl blissfully paddling my canoe alone on Lake Tahoe, early in the morning before anyone else was out there to disturb my solitude, I would drift across the waters of that lake, then still clear, where one could see everything on the bottom even quite far out. But suddenly the lake bottom drops away, to what depth, they say, or said then, nobody knows. The bottom is already a dozen or more meters deep when it vanishes from sight, so in practical terms of actual safety that dark edge far underwater makes no difference at all. I knew that, but I found both excitement and fear in crossing from the pale blue waters to the bottomless dark, as though something must be invisibly down there, waiting. When contemplating the shifting aspects of the Goddess icon presented in this book, I have occasionally encountered the same feeling, a terrorized *elastic* sense of reaching out to perceive something much farther away than my mind can, or wishes to, stretch. Thinking in a refined and scholarly way about the Castaway Queen in her sure-to-end-happily romance, discovering her comprehensible Christian and classical backgrounds in works one can analyze, is in its way reassuring. One can see to the bottom, or pretend to. One can find a charter myth there, glittering and usable, the precious stone that rewards our quest.

But dark beyond the edge of what we know, in the deep reaches of our own inscrutable past, lingers a huge, indistinct shape, faceless, without star or ship, perhaps without arms or hands or else with huge hands outstretched, mysterious of motive. She is at one with nature and finitude, yet, as we perceive her, unfathomable and uncontained. In postmodernist terms she is "undecidable," hence open to many possibilities, like being adrift, like nature itself. Ominous though she appears in the shadowy depths of her antiquity, she empowers the woman on the open seas of life in the world. "More distant than stars and nearer than the eye," alien and yet familiar as oneself, she terrifies and empowers us all.

Notes

CHAPTER I: THREE TALES OF CASTAWAY QUEENS

1. The term "Accused Queens" was formalized by Margaret Schlauch in her sympathetic and finely researched book, *Chaucer's Constance and Accused Queens*. Schlauch's stated purpose in this work, which she presents as primarily concerned with the folktale context, is to provide "a systematic study of the accusations brought against all queens in romance, and of the motives of the accusers" (7). More recently, Carolyn Hares-Stryker has studied the "woman adrift" theme of the medieval romances within a worldwide folklore context (*Sleeping* and "Adrift"). My study takes a different direction from hers. Defining the same theme more narrowly, specifically as the woman cast adrift in relation to incest, I follow it to the written, as opposed to folkloric, classical antecedents of the three romances of this book, and beyond. Whereas Hares-Stryker casts her nets wide to discover universals, I follow a particular trail.

2. Grimm named this story *Das Mädchen ohne Hände*, "The Handless Maiden." Otto Rank associates the mutilation of hands with punishment for masturbation, an activity that replaces and thereby threatens the lustful father (322). I see it as a vivid symbol of powerlessness. This theme of the story will be explored in chapter 3. Though the theme of severed hands occurs frequently in fairytales and romances outside of England, only the earliest version of the story known in England displays it (*The Life of Offa I*).

3. The twelve-line "tail-rhyme" stanza used by the poets of *Emaré* and *Florence* contains four sets of triplets rhyming aab-ccb-ddb-eeb, with the rhyming couplets in tetrameter and the link-rhyme lines (here marked "b") in trimeter. For the *Man of Law's Tale* about Custance, Chaucer, who introduced iambic pentameter into English, uses his loftier "ryme royal," a seven-line iambic pentameter stanza rhyming ababbcc. These stanzaic forms enhance the rapidity of the narrative; a prose translation gives an entirely different impression of the story, losing what Valerie Krishna describes as "the folksiness and fun of verse narrative" (5). It may be that those who dis-

like these romances are incapable of grasping the liveliness of the verse form. Someone in that predicament might find it a help to read with the rhythms of musical comedy in mind.

4. In "Middle English Romance: The Limits of Editing, the Limits of Criticism," A. S. G. Edwards argues against the usefulness of modern critical methods in interpreting the metrical romances as "poems," both because the texts themselves are so uncertain and because this uncertainty together with the romance authors' preference for formula over originality "limits the role of the literary critic who also has to confront the untranscendable banality of such texts" (94).

5. The Middle English text is from Dunn and Byrnes, 467. Since *Romancing the Goddess* is intended partly for those who may not be skilled in reading Old and Middle English and will therefore value translations of medieval English poems, poetry in the commentary will be presented in translation, with the original verses afterwards in brackets.

Believing that the formal structures of rhyme or alliteration add to the narrative a vital element of delight ("art" is a more ambiguous term), I attempt to imitate those formal structures. Readers should be reminded, however, that no translation is an accurate representation of its original, and an attempt to imitate formal structures will distort the poem's semantic content even further. The reader may wish carefully to compare this stanza of *Thomas of Erceldoun* with the original, which is not difficult to read, in order to be aware of the kind of distortion provoked by imitation of rhyme and meter. This caveat applies also, of course, to the three romances translated in the main text.

6. Gravdal has documented the frequency with which women in the medieval French pastourelle are forced actually to succumb to the violence merely threatened by Thomas: "In a variant of the classical 'encounter' type [of medieval pastourelle], the songs become lyric variations on the themes of gender, power, and sexual violence. This type repeatedly narrates the same event: a knight is riding down the road when he sees a comely shepherdess alone in a meadow. The bucolic mode is interrupted by the spectre of a potential act of violence that is anomalous in the context of the pastoral tradition: rape. In approximately 18 percent of the extant Old French pastourelles (thirty-eight of the one hundred and sixty texts included in my count), the shepherdess is raped by the medieval knight" (105). The supposed "shepherd's daughter" is similarly raped by a knight in Child ballad 110, "The Knight and the Shepherd's Daughter," which has affinities with the rape story in Chaucer's Wife of Bath's Tale. In stories of classical antiquity, especially those retold by Ovid, the percentage of rapes as male and female meet in a bucolic setting would be even higher. Rank perhaps adds to the safety of the lady Thomas confronts, as to that of the queens in the romances, even though the latter often keep their identity secret.

7. For just one example of such comparison, Trevet has Custance, like Emaré, change her own name in the story, to Custe; otherwise he seems to use Custance and Constance interchangeably. Chaucer chooses the name Custance, Gower chooses Constance, and neither of them recounts the name-changing episode.

8. The close resemblances of the two stories are shown by the comparative lists of motifs in Gough's "Constance Saga," 31.

9. Anne Thompson Lee gives some brief but useful examples of the English *Florence's* differences from the lengthy French romance. The greater length of the French version accommodates, for example, "a highly specific knowledge of social and military background as well as a great interest in astrology and magic, but the English author has little interest in either of these areas" (344). The English author does have, however, an intriguing interest in the geography of the romance, making it more specific than the French poet does (see my note to stanza 158). In the interest of moving the action along, the English author also omits the extensive biblical references of the source, as well as passages demonstrating Florence's Christian learning.

10. Christine's abbreviated version, while emphasizing Florence's beauty and skill at healing, has a slightly different plot and is less dramatic and bloodthirsty than the romance; for example, in Christine's concluding scene Florence succeeds in prevailing upon her husband not to put all her tormenters to death. Nevertheless, the fact that such a concluding scene does take place, in which all the malefactors are gathered together and the couple reconciled, aligns Christine's story with the English and French romance versions rather than, for example, the Miracle version recorded by John of Garland in Latin meter in his *Stella Maris* of the mid-thirteenth century. In this version "the Chaste Empress" prefers to remain a nun rather than returning to her husband (Wilson 109–13, 168–70). The empress is not named in John's story or in most others, even including the late medieval French play, "Miracle de L'Empereris de Romme," collected by Gaston Paris and Ulysse Robert in their *Miracles de Nostre Dame, par personnages.*

11. See Weisl, who argues that "All of Chaucer's romances that end, end happily" (118–20). A recent series of essays by modern writers of romance novels confirms that the happy ending remains preferred for this genre. A number of the writers voiced the opinion expressed here by Suzanne Simmons Guntrum: "We also read romance novels . . . because in the end there is no ambiguity, no tragedy, no defeat. There is ambiguity enough, tragedy enough, defeat enough in real life. We do not read romances to be reminded of these realities. In a romance novel we know that, whatever the odds against them, the hero and heroine will come together in the end and live happily ever after. Indeed, if the above is *not* true, then either the book is flawed or it isn't a romance" (in Krentz 152–53).

12. "Making the Mold: The Roles of Women in the Middle English Metrical Romance, 1225–1500." DAI 37 (1977): 5812A (NYU). Elizabeth Archibald goes so far as to ask whether "any medieval narrative of adventure with a single female protagonist [can] be described as romance" ("Case" 14).

13. See also Kevin Roddy's earlier discussion, "Mythic Sequence in the *Man of Law's Tale*," in which the myth he discovers is a Christian one revealing that "Custance is meant to be read as the Christian soul" (21–22), and Johannes Wilhelmus Smit's *Studies on the Language and Style of Columba the Younger (Columbanus),* in which he dedicates a section to "the turbulent sea," with copious quotation from Patristic sources concerning "the *navigatio* of the church across the sea of the world" (189).

14. Christine de Pisan herself makes the comparison in 1405 C.E.: "The noble Florence, empress of Rome, endured great adversity with amazing patience and greatly resembled Griselda" (Christine 176). Griselda is that archetype of wifely stoicism who determinedly survives without demur her husband's cruel and obsessive "testing" of her patience. She is made famous to modern readers as the protagonist of Chaucer's Clerk's tale, derived, as he says, from Petrarch, but the story is also traditional.

15. Although over-reacting against the "secular hagiography" view of these romances by making the heroines morally flawed pilgrims "voyaging through a flawed universe in which no one is blameless" (199), Hares-Stryker does offer a fresh look at Florence when she criticizes previous descriptions: "Despite Hibbard's view that 'the Middle English redactor of *Florence* was of a strong religious cast of mind and . . . tells his story not for the sake of diversion, but for the picture it gives of Christian fortitude,' in this late fourteenth-century English version Florence may be pious but she is also self-willed" (212). She is too self-willed for her own spiritual health, Hares-Stryker believes. Hares-Stryker refers to Anne Thompson Lee's analysis demonstrating that the English *Florence* is some four thousand lines shorter than the French version "due in great part" to elimination of allusion to biblical material (212), and she concludes that Florence's "suffering does not occur because of her Christian decision not to submit to sin, but because of her refusal to submit to anything" (213). Yet even Hares-Stryker neglects the heroine's active management of the end of the story, which is almost universally described with passive expressions such as Donovan's concerning Emaré: "Her union with the King is effected through Segramore" (Severs's *Manual* 137). Emaré is the agent here, actively arranging the occasion and using her son Segramore as a tool.

16. Georgiana Donavin points out that in his version of the Constance story Gower, Chaucer's friend, specifies envy as the motive of the Sultan's mother's violence and setting of Constance adrift; on the principle that the second mother-in-law episode is a doubling of the first, she posits again "a latent romantic passion for her son" as the motive of Allee's [Alla's] mother

when she exchanges the letters, leading to Constance being set adrift for a second time (46).

17. For an examination of the worldwide folklore on the theme of setting adrift, including the *imrama* or voluntary setting of the self adrift in a boat practiced by Irish monks and others and made famous by St. Brendan, the reader is recommended to Carolyn Hares-Stryker's 1990 dissertation, "Sleeping in the Midst of the Sea." Otto Rank recounts and analyzes a good number of the same woman-adrift tales and others, both folk and literary, and relates them to contemporary cases and news accounts in chapter 11 of his classic work, *The Incest Theme in Literature and Legend:* "The Relationship between Father and Daughter in Myth, Folktales, Legends, Literature, Life, and Neurosis" (300–337). The chapter refers specifically to our tale-type from page 315 on, beginning with the Swedish folktale of "The Russian King's Daughter." This tale is worth recounting here for the sake of comparison. The pope decrees that the lustful king may marry his daughter. To prevent this, the daughter mutilates herself, so the king in anger casts her to sea in a barrel. It carries her to Greece. There she marries the king (which Rank calls "doubling," claiming that in effect she is marrying her father), and she bears his child in his absence. His wicked mother exchanges the letter reporting the birth for a letter saying she has borne a monster; in response the king commands mother and child to be exposed in a barrel thrown into the sea. It is carried to Rome. Both kings go to Rome in penance. The pope, upon hearing their stories, puts two and two together and reunites the family (315). In this version of the tale, after her first and only active response to her situation, the woman can hardly be called a protagonist. At least as Rank retells the story, she is merely the object of men's desires and manipulations.

18. Overing summarizes the various scholarly judgments upon the passage (101–4).

19. It has been variously argued that modþryþo could be a name, a descriptive epithet, or an adjectival phrase (Sisam: "violence of character"), or even subject and object with the verb *wæg:* "Courage (mod) had strength (thryth)." I like very much the suggestion of Fred C. Robinson, offered in a private communication, that the subject may be Queen Hygd in the previous lines of *Beowulf,* the words *mod þryþo wæg* meaning that she, Hygd, "weighed [i.e., thought about] the arrogance of Thryth." Thus I have translated, partly convinced by the fact that the eighth-century Mercian King Offa, of whom the continental Offa here is a famous ancestor, had a wife Cynethryth, called Drida (Latin for Thryth) in the story told circa 1200 by a monk of St. Albans in terms that seem to fit with the story in *Beowulf.* I believe that further attention to the stories about Thryth might prove profitable, less to prove how the tale spread, if that is indeed possible, than to observe how various parts of the story were emphasized or suppressed under different sociohistorical circumstances. When R. W. Chambers examines (36–40) and as-

sembles (206–37) the several Latin versions of the story in his *Beowulf: An Introduction*, he neglects the subject of incest, which the *Beowulf*-poet suppresses, like Chaucer, both in this story and elsewhere. Sisam considers that there is no connection between the Thryth digression in *Beowulf* and the *Lives of the Offas* (83–84).

20. "Great lord" is my guarded translation of *sinfrea*, a word explained by Klaeber as referring to "either the 'father' or 'husband'" (199). But he clearly must be the father, since he suggests that Thryth marry Offa. The fact that *sin* in Old English usually has no connection with evildoing helped me to control my impulse for an echoing translation, "sin-lord," in order to allude to the incest stories under discussion; yet I waver on this decision in view of Robinson's recent interpretation of the word *synsnædum* in *Beowulf* as "sinful morsels" (Robinson 143–46). Certainly lines 1932–43 suggest comparison with the opening scene of *Apollonius of Tyre*, where would-be suitors are put to death on a pretext so as not to separate the daughter from her father (the possible similarity is further discussed below). Overing speaks of Thryth's "rejection of the female peace-weaver role" in lines 1931–44 (103–4), but it seems more accurate to say that Thryth does not discover her appropriate role, and the better life that goes with it, until she goes to Offa and finds in him a suitable mate.

21. Chambers's discussion is also detailed (31–40), and he furnishes the relevant materials in Latin (206–44); most are translated by Simpson (222–37), though she merely summarizes the parts most interesting in the present context since they are irrelevant to *Beowulf*, the topic with which she is concerned. Schlauch's discussion (64–68) supplements these texts and translations.

22. Rickert additionally attempts to bring into the argument the Old English poem that is today editorially titled "The Wife's Lament." Following W. W. Lawrence in calling it by an earlier designation "The *Banished* Wife's Lament" (my emphasis), which already biases a reading of the poem, she argues that it and the other so-called elegies as well make the best sense as fragments from epics ("Offa Saga" II, 45–55). It seems to me that her argument, rather than proving her point, shows instead how easy it is to adopt such floating fragments into a structure where they may be made to fit. (Even though this poem is not considered a fragment, *per se*, Alain Renoir's argument about "the apprehension of fragments" in his article "Fragment: An Oral-Formulaic Nondefinition" offers some useful suggestions for reading such noncontextualized materials.) If one translates "The Wife's Lament" so that her husband is an enemy who forces her into the wilderness, rather than, as I understand the poem, her concerned husband attempting to protect her from his family by advising a wilderness retreat, the situation can indeed be fitted into the version of the "woman adrift" (in the wilderness) found in the Offa story. I suspect, however, that Rickert's elaborate study of the Offa

story has itself influenced much scholarly understanding of the situation in "The Wife's Lament"; see Barrie Ruth Straus's interpretation of the poem as opposed to Wentersdorf's, both included in *Old English Shorter Poems: Basic Readings*, edited by O'Keeffe.

23. Overing discusses the ways in which she disturbs in *Language, Sign, and Gender in Beowulf*, 101–7.

24. I am convinced by Elizabeth Archibald, who argues "that the flight from incest does have [despite Schlauch's statement to the contrary] an ancient and lasting connection with the Accused Queen theme, and that this can be demonstrated by considering two late classical texts which do not contain the Exchanged Letter but do use incest as the catalyst for the flight of a protagonist, and also contain other Constance motifs. These texts are the *Clementine Recognitions* and *Apollonius of Tyre*" ("Flight" 259).

25. Against Rohde, who was persuaded that the opening incest scene "was a later addition to the original story, intended to motivate Apollonius' flight from Tyre," Archibald maintains that "the death of Antiochus and his daughter is the catalyst for the second half of the story" and "all the male authority figures in [*Apollonius of Tyre*] have only daughters.... Their attitudes to and treatment of their daughters are crucial to the plot" (15). Archibald's argument for the way the author knits together the threads of the story is sound, but at the more elementary level of the plot the two strands appear distinct. Perry, whose views are outlined below, suggests an alternative scenario in which the *Apollonius* author is altering a traditional tale that was previously better integrated.

26. See also Goepp, 168–69. Perry says, "It appears that the author of *Apollonius* must have made one radical change in the terms of the original myth about incest, whatever it was, whether written or oral, upon the basis of which his own story of Antiochus was fashioned: he substituted a suitor (Apollonius) in place of one of the parties to incest (the daughter of Antiochus) as the victim of the aggressor's persecution. This he did for the purpose of motivating the travels of his hero Apollonius, whose adventures were shaped by him on the model of other sources, both Greek and Latin; and, in so doing, the fate of Antiochus' daughter was necessarily, but conspicuously, ignored" (301).

27. Perry devotes Appendix 1 of *Ancient Romances* to the texts and sources of the story, a retelling, and a brief analysis (285–93); Archibald also retells it and discusses its implications in "Flight" (264–65).

28. Thomas Mann introduces the story into chapter 31 of *Doktor Faustus* as a puppet show and later parodies it in *Der Erwähte*, translated as *The Holy Sinner*. I am grateful to Mary Frances Fahey for furnishing information about the German stories and lending me the texts.

29. Jocelyn Wogan-Browne, who is among the few who have done research on the audience of the romances (she lists others, 85 n.6), shows that "recent

work on manuscripts and social history emphasizes at least overlap, and frequently identity, among medieval audiences and social contexts for romance and hagiography" (85), and she draws particular attention to the fact that the manuscripts of the hagiographical legends she has researched are monastic, "but their patronage is female" (89). She sees the Anglo-Norman legend of Clement (essentially the same story as the *Clementine Recognitions* discussed earlier) "as a narrative socially grounded in the bio-politics of chastity—in the disposition of territorial and genealogical resources between the biological and institutional successions of family and church—and as a narrative for socializing younger brothers by exemplary career romance" (90).

30. Florence's situation requires further comment, since what she next does, or rather refuses to do, will puzzle a modern reader. She becomes betrothed to Emere and then refuses to sleep with him, not until they are married, as we might think normal, but until he has slain Garcy. The implicit assumption that she would ordinarily sleep with him before the formal celebration of matrimony may be explained by the fact that the betrothal itself was considered binding, and need not even be public: "Gratian's *Concordance of Discordant Canons* declared that a valid marriage was constituted when the lovers consented to their union and spoke words to that effect. Strictly defined, the words spoken by the lovers alone, without benefit of banns, witnesses, or clergy, constituted a legitimage, binding union, indeed a sacrament" (Hudson 86). This understanding of marriage radically undermined both parental and institutional roles. The Fourth Lateran Council, mentioned above, decreed that private marriages were clandestine, hence punishable, but valid, while prescribing "a more public and protracted chain of events through which the marriage was made" (ibid.). Finally, in the sixteenth century the Council of Trent decreed clandestine marriages invalid, and parents and the church were back in charge. The fourteenth and fifteenth centuries must have been fraught with discussions of exactly what forms acceptably constituted marriage, with generations siding against each other on this heated topic.

31. In the Icelandic *Egil's Saga*, the sea-burial of emigrating Kveldulf is used to divine the location of his descendants' home in Iceland. Before he dies he tells his crew to throw his coffin overboard and to tell his son that "he's to build his homestead close to the place where I come to land" (chapter 27). Such site-divination in the sagas was usually done by tossing overboard the inherited pillars of the family highseat, brought from the homeland as a symbol of that family's continued existence; the pillars' landfall marked the site destined for the new family home. This custom further confirms the power of the sea to determine human fate. With typical arrogance yet also appropriately, Kveldulf uses his own body to symbolize the lineage of his kindred and discover the site where it may flourish in the new land.

32. Several of my students have pointed to modern stories that contain

similar motifs and themes, such as *Jane Eyre* and the movies *Thelma and Louise* and *The Piano*. It is unlikely that these bear any direct relationship to the Castaway Queen tales. Although to a degree they address similar issues, even down to sometimes startling details, they do so from perspectives absolutely of nineteenth- and twentieth-century women (not in every respect demanding to be admired, as the poets of medieval romance require us to admire the pure good will of their own heroines). In the film *The Secret of Roan Inish* a "setting adrift" in a supernaturally propelled little boat is a central feature of the plot, but the ancient Celtic tales upon which this film draws concerning silkies (seals) taking their half-breed children back to the sea is a strand of folklore alien to this study (See Leavy).

CHAPTER 2: THE ROMANCES RHYMED IN MODERN ENGLISH

Emaré

1. Denise MacLachlan introduced me to the romance titled *Emaré* in a graduate seminar paper about the meanings of the names by which Emaré changes and embroiders her identity. I refer to these names in the notes that follow. In a later seminar, Emma Cornell, a graduate student accustomed to performing medieval music, composed a medieval-sounding melody to which she sang a portion of the romance in Middle English. Her effective presentation gave us some idea of what listening to such a romance might be like.

As the attributions indicate, many of the following notes are indebted to those of Gough and Rickert. I include their consecutive line numbers followed in parentheses by a numbering by stanza and line.

1–12 (1:1–12) The opening prayer is the longest in any English romance (Rickert).

23 (2:11) According to Gough, the name Emaré derives from Old French *esmarie*, "the bewildered, distressed woman." Rickert argues for another meaning, "pure, refined (as gold), with rare qualities" as in "La Blonde Esmerée" in *Li Biaus Disconneus* (edition xxix). The change of the main vowel to "a" makes it hard to disregard the Latin *e mare* "from the sea" as a possible nuance.

33 (3:9) Ivory: The *whales bane* of the original is probably walrus ivory, "a frequent comparison" (Gough).

34 (3:10) Erayne: Gough suggests that the name is a variant of "Irene." Rickert refers to the famous Empress of Constantinople named Irene who was contemporary with Charlemagne, but she prefers to associate the name with Elayne (Helen) or Igraine (Arthur's mother).

57 (5:9) Concerning the foster mother's name Abró, Rickert observes that *abra* is a medieval Latin word for "female servant."

58–60 (5:10–12) Rickert compares Emaré's "feminine" skills to the formidible learning acquired by Trevet's Constance and by Florence in lines 58–63 of that romance (a part not translated in this book); by the time she is fifteen Florence knows how to read and write well and to play the harp and psaltry. Probably the most learned of all medieval romance ladies, however, is Guy of Warwick's lady Felice.

78 (7:6) The reference to "play," says Rickert, "evidently alludes to the emperor's licentious character." In this romance the word "play" insistently suggests "have intercourse."

79–187 (stanzas 7–15) The visit of the Saracen (but converted) prince is, according to Gough, "the only incident peculiar to *Emaré*," which in most respects is a very traditional version of the story. For possible justification of the long passage about the cloth that Sir Tergaunt brings, see Donovan, "Cloth Worthily Wrought." Rickert mentions the length of the description and refers to the similarly long description of the coronation robe in Chrétien's *Erec et Enide* (ll. 6735–6809). Erec's robe also has a fourfold design, but one that is based upon the four liberal arts rather than lovers (see Owen's translation 89–90). A magic robe occurs in several versions of the Castaway Queen tale, such as *La Belle Hélène, Mai und Beaflor,* and Enikel's *Chronicle,* as Gough points out. In my view this special robe may be associated with the "sky robe" of both Isis and the Virgin Mary, Mary's blue robe being traditionally adorned with stars (see chapter 3). John Speirs uses Emaré's robe as the basis for his interpretation of her as a fairy (157–61), and clearly there is some overlap here (or what folklorists would call "contamination") with tales like those of swan maidens and other animal wives, in which the woman's garment contains most of her power and the means of escape from intolerable male or mother-in-law dominated domestic existence (see Leavy *passim*). The garment is taken away from the animal wife, however, whereas Emaré retains hers.

94 and 142 (8:10 and 12:10) The toadstone (French *crapaudine)* was a stone supposed to be secreted in the head of a toad and to possess magic properties. Rickert lists the magical powers attributed to several of the other stones mentioned, though not this one, deriving her information from French lapidaries.

97–101 (9:1–5) The blinding glare of the gems may be compared to a passage in *Erec et Enide* immediately after the lengthy description of the robe. Two massive golden gem-studded crowns are brought in for the lovers, so dazzling with carbuncles that for a long time those in the hall can see nothing (Owen's translation 90).

109–68 (10–14) While it is unlikely that any cloth ever existed so elaborately bejewelled as this in *Emaré*, the embroidering of narrative subjects upon fabric is an ancient art. One hears in the Icelandic sagas of long embroidered panels illustrating myths or commemorating great deeds, and the spectacular Bayeux Tapestry verifies that such embroideries actually existed. In later times the narrative subjects were often, of course, those of romance. Henry Thomas writes, "One of the most peculiar illustrations of the hold which these romances had obtained in Italy is to be found in the *Letters* of Andrea Calmo" (died 1571). A list of gifts that this gentleman is presenting to a lady begins with a *camise* made by a Hebrew woman upon which were embroidered scenes from classical fables. The list concludes with a kerchief or shawl on which were woven (quoting Thomas's translation of the letter) "all the war the pagan King Agramante had with Charlemagne King of France, the death and avenging of Julius Caesar, the history of Palmerin de Oliva, Emperor of Constantinope, and the brave deeds of Amadis of Gaul, with all the adventures of the knights of King Arthur's Round Table, and in the middle the wise Atlas, holding the world on his shoulders, and surrounded by the great doctors in astrology" (193–94). One hopes that the lady was suitably impressed.

122 (11:2) Though Gower mentions "Amadas and Ydoyne" in his *Confessio Amantis* (6:879), and in "Sir Degrevant" the story is embroidered on a bed-tapestry (ll. 1477–78), the romance about these lovers is known only in its Continental forms. The English romance "Sir Amadas" borrows only the name.

124 and 125 (11:4 and 11:5) The "honest" love and the "true-love" flowers depicted upon the cloth provide a standard against which to measure the incestuous love displayed later by Emaré's father.

125 and 149 (11:5 and 13:5) The true-love flower is the herb-paris, *paris quadrifolia*, which was used as a love charm.

134 (12:2) *Tristram* (or Tristan) *and Isolde* is probably the best-known and most widely distributed medieval love story. The standard modern English version is Belloc and Rosenfeld's translation of the French scholar Bédier's careful retelling and weaving together of episodes from the various earlier medieval versions. Currently other translations are becoming available.

146 (13:2) The Middle English *Floris and Blancheflor* is edited by Bennett and Smithers (text 40–51 and notes 282–88) and by Stevick (98–139).

151 (13:7) As Rickert says, these "knyȝtus and senatowres" (knights and senators) intrude suddenly where names of stones might be expected. She suggests that if the line was taken down from hearing, it might have been corrupted from "Ther wer onyx and centaureus," rhyming with Middle English "vertues" in the next line.

164 (14:8) The unicorn is traditionally tamed by the presence of a virgin, as mentioned in the *Physiologus* and depicted on the famous "Unicorn Tapestry" of the Musée de Cluny in Paris.

326 (28:2) Emaré drifts to land in "a little over a seven-night," much as the heroine of *La Manekine* drifts from Hungary to Berwick in eight days (l. 1168) and from Berwick to Rome in twelve (l. 4761). Trevet, followed by

Chaucer, has Constance adrift "first three, and then five years at sea" (Rickert).

338 (29:2) Galys: Most likely Wales or Galloway on the Scottish border (the names are etymologically related). Gough cites Suchier in arguing that Galys is Galicia in Spain. Rickert observes that "this form [Galys] occurs, alike for either country [Wales or Galicia], with the accent on either syllable," and in a note on stanza 41 (ll. 481 and following) she adds historical arguments for Galicia. The west coast of Britain nevertheless seems more probable in an English romance and above all in this romance-type where the heroine traditionally comes to British shores, though usually in the north of England (hence Galloway is attractive). As Gough observes in his essay *The Constance Saga*, "While *Emaré* substitutes *Galys* for Northumbria, *Manekine* preserves the locality of [the other stories of this group]" (31).

351 (30:3) "Fey" means magical, frightening.

376–78 (32:4–6) "She taught the women how to sew . . ." In many of these romances the protagonist must earn her living for a time by the skill of her hands. From an undergraduate essay comes the illuminating remark that this "woman who overcomes troubling situations . . . can be compared to a single working mother today."

504 (42:11–12) The most famous "king's mark" in Middle English literature is the glowing cross on the hero's right shoulder in *Havelok* (ll. 604 and 2139–47), where it affects the plot. The "double royal mark" on Emaré's child may be intended as a sign of the royal blood of both parents; Emaré has not yet revealed her identity as the daughter of an emperor (see line 73).

524 (44:8) "Forty shillings" recalls the *quarante sols* paid by the old queen in *La Manekine* (l. 3060).

539 (45:10–12) Rickert observes that this false description of the newborn child, a traditonal motif in the story, depicts "the most monstrous creature in any version."

689 (57:7) In *Mai und Beaflor*, *La Manekine*, and Enikel's *Chronicle*, the heroine's boat "drifts miraculously up the Tiber" (Gough). In *Emaré* Rome seems to be situated by the sea.

713 (59:8) Egarye (Egaré): "outcast."

799 (67:7–12) Concerning the wicked mother-in-law's exile, Rickert observes that "the remission of punishment is peculiar to *Emaré*." In other versions she is immured, or killed by the sword as in Trevet's version of *Constance* (Chaucer has Alla merely "slay" her at line 895), or, in most versions, burnt.

822 (69:5) The king's penance is explained by Trevet and others as prompted by remorse for slaying his mother. Both Gough and Rickert point out that he has no need to blame himself for this in *Emaré*, but we are not told that

he does. Instead, this storyteller takes a different tack, offering the king's strange idea that Emaré's supposed death by drowning was intended to save his soul from death, perhaps in the sense of Christ's sacrifice for mankind. This prompts him to go to Rome on a penitential journey to "save his soul."

864 (72:12) Rickert compares *lufsumme vnder lyne* ("lovesome under linen") to other alliterative expressions concerning clothing and fabrics such as "seemly under sark" (l. 501) and "goodly under gore" (ll. 198 and 938). I have paraphrased or omitted all of these phrases since they would make no sense to a modern audience.

1030 Breton lay: This designation may be questioned, or more precisely the genre of *Emaré* may be associated with the tail-rhymed "pseudo-lays" (Graham Johnston's term) in vogue late in the medieval period in England.

1032 (86:12) "The Complaint of Garye": Middle English *playn* or *complaynt* means "lament." Most editors emend or annotate the manuscript reading *playn þe garye*. Rumble's *playn d' Egarye* makes good sense. He explains that "the scribe appears to be imitating a French form of the title" (133). Reading the *gar-* element as in our modern French-derived word "garage," I retain the manuscript "Garye" on the somewhat dubious principle that the former outcast *Egarye* has now found shelter (hence, "garye").

Florence

Many of the following notes for *Le Bone Florence of Rome* are based upon those provided by Heffernan in her edition, which I follow closely in my translation. Nicolas Jacobs warns, however, that the unique surviving manuscript of this text offers "a number of readings in which the text is remarkably difficult either to construe or to interpret," adding in a footnote "despite the silence of the most recent editor [Heffernan]" (281). As before, the notes are numbered first according to consecutive line numbers, then in parentheses according to stanza number and line. I should like to repeat here how grateful I am to Carolyn Hares-Stryker for bringing this romance to my attention in a graduate seminar.

1292 (108:11) Calumny and deceit mark Miles from the beginning of this section as the wicked one of the two brothers. As explained in chapter 1, *Florence* belongs to a group of the Castaway Queen romances having a different basic form from *Emaré* yet borrowing across these forms as far back as the classical period. Whereas Emaré's journey is instigated by the wrath of an incestuous father, Florence's is instigated by the conniving of her incestuous brother-in-law Miles, who begins his series of deceits by maligning Egravain and Florence at line 1303 (109:10).

1361 (114:11) The Middle English text inserts a Latin phrase here, "And he assoyled me *a pena et culpa*," about which Heffernan has an interesting note based on two entries in *The Catholic Encyclopedia*, first the article on

"Penance" (XI, 619f.) then that on "Abduction" (I, 32 and following). Apparently Egravain's guilt is in being an accomplice, however unwilling, in the sin of *raptus violentiae* (abduction by violence), having been forced to swear allegiance to Miles when that villain tried to make Florence marry him and incarcerated her when she attempted to flee (114:1–8). The sin of *raptus violentiae* "is committed when a reluctant woman is forcibly transferred with a matrimonial intent from a secure and free place to a morally different one and there held by threats, great fear, or fraud equivalent to force" (*Cath. Encyc.* I, 32 and following, s.v. "Abduction"). Heffernan continues, "It is not necessary that actual change of locality occur. Some jurists claim 'virtual change' from a state of freedom to that of subjection to be sufficient to constitute 'abduction.'" The question this explanation raises in my mind concerns Chaucer, whether the *raptus* of Florence, in which Egravain is implicated by swearing loyalty to Miles, can be compared to the mysterious *raptus* with which Cecelia Champagne charges the famous poet. (For an account of that event see Howard 317–20.)

1444 (121:10) The Middle English text has: "Hys lykyng vanysched all away," which I have made more explicitly phallic by translating *vanysched* "withered." In view of Miles's accusation of witchcraft at line 1507 (127:1), it seems clear that the romancer intends us to imagine detumescence here. In her note on these lines Heffernan emphasizes the Virgin Mary's power that protects Florence's chastity both here and later (ll. 1499–1500, 1852–59), underscoring "the ties that *Florence* has to Tales of the Virgin." (See chapter 1 above.)

1534–40 (129:4–10) As Heffernan remarks, "The beauty of Florence, like that of Emaré, has something celestial about it. . . . [It] is here raised to a visible symbol of her virtue." Villains in both stories, however, claim that the heroine's gleaming attire betrays her "demonic nature" (in *Florence* see ll. 1666–69, 140:7–10, in *Emaré*, ll. 438–47, 37:6 to 38:3), thus displaying their own sinful perception of innocent beauty.

1567–72 (132:1–6) Florence's attitude toward men here seems psychologically believable as the reaction of an emotionally and physically mistreated woman.

1592 (134:3). Macary (Macaire) is the name of a persecuting villain in other romances of this genre, particularly those associated with the "Charlemagne's wife" group of tales. The name appears ultimately to derive from Canacee's incestuous brother Macarius in the story of that maiden told by Ovid in his *Heroides* (and later by Gower). It is interesting that lustful Macary should make his appearance in this romance just as we are told that Garcy has died, the second evil suitor taking the place of the first.

1603 (135:1) The stone is probably there for bed-warming, in which case it would have been heated in the fireplace, wrapped in a cloth, and put into the bed, then kicked out when no longer useful. (We still sometimes used heated bricks in Yorkshire when I lived there.)

1605 (135:3) In the French romance titled *Macaire*, the name of its major villain, a dwarf acts as go-between between that wicked courtier and the lady, who rejects him. In the related Dutch folk-book and Spanish prose romance about Sibille, both possibly derived from a French folk-book, "the dwarf is rejected with a blow on the mouth when he approaches the queen" (Schlauch 104–5). This analogue suggests that the villain named Macary and the well-aimed blow are associated themes.

1624 (137:1) The specious evidence of the bloody knife also appears in Chaucer's *Custance* (and in Trevet's chronicle), but not in *Emaré*, where the heroine is instead betrayed by her mother-in-law's forged letters. Christine de Pisan makes the victim a child (Richards translation 177). She gets her version from Gautier de Coinci's collection of miracles of the Virgin; Richards gives a detailed citation (266).

1639–47 (138:4–12) As Heffernan comments, this description of Sir Terry's prophetic dream and his anxious walk by candlelight through the halls to his daughter's bed is "masterly."

1669 (140:10) A devil in disguise: See note on lines 1534–45 above.

1744 (147:1) A burgess is simply a city-dweller. The -ess suffix does not denote gender.

1875 (157:12) My "reef" is obviously dictated by the modern English rhyme; in the Middle English text Florence is cast upon a *roche*. This feature recalls to Heffernan the rock in the middle of a river upon which the heroine is exposed "in the twelfth-century Latin Miracle version of the tale." Iconographically, it may bring to mind the image of bound Andromeda mentioned in the introduction, but in terms of stories of persons set adrift a closer early analogue is the rock of the saintly Gregory's long sojourn in the sixth-century Latin tale more famously retold by Hartman von Awe and Thomas Mann (see chapter 1, under "Analogues").

1882 (158:7) About the name of the convent Beuerfayre, Heffernan comments that the English romancer "evidently means to Anglicise the French name for the convent, Beau Repaire [in *Florence de Rome*]." The English romancer substitutes f for p in the name.

1883–84 (158:8–9) The Middle English text describes the convent standing "on the watur of Botayre, / That rennyth in to the grekys see." The exact location in Macedonia indicated in my translation constitutes my main contribution to the close textual study of this romance (see map). The French romance, lacking such specificity, merely locates the convent vaguely upon the east coast of central Italy (Wallensköld 1:47). The English text's precision suggests that the poet has some knowledge of a particular site, perhaps the sister house of an English convent, or perhaps a way station for pilgrims run by an order of English nuns, since the poem locates Beuerfayre on the *Via Ignatia,* the main land route to Jerusalem via Constantinople. It was a difficult alternative for those who preferred not to travel by sea.

1888 (159:1) Sir Lucius Ibarnius, the founder of the convent, replaces the French text's anachronistic Julius Caesar, who was murdered in 44 B.C.E. (Though a pagan temple of healing could well have been established at the Lake Bottiaea location during Caesar's reign, it is unlikely that either the French or English poet would have known about it. The site is in fact not far from the great healing temple of Sarapis in Thessalonica.) Besides re-locating the convent from Italy to the more specific Macedonian site, the English poet makes its founder the first pagan in England to be converted to Christianity, according to Bede in the year 167 C.E. The same name is used for King Arthur's Roman antagonist in several stories about that hero, beginning with Geoffrey of Monmouth.

1895 (159:8) The feast day of Saint Hilary, Bishop of Poitiers, is January 13 (which marks the beginning of "Hilary Term" at Oxford University). The twentieth day of Yule mentioned in this line, that is, the twentieth day after Christmas, coincides with this date.

1910 (160:10) A "habit" is the traditional garment of a nun.

1923 (161:11) Florence's vocation as healer reflects a role that nuns "occasionally play . . . in medieval romances," observes Heffernan; she refers to M. Hughes, *Women Healers in Medieval Life and Literature.* Nuns played (and play) this role in real life as well. But the theme of the Castaway Queen becoming a healer at the holy site to which she drifts for the last time appears to be an element in the classical story to which the medieval romance is indebted. In the later Miracle of the Virgin story told by Christine de Pisan, the Virgin instructs Florence in a dream to pluck the herb under her pillow, and it is with this herb that she effects her cures. Our "English" Florence apparently cures people with a laying on of hands.

1965 (165:6) We might understand "Gyllam of Pole" better as "William of Apulia." Apulia is located in Italy.

2032–37 (171:1–6) In various classical cults an open confession of sin was often required before healing was effected. In the first of his *Epistolae ex Ponto,* for example, Ovid describes persons confessing before Isiac altars (Griffiths, *Apuleius* 271).

2117 (178:2) " 'It was a plot!' exclaimed Emere." Heffernan has: "He seyde, 'Y fynde yow iiii in fere.' " This may be translated, "He said, 'I find you four in company,' " which I take to mean "in conspiracy." Jacobs uses this line to illustrate one of his "creative misreadings," remarking that the manuscript reading "gives a trivial sense . . . and we should perhaps read *þe fende yow fonge in fere; fecche* would be more idiomatic, but *fonge* gives a more likely homeograph" (284). His substituted phrase may be translated, "The fiend take you all together!" I prefer to be more conservative about the text when possible.

2147 (180:8) The *Te deum laudamus* is a famous Latin hymn of thanksgiving traditionally attributed to St. Ambrose.

2173 (182:10) Pope Simon (Symond in the original) did not write this story, nor is it in the chronicles of Rome, though there is a famous thirteenth-century chronicler of the north of England called Symond of Durham.

2181 (183:5) "Wend" is an archaic word meaning "go" (as in "to wend one's way").

2185 (183:10) Heffernan suggests that this "good" romance offers a model for those who wish to follow the moral example of the saintly Florence.

Custance

Many of the following explanations for Chaucer's *Custance* are condensed from the excellent Explanatory Notes provided for the *Man of Law's Tale* by Patricia J. Eberle in *The Riverside Chaucer*. Not everything is covered in the notes below. For example, Chaucer's complex astronomy and astrology in particular are scanted (though not ignored), nor do these notes normally provide explanations of persons mentioned simply as examples. The reader is referred to Eberle's more comprehensive notes for detail in these areas.

135 (1:2) The merchants are added to the story by Chaucer.

162–68 (5:1–7) The moral beauty of the heroine is typical of romance.

190–203 (stanzas 9–10) The source of this "book of the sky" passage, like that of many others, is provided by a Latin scribal gloss in one of the manuscripts, in this case referring to Bernardus Silvester's *Megacosmos*. The major changes Chaucer makes are to give most of the details a negative twist, stressing the deaths of the heroes Turnus, Hercules, Achilles, Pompey, Julius Caesar, Sampson, and Socrates, and radically to change the conclusion at the end. Whereas Bernardus says that in the stars God provided a cipher that allows us to behold in advance ages to come, Chaucer adds that as limited human beings we are *not* able to read that cipher, a theme that he repeats later (see notes on lines 315 and 482–83).

220–21 (13:3–4) The disparity between the two countries' cultures refers to the *disparitas cultus* of canon law, specifically to the difference in religion between persons baptized and unbaptized, which creates an impediment to marriage.

224 (13:7) Mohammed (570?–632 A.D.), the founder of Islam, is not mentioned in the part of Trevet's *Chronicles* about the life of Constance, but he is mentioned later on where Trevet recounts the life of Constance's son Maurice.

272–73 (20:6–7) In this passage important for tone, Chaucer's irony clearly breaks through the emotional narrator's voice.

286–87 (22:7–8) This couplet is the most overtly patriarchal statement in

the tale. Commenting on how little Custance actually says in this ro-
mance ("the most generous account" gives her sixty-five lines in a narra-
tive of 1129 lines), A. S. G. Edwards indicates doubt that even that many
lines "can be confidently attributed" to her, and he says that he is "par-
ticularly uncertain" about this famous couplet, "lines which seem more
consistent in tone and sentiment with the narrator [the Man of Law] than
with Constance herself" ("Chaucer" 64, n.10). This is true especially in
the context of the two lines about husbands noted just above (ll. 272–
73). For another view, that such statements are "illocutionary acts," see
Dawson.

295–301 (stanza 24) In the simplest terms, this stanza refers to the astro-
nomical fact that precession very gradually, over the course of centuries,
moves the visible stars west to east, against the apparent daily and the
slower annual movement of the sky east to west. What makes Chaucer's
narrator's lament remarkable is the way he bemoans this movement rather
than regarding it more traditionally as harmonious. The friction of the
spheres as they were imagined to move against each other was usually
thought to be the source of the "music of the spheres."

301 (24:7) "Cruel Mars," imagined as the planet as well as the god of vio-
lence, has passed into an astrological configuration among the stars that
gives him a special potency.

302–8 (stanza 25) This astonishingly technical stanza would have been as
obscure to most people in Chaucer's time as it is to modern readers. The
Riverside Chaucer devotes a full page of small type to the stanza (revealing
that what Chaucer means by *atazir* is uncertain here) (858–59). The point
of it is made clear in the next stanza: astrologically, this is a bad time to be
setting out on a journey.

315 (26:7) Again Chaucer's narrator laments the fact that although the stars
may encode the secret of our destiny, we humans are incapable of reading
it. There may be some authorial irony when, despite the narrator's impas-
sioned despair about the configurations of the stars, Custance does survive
her journey.

321–22 (27:6–7) Though similarly abrupt "meanwhile back at the ranch"
transitions are also found in the other two romances, they are an element
of Chaucer's style of which he is probably conscious in a way that the other
authors are not.

360–61 (33:3–4) In medieval art, especially in pictures of Adam and Eve
standing beside the fatal tree, Satan is often depicted as a serpent having
the face of a young woman.

383 (36:5) Chaucer, with his consciousness of the power of gesture, adds the
effective detail of the sultan kneeling to his mother in gratitude.

404 (39:5) Because it poisons its victims with its tail rather than "more hon-
estly" from its mouth, the scorpion is a symbol of treachery. The image of

the mother as scorpion also echoes that of the sweet-faced Satan with his
serpent body in lines 360–61.

437–41 (44:3–7) In his argument that the Man of Law is a suitable teller for
this tale, Scheps points out that "the sultaness sees Custance as a threat
to the 'olde lawe' and uses a legal punishment to get rid of her" (292). See
the discussion of "setting adrift as legal punishment" at the end of chapter 1.

449–62 (stanzas 46–47) Custance's prayer to the Cross before beginning her
voyage may be meant to remind the reader of "the votive Mass invoking
the aid of the Cross for protection for travelers" (Eberle).

463–90 (stanzas 48–51) The motifs of Daniel, Jonah, and the crossing of the
Red Sea are often found together both in Christian art and liturgy, and in
art "the group is often joined by the figure of a woman praying" (Eberle).

482–83 (50:6–7) Again the narrator makes a contrast between a large de-
sign that surrounds us (in this case God's plan) and our inability as humans
to understand that design.

491–94 (52:1–4) These four angels of the winds are biblical, found in Reve-
lation 7:1–3 and represented on early maps.

500–503 (53:3–6) "Egyptian Mary" was a desert hermit said (in the *South
English Legendary*) to have lived off the land for forty-seven years after
taking only two and a half loaves of bread into the desert with her; Jesus'
famous miracle of feeding his five thousand hungry listeners with what
was on hand, five loaves and two fish, is recounted in all four gospels.

507–8 (54:3–4) It has been suggested that Chaucer "cannot name" this
castle that Trevet situates near the Humber because it evoked his patron
John of Gaunt's castle Pontefract, and that for the same reason he sup-
presses the placename Knaresborough in line 786 (94:2) below; both would
have aroused comparison of Custance with John's wife Constanza (Con-
stance) of Castile. But Chaucer suppresses the castle name so blatantly
that it seems he is aware that such a comparison is inevitable. Like Cust-
ance, Constanza was a foreign princess married to an Englishman whose
language she did not speak. Chaucer would have known the duchess fairly
well, since his wife Philippa was her lady-in-waiting, and he must have had
at least a minimal knowledge of Spanish, having been sent to Spain on a
diplomatic mission in 1366. Constanza died on March 25, 1394, around
the time that Chaucer may have been working on the *Man of Law's Tale*
(1390–94; see Eberle's note on the "Prologue," 856). Constanza's obsession
with her father, Don Pedro of Castile, may even have had something to do
with Chaucer's conscious omission of the incest theme, though in this he
is also following Trevet.

519 (56:1) "Corrupt Latin" seems to be a standard designation for the Ro-
mance languages. An equivalent term is used, for example, in the Anglo-
Norman romance of *Fouke le fitz Waryn*, where a young shepherd greets
Fulk and his brothers in "un latyn corumpus" (43). Like Custance in speak-

ing Italian, John of Gaunt's wife Constanza would have spoken a "corrupt Latin" in speaking Spanish. Trevet's better-educated Constance spoke Saxon among her several languages, useful when cast ashore in Anglo-Saxon Northumbria.

540–45 (59:1–6) Since Celtic Christianity had been established in Britain before the coming of the Germanic invaders, the situation presented here is perhaps not too far from the truth.

578 According to the Venerable Bede, Ælla reigned as King of Deira (in Northumbria) from 560 to 588 C.E.

585–88 (65:4–7) This lustful knight is analogous to Macary in *Florence*. Chaucer does not bother, however, to give him any name or personality.

600–601 (67:5–6) The same scene occurs in *Florence*, only with a daughter as the victim instead of a wife. The "Empress of Rome" tale told by Christine de Pisan makes the victim a child. (See note for *Florence*, l. 1624.)

630 (71:7) The "fight" is an ordeal by combat. The accused is responsible for obtaining a champion, a surrogate to fight on her behalf, and the outcome will determine whether she should be punished or not. The most famous of all such medieval trials by ordeal is Guenivere's trial when she has apparently poisoned a knight visiting Arthur's court. At the last moment Lancelot comes to her rescue, "proving" her innocence as he wins the combat.

639 (73:2) The biblical Suzanna was also falsely charged, and divinely rescued by God speaking through the young prophet Daniel. Her story is told in the thirteenth chapter of the book of Daniel.

645–51 (stanza 74) Chaucer's analogy here has been pointed out as one of the most effective moments in this emotional story.

669 (77:4) God's hand descending from the clouds is a motif frequently seen in medieval art, more commonly (though not always) in a gesture of blessing rather than striking. See figure 7.

675–77 (78:2–4) Attention has been drawn to Psalm 49:2 (AV 50:3), but the Psalmist says there that God shall *not* keep silent (i.e., hold his peace), the opposite of what God says in the tale. This discrepancy is curious, and I cannot account for it. Kolve bases much of his allegorical interpretation of Custance upon God's claiming of her here as the "Daughter of Holy Church."

723 (85:2) Trevet attached the Castaway Queen story to historical personages, having his Constance be Constantia, the daughter of the Byzantine Emperor Tiberius Constantinus, who died in 582 C.E., and casting her son as Mauricius Flavius Tiberius (ca. 539–602), who succeeded him. The real Mauricius was not born in Northumbria. Stories like this of the Castaway Queen are several times attached to the mothers of popes, saints, and emperors in order to provide the famous son with a birth story (see chapter 3).

771–77 (stanza 92) This stanza is one of many passages in the text based upon the *De contemptu mundi.* The text is glossed in some manuscripts with the Latin original, which is identified there by its title. This passage is found in Innocent III's *De miseria condicionis humanae* (2.12.1–4), which Chaucer was apparently translating at the time he wrote, or revised, the *Man of Law's Tale.* He offers the title himself in the list of his works in the F Prologue of *The Legend of Good Women:* "Of the Wreched Engendrynge of Mankynde / As man may in pope Innocent yfynde" (ll. 144–45).

834–68 (stanzas 101–5) Eberle points out how Chaucer changes this scene radically from that by Trevet, who merely says ironically: "Then, on the fourth day she was exiled with Maurice her dear son, who (thus) learned sailing at a tender age." Like Chaucer, Gower presents an emotionally affecting scene at this point. The reader's attention is directed to Chaucer's sense of gesture in lines 837–38 (101:4–5).

847 (102:7) There is a question whether the word "woman" in the original text should be read as one word or two ("wo man"), that is, as I have translated it, or as follows: "And there is no comparison between / Your woe and any *woe man* may sustain." "Woman" seems to me the more likely reading, since Custance is referring to Christ's crucifixion at this point, and she is being very sensitive in comparing her own woe to that of the Virgin Mary.

904–24 (stanzas 111–13) This briefly told adventure corresponds to Florence's struggle with the sea captain (stanzas 155–57), where that heroine also is aided by the Virgin. Both women, however, are very active in struggling to protect themselves, *not* passive victims!

925–31 (stanza 114) Again, this is a translation from Pope Innocent's work, glossed in Latin and identified in the manuscript as *De contemptu mundi.*

947 (117:2) "Septe" (pronounced Sept-ay) refers to the seven-peaked ridge, the *septem fratres,* or "seven brothers," opposite Gibraltar, a famous landmark important to navigators.

971–73 (120:5–7) Like Emaré, Custance prefers to keep her identity a secret.

974–75 (121:1–2) The heroine of these romances frequently spends some time in domestic service.

980 (122:1) The coincidental relationship explains why the senator who has given Custance shelter knows her father Alla when he comes to Rome. In Trevet's version the senator's wife is Constance's cousin.

1048–50 (131:5–7) Custance still believes that Alla had intended her and her child to be killed by being set adrift. In the story that Christine de Pisan tells, the husband does specifically order his wife to be slain. No wonder that at the end of that version of the story she chooses to remain a nun!

1086–92 (137) This stanza is surely a comment on other versions of the story.

1121 (142:1) See the note for line 723 (85:2).

1126–27 (142:56–7) "Apparently a reference to Roman history in general . . . rather than to the *Gesta Romanorum*, where the life of Maurice does not appear" (Eberle). Perhaps this is even a reference to Trevet's *Chronicle*, with which Chaucer had been working.

1132–38 (143:5–144:4) Several Latin glosses appear on these lines, all from Innocent III's *De miseria*.

1153 (146:5) Note that Custance is not kneeling submissively to her father, as has been assumed, but gratefully to God for bringing her home.

CHAPTER 3: BACKTRACKING THE GODDESS

1. I use "icons" in the sense proposed by Victor and Edith Turner in *Image and Pilgrimage*, as "heraldic or conventional emblems" (142), but including that additional element of mystery and radiance that one finds in Russian icons.

2. In contrast to this assertion, Carol P. Christ eloquently questions the dependability of written texts and defends meanings gleaned from careful attention to artifacts in her article "Mircea Eliade," 86–87.

3. It is significant for this transmission of the classical material to the medieval period that in the medieval romances the name "Machary" for a villain unrelated to the heroine who attempts to rape her, a name occurring in other stories as well as that of Florence, is the brother's name in the classical story of sibling incest that Ovid tells of Canacee and Macarius in his *Heroides* (64–69: *Canace Macareo*). This is a story that Chaucer, according to his Man of Law, would not think of telling ("Introduction to the Man of Law's Tale," ll. 77–80).

4. See Archibald, *Apollonius* 37–44, for discussion of the historical associations of this late classical romance.

5. For various perspectives on this political aspect of Mary's story and its implications see, among others, Stone, *When God Was a Woman* (the book is inspired by her concerns about this appropriation), Spong (201–24), Baring and Cashford (547–608), and most importantly Warner.

6. In many myths, instead of being cast adrift with his mother as in the myth of Perseus and in *Emaré* and *Custance*, the child destined to be hero or ruler arrives alone—in a boat (Scyld Scefing in *Beowulf*), or basket (Moses), or leather bag (Taliesin), or naked on the wave (Tennyson's King Arthur), or flying house (Dorothy in Oz; she is one of the rare female benefactors thus to arrive), or alien spacecraft (Superman). These are just a few of such heroes famous within our culture; each story shows aspects of the same arrival myth. This mysterious arrival from "elsewhere" is a worldwide theme, as Hares-Stryker has shown with examples from several unrelated cultures

("Adrift" 85–88). She evocatively concludes, "Heroes enter the world not born of flesh but borne by vessels that logic dictates would sink like stones if they were the bearers of cargo less precious" (ibid. 88). Besides adding "the magical and mystical element" (ibid. 85) to a hero's life-story, however, the theme of the child borne thus to the shore where he or she is needed often has the political function of making the establishment of a religion or dynasty appear ineluctably fated, or desired and enforced by a supernatural agency. Also important to this theme is the fact that children really were (and are) abandoned for various reasons, often because they are the result of an unsanctioned relationship or to save them from danger in their present situation. Setting a child adrift where it was sure to come to shore could assuage the mother's conscience and give her hope that it would encounter the kindness of strangers.

The mysterious journey by sea features also at the end of numerous hero-king stories as part of his mystique, in some stories (those of King Arthur and Quetzalcoatl, for example) allowing for the possibility of return at his people's hour of greatest need. Stories *always* reflect in some way certain social conditions, structures, and desires of the society in which they are told. They may also reflect the more simple facts of life, like the changing of the seasons, as these are incorporated into the patterns of a culture. Mandt offers Oscar Almgren's 1927 reading of the god (hero, etc.) in the boat as a seasonal myth, probably reenacted in ritual: "According to old myths and legends the fertility god celebrated his wedding when visiting his people. He was killed by a rival, however, and his dead body was taken on a ship to an island. This happened in the autumn, and the vegetation died simultaneously. In the following spring, however, the god rose from the dead and sailed back to his people, and the vegetation revived" (45).

7. I use this careful term because the Virgin Mary, to whom the ritual is transferred, is not, strictly speaking, a goddess. The Second Council of Nicaea in 787 C.E. decreed that the Virgin Mary might be adored but was not to be worshiped as divine. The word "numinous," made popular by Rudolph Otto in *The Idea of the Holy,* meaning "mysterious, divine," comes from the Latin *numen,* "a god or presiding spirit," and is related to Sanskrit *návate,* "moves." For me it also contains a hint of its rhyme-word "luminous," thus referring to the special radiance of a saintly person that is indicated in art by a halo.

8. Marina Warner explains that the phrase *Ave Maris Stella* in the Office of the Virgin comes from a misunderstanding of Jerome's identification of the Hebrew name Miriam as *stilla maris,* a drop of the sea. "The sway of astronomy over the medieval imagination was so strong, and the Virgin so closely identified with the heavens, that the slip of a scribe's hand introduced into Marian literature and art one of its most suggestive and beautiful metaphors.

For an early copyist wrote *stella maris,* star of the sea, instead of *stilla maris,* a mistake that persisted until the most recent edition of Jerome's *On the Interpretation of Hebrew Names*" (262).

9. Not every representation of a woman in a boat in Europe and the Near East is included in this discussion. A striking omission is the representation on a Roman altar in Holland of the apparently Germanic goddess Nehalennia, standing with one foot in a little boat, the other on shore beside her hound. Mandt offers a fine photograph of this altar (45, fig. 19). Since we possess no context for Nehalennia, anything said of her must be guarded, as are Mandt's words: "Many of the myths [of seasonal renewal associated with a god in a boat] describe a male deity as the leading character of the drama, but significantly several . . . sources refer to or depict a woman as the main participant, associated in some way with a boat. Included are the Roman goddess Isis and the German goddess Nehalennia" (45–46). The last pages of this chapter will offer a further context in which some may wish to place Nehalennia.

10. For example, "what must have been one of the greatest Isis-Serapis sanctuaries in the Graeco-Roman world" (Wild 275) existed at Thessalonica, not far from Lake Loudias, or Volvi as it was formerly called. At this sanctuary a tablet was found recording a ceremony like the Navigium Isidis in the second century B.C.E. A water facility there bears a first century B.C.E. dedication to "Isis and all the other gods," and nearby stand buildings of later construction including a crypt possibly used for initiation—in Wild's view "the most interesting of all [such] structures" (190, see fig. 30). Because of the death of the chief investigator before he published his findings, most of the material, including eighty or so inscriptions, had not been published by 1981, the date of Wild's book (275). I suspect the research potential of this area is relatively untapped by scholars. There are numerous hot sulphur springs on the *Via* east of the city and along Lake Volvi, where a modern spa provides facilities at Nea Apollonia, my imaginary site for Florence's convent.

Heffernan notes in connection with the *roche* upon which shipwrecked Florence lands (stanza 161:6), "In the twelfth century Latin Miracle version of the tale the empress is exposed on a rock in the middle of a river" (148). Changing the site to a named lake, or at this time an inlet of the sea (its entrance became silted up to form a lake later, and it has now been drained for pastureland), would seem to be part of the English poet's strategy to give precise location to the romance.

11. Those familiar with the story of *Beowulf,* the Anglo-Saxon poem about a hero who kills three monsters—first in Denmark the man-eating, troll-like Grendel, then Grendel's Mother in her lake, and then, fifty years later and far away, a dragon—may have been reminded of that story here.

Although it is very unlikely indeed that the *Florence* author knew either of *Beowulf*, which did not have the wide availability of a folk epic, or of the goddess Bolbe, it is nevertheless fascinating to see here a distant cousinhood between this Greek lake goddess with her son nearby on land and Grendel's Mother in her lake or mere. Both Bolbe and Grendel's Mother seem related to an earlier goddess of abundance of whom the Greek Bolbe is, one might say, a daughter, and to whom in turn Grendel's unnamed mother in her Danish appearance is the deformed and troll-like cousin several times removed. Through the lenses of cultural change and the Christian poet's background, the Greek sacrifice to honor the son has become in *Beowulf* the monster Grendel's cannibalism, and the Mother has become demonized, a candidate for the heroic slaying.

12. In 431 the Council of Ephesus decreed that she had been there and proclaimed Mary *Theotokos* (Warner 87). Marina Warner recounts the story of the nineteenth-century German mystic named Catherine Emmerich (died 1824), whose visions apparently resulted in a find offering warranty for this Ephesian claim. The young woman's visions revealed to her "the house and tomb of the Virgin at Ephesus, a place she had never visited. Her revelations, published in 1876, sent eager archaeologists to the sites described, where they did indeed find some very ancient foundations—including a tiny first-century house, believed to be the Virgin's" (88).

13. Accompanying it with a fine plate (22), Harrison tells the story: "For a long time no one thought to doubt that these bulbs were breasts symbolizing the goddess's superabundant fertility, but then someone looked closer and remarked on their strange lack of plastic realism. In short, a group of Austrian archaeologists recently confirmed that these protrusions do not represent breasts after all but rather the testicles of bulls. The fact is corroborated by evidence uncovered at Ephesus which indicates that on her festival days Artemis's priests would castrate several bulls, string the scrotums together, and then place the gruesome garlands around a wooden image of the goddess, which her votives would then follow in an ecstatic procession from her sacred altar to the center of the city" (20–21).

14. In a private communication, Miriam Robbins Dexter calls my attention to the Hebrew Song of Songs (7:8), "in which the breasts of the beloved are compared to clusters of dates." In the King James Version of the Bible, the translation chosen is "grapes." Carol P. Christ describes the objects on the upper torso of Artemis as her "many egg breasts" ("Mircea Eliade" 92).

15. The song implies a real sea, but the sea in its violent aspect often served as a metaphor for human torment more generally, and Mary could be called upon as sea-savior in that regard as well. Marina Warner quotes Petrarch's *canzone* in which he invokes the Virgin "as the star that holds sway over his life, and pleads for her help" (263). I give only the translation that

she offers: "Bright virgin, steadfast in eternity, / Star of this storm-tossed sea, / Trusted guide of every trustful pilot / Turn your thoughts to the terrifying squall / In which I find myself, alone and rudderless."

16. Rickert develops her argument, incorporating that of Gough, in her long, and to an Anglo-Saxonist fascinating, section on "Origins" (edition xxxii–xlvii). Despite my disagreement with her conclusions in the light of evidence chiefly by Schick and Archibald, the northern associations of several of these romances, both English and Continental, may be significant in some way. Perhaps one should take account of the fact that a cultic water site was dedicated to Isis at York in the second or third century c.e., the inscription still legible today (Wild 209). The Alla whom Custance converts to Christianity is based on King Ælla of Deira, the kingdom in which York lies; he is the king who with his province and his people inspired Gregory the Great's famous "Angles/Angels" wordplay sanctioning the pope's wish to convert the English in the story recounted by Bede (99–100). Gregory sent Augustine as his missionary in 597 c.e. to a country whose displaced population was already partially Christian (as noted in Custance's story). When Erasmus visited England in the early sixteenth century, he saw in a manuscript an account from the time of Ethelbert of Kent of "a ceremony of depositing a deer's head upon the altar of St. Paul's church, which was built upon the site of a temple of Diana" (Clarke 2:139n). Ethelbert built a church dedicated to Saint Peter and Saint Paul in 602 c.e. according to Bede (91), but he does not mention the goddess Diana, and I cannot imagine what manuscript Erasmus saw. Nevertheless, his comment suggests a long and continuous history of interest in pagan antiquities in England. Though, as we have seen, Gough, Rickert, and Schlauch are mistaken in assigning the origins of the basic plot of the "Constance saga" to the north of England, it is nevertheless the case that local lore and native chronicle traditions of northern history had a strong effect on the stories these romancers told.

17. I owe thanks to Miriam Robbins Dexter for drawing my attention to this poem.

18. Compare, for example, Stone in *When God Was a Woman*, Ruether in *Gaia and God*, 115–201, and Renfrew, "Origins," 110–14.

19. Heyob begins her chapter on "Morality and the Cult of Isis" with the following statement: "Until the recent outburst of scholarship on the cult of the Egyptian deities, mention of the goddess Isis seems primarily to have evoked thoughts of the sexual immorality of her adherents" (111). She then proceeds to place the negative statements of the elegiac poets Martial and Juvenal and the historian Josephus into their proper perspective, demonstrating that, while "certain possibilities for immoral actions did exist within the confines of the temple of Isis . . . the religion was not a cult of the demimonde, nor was sexual freedom a characteristic of the cult" (126). Tannahill sums up the situation well: Isis became a favorite goddess of the Roman ma-

trons, "so that misogynists inevitably attributed all the trappings of female sensuality to her worship. They had a field day in A.D. 19 when a gullible young matron, Paulina, believing that she had spent the night in holy intercourse with Isis's associated god Anubis, discovered that the god's part had been played by one of her own entirely mortal admirers. [Because they allowed this to happen,] the outcome was crucifixion for the priests of Isis, and the deportation of a great number of worshipers to the mosquito-ridden island of Sardinia, where, as Tiberius said, 'If the climate killed them they would not be missed'" (120). The first century historian Josephus tells the story of the scandal in a section of Book 18 of his *Jewish Antiquities,* which Meyer anthologizes (193–96).

20. I am indebted to Anne Sullivan for directing me to this passage and to that by George Eliot quoted in chapter 1 and again shortly below.

21. The rock carvings of this culture, which on their warriors feature the male genitalia so strikingly, often seem to distinguish women by cupmarks between their legs. See Mandt, especially 40–41 and 47–48.

22. A watered-down version apparently of the same goddess occurs in the person of Mere-Ama, venerated by the Finns and Lapps according to Patricia Monaghan. She tells us that Mere-Ama "ruled sea creatures, especially the fish on whom her people depended for food. To woo her good nature, humans only had to pour liquor into the sea, then many fish would bite when fishing began, for Mere-Ama loved brandy" (201–2). I have it on good authority that similar libations are made to certain lake-goddesses in the north. I am inclined to think these goddesses of the waters may bear some relationship to Inuit Sedna, since certain rituals and stories of the far north appear to have a circumpolar dispersal.

23. The psychological power of this tale of severed hands is emphasized by two books published recently by Jungian psychologists. Instead of including them in the general list of Works Cited, I give full citations here. In *Here All Dwell Free: Stories to Heal the Wounded Feminine* (New York: Fawcett Columbine, 1991), Gertrud Mueller Nelson, who studied at Jung's Institute in Zurich with his student Marie-Louise von Franz, meditates upon a Swahili analogue to discover in the maiden's loss of hands a *choice* to be feminine and "helpless." In Part 4 of her book, she provides an interesting international collection of tales related to the version by Grimm with which she begins, and on page 333 she refers to a depth-psychology study by Eugen Drewermann: *Das Mädchen ohne Hände: Grimms Märchen Tiefenpsychologische Gedeutet* (Breisgau, Germany: Walter-Verlag, 1981). Robert A. Johnson suggests a similar approach to what he terms "the wounded feeling function" in *The Fisher King and the Handless Maiden: Understanding the Wounded Feeling Function in Masculine and Feminine Psychology* (San Francisco: Harper SanFrancisco, 1993). In a footnote on page 9 he graciously defers to his predecessor: "I am reasonably at home in discussing the mas-

culine dimension of this ubiquitous problem, but I embark on the feminine dimension of it with some trepidation. I refer the reader to Gertrude Nelson's book . . . for her feminine wisdom on this dimension of the wound."

24. As I cite Walter Burkert throughout this section, it should be noted that I make no effort to relate what I take from him to his more general discussion. His *Homo Necans* offers a new theory of religion that is a subject too vast to take up here. What he describes there as a "Copernican Revolution" (37), however, is a way of looking at myth that informs my own discussion throughout, especially in this section. He sums up that revolutionary new way of looking in a more recent essay, "The Problem of Ritual Killing": "Ritual is not to be understood as incorporating an 'antecedent idea,' not as the secondary manifestation of spiritual belief, but as communicative activity prescribed by tradition; ideas and beliefs are produced by ritual, rather than vice versa" (156). Stories, above all, may be produced to explain and justify or give a narrative dimension to ritual.

CHAPTER 4: GODDESS OF THE HUMAN DAWN

1. Such blanket identifications of all the small statues of prehistoric cultures as representing a single "Goddess" receive just criticism: "Certainly, the worship of a goddess of some kind is very probable for Neolithic Çatal Hüyük, where fertility cults and a Mother Goddess are historically attested for later periods. . . . But if it is reasonable to assert that a goddess of some kind was worshipped in this Neolithic village, can the same explanation be given for *all* the figurines found for the Paleolithic and Neolithic?" (Biehl 34, her emphasis). Thirty years ago the prehistorian André Leroi-Gourhan similarly objected to describing these figures uniformly as "Venuses," thus evoking a sexuality that some even thought pornographic: "In reality one knows nothing about the deep meaning that the Paleolithic peoples gave to their 'Venuses,' who could just as well be 'Junos' or 'Proserpines.'" [En réalité on ne sait rien sur le sens profond que les Paléolithiques donnaient a leurs "Vénus" qui pouvaient aussi bien être des "Junons" ou "Proserpines"] (124). The most skeptical voice I have encountered to date is that of Douglass W. Bailey: "Traditionally archaeologists have read prehistoric anthropomorphic figurines as images of gods, goddesses or ritual supplicants. These readings have neither philosophical nor archaeological support" (321). Bailey reads the figures as "individual identities" (327–29). Ehrenberg offers a spectrum of interpretations (73–76).

2. Campbell expresses doubt about the mammoth-ivory medium (166), but a more recent find makes the association between "goddess" and mammoth-hunting more explicit: "At a site in Siberia, twenty-seven mammoth skulls were found set up in a circle around a central point where a female statuette lay buried beneath a pile of bones and partially worked tusks"

(Burkert, *Homo Necans* 14). Gimbutas shows three of the geese in *Language* (4, fig. 8), and Alfred Salmony provides excellent plates including all the major carvings in his 1931 article on the women-with-geese find. The small figures of women are more elongated than the famous "Venus" figures of farther south, a shape perhaps dictated by the bone from which they are carved. Although the geese carved in the round are the "artistic highpoint" [künstlerischen Höhepunkt] of the find according to Salmony (5), making it unique in its quality, the figures of women are not unusual for the period: "'Venus' figurines are relatively common on leptolithic sites; indeed a high proportion of all the known Venuses came from the USSR" (Whitehouse and Whitehouse 36). Baring and Cashford assume the mammoth-ivory medium of these statues throughout their discussion (e.g., 13) and date the Siberian site between 16,000 and 13,000 B.C.E. (referring to no authority, 24). Stone omits northern Eurasia entirely from her schematic date charts for archaeological finds in *When God Was a Woman*, 242–45.

3. Jacques Cauvin's thesis challenges V. Gordon Childe's classical theory of a "Neolithic revolution" (Childe's term), which posited a change in climate followed by the beginnings of sedentary agriculture and an ensuing population explosion. Cauvin argues instead that a slow cultural and religious evolution (not a change in climate) established the conditions that were to create agriculture, and that the "goddess" figures constitute a major witness to this evolution (Cauvin "L'Apparition" and *Naissance*). While some retain the model of radical change, perhaps a change due to a clash of cultures like that caused by Gimbutas's proposed Kurgan hordes, other modern archaeologists argue, similarly to Cauvin but from different premises, for a "processual" evolution rather than dramatic sudden change (e.g., Renfrew).

4. Luhrmann writes concerning this question of belief among modern practitioners of the Craft in England: "Witches have talked to me about the 'duality' of their religious understanding, that on the one hand the Goddess merely personifies the natural world in myth and imagery, and that on the other hand the Goddess is there as someone. . . . I suspect that for practitioners there is a natural slippage from metaphor to extant being, that it is difficult—particularly in a Judaeo-Christian society—genuinely to treat a deity-figure as only a metaphor, regardless of how the religion is rationalized. The figure becomes a deity, who cares for you" (47).

5. Townsend explains, "We can begin to talk about a shift in the conceptualizing of deities into a hierarchical pantheon or a single paramount deity, something like what we are familiar with, about 5,000 B.C.E. or slightly earlier" (94).

6. This dualism results in a curious conflict of attitudes. On the one hand Eliade presents his early "man" as terrified by expanse, "an apparently limitless, unknown, and threatening extension" (Christ, "Mircea Eliade" 82, quoting him), which Christ rightly condemns as anachronistic in the way it

displays an existentialist sense of alienation from nature and community (83). But on the other hand he presents transcendence as the supreme (paternal) good, while conceiving of it spatially as "height" (80). This may be one of those points at which standard metaphor and personal feeling come into conflict: led by Western concepts of God as a sky god up there, beyond, Eliade thinks of transcendence in those terms, while probably suffering, as his sympathetic projection of the fears of early "man" suggests, from mild agoraphobia himself. Spatial concepts are particularly important in this chapter.

7. In the Near East especially there are clear links between trees and other Goddess symbols; see Levy (89–122) and Neumann (240–67) for discussion and pictures, and Stone, *When God Was a Woman* (214–18) for implications of the Goddess-tree connection for the Eden story. In the Meso-American myth of Mayahuel comes an episode of women (goddesses) eating from the virgin-tree, the goddess Mayahuel in tree form, that echoes Stone's feminization of the Eden story (Markman and Markman 214).

8. This unabashedly sentimental projection, that a skeptic like Biehl might with justice describe as "more characteristic of Disneyland exhibitions than authentic folk traditions" (47), is nevertheless based on the fact that bird-goddesses (for example valkyries and angels) are often imagined as agents conveying the souls of the dead between realms of being. What is one to make, however, of the "disquieting evidence of human sacrifice in these early cultures," including "infant graves" that to Gimbutas herself "suggest a ritual offering of small children"? (Biehl, citing Gimbutas, 32). The Goddess is not always so benign as I imagine her at the Baikal burial.

9. The Episcopalian bishop John Shelby Spong severely criticizes the church's promotion of Mary as the ideal woman: "Who can be such an ideal? Who can be a virgin mother? A virgin mother is a contradiction in terms. If that was to be the feminine ideal, accepted and saluted by church and world alike, then in one stroke every other woman was and is rendered inadequate, incomplete, incompetent. Celibate males who constituted the decision-making body of the church had succeeded in defining the ideal woman in such a way as to universalize guilt among women" (Spong 218). At the end of his eloquent book he says, "The only hope for the survival of the virgin Mary as a viable symbol is her redefinition by the new consciousness. A male-dominated church will resist this with its dying breath" (224).

Yet the Virgin of Guadalupe is one such redefinition that has sustained generations of Latin Americans, men and women alike. Rodriguez argues that this is in great part due to her assimilation to native culture. For example, the site at which Juan Diego's visionary Virgin wished her temple to be built was the hill called Tepcyac, which "had previously been the shrine of Tonantzin, an earth goddess and one of the major divinities of the Aztec people" (Rodriguez 41). Other features of the story, including the representation of the Virgin herself in the painting on Juan's coat, further connect her with powerful myths established within the culture. At the same time, the out-of-season roses at the top of the hill, which the Virgin instructs Juan to gather to confirm the miracle of his vision, represent an old-world symbol long associated with the Virgin Mary, and before her connected with the divine power of Isis to transform and regenerate. The living power of that symbol may be seen in figure 4.

Through passages from the Book of Wisdom and other Old Testament sources that seemed to apply to her, Mary became associated with the concept of Sophia, personified Wisdom (Johnson 100). Sophia in turn also owes much to Isis: "There is very little doubt among scholars that Jewish authors both at home and abroad transferred characteristics of the mighty Isis to the figure of Sophia in a creative effort to counteract the religious and social attractiveness of this most popular deity" (ibid. 92–93; see also Warner *passim*). There are thus powerful goddesses of both European and American cultures that have become part of the post-biblical understanding of the Virgin Mary, suggesting that further redefinition along such lines is possible.

10. The hymn "In the Garden" composed by Austin Miles in 1913 follows the convention of capitalizing "He" to indicate the divinity of Christ, who is, of course, the hymnist's friend in the garden. I prefer in this context to retain the more usual lower-case spelling of the pronoun because there was no sense in my experience that the comforting presence was divine. On the other hand, since I am speaking throughout this book of a figuration of the divine in female form, I capitalize the word "Goddess" when using it in this way.

11. Actually, the *advice* of Don Juan reminded me to become aware of my hands, but I restored them (i.e., my ability to function) myself, aware all along that Don Juan was a fictive character. I am using "saint" here only to align the experience with that of the Castaway Queen in those versions of the stories where she loses her hands, or their use, eventually to be healed supernaturally. Laurie Hatch has observed to me that both of my figures that represent a healing process within, Don Juan and the woman in the wheat, appeared to me as "externalized projected benevolences . . . like so much of religion that has a deity in it." Recent feminist religious discourse repeatedly refers to the Goddess as representing a strength within rather than an objective deity. Nevertheless, as James Hillman argues in his book *Re-Visioning Psychology*, projection is one way of finding out what is going on inside: "Our point here is not to reduce demons to complexes or complexes back to an old demonology, but to insist that *psychology so needs mythology that it creates one as it proceeds. A mythic manner of speaking is fundamental to the soul's way of formulating itself*" (20, his emphasis). The difficulty is to maintain awareness that the projection is mythic.

12. I enjoy being given a story that makes narrative sense out of the rich materials of the find that Gimbutas works with at Çatal Hüyük. I like the

epic drama of her particular story and the way it makes sense of the vanishing of the goddess figures, and also of the way the later myth reduces goddesses to mothers and daughters of gods—as a result of the invasion of those Sky-Father-worshiping Indo-European "hordes." It all makes sense in a narrative that holds together; see *Civilization* (352) for a recent summary version of the story. On the basis of converging data from a variety of disciplines, Colin Renfrew has proposed an alternative, less dramatic, story of a spread of agriculture and language changing cultures more gradually from within, and flowing from Anatolia north to affect those hordes of the Steppes themselves. For a critique of his views, see Everson. Indo-Europeanists are still discussing the evidence and trying to account for it in various ways.

13. For the supposed male conspiracy to suppress Goddess-worship itself, see Merlin Stone, *When God Was a Woman*, which also, however, contains much fascinating material and is persuasive concerning the designs of the Levite priesthood in particular (198–223). Concerning the other male conspiracy, to cover up modern scholarly data proving the existence of these matristic, Goddess-worshiping cultures, I refer to Sally R. Binford's ironic and cynical discussion: "In recent years, several women authors such as Elizabeth Gould Davis in *The First Sex* and Merlin Stone in *When God Was a Woman* have revived the notion that humanity experienced a golden age of matriarchy in the past. This belief has been combined with the assertion that there is a conspiracy against its acceptance, making those who question the faith subject to suspicion of being co-conspirators. I am the last to deny that anthropology—perhaps even more than other academic enterprises—is dominated by sexist males. I am, however, equally persuaded that if a male anthropologist discovered evidence of past matriarchies, he would publish his findings rather than suppress them. . . . The unique discovery of matriarchal cultural systems would also guarantee research grants, and I cannot believe that any academic male social scientist would suppress his findings on principle, thereby denying himself funding" (Binford 544). She goes on to say that "myths are not appropriate primary data for reconstructing the past" (544), pointing out that the Noah story "tells us nothing of past geologic processes" (545).

The surprisingly virulent responses printed after Binford's article confirm what Binford calls (slightingly, it is true) "the New Feminist Fundamentalism" (547). Merlin Stone claims that Binford's "own reference to belief in Goddess reverence as 'madness' not only reveals an intolerable religious bigotry but perhaps explains her problem in absorbing and comprehending this massive body of information" (551). Binford had referred to a conference at the University of California at Santa Cruz as concerned with "the Mother Goddess/Matriarchy madness" (543), and she does use language likely to stir heated response. Charlene Spretnak, the editor of the volume, concludes the discussion with a further scathing (and essentialist, see 560–61) dismissal of Binford's views as exhibiting "patriarchal thought" (554).

14. In her book *Of Witches,* Janet Thompson offers an eloquent evocation of "the experience of witchcraft as a healing and gentle religion" (xiv), wholly rejecting the negative elements of Satanism.

15. Rupprecht summarizes a theory, "transitionally," that rejects "the mental process of analytical separation, categorization, and claims of objectivity in order to include the effects of unconscious processes on cognitive ones" (Lauter and Rupprecht 236), endorsing it as one important way of regarding female experience.

16. This sense of amplitude or extension is not required by everyone. Carol P. Christ informs us that "some would assert that the Goddess definitely is *not* 'out there,' that the symbol of a divinity 'out there' is part of the legacy of patriarchal oppression, which brings with it authoritarianism, hierarchicalism, and dogmatic rigidity associated with biblical monotheistic religions." But then she adds, "They might assert that the Goddess symbol reflects the sacred power within women and nature, suggesting the connectedness between women's cycles of menstruation, birth, and menopause, and the life and death cycles of the universe" ("Why Women Need" 76). This definition suits me just fine. The universe to which she refers seems pretty thoroughly "out there" (visible through a telescope), yet the Gaia principle, which is receiving increasing attention often in association with the Goddess symbol, would embrace it in a connectedness extending within and without. The startling extension of the universe currently being revealed by modern astronomy is also part of "Gaia." Starhawk, whose very name soars us away, "out there," asserts the inner-outer continuum when defining the Goddess in contrast to the Christian God, imagined as wholly Other: "The symbolism of the Goddess is not a parallel structure to the symbolism of God the Father. The Goddess does not rule the world; She *is* the world. Manifest in each of us . . ." (51). An objection to a deity having "outside" extension on the basis that such extension is an androcentric "othering" marks a phase of religious feminism establishing the Goddess as non-God (i.e., not a male Sky-Father) and may now be regarded as exclusionary in a manner contrary to the religious and ethical ideas that the Goddess discussion on the whole is proposing.

17. When I mentioned to another scientist my skepticism about the assertion that there "must" be life out there (not necessarily intelligent life), he agreed with my astronomer-brother and quoted to me the scientists' maxim, "Once is a miracle, twice is a statistic." Yet how far does one take this? Is intelligent life then a "miracle" (in the popular understanding of the term)?

18. The name by which we know this most famous manifestation of the

Virgin in the Americas, the "Virgin of Guadalupe," is the result of a further cultural assimilation. The Spaniards listening to Juan Diego's account heard the Nahuatl word *Tlecuauhtacupeuh* as "Guadalupe," a name from the landscape of Spain with which it resonates (Rodriguez 45). Yet this probably inadvertent appropriation through naming has by no means subverted the power of the image for native worshipers, who still can see with their own eyes that this *virgencita* is one of them. Rodriguez documents and analyzes how this perception helps Mexican-American women in particular to affirm their sense of self-worth (61–158).

Works Cited
and Selected Editions

Allen, Richard Hinckley. *Star Names: Their Lore and Meaning.* New York: Dover, 1963.

Apollonius of Tyre. See Archibald.

Apuleius. *The Golden Ass.* Trans. P. G. Walsh. Oxford: Clarendon Press, 1994.

Archibald, Elizabeth. *Apollonius of Tyre: Medieval and Renaissance Themes and Variations, Including the Text of the Historia Apollonii Regis Tyri with an English Translation.* Cambridge: D. S. Brewer, 1991.

———. "The Case of the Female Foundling: Gender and Genre in Lai le Freine" (conference abstract). *Chronica* (Journal of the Medieval Association of the Pacific) 53 (1996): 14.

———. "The Flight from Incest: Two Late Classical Precursors of the Constance Theme." *Chaucer Review* 20 (1986): 259–72.

———. "Incest in Medieval Literature and Society." *Forum for Modern Language Studies* 25 (1989): 1–15.

Auerbach, Erich. *Mimesis: The Representation of Reality in Western Literature.* Trans. Willard R. Trask. Princeton: Princeton University Press, 1953.

Bailey, Douglass W. "Reading Prehistoric Figurines as Individuals." *World Archaeology* 25:3 (Feb. 1994): 321–31.

Bárðar Saga. Ed. and trans. Jón Skaptason and Phillip Pulsiano. New York: Garland, 1984.

Baring, Anne, and Jules Cashford. *The Myth of the Goddess: Evolution of an Image.* London: Viking Arkana, 1991.

Barron, W. R. J. *English Medieval Romance.* London: Longmans, 1987.

Barstow, Anne L. "The Prehistoric Goddess." In Olson, 7–15.

Barthes, Roland. *Mythologies.* Trans. Annette Lavers. London: Jonathan Cape, 1972.

Basso, Keith H. *Portraits of "The Whiteman": Linguistic Plan and Cultural Symbols among the Western Apache.* Cambridge: Cambridge University Press, 1979.

Bede. *A History of the English Church and People.* Trans. Leo Sherley-Price, rev. R. E. Latham. Harmondsworth: Penguin, 1968.

Bédier, Joseph. *The Romance of Tristan and Iseult.* New York: Pantheon, 1964 [1945].

Begg, Ean C. M. *The Cult of the Black Virgin.* London: Arkana, 1985.

Bennett, J. A. W., and G. V. Smithers. *Early Middle English Verse and Prose.* 2d ed. Oxford: Oxford University Press, 1982.

Benson, C. D., and E. Robertson, eds. *Chaucer's Religious Tales.* Cambridge: D. S. Brewer, 1990.

Benson, Larry D., ed. *The Learned and the Lewed: Studies in Chaucer and Medieval Literature.* Harvard English Studies 5. Cambridge: Harvard University Press, 1974. (See Donovan and Lee.)

Beowulf and the Fight at Finnsburg. Ed. Fr. Klaeber. Boston: D. C. Heath, 1950.

Biehl, Janet. *Rethinking Ecofeminist Politics.* Boston: South End Press, 1991.

Binford, Sally R. "Are Goddesses and Matriarchies Merely Figments of Feminist Imagination? Myths and Matriarchies." In Spretnak, 541–49.

Birnbaum, Lucia Chiavola. *Black Madonnas: Feminism, Religion, and Politics in Italy.* Boston: Northeastern University Press, 1993.

Blanch, Robert J., and Julian N. Wasserman. *From Pearl to Gawain: Forme to Fynisment.* Gainsville: University Press of Florida, 1995.

Bleeker, C. J. "Isis as Saviour Goddess." In Brandon, 1–16.

Boccaccio, Giovanni. *Concerning Famous Women.* Ed. Guido A. Guardino. New Brunswick, N.J.: Rutgers University Press, 1963.

Bonnefoy, Yves. *Mythologies.* Trans. under the direction of Wendy Doniger. 2 vols. Chicago: University of Chicago Press, 1991.

Boswell, John. *The Kindness of Strangers: The Abandonment of Children in Western Europe from Late Antiquity to the Renaissance.* New York: Pantheon, 1988.

Brandon, S. G. F., ed. *The Saviour God: Comparative Studies in the Concept of Salvation.* Manchester: Manchester University Press, 1963.

Burkert, Walter. *Ancient Mystery Cults.* Cambridge, Mass.: Harvard University Press, 1987.

———. *Homo Necans: The Anthropology of Ancient Greek Sacrificial Ritual and Myth.* Trans. Peter Bing. Berkeley: University of California Press, 1983.

———. "The Problem of Ritual Killing." In *Violent Origins: Ritual Killing and Cultural Formation,* ed. Robert G. Hamerton-Kelly, 149–76. Stanford: Stanford University Press, 1987.

Campbell, Joseph. *The Flight of the Wild Gander: Explorations in the Mythical Dimension.* South Bend, Ind.: Regnery/Gateway, Inc., 1969.

Carroll, David, ed. *George Eliot: The Critical Heritage.* New York: Barnes and Noble, 1971.

Cauvin, Jacques. "L'Apparition des premieres divinités." *La Recherche* 18 (Dec. 1987): 1472–80.

———. "Naissance des divinités, naissance de l'agriculture." Paris: CNRS Editions, 1994.

Chambers, R. W. *Beowulf: An Introduction to the Study of the Poem.* Cambridge: Cambridge University Press, 1963.

Chaucer. *The Riverside Chaucer.* Gen. ed. Larry D. Benson. New York: Houghton Mifflin, 1987.

Chrétien de Troyes. *Arthurian Romances.* Trans. D. D. R. Owen. London: Dent (Everyman Classics), 1987.

Christ, Carol P. "Mircea Eliade and the Feminist Paradigm Shift." *Journal of Feminist Studies in Religion* 7 (Fall 1991): 75–94.

———. "Symbols of Goddess and God in Feminist Theology." In Olson, 231–51.

———. "Why Women Need the Goddess: Phenomenological, Psychological, and Political Reflections." In Spretnak, 71–86.

Christine de Pisan. *The Book of the City of Ladies.* Trans. Earl Jeffrey Richards. New York: Persea Books, 1982.

Clarke, Edward Daniel. *Travels in Various Countries of Europe, Asia, and Africa. Part the Second: Greece, Egypt, and the Holy Land.* 4th American ed. New York: D. Huntington, 1814.

Clover, Carol. "The Politics of Scarcity: Notes on the Sex Ratio in Early Scandinavia." In Damico and Olson, 100–134.

Coghill, Nevill. *The Collected Papers of Nevill Coghill, Shakespearean and Medievalist.* Ed. Douglas Gray. New York: St. Martin's Press, 1988.

Coles, John. *Images of the Past: A Guide to the Rock Carvings and Other Ancient Monuments of Northern Bohuslän.* Uddevalla, Sweden: Risbergs Tryckeri, 1990.

Crane, Susan. *Insular Romance: Politics, Faith, and Culture in Anglo-Norman and Middle English Literature.* Berkeley: University of California Press, 1986.

Cristofol, Jean. Personal letter to the author, September 27, 1994.

Cumont, Franz. *The Oriental Religions in Roman Paganism.* New York: Dover, 1959.

Curtius, Ernst Robert. *European Literature and the Latin Middle Ages.* Trans. Willard R. Trask. New York: Bollingen Foundation, 1953.

Custance. See Chaucer.

Daly, Lloyd W., trans. *Aesop Without Morals: The Famous Fables and a Life of Aesop.* New York: Thomas Yoseloff, 1961.

Damico, Helen, and Alexandra Hennessey Olsen, eds. *New Readings on Women in Old English Literature.* Bloomington: Indiana University Press, 1990.

Davidson, Hilda Ellis. *The Lost Beliefs of Northern Europe.* London: Routledge, 1993.

Dawson, Robert B. "Custance in Context: Rethinking the Protagonist of the *Man of Law's Tale.*" *Chaucer Review* 26 (1992): 293–308.

Delany, Sheila. *Writing Woman: Women Writers and Women in Literature, Medieval to Modern.* New York: Schocken Books, 1983.

Dexter, Miriam Robbins. "Reflections on the Goddess *Donu." *Mankind Quarterly* 31 (1990): 45–58.

———. *Whence the Goddesses: A Source Book.* New York: Pergamon Press, 1990.

Diamond, Arlyn. "Unhappy Endings: Failed Love/Failed Faith in Late Romances." In Meale, 65–81.

Donavin, Georgiana. *Incest Narratives and the Structure of Gower's "Confessio Amantis."* ELS Monograph Series. English Department, University of Victoria, British Columbia, 1993.

Donovan, Mortimer J. "Breton Lays." In Severs's *Manual* (see Severs), 133–43.

———. "Middle English *Emaré* and the Cloth Worthily Wrought." In Benson, 337–42.

Dunn, Charles W., and Edward T. Byrnes, eds. *Middle English Literature.* New York: Garland, 1990.

Eberle, Patricia. [Notes on the Man of Law's Tale (*Custance*).] See Chaucer.

Edwards, A. S. G. "Chaucer and the Poetics of Utterance." In *Poetics: Theory and Practice in Medieval English Literature: The J. A. W. Bennett Memorial Lectures,* ed. Piero Boitani and Anna Torti, 57–67. Woodbridge, Suffolk: Brewer, 1991.

———. "Critical approaches to the *Man of Law's Tale.*" In *Chaucer's Religious Tales,* ed. C. David Benson and Elizabeth Robertson, 85–94. Cambridge, England: D. S. Brewer, 1990.

———. "Middle English Romance: The Limits of Editing, the Limits of Criticism." In *Medieval Literature: Texts and Interpretation.* Binghampton: Medieval and Renaissance Texts and Studies (MRTS), 1991, 91–104.

Egil's Saga. Trans. Hermann Pálsson and Paul Edwards. Harmondsworth: Penguin, 1976.

Ehrenberg, Margaret. *Women in Prehistory.* London: British Museum Publications, 1989.

Eingartner, Johannes. *Isis und ihre Dienerinnen in der Kunst der Römischen Kaiserzeit. Supplements to Mnemosyne: Bibliotheca Classica Batava.* Leiden: E. J. Brill, 1991.

Eliade, Mircea. *Cultural Fashions in History of Religions.* Chicago: Wesleyan University Center for Advanced Studies, 1967.

———. *Shamanism: Archaic Techniques of Ecstasy.* Trans. Willard R. Trask. Princeton: Princeton University Press, 1972.

Eliot, George. *The Mill on the Floss.* Ed. Gordon S. Haight. Oxford: Oxford University Press [World's Classics], 1981.

———. *Romola.* Ed. Andrew Sanders. Harmondsworth, England: Penguin, 1980.

Eliot, T. S. "Marina." In *The Complete Poems and Plays.* New York: Harcourt, Brace and Company, 1952.

Emaré (editions). See Gough, Rickert, Rumble.

Everson, Michael. "Picture Out of Focus: Colin Renfrew's Archaeology and Language—The Puzzle of Indo-European Origins." *Mankind Quarterly* 30 (1989): 159–73.

Farnell, Lewis Richard. *The Cults of the Greek States.* 3 vols. Reprint. New Rochelle, N.Y.: Cartzas Brothers, 1977.

Ferguson, John. *Among the Gods: An Archaeological Exploration of Ancient Greek Religion.* London: Routledge, 1989.

Fichte, Joerg O. "Grappling with Arthur, or Is There an English Arthurian Verse Romance?" In *Poetics: Theory and Practice in Medieval English Literature: The J. A. W. Bennett Memorial Lectures,* ed. Piero Boitani and Anna Torti, 149–63. Woodbridge, Suffolk: D. S. Brewer, 1991.

Field, Rosalind. "Rescuing Romance" (book review), *English* 38 (1989): 251–55.

Florence (editions). See Heffernan, Lee (1974).

Florence de Rome. Ed. A. Wallensköld. Paris: F. Didot, 1907–9.

Forbes, Alexander Penrose, trans. *Lives of S. Ninian and S. Kentigern.* Edinburgh: Edmonston and Douglas, 1874.

Fouke le Fitz Waryn. Ed. E. J. Hathaway, P. T. Ricketts, C. A. Robson, and A. D. Wilshere. Oxford: Blackwell (for the Anglo-Norman Society), 1975.

Frye, Northrup. *The Secular Scripture: A Study of the Structure of Romance.* Cambridge, Mass.: Harvard University Press, 1976.

———, Sheridan Baker, and George Perkins. *The Harper Handbook to Literature.* New York: Harper and Row, 1985.

Garmonsway, G. N., and Jacqueline Simpson, trans. *Beowulf and Its Analogues.* London: J. M. Dent & Sons Ltd., 1968.

Gibbs, A. C., ed. *Middle English Romances.* London: Edward Arnold (York Medieval Texts), 1966.

Gimbutas, Marija. *The Civilization of the Goddess.* Ed. Joan Marler. San Francisco: Harper San Francisco, 1991.

———. *The Goddesses and Gods of Old Europe, 6500–3500: Myths and Cult Images.* Berkeley: University of California Press, 1974.

———. *The Language of the Goddess.* New York: Harper and Row, 1989.

Glueck, Nelson. *Deities and Dolphins: The Story of the Nabataeans.* London: Cassell, 1966.

Goepp, P. H. "The Narrative Material of *Apollonius of Tyre.*" *ELH* 5 (1938): 150–72.

Goldenberg, Naomi. "Feminist Witchcraft: Controlling Our Own Inner Space." In Spretnak, 213–18.

Goodman, Frederick. *Zodiac Signs.* London: Brian Trodd Publishing House Ltd., 1990.

Gough, A. B. "The Constance Saga." *Palaestra* 23 (1902): 1–84.

———. *Emaré,* in *Old and Middle English Texts,* vol 2. London: Sampson Low Marston, 1901.

Gower, John. *The English Works of John Gower.* 2 vols. EETS, e.s., 81–82. Oxford: Oxford University Press, 1900–1901. Reprint, 1957.

Gravdal, Kathryn. *Ravishing Maidens: Writing Rape in Medieval French Literature and Law.* Philadelphia: University of Pennsylvania Press, 1991.

Gregorius. See Hartmann von Aue.

Griffiths, J. Gwyn. *Apuleius of Madauros: The Isis-Book (Metamorphoses, Book 11).* Leiden: E. J. Brill, 1975.

———. See Plutarch.

Grimm, Jacob and Wilhelm. *The Complete Fairy Tales of the Brothers Grimm.* Trans. Jack Zipes. Toronto: Bantam, 1987.

Hanning, Robert, and Joan Ferrante, trans. *The Lais of Marie de France.* New York: Dutton, 1978.

Hares-Stryker, Carolyn. "Adrift on the Seven Seas: The Mediaeval Topos of Exile at Sea." *Florilegium* 12 (1993): 79–98.

———. "Sleeping in the Midst of the Sea: The Motif of the Heroine Adrift in Medieval Romance." Ph.D. diss., University of California, Davis, 1990.

Harper Handbook. See Frye.

Harrison, Robert Pogue. *Forests: The Shadow of Civilization.* Chicago: University of Chicago Press, 1992.

Hartmann von Aue. *Gregorius: The Good Sinner* (bilingual ed.). Trans. Sheema Zeben Buehne. New York: Frederick Ungar, 1966.

Haskins, Susan. *Mary Magdalene: Myth and Metaphor.* New York: Harcourt, Brace and Company, 1993.

Heffernan, Carol Falvo. *Le Bone Florence of Rome.* Manchester: Manchester University Press, 1976. New York: Barnes and Noble, 1976.

Hesiod. *The Poems of Hesiod.* Trans. R. M. Frazer. Norman: University of Oklahoma Press, 1983.

Heyob, Sharon Kelly. *The Cult of Isis among Women in the Graeco-Roman World.* Leiden: E. J. Brill, 1975.

Hibbard, Laura A. *Medieval Romance in England: A Study of the Sources and Analogues of the Non-Cyclic Metrical Romances.* New York: Burt Franklin, 1960.

Hillman, James. *Re-Visioning Psychology.* New York: Harper & Row, 1975.

Holzberg, Niklas. *The Ancient Novel: An Introduction.* Trans. Christine Jackson-Holzberg. London: Routledge, 1995.

Hornstein, Lillian Herlands. "Eustace-Constance-Florence-Griselda Legends." In Severs's *Manual* (see Severs), 120–32.

Howard, Donald R. *Chaucer: His Life, His Works, His World.* New York: Dutton, 1987.

Hudson, Harriet E. "Construction of Class, Family, and Gender in Some Middle English Popular Romances." In *Class and Gender in Early English Literature: Intersections,* ed. Britton J. Harwood and Gillian R. Overing, 76–94. Bloomington: Indiana University Press, 1994.

Hughes, Muriel Joy. *Women Healers in Medieval Life and Literature.* New York: King's Crown Press, 1943.

Hurtado, Larry, ed. *Goddesses in Religions and Modern Debate.* Atlanta: Scholars Press, 1990.

Jacobs, Nicolas. "Some Creative Misreadings in *Le Bone Florence of Rome*: An Experiment in Textual Criticism." In *Medieval Studies Presented to George Kane,* ed. Edward Donald Kennedy, Ronald Waldron, and Joseph S. Wittig, 279–84. Woodbridge, Suffolk: D. S. Brewer, 1988.

Jameson, Fredric. *The Political Unconscious: Narrative as a Socially Symbolic Act.* Ithaca: Cornell University Press, 1981.

Jocelin, *The Life of St. Kentigern.* See Forbes.

John of Garland. See Wilson.

John of the Cross, Saint. See Juan de la Cruz.

Johnson, Elizabeth A. *She Who Is: The Mystery of God in Feminist Theological Discourse.* New York: Crossroad, 1993.

Johnston, Grahame. "The Breton Lays in Middle English." In *Iceland and the Medieval World: Studies in Honor of Ian Maxwell,* ed. Gabriel Turville-Petre and John Stanley Martin, 151–61. Victoria, Australia: Wilke, 1974.

Juan de la Cruz, San. *Poesía completa y comentarios en prosa.* Ed. Raquel Asún. Barcelona: Planeta, 1989.

Kee, Howard Clark. *Miracle in the Early Christian World: A Study in Socio-historical Method.* New Haven: Yale University Press, 1983.

Kelly, Fergus. *A Guide to Early Irish Law.* Dublin: Dublin Institute for Advanced Studies, 1988.

Kenworthy, Eldon. *America/Américas: Myth in the Making of U.S. Policy toward Latin America.* University Park: Pennsylvania State University Press, 1995.

Krentz, Jayne Ann, ed. *Dangerous Men and Adventurous Women: Romance Writers on the Appeal of the Romance.* Philadelphia: University of Pennsylvania Press, 1992.

Krishna, Valerie, trans. *Five Middle English Arthurian Romances.* New York: Garland, 1991.

Knight, Stephen. "The Social Function of the Middle English Romances." In *Medieval Literature: Criticism, Ideology, and History,* ed. David Aers, 99–122. Brighton: Harvester Press, 1986.

Knobbe, Albert. *Über die mittelenglische Dichtung Le Bone Florence of Rome.* Marburg, 1889. The introduction only is included in Viëtor; see below.

Kolve, V. A. *Chaucer and the Imagery of Narrative.* Chapter 7: "The Man of Law's Tale: The Rudderless Ship and the Sea." Stanford: Stanford University Press, 1984.

Lauter, Estella, and Carol Schreier Rupprecht, eds. *Feminist Archetypal Theory: Interdisciplinary Re-Visions of Jungian Thought.* Knoxville: University of Tennessee Press, 1985.

Leavy, Barbara Fass. *In Search of the Swan Maiden: A Narrative on Folklore and Gender.* New York: New York University Press, 1994.

Le Bone Florence of Rome. See Heffernan and Lee.

Lee, Anne Thompson. "*Le Bone Florence of Rome:* A Critical Edition." Ph.D. diss., Harvard University, 1974.

———. "*Le Bone Florence of Rome:* A Middle English Adaptation of a French Romance." In Benson, 343–54.

Lefkowitz, Mary R. "The New Cults of the Goddess." *The American Scholar* 62 (1993): 261–68.

Lerner, Gerda. *The Creation of Patriarchy.* New York: Oxford University Press, 1986.

Leroi-Gourhan, Andre. *Prehistoire de l'art occidental.* Paris: L. Mazenod, 1965.

Leroux, Odette, Marion E. Jackson, and Minnie Aodla Freeman, eds. *Inuit Women Artists.* Vancouver: Douglas and McIntyre, 1994.

Levy, Gertrude Rachel. *The Gate of Horn: A Study of the Religious Conceptions of the Stone Age and Their Influence upon European Thought.* London: Faber, 1948.

"Lives of Offa I and II." In Chambers, 217–43.

Lucian, of Samosata. *The Syrian Goddess* (De dea Syria); attributed to Lucian. Trans. Harold W. Attridge and Robert A. Oden. Missoula, Mont.: Scholars Press for the Study of Biblical Literature, 1976.

Luhrmann, T. M. *Persuasions of the Witch's Craft: Ritual Magic in Contemporary England.* Cambridge, Mass.: Harvard University Press, 1989.

Mandt, Gro. "Female Symbolism in Rock Art." *AMS* [Arkeologisk Museum i Stavanger] *Varia* 17: 35–53.

Mann, Jill. *Geoffrey Chaucer.* New York: Harvester Wheatsheaf, 1991.

Mann, Thomas. *Doctor Faustus.* Trans. H. T. Lowe-Porter. New York: Knopf (Everyman), 1992.

———. *The Holy Sinner.* Trans. H. T. Lowe-Porter. Berkeley: University of California Press, 1992.

Marie de France. *The Lais of Marie de France.* Trans. Robert Hanning and Joan Ferrante. Durham, N.C.: The Labyrinth Press, 1978.

Markman, Roberta H., and Peter T. Markman. *The Flayed God: The Meso-

american Mythological Tradition. San Francisco: Harper San Francisco, 1992.

Mattingly, Harold. *Tacitus on Britain and Germany.* Trans. and revised by S. A. Handford. Harmondsworth: Penguin, 1970.

McCance, Dawne. "Understandings of 'the Goddess' in Contemporary Feminist Scholarship." In Hurtado, 165–78.

Meale, Carol M., ed. *Readings in Medieval English Romance.* Cambridge: D. S. Brewer, 1994.

Mediz Bolio, Antonio. *La Tierra del Faisán y del Venado,* in *Mundo Indígena Mesoamericano.* Mexico D.F.: Organizacion Editorial Novaro, 1974.

Mehl, Dieter. *The Middle English Romances of the Thirteenth and Fourteenth Centuries.* London: Routledge & Kegan Paul, 1968.

Meyer, Marvin W. *The Ancient Mysteries: A Source Book.* San Francisco: Harper and Row, 1987.

Milton, John. *Complete Poems and Major Prose.* Merritt Y. Hughes, ed. New York: Odyssey, 1957.

Monaghan, Patricia. *The Book of Goddesses and Heroines.* New York: E. P. Dutton, 1981.

Murphy, Patrick D. *Literature, Nature, and Other: Ecofeminist Critiques.* Albany: State University of New York Press, 1995.

Neumann, Erich. *The Great Mother: An Analysis of the Archetype.* 2d ed. Trans. Ralph Manheim. Princeton: Princeton University Press, 1963.

Newstead, Helaine. "Romances: General." In *A Manual of the Writings in Middle English, 1050–1500,* J. Burke Severs, gen. ed., 11–16. New Haven: Connecticut Academy of Arts and Sciences, 1967.

Nicholson, Peter. "Chaucer Borrows from Gower: The Sources of the *Man of Law's Tale.*" In *Chaucer and Gower: Difference, Mutuality, Exchange,* ed. R. F. Yeager, 85–99. Victoria, B.C.: English Literary Studies, University of Victoria, 1991.

———. "Man of Law's Tale." In *The Chaucer Encyclopedia.* [Forthcoming.]

———. *"The Man of Law's Tale:* What Chaucer Really Owed to Gower." *Chaucer Review* 26 (1991): 153–74.

Ogilvy, J. D. A. *Books Known to the English, 597–1066.* Cambridge, Mass.: Medieval Academy of America, 1967.

O'Keeffe, Katherine O'Brien, ed. *Old English Shorter Poems: Basic Readings.* New York: Garland, 1994.

Olson, Carl, ed. *The Book of the Goddess, Past and Present: An Introduction to Her Religion.* New York: Crossroad, 1990.

Ondaatje, Michael. *The English Patient.* New York: Knopf, 1992.

Onions, C. T., ed. *The Oxford Dictionary of English Etymology.* Oxford: Clarendon, 1966.

Orenstein, Gloria Feman. *The Reflowering of the Goddess.* New York: Pergamon Press, 1990.

Osborn, Marijane. "Ransom" (poem). *Studia Mystica* 9 : 3 (1986): 81.

———. "The Real Fulk Fitzwarine's Mythical Monster Fights." To be published in *Words and Works: Essays in Honor of Fred C. Robinson*, ed. Peter Baker and Nicholas Howe. Toronto: University of Toronto Press, 1997. [Forthcoming.]

Otto, Rudolph. *The Idea of the Holy.* Trans. John W. Harvey. New York: Oxford University Press, 1950.

Overing, Gillian. *Language, Sign, and Gender in Beowulf.* Carbondale: Southern Illinois University Press, 1990.

Ovid. *Heroides.* Ed. Arthur Palmer. Hildesheim: Georg Olms Verlagsbuchhandlung, 1967.

Owen, D. D. R., trans. *Arthurian Romances by Chretien de Troyes.* London: Dent, 1987.

Paris, Gaston, and Ulysse Robert, eds. *Miracles de Nostre Dame, par personnages.* Vol. 4. Paris: Librairie de Firmin Didot, 1879.

Paris, Ginette. *Pagan Meditations: Aphrodite, Hestia, Artemis.* Trans. Gwendolyn Moore. Dallas: Spring Publications, 1986.

Perry, Ben Edwin. *The Ancient Romances: A Literary-Historical Account of Their Origins.* Berkeley: University of California Press, 1967.

———. *Studies in the Text History of the Life and Fables of Aesop.* Haverford, Penn.: American Philological Association, 1936.

Plutarch. *Plutarch's De Iside et Osiride.* Trans. J. Gwyn Griffiths. Cambridge: University of Wales Press, 1970.

Poulain, Dominique. Personal letter to the author, February 4, 1996.

Primack, Joel R., and Nancy Ellen Abrams. " 'In a Beginning . . . ': Quantum Cosmology and Kabbalah." *Tikkun* 10 : 1 (1995): 66–73.

Radway, Janice A. *Reading the Romance: Women, Patriarchy, and Popular Literature.* Chapel Hill: University of North Carolina Press, 1984.

Ramsey, Lee C. *Chivalric Romances: Popular Literature in Medieval England.* Bloomington: Indiana University Press, 1983.

Rank, Otto. *The Incest Theme in Literature and Legend: Fundamentals of a Psychology of Literary Creation.* Baltimore: Johns Hopkins University Press, 1992.

———. *The Myth of the Birth of the Hero: A Psychological Interpretation of Mythology.* Trans. Drs. F. Robbins and Smith Ely Jelliffe. New York: R. Brunner, 1952.

Reardon, B. P., ed. *Collected Ancient Greek Novels.* Berkeley: University of California Press, 1989.

Reid, T. B. W. "A Note on Homonymic Convergence: aimer/esmer." In *Studies in Medieval Literature and Languages in Memory of Frederick Whitehead*, ed. W. Rothwell et al. Manchester: Manchester University Press, 1973.

Reinhard, J. R. "Setting Adrift in Medieval Law and Literature." *PMLA* 56 (1941): 33–68.

Renfrew, Colin. "The Origins of Indo-European Languages." *Scientific American* 261:4 (Oct. 1989): 106–14.

Renoir, Alain. "Fragment: An Oral-Formulaic Nondefinition." *New York Literary Forum* 8–9 (1981): 39–50.

Richmond, Velma Bourgeois. *The Popularity of Middle English Romance.* Bowling Green, Ohio: Bowling Green University Popular Press, 1975.

Rickert, Edith. "The Old English Offa Saga." *Modern Philology* (part 1, 1904): 29–76; (part 2, 1905): 321–76.

———. *The Romance of Emaré.* Early English Text Society, Extra Series 99. London: Kegan Paul, Trench, Trübner, 1908. Reprint. Oxford University Press, 1958.

Riedinger, Anita. "The Englishing of Arcestrate: Women in *Apollonius of Tyre.*" In Damico, 292–306.

Roberts, Nanette McNiff. "Making the Mold: The Roles of Women in Middle English Metrical Romance, 1225–1500." DAI 37 (1977): 5812A (NYU).

Robinson, Fred C. *The Tomb of Beowulf and Other Essays on Old English.* Oxford: Blackwell, 1993.

Roche, Paul, trans. *The Orestes Plays of Aeschylus.* New York: New American Library (Mentor), 1962.

Roddy, Kevin. "Mythic Sequence in the *Man of Law's Tale.*" *Journal of Medieval and Renaissance Studies* 10 (1980): 1–22.

Rodriguez, Jeanette. *Our Lady of Guadalupe: Faith and Empowerment among Mexican-American Women.* Austin: University of Texas Press, 1994.

Rohde, Erwin. *Der griechische Roman und seine Vorläufer.* Hildesheim: Georg Olms, 1960.

Rudd, Niall (trans.), and William Barr. *Juvenal: The Satires.* Oxford: Clarendon Press, 1991.

Ruether, Rosemary Radford. *Gaia and God: An Ecofeminist Theology of Earth Healing.* San Francisco: Harper San Francisco, 1992.

Rufus, Anneli, and Kristan Lawson. *Goddess Sites: Europe.* San Francisco: Harper San Francisco, 1990.

Rumble, Thomas C. *The Breton Lays in Middle English.* Detroit: Wayne State University Press, 1965.

Salmony, Alfred. "Die Kunst des Aurignacien in Malta (Sibirien)." IPEK: Jahrbuck für Prähistorische & Ethnographische Kunst. Berlin: Klinkhardt & Biermann, 1931.

Scheps, Walter. "Chaucer's Man of Law and the Tale of Constance." *PMLA* 89 (1974): 285–95.

Schibanoff, Susan. "Worlds Apart: Orientalism, Antifeminism, and Heresy in Chaucer's Man of Law's Tale." *Exemplaria* 8 (1996): 59–96.

Schick, Von. J. "Die Urquelle der Offa-Konstanze-Sage." In *Britannica: Max Förster zum sechzigsten geburtstage.* Leipzig: B. Tauchnitz, 1929.

Schlauch, Margaret. *Chaucer's Constance and Accused Queens.* New York: Gordian Press, 1969.

Schulenberg, Jane Tibbetts. "The Heroics of Virginity: Brides of Christ and Sacrificial Mutilation." In *Women in the Middle Ages and the Renaissance,* ed. Mary Beth Rose, 29–72. Syracuse: Syracuse University Press, 1986.

Schwabe, G. T. Personal letter to the author, March 1, 1996.

Severs, J. Burke. *A Manual of the Writings in Middle English, 1000–1500.* (Based upon John Edwin Wells, *A Manual of the Writings in Middle English, 1050–1400.*) New Haven: Connecticut Academy of Arts and Sciences, 1967.

Shakespeare, William. *Pericles.* Ed. G. Blakemore Evans in *The Riverside Shakespeare.* Boston: Houghton Mifflin Company, 1974.

Simpson, Jacqueline. See under Garmonsway.

Sir Gawain and the Green Knight. Middle English text in Dunn and Byrnes, 376–459. See Tolkien for translation.

Sir Orfeo. Middle English text in Dunn and Byrnes, 216–30. See Tolkien for translation.

Sisam, Kenneth. *The Structure of Beowulf.* London: Oxford University Press, 1965.

Skármeta, Antonio. *The Postman.* New York: Miramax Books (Hyperion), 1993.

Smit, Johannes Wilhelmus. *Studies on the Language and Style of Columba the Younger (Columbanus),* 172–89. Amsterdam: Adolf M. Hakkert, 1971.

Solmsen, Friedrich. *Isis among the Greeks and Romans.* Cambridge, Mass.: Harvard University Press, 1979.

Speirs, John. *Medieval English Poetry: The Non-Chaucerian Tradition.* London: Faber and Faber, 1971.

Spong, John Shelby. *Born of a Woman: A Bishop Rethinks the Birth of Jesus.* San Francisco: Harper San Francisco, 1992.

Spretnak, Charlene, ed. *The Politics of Women's Spirituality: Essays on the Rise of Spiritual Power within the Feminist Movement.* Garden City, N.Y.: Anchor Books, 1982.

———. "Response" and "Post-Counter-Response" [to Binford]. In Spretnak, 552–57 and 560–61.

Starhawk. "Witchcraft as Goddess Religion." In Spretnak, 49–56.

Steinfells, Peter. "Idyllic Theory of Goddesses Creates Storm." *New York Times,* Tuesday, Feb. 13, 1990: C1 and C12.

Stenton, F. M. *Anglo-Saxon England.* Oxford: Clarendon, 1971.

Stevick, Robert D., ed. *Five Middle English Narratives*. Indianapolis: Bobbs-Merrill, 1967.

Stone, Merlin. "Response" [to Binford]. In Spretnak, 550–51.

———. *When God Was a Woman*. San Diego: Harcourt and Brace, 1976.

Straus, Barrie Ruth. "Women's Words as Weapons: Speech as Action in *The Wife's Lament*." In O'Keeffe, 335–56.

Tacitus. See Mattingly.

Tannahill, Reay. *Sex in History*. New York: Stein and Day, 1982.

Thomas, Henry. *Spanish and Portuguese Romances of Chivalry*. Cambridge: Cambridge University Press, 1920.

Thomas of Erceldoun. In Dunn and Byrnes.

Thompson, Janet. *Of Witches: Celebrating the Goddess as a Solitary Pagan*. York Beach, Maine: Weiser, 1993.

Toews, John E. "Male and Female Perspectives on a Psychoanalytic Myth." In *Gender and Religion: On the Complexity of Symbols*, ed. Caroline Walker Bynum, Stevan Harrell, and Paula Richman, 289–317. Boston: Beacon Press, 1986.

Tolkien, J. R. R., trans. *Sir Gawain and the Green Knight, Pearl, and Sir Orfeo*. Boston: Houghton-Mifflin, 1975.

Townsend, Joan B. "The Goddess, Fact, Fallacy, and Revitalization Movement." In *Goddesses in Religions and Modern Debate*, ed. Larry W. Hurtado, 179–203. Atlanta: Scholars Press, 1990.

Turner, Victor, and Edith Turner. *Image and Pilgrimage in Christian Culture*. New York: Columbia University Press, 1978.

Viëtor, Wilhelm. *"Le Bone Florence of Rome."* Ph.D. diss., University of Marburg, 1893. Text only published in Marburg, 1899; the introduction is in a separate volume by Knobbe, cited above.

Vitae Duorum Offarum. In Chambers.

Wallensköld, A. *Florence de Rome: Chanson d'aventure*. 2 vols. Paris: Firmin-Didot et cie, 1909.

Warner, Marina. *Alone of All Her Sex: The Myth and Cult of the Virgin Mary*. New York: Vintage Books, 1976.

Weaver, Mary Jo. *Springs of Water in a Dry Land: Spiritual Survival for Catholic Women Today*. Boston: Beacon Press, 1993.

Weisl, Angela Jane. *Conquering the Reign of Femeny*. Chaucer Studies 22. Woodbridge, Suffolk: D. S. Brewer, 1995.

Wentersdorf, Karl P. "The Situation of the Narrator in the Old English *Wife's Lament*." In O'Keeffe, 357–407.

Whitehouse, David, and Ruth Whitehouse. *Archaeological Atlas of the World*. San Francisco: W. H. Freeman and Company, 1975.

Wild, Robert A. *Water in the Cultic Worship of Isis and Sarapis*. Leiden: E. J. Brill, 1981.

Wilson, Evelyn Faye, ed. *The Stella Maris of John of Garland.* Cambridge, Mass.: Medieval Academy of America (with Wellesley College), 1946.

Witt, Rex E. *Greece the Beloved.* Thessalonike: Institute for Balkan Studies, 1965.

Wittig, Susan. *Stylistic and Narrative Structures in the Middle English Romances.* Austin: University of Texas Press, 1978.

Wogan-Browne, Jocelyn. "'Bet . . . to . . . rede on holy seyntes lyves . . .': Romance and Hagiography Again." In Meale, 83–97.

Zimmerman, J. E. *Dictionary of Classical Mythology.* New York: Bantam, 1964.

Index

Abduction, 261–62

Abrams, Nancy Ellen, 245

Abró, meaning of, 257

Abuse, 26; transcended by Castaway Queen, 247

Accusation, medieval source of: against innocent woman, 39–40

Accused Queen, 249n1, 255n24

Adequate symbolization, 241

Aegean Sea: as location of Florence's convent, 190

Ælla (king of Deira), 268, 274n16

Æschylus, 192

Aesop: incest story, 208

Agamemnon: sacrifices Iphigenia to Artemis, 192–93

Aldhelm: alludes to *Clementine Recognitions*, 182

Allegory: in *Custance*, 21, 268

Allen, Richard Hinckley, 191

Almgren, Oscar, 271n6

Ambrose, Saint, 24, 265

Amplitude: as essential element of religious experience, 232, 236, 242

Analogues: to Castaway Queen romances, 11–12, 27–40

Ancient stories: remodeled into medieval romances, 48

Androcentric theories, 230

Aphrodite, 181; birth legend, 199, 212; goddess of love and generation, 199

Apollonius, wife of: at temple of Artemis, 191

Apollonius of Tyre, 35, 175–76, 254n20, 255n24; affinities to Castaway Queen tale-type, 36–38; incestuous father punished, 45; influence of, 36; plot summary of, 36–37; source of, 40

Apotheosis of female protagonist, 181; in Sedna legend, 218

Apuleius, 201–2, 204–5, 222

Archibald, Elizabeth: Apollonius and history, 270n4; gender and definition of romance, 252n12; generic story, 38; incest, 41, 42, 45, 46, 175, 255nn24–25; late classical romance origins, 274n16; story precedes *Apollonius of Tyre*, 40

Aristophanes, 209

Arrival myth, 270–71n6

Artemis, 181, 273n14; demands sacrifice of Iphigenia, 192–93; statue with bull testicles, 273n13; temple of, at Ephesus, 191–92; as water- or wilderness-goddess, 192–93. *See also* Diana

Arthur, King, 44–45

Astrology: in *Custance*, 265

Athena, birth legend of, 212

Audience: female, of hagiographical legends, 256n29; of the Middle Ages, 49

Auerbach, Erich, 21

Augustine, 24, 274n16

Ave Maris Stella, 271n8

Baikal bird figures, 235
Baikal women, 227–28
Bailey, Douglass W., 276n1
Baring, Anne, 186, 227, 270n5,
    277n2
Barr, William, 198–99
Barron, W. R. J., 15, 26
Barstow, Anne L., 247
Barthes, Roland, 180
Bastian, Adolph, 229
Bayeux Tapestry, 259
Bede, 39, 182, 190, 264, 268, 274n16
Bédier, Joseph, 259
Begg, Ean C. M., 184
Belief: defined, 229
Bennett, J. A. W., 259
Beowulf, 30–36, 253–54n19,
    272n11
Beuerfayre, 263–64
Biehl, Janet, 230, 239, 240, 276n1,
    278n8
Binford, Sally B., 280n13
Bird-goddesses, 278n8
Birnbaum, Lucia Chiavola, 184
Birth, androgenetic, 212
Black Madonnas, 184, 185–86
Blanch, Robert J., 206
Bleeker, C. J., 200
Blessed Virgin Rescuing a Floundering
    Ship, 198
Boas, Franz, 216
Boat(s): carrying surrogate maiden sac-
    rifice, 224; cult-, 4–5, 187, 271n6; in
    Iron Age rock carvings, 214; rudder-
    less, 6
Boat-Virgins: Mediterranean refer-
    ences to, 185–86
Boccaccio: account of Isis, 200–201
Bolbe (Greek lake goddess), 190–91,
    273n11
Bone Florence of Rome, Le. See
    Florence
Bonnefoy, Yves, 187, 214
Boswell, John, 46
Botticelli, 199
Breton lay, 10–11, 16, 39, 51, 261
Britain: as remote island, 182

Burkert, Walter, 191, 203, 219–20,
    224, 228, 276n24, 276–77n2
Byrnes, Edward T., 250n5

Calmo, Andrea: letters of, 259
Campbell, Joseph, 181, 227, 228, 229,
    244; doubts Baikal carvings are
    ivory, 276n2
Canacee, 262
Canciones del alma, 20
Cantigas de mujer, 19
Carroll, David, 221
Carvings: of women and geese, 235
Cashford, Jules, 186, 227, 270n5,
    277n2
Castaneda, Carlos, 238, 241–42
Castaway Queen: attached to histori-
    cal personages, 268; happy ending
    for, 248; as healer, 264; journey of,
    233; maintenance of personal integ-
    rity, 247; modern analogues,
    257n32; as motif, 181; parallel
    experience in life of author, 238–39;
    relationship to Isis and Mary, 207
—romances, 261; analogues to, 11–12,
    27–40 passim; authors of, unaware
    of source, 223–24; different from
    saints' lives and miracles of the Vir-
    gin, 204; as gateway to the Goddess,
    210, 229, 246–47; and Isis, 187, 201,
    209; magical robe in, 258; Mediter-
    ranean roots of, 182; mutilation of
    hands in, 213, 279n11; as narration
    of maiden sacrifice, 220; Provençal
    legend's influence on, 189–90
—tale-type: and *Apollonius of Tyre*,
    36, 38; backtracking story, 180; con-
    nected with Offa stories, 33; and
    contemporary unrest, 41; and in-
    cest, 42; incest and setting adrift in,
    40–41; previous designation for, 7;
    redeployment of plot, 179; sea as es-
    cape in, 177; as subset of Greek ro-
    mance, 176–77
Çatal Hüyük, 276n1, 280n12
Catullus, 210
Cauvin, Jacques, 228, 277n3

Chambers, R. W., 253n19, 254n21

Champagne, Cecelia, 262

Character(s): child of accused queen, 28; father who sets daughter adrift, 7; female romance heroine, 9; goddess Diana, 37; good merchant, 28; holy figure who aids reconciliation, 177; incestuous brother-in-law, 261; incestuous father, 10, 33, 40, 44, 45, 249n2, 253n17; knight, 15; male, and creation of interesting birth story, 178; priestess, 37; rejected suitor, 8; reluctant daughter, 45; Saracen prince, in *Emaré*, 258; thwarted suitor, 28, 39; wicked foster mother, 37
—wicked mother-in-law, 6, 8, 10, 28, 29, 39, 252–53n16, 253n17; exile of, in *Emaré*, 260; murders son in *Custance*, 44

Charlemagne, 257

Charter myths, 12

Chastity: bio-politics of, 256n29; Florence's, 262

Chaucer, Geoffrey, 252n14, 267; and Cecelia Champagne, 262; omission of incest in *Custance*, 127

Chaucer, Philippa, 267

Child adrift, 271n6

Child ballad 110: "The Knight and the Shepherd's Daughter," 250n6

Childe, V. Gordon, 277n3

Children: foundling, adoption of, 46; unwanted, abandonment of, 45–46

Chrétien de Troyes, 258

Christ: death of, 234; as supernatural helper, 224

Christ, Carol P., 229–30, 231, 232, 233, 270n2, 273n14, 277–78n6, 281n16

Christianity: Celtic, 268

Christian legends: as transmitters of Castaway Queen story, 182–83

Christine de Pisan, 92, 251n10, 252n14, 263, 264, 268, 269; version of *Florence* by, 12–13

Church: as ship, 252n13

Civilization: of the Goddess, 239

Clarke, Edward Daniel, 274n16

Class structure: in romance, 15, 16

Clementine Recognitions, 12, 175–76, 182, 255n24, 256n29; loss of control of hands in, 213; summary of, 38

Clement of Alexandria: story of parentage, 38, 178

Clerk's Tale, The, 252n14

Clover, Carol, 46

Coghill, Nevill, 16

Coles, John, 215

Confession of sin: as prerequisite for healing, 264

Consanguinity laws, 42

Constance: regarded as historical during Middle Ages, 39

Constance Saga, origins of, 274n16

Constantine the Great: story of parentage, 38–39

Contritionism, 41

Cosmological fictions, 233

Council of Ephesus, 273n12

Council of Trent, 256n30

Crescentia of Rome, 11–12

Criminals, exposure of, 45

Cristofol, Jean, 228

Cult destination of heroine's ship, 204

Cult practice: narrated into story, 204

Cult site, lack of: in *The Mill on the Floss*, 221

Cultural syncretism, 246

Cumont, Franz, 204

Custance, 6; analogous to Virgin Mary, 186; changes name, 251n7; as Christian soul, 252n13; converts Alla to Christianity, 274n16; as devotee of Virgin Mary, 179; helped by God while adrift, 206; length of time adrift, 259–60; mother of emperor Mauricius Flavius Tiberius, 39; protected by the Hand of God, 215; separation from parental domination, 44; set adrift into God's hands, 47; as victim, 128; as woman of power, 21, 27, 206

Custance, 18, 51; ambiguities of power structure in, 128; as birth story of Mauricius, 178; bloody knife in, 263; Chaucer's departures from the traditional tale-type, 126–27; compared to *Emaré* and *Florence,* 13–14; concern with etiology in, 177; critics' opinions of, 8; culmination of story-type, 26–27; date of, 13; hand of God in, 206; importance of Fortune, Providence, Satan, and God in, 128; omission of incest in, 127; sources and analogues of, 10, 13; stanza form and meter, 126, 249n3; textual notes for, 265–70
Cybele (goddess), 210

Daly, Lloyd W., 208
d'Ancona, Alessandro, 41
Davidson, Hilda Ellis, 233
Davis, Elizabeth Gould, 280n13
Dawson, Robert B., 128, 266
Deity: as organic extension, 232
Delany, Sheila, 27
Detumescence, 262
Devil: in vision of author, 244
Dexter, Miriam Robbins, 193, 212, 228, 273n14, 274n17
Diamond, Arlyn, 15
Diana: as moon-goddess, 193; many-breasted, 193; temple of, 274n16. *See also* Artemis
Dijon: as location of Sequanna statue, 189
Diodorus Siculus, 200, 201
Donavin, Georgiana, 42, 44, 45, 46, 252n16
Don Juan, 238–39, 241–42, 279n11
Donovan, Mortimer J., 252n15, 258
Dream, prophetic: in *Florence,* 263
Drewermann, Eugen, 275n23
Drida, 33–34, 253n19
Drugs, 243–44
Dualism, androcentric, 232; associated with transcendence, 231
Dunn, Charles W., 250n5

Ebba, Abbess, 24–25
Eberle, Patricia J., 34, 128, 265–70
Edwards, A. S. G., 8, 250n4, 266
Egil's Saga, 256n31
Ehrenberg, Margaret, 41, 276n1
Eingartner, Johannes, 236
Elementary Ideas, narration of, 229
Eliade, Mircea, 229–30, 231, 232–33, 235, 277–78n6
Eliot, George, 4, 220–22; Maggie Tulliver as saviour goddess, 221
Emaré, 6, 252n15; analogous to Virgin Mary, 186; associated with sky-goddesses by her magical cloak, 205–6; correspondence to our assumptions, 26; as devotee of Virgin Mary, 179; glittering robes of, 200; mother of emperor Segramor, 39; papal dispensation to marry father, 42; pronunciation of name, 52; resemblance to Virgin Mary, 193; separation from parental domination, 44; set adrift as presumed criminal, 47; skills compared to Constance's and Florence's, 258; variant spellings of name, 52; as woman of power, 27
Emaré, 18, 51; accompanying music, 257n1; concern with etiology in, 177; critics' opinions of, 8; as fairy tale, 20; incestuous father repents, 45; magical robe in, 258; main plot elements of, 10; name changes in, 257n1; ramifications of, 29; as song, 11; source, provenance, dialect, and date of, 10, 52; stanza form of, 52, 249n3; textual notes to, 257–61
Emmerich, Catherine, 273n12
Ephesus, 191–92, 273n13
Erasmus, 274n16
Erayne: meaning of name, 257
Erec et Enide, 258
Euripides, 193
Everson, Michael, 280n12
Exiled woman: in Aesop story, 208
Ex voto offerings, 195, 224

Fabric: narrative subjects embroidered
on, 258–59
Family dysfunction, 9
Farnell, Lewis Richard, 192
Felice (Guy of Warwick's lady), 258
Female, numinous, 179
Female body, power of the, 230
Female protagonist, 181
Female statues, 247; in Egypt, 230–31;
Paleolithic, 227–28
Feminine power, control of, 25–26
Feminist aspects of medieval ro-
mance, 18
Ferguson, John, 192
Fermicus Maternus, 204
Fichte, Joerg O., 14–15, 16
Field, Rosalind, 15
Figures of women, 227–28
Florence: as active manager, 252n15;
Christian learning of, 251n9; com-
pared to Griselda, 252n14; connec-
tion with sea-virgin, 6; control of
raping penis, 210, 211–12; defending
herself from rape, 43; demand for
confession before healing, 203; as
devotee of Virgin Mary, 179; glitter-
ing robes of, 200; as healer, 264; and
Mary Pelagia, 206; as mother of Em-
peror Otis, 39; refusal to consum-
mate marriage, 256n30; rejection of
incestuous-father surrogate, 44;
resemblance to Virgin Mary, 193; as
sanctified character, 177; separation
from parental domination, 44; set
adrift into God's hands, 47; as too
self-willed, 252n15; as woman of
power, 27, 205–6
Florence: concern with etiology in,
177; critics' opinions of, 8; generic
or structural confusion of plot, 18;
less traditional than Emaré, 26; lo-
cation of convent, 190–91, 272n10;
main plot elements of, 11; plot of
chivalrous first part, 91–92; as polit-
ical commentary, 20–21; prove-
nance, manuscript, dialect, and date

of, 11, 91; sources and analogues of,
10, 12–13, 251n9; stanza form of,
93, 249n3; story of, included by
Christine de Pisan in Book of the
City of Ladies, 92; textual notes to,
261–65; variation on incest plot, 51
Florence de Rome: as analogue of Flor-
ence, 12, 91, 251n9
Floris and Blancheflor, 259
Folktale context of Custance, 249n1
Forbes, Alexander Penrose, 40
Forest exposure, 47
Fortune, 222–23
Fourth Lateran Council, 42, 45,
256n30
Freud, Sigmund, 234–35
Frye, Northrop, 15, 19, 21, 23, 37–
38, 49

Gaia principle, 281n16
Galys, location of, 260
Garden: as refuge for author, 237, 238,
242, 243; in hymn, 279n10
Geese: carved from ivory, 277n2
Gibbs, A. C., 8
Gimbutas, Marija, 210, 227, 239, 240,
277nn2–3, 278n8, 279–80n12
Glueck, Nelson, 223
God: Christian, 281n16; importance
of, in Custance, 128; as judge in sea-
exposure, 47; on the side of romance
heroines, 25; as sky-father, 233,
278n6, 280n12, 281n16; as super-
natural helper, 224
Goddess: ability to subdue lust, 213;
as ancestor of romance heroine, 174;
association with Castaway Queen,
190, 246–47; benignity of, 278n8;
bird-, 278n8; in a boat, 189; with
boat, 201; capitalization of, 279n10;
development of agricultural mother
into Mary Pelagia, 180; as healer of
mutilated hands, 218; image associ-
ated with chaotic flux, 230; inscru-
tableness of, 248; link to Castaway
Queen, 209; manifestations of, 3–8;

and modern witches, 277n4; Neolithic desires behind, 228–29; not "out there," 281n16; personal quest for, 236; as source of medieval romance, 241; subordination of, to male pantheon, 212; Tree as body of, 233; in vision of author, 244; on the waters as helper, 224; and World Tree, 232; worshiped near location of Florence's convent, 191
—ancient, 247; modern conceptions of, 230
—archaic, 181, 211, 237, 239; Isis as, 202
—sea-: transformed into Virgin Mary, 179
—sky-: with moon boat, 195
Goddess adrift, 220; as sacrifice, 178
Goddess culture, modern, 240
Goddess feminism, 235–35
Goddess feminists, 231; assumptions about Mother Goddess religion, 233, 239
Goddess icon, 248
Goddess reverence, 280n13
Goddess rhetoric: demanding uncritical belief, 239–40
Goddess rituals, 40
Goddess statues, 185, 227, 228, 230, 233, 280n12; criticism of blanket term for statues, 276n1
Goddess symbol, 281n16; and trees, link between, 278n7
Goddess-worship: supposed male conspiracy against, 240, 280n13
Goepp, P. H., 255n26
Golden Ass, The, 202
Goldenberg, Naomi, 240, 241
Goodman, Frederick, 195
Gough, A. B., 30, 182, 251n8, 257–58n1, 274n16
Gower, John, 44, 252n16
Gravdal, Kathryn, 25, 43, 250n6
Gregory the Great, 263, 274n16; story of parentage, 38
Griffiths, J. Gwyn, 187, 202, 264
Grimm, Jacob, 249n2, 275n23

Grimm, Wilhelm, 249n2, 275n23
Griselda: comparison to Florence, 252n14
Guntrum, Suzanne Simmons, 251n11
Guy of Warwick, 258
Gypsies, patron saint of, 184

Hagiography, 256n29; secular, 252n15
Haight, Gordon S., 221
Handless Maiden: as tale-type, 249n2
Hand of God, 206, 268; in *Custance,* 215
Hands: in dream of author, 238, 239, 243; healed by Goddess, 218; laying on of, by heroine, 264; as love-inducing feature, 213–14; mutilated, 213–18; in rock carvings, 215; self-mutilation after incest, 213–14; skill of, as means of heroine earning her living, 260
—mutilation of, 210; backfiring, 215–18; in *Clementine Recognitions,* 38; as punishment for masturbation, 249n2; renders protagonist helpless, 218; as symbol of powerlessness, 249n2
—severed, 28, 176, 201, 275n23; associated with male sexual aggression, 214; in Castaway Queen, 279n11; in dreams indicating ritualized sexual abuse, 218; in "Offa Saga," 33; to prevent shamanic power, 215; to prevent victim from crossing self, 214; as proof of death, 214; as punishment for infanticide, 214
—uplifted: in Iron Age rock carvings, 214
Hands of Sedna, severed: transformed into marine life, 217
Hares-Stryker, Carolyn, 18, 40, 207, 249n1, 252n15, 253n17, 270–71n6
Harrison, Robert Pogue, 273n13
Hartmann von Aue, 263
Haskins, Susan, 187–89
Hatch, Laurie, 279n11
Hathor (goddess), 187, 201
Havelok, 260

Healing: in Christine de Pisan's *Florence*, 251n10
Heffernan, Carol Falvo, 91, 93, 190, 261–65, 272n10
Hero, arrival of: alone while a child, 270–71n6
Heyob, Sharon Kelly, 213, 222, 274n19
Hibbard, Laura A., 252n15
Hieratic female, 244
Hilary, Saint (Bishop of Poitiers), 264
Hildeburh (in *Beowulf*), 30
Hillman, James, 279n11
Holy site: where woman drifts ashore, 207
Holzberg, Niklas, 19
Hornstein, Lillian Herlands, 26
Horus (god), 200
Howard, Donald R., 262
Hudson, Harriet E., 43–44, 256n30
Hughes, M., 264
Hygd (in *Beowulf*), 31, 253n19; and Thryth, comparison between, 30

Iceland, site-divination in, 256n31
Icons: defined, 270n1
Image, mythic: in *The Mill on the Floss*, 221
Incest: in *Apollonius of Tyre*, 36, 37, 255n25; in the Arthurian cycle, 44–45; in Castaway Queen tale-type, 40–41; as catalyst, 41, 45; in *Clementine Recognitions*, 38; committed unwittingly, 42; connections between medieval and classical plots, 175; as crime to be expiated, 45; defined, 42; flight from, 48, 255n24; in Greek myth, 41; in Isis legend, 201; leading to loss of social connections, 44; legally punished by setting adrift, 46–47; as male control, 177; in matrilineal cultures, 41; in Middle Ages, 11, 40, 41–42; in *The Mill on the Floss*, 221; as motivation for exposure, 28; mutilation of hands after, 213; omission of, in *Custance*, 127; in parentage stories of great men, 38–39; possible, in

Thryth digression in *Beowulf*, 34–35, 254n19; in Ptolemaic dynasty, 201; in relation to woman adrift theme, 249n1; in story of Canacee, 262; in story told by Aesop, 208, 209; threat of, in *Emaré*, 10; thwarted, 176;
Incest motif: popularity of during Middle Ages, 41; double incest motif, 45
Incest scandals, real, 42
Incest theme, classical source of, 39
Incestuous love: by Emaré's father, 259
Indo-European hordes, 240, 280n12. *See also* Kurgan hordes
Infanticide: punished by severing of hands, 214
Innocence: as protection against danger, 47
Innocent III (Pope), 269, 270
Inuit story of Sedna: mutilation of hands in, 215–18
Iphigenia: sacrificed to Artemis, 192–93
Iron Age Scandinavian rock carvings, 214–15
Irony: in *Custance*, 265
Isarn, Abbé, 186
Isian ritual: boat is launched as civilized version of sacrifice, 220
Isis, 223; associated with Fortune, 223; in a boat, 181, 187, 272n9; connection to Mary, 186; connection to Sophia, 279n9; as consoler, 203; cultic site at York, 274n16; as divine healer, 190, 203; emphasis on chastity in romances, 213; fabrication of gold penis for Osiris by, 213; as goddess of flooding Nile, 187; hand detached as sign, 214; honored in Alexandria, 187; Isis Pelagia, 187, 200; legends about, 199–200; linked to cow-goddess, 201; as magician, 210; as many goddesses, 201, 202, 246; *Navigium Isidis*, 187; relationship to Castaway Queen, 207; as rescuer,

206, 207; Roman women emulated, 236; as saviour-goddess, 200, 203, 222; as sea-protectress, 187, 210; secret initiation rites of, 204–5; and sexual immorality, 274–75n19; ship as emblem, 214–15; sky-robe of, 203, 258; source of aspects of Mary Pelagia, 198–99; transformed into goose, 228; virgin goddess of Mediterranean, 199; water facility dedicated to, 272n10; worshiped in Provence, 185

Ivory, statues carved from, 276–77n2

Jacobs, Nicholas, 261, 264–65
Jameson, Fredric, 16
Jerome, Saint, 24, 25, 271–72n8
Jocelyn de Brakelond, 40
John of Garland, 251n10
John of Gaunt, 267
Johnson, Elizabeth A., 279n9
Johnson, Robert A., 275–76n23
Johnston, Graham, 261
Jones, Ernest, 235
Josephus, 274–75n19
Journey: of bird-woman, 235; divinely protected, 229; by sea, 271n6
Juan de la Cruz, San, 19–20
Juan Diego of Tepeyac, 244, 278–79n9, 282n18
Julius Caesar, 264
Jung, Carl, 275n23
Juvenal, 198–99, 274n19

Kee, Howard Clark, 187, 200, 201, 203, 204, 205, 213, 222
Kelly, Fergus, 46–47
Kentigern, Saint: parentage story of, 40
Kenworthy, Eldon, 179, 180
Klaeber, Fr., 254n20
Klein, Melanie, 235
Knight, Stephen, 25–26
"Knight and the Shepherd's Daughter, The," 250n6
Knight of the Cart, The: as male-centered romance, 22

Kolve, V. A., 10, 21, 39, 127, 128, 178, 189, 268
Krentz, Jayne Ann, 251n11
Krishna, Valerie, 249n3
Kurgan hordes, 239, 277n3. See also Indo-European hordes
Kveldulf, 256n31

Lake Baikal, 247, 278n8
Lake Bolbe: as location of Florence's convent, 190. See also Lake Volvi
Lake Bottiaea: as location of Florence's convent, 190, 264
Lake Loudias, 190, 272n10
Lake Tahoe, 248
Lake Volvi, 190, 272n10
Latin, "corrupt," 267–68
Lauter, Estella, 281n15
Lawrence, W. W., 254n22
Leavy, Barbara Fass, 228, 257n32, 258
Lee, Anne Thompson, 251n9, 252n15
Lefkowitz, Mary R., 174
Legendary mothers: of popes, saints, and emperors, 38–39
Lerner, Gerda, 174
Leroi-Gourhan, André, 276n1
Leroux, Odette, 216
Les-Saintes-Maries-sur-Mer, 183–85
Levite priesthood, 280n13
Levy, Gertrude Rachel, 278n7
Life of Aesop: dating of, 209; woman adrift in, 207
Life of Saint Kentigern, 40
Lives of the Two Offas, 32–34
Location: cult site, 177, 180
Lollards, 42
Lucian of Samostrata, 201
Lucius Ibarnius, 190, 264
Luhrmann, T. M., 277n4
Lydgate, John, 16

Macary, 268; common name for villain in romance, 262; and well-aimed blow, 263
Machary, 270n3
Madonna and Child, 184
Magical robe: in Castaway Queen, 258

Male assumptions about unaccompa-
nied women, 9
Male conspiracy against Goddess-
worship, supposed, 240
Male desire for dominance, 26
Male sexual desire: as reason for
woman being set adrift, 29
Male violence, 43; thwarted, 26
Mammoth ivory, statues carved from,
227–28, 276–77n2
Mandt, Gro, 271n6, 272n9
Mann, Jill, 27
Mann, Thomas, 255n28, 263
Man of Law, 266, 267; as narrator of
Custance, 127–28
Man of Law's Tale. See *Custance*
Manuscript: of Emaré, 52; of *Flor-
ence*, 91
Marian ritual: boat is launched as civi-
lized version of sacrifice, 220
Marie de France, 10
Markman, Peter T., 278n7
Markman, Roberta H., 278n7
Marriage in the Middle Ages, 41–45;
control of, 41, 43, 45; generational
conflict over, 44; restricted pool of
partners for aristocracy, 42; valid,
medieval definition of, 256n30
Mars, 266
Marseille, 184; location of Mary Mag-
dalen's landing, 188–89; ship mu-
seum of ex voto models, 195
Martial, 274n19
Martin of Tours, Saint: story of parent-
age, 39
Martyrdom: as preferable to rape, 25
Mary ("the Egyptian"), 267
Mary (Virgin): ancient ritual, 187; as-
similation of Artemis's attributes,
193; associated with North Star and
planet Venus, 200; association with
sea, 179; in boat in literature, 4;
borrows features of Isis, 199, 209;
buried/bodily assumption at Ephe-
sus, 191; chastity of, 213; with child
in boat, 186, 189; as consoler, 203;
contradiction in terms, 278n9;

Custance compared to, 269; de-
clared *Theotokos*, 273n12; depicted
as sky-goddess standing on crescent
moon, 193; development of legends
about, 178; as divine woman in
boat, 181; as focus for female em-
powerment, 236; not goddess,
271n7; as Hebrew virgin, 209, 179;
legend of Provence, 183–85; in *The
Mill on the Floss*, 220–21; miracles
of, 190; political aspect of, 270n5; as
powerful Mediterranean goddess,
179; as protector of chastity, 262;
as protectress, 3, 195, 198, 207,
209; as Queen of Heaven, 194;
representations of, 193–99; sea-
voyage with Mary Magdalen, 188;
on side of romance heroines, 25;
sky-robe of, 258; as supernatural
helper, 224
Mary Magdalen: connection to sea-
goddess, 187–89
Mary Pelagia, 179, 195, 222, 236;
invoked by Florence, 206; as sea-
saviour, 209, 273n15
Matriarchy: defined, 41, 280n13
Matriliny: defined, 41
Matrisic: defined, 240; opposed to ma-
triarchal, 240
Mauricius Flavius Tiberius, 268; birth
story of, 178
Mayahuel (goddess), 278n7
Meaning, religious: of Custance, 27
Mediz Bolio, Antonio, 228
Men: as protagonists in romance, 9
Mere-Ama, 275n22
Meyer, Marvin W., 204, 275n19
Miles, Austin, 279n10
Milton, John, 47
Modthryth, 253n19. *See also* Thryth
(in *Beowulf*)
Mohammed, 265
Monaghan, Patricia, 275n22
Murphy, Patrick D., 231–32
Myth(s): adopted into genealogy, 237;
bird-women in, 228; charter, 180,
248; to comprehend void, 243; cos-

mological, 246; in *Custance*,
252n13; deep past of, 190; defined,
179, 245–46; feminist, of the Neo-
lithic, 231; of hero's arrival, 270–
71n6; inadequate as data for recon-
structing past, 280n13; incest, in
Apollonius of Tyre, 255n26; life-
enhancing, 241; Oedipus, 234–35;
primary, 246; restructuring of, for
particular culture, 222; Sedna, 215–
18; selective readings of, 229; as
source for romance, 175; as support
for author, 239; usefulness of, 242

Narrative subjects: embroidered on
fabric, 258–59
Navigium Isidis, 205, 272n10; cere-
monial setting adrift of boat, 207
Nehalennia (goddess), 272n9
Nelson, Gertrud Mueller, 275–76n23
Neolithic, 230, 241; desires, 228; femi-
nist, as revisionist cosmology, 233;
feminist vision of, 231; statues, 174,
227
Neumann, Erich, 187, 195, 278n7
Newstead, Helaine, 14
Nicholson, Peter, 127, 128
Notre-Dame de Confession Parée (in
Marseille), 186
Numinous power, 218; defined,
271n7; source of Goddess's, 247
Nuns: as healers, 264; self-mutilation
of, to prevent rape, 24–25
Nut (goddess), 203

O'Keeffe, Katherine O'Brien, 255n22
Offa I, 31, 249n2; *Life* as earliest ver-
sion of accused queen tale-type in
Castaway Queen story, 32–33; and
Offa II, 253–54n19, 254nn20, 22
"Offa-Constance Saga": Mediterra-
nean roots of, 182
Office of the Virgin, 271n8
Offspring of romance heroine: as his-
torical personage, 12
Ogg, Saint: and his Virgin, 4, 221

Ogilvy, J. D. A., 182
Olson, Carl, 236, 237
Ondaatje, Michael, 4
Orenstein, Gloria Feman, 240
Osiris (god), 187, 199–200, 201; find-
ing of, 204
Otto, Rudolph, 271n7
Our Lady of Solitude, 197
Overing, Gillian, 253n18, 254n20,
255n23
Ovid: story of Canacee in *Heroides*,
262
Owen, D. D. R., 258

Pagan past: link between Christian
romance and, 175
Paleolithic female statues, 227–28
Papal dispensations: to allow consan-
guinous marriage, 42
Paris, Gaston, 251n10
Paris, Ginette, 192
Pastourelle, French, 250n6
Patriarchal oppression, 239
Patriarchy, 243; as cultural construc-
tion, 231; rise of, 233
Patricide, 234
Paul, Saint: opposition to Diana (god-
dess), 193
Pausanias, 191
Peace-weaver, 31
Penance, 261–62
Pericles, 8
Perry, Ben Edwin, 36–37, 38, 208, 209,
255nn25–27
Peter, Saint, 38
Petrarch, 252n14, 273n15
Physiologus, 259
Plot: Accused Queen, 11–12; attached
to historical situation, 177; Cast-
away Queen, 27; Castaway Queen,
modified in *Florence*, 11; double
journey, 28–29; genealogical, 177
Plot event: exchange of letters, 28;
false accusation, 6; forged letter, 10;
framed for murder, 8; hands cut off, 8
Plutarch: Isis history, 201

Portugal: Madonna procession, 186
Postino, Il (film), 4–5
Poulain, Dominique, 186
Power: and severing of hands, 249n2;
    of women, 6
Power structure: ambiguities of, in
    Custance, 128
Primack, Joel R., 245
Pronunciation: in *Emaré*, 52
Protagonist-saviour: successful, in
    Romola, 221
Provence: legend of two Maries, 183–
    85
Psychotropic drugs, 243–44
Ptolemaic dynasty: incest in, 201

Quest: for adventure, distinct from
    setting adrift, 48; associated with
    bird figures, 228; for beloved, 200;
    female, transformed into son's birth
    story, 177; for the Goddess, 175,
    233, 235–36; Isis's, to gather Osiris's
    parts, 201; spiritual, 244, 248; of
    woman, 20

Ra: site in Provence, 185
Radway, Janice A., 18–19
Rank, Otto, 29, 38, 249n2, 253n17
Rape, 23; in classical stories, 250n6;
    in French pastourelles, 250n6; in
    modern romance, 43; prevented
    by Mary, 210, 206; in story told by
    Aesop, 208
Raptus violentiae, 262
Rasmussen, Knud, 216
Ratis: site in Provence, 185
Reardon, B. P., 176, 177
Reinhard, J. R., 46–47, 48
Renfrew, Colin, 240, 274n18, 277n3,
    280n12
Renoir, Alain, 254n22
Richards, Earl Jeffrey, 263
Richmond, Velma Bourgeois, 8
Rickert, Edith (editor of *Emaré*), 189–
    90; incest in *Emaré*, 34, 36; location
    of *Emaré* in England, 36, 182,

254n22, 274n16; location of ms.
    dialect, 10, 52; ramifications of
    Emaré, 29, 30; recognition scene in
    Emaré, 39; textual notes to *Emaré*,
    257–61n1; Thryth digression in
    Beowulf, 32–33; woman in boat
    theme, 183–84, 206
Ritual: as communicative activity,
    276n24; as precedent for beliefs, 228
Robert, Ulysse, 251n10
Roberts, Nanette McNiff, 17
Robinson, Fred C., 30, 253n19,
    254n20
Roche, Paul, 192
Rock carvings: depiction of men and
    women, 275n21
Roddy, Kevin, 252n13
Rodriguez, Jeanette, 236, 244, 278n9,
    282n18
Roger of Wendover, 24–25
Rohde, Erwin, 255n25
Romance: as allegory, 19; appeal to au-
    dience of Middle Ages, 49; Arthu-
    rian, and incest in, 44–45; attached
    to historical situation, 40, 177; audi-
    ence of woman-centered, 43–44;
    Castaway Queen, classical roots
    of, 182; classical, and affinities to
    miracles of the Virgin, 204; and clas-
    sical associations, 175, 209, as con-
    duit for social concerns, 41; distinct
    from real dangers, 25; early, 222; as
    escape, 18–19; female- vs. male-
    centered, 21–23, 27; formula for, 15;
    functioning of families, relation to,
    25–26; happy ending of, 15–16, 43,
    248; ideal Greek, 176; Greek, and re-
    lation to Isis, 203; link between
    pagan past and Christian, 175; liter-
    ary association with earlier texts,
    176; male-centered, 21–23; and
    Marxian view of history, 16; metri-
    cal, and preference for formula over
    originality, 250n4; mutilation of
    hands renders protagonist helpless,
    218; non-gender-specific definition

of, 15; religious aspect of, 179–80; role of males in, 14–15; similarities between medieval and modern, 18; stanza form, 52; themes in *Romola*, 221–22; typical outcome, 9; verse structure of, 14–15; woman-centered, 22–23, 48
—medieval: connected to the Goddess, 241; defined, 14–17; distinct from *The Mill on the Floss*, 221; plot of, 207; woman adrift theme in, 249n1
—modern, 251n11; defined, 14, 17–18; rape scenes in, 43
Romance as propaganda, 203
Romance heroine: associated with the Goddess, 174, 177; cult destination for, 204; Middle English, 205; roles of, 17
Romance languages, 267–68; influence on romance, 14
Roman matrons: Isis-worship of, 274–75n19
Romany race, patron saint of, 184
Rome: as location of Isis cult, 187
Royal succession: through the woman, 41
Rudd, Niall, 198–99
Ruether, Rosemary R., 233, 274n18
Rumble, Thomas C., 52, 261
Rupprecht, Carol Schreier, 281n15

Sacrifice: of animals, in lieu of maidens, 219; human, 278n8; human, to Artemis, 192–93; of maidens, 219, 220; primitive, associated with Oedipus, 234
Sacrificed maiden: transformation into saviour goddess, 220
Sacrificial ritual for goddesses, 191
Saint as healer, 8
Saints' lives: distinct from Castaway Queen, 204
Salmony, Alfred, 277n2
Sanctuary, 28, 29
Santa Maria della Navicella (church in Rome), 186

Sara, Saint (Egyptian), 184–85, 187, 188; ceremony with, 186
Satan: depicted as serpent with woman's face, 266, 267
Satanism, 240
Saviour god, 239
Scheps, Walter, 128, 267
Schibanoff, Susan, 27
Schick, Von. J., 38, 182–83, 274n16
Schlauch, Margaret: Accused Queen theme, 11–12, 176, 249n1, 255n24, 263; appreciation of woman-centered romances, 8; location of story-type in England, 36, 274n16; matriarchy, 41; Offa stories, 254n21; ramifications of tale, 29–30; retells *La Belle Hélène*, 39; severed hands, 214
Schulenberg, Jane Tibbetts, 23–25
Schwabe, G. T., 186
Sea as arbiter of justice, 46, 256n31
Sea-burial: distinct from setting adrift, 48
Sea-exposure, 46
Sea-journey, 271n6
Sea-voyage: in Sedna legend, 215
Second Council of Nicaea, 271n7
Sedna, 181, 217, 275n22; as maiden sacrifice, 219; as mistress of sea-creatures, 217; mutilation of hands, 215–18; subject of women's art, 216
Self-mutilation: as preferable to rape, 23–25
Semitic descendants of Indo-Europeans, 240
Sequanna (goddess of Seine), 181, 189; resemblance to Virgin Mary, 193
Set (god), 201
Setting adrift: of criminals or presumed criminals, 46–47; distinct from quest for adventure and sea-burial, 48; of innocent persons unwanted in community, 46–47; as legal punishment in Middle Ages, 45–47; as male control, 177; of non-criminals placed in God's hands, 46; worldwide folklore on, 253n17

Severs, J. Burke, 252n15
Sexual violence: in Sedna legend, 215–18
Shakespeare, William, 8
Shaman(s), 215, 243; Sedna placated by, 217–18
Shamanic rock carvings, 214–15
Shamanism, 232–33, 235, 238; associated with bird figures, 228
Ship: associated with archaic Goddess, 211; as emblem for Isis, 214–15; in secret initiation rites of Isis, 205
Simpson, Jacqueline, 33–34, 254n21
Sinfrea (word in *Beowulf*), 254n20
Sir Gawain and the Green Knight: as feminized male-centered romance, 22
Sirius (star), 200
Sir Orfeo: as male-centered romance, 21–22; turned into romance, 16–17
Sisam, Kenneth, 30, 253n19, 254n19
Smit, Johannes Wilhelmus, 252n13
Smithers, G. V., 259
Social concerns: reflection of, in romances, 41
Social structures: of early societies, 228, 230
Solmsen, Friedrich, 201, 203
Sophia (personification of Wisdom), 279n9
Sophocles, 192
Sources: remodeled into medieval romance by current concerns, 48
Southern, R. W., 40
Speirs, John, 258
Spica (star), 195, 200; temple of Artemis oriented on, 191
Spong, John Shelby, 177–78, 179, 270n5, 278n9
Spretnak, Charlene, 239, 240, 280–81n13
Starhawk, 239, 281n16
Statues: of human beings, 228; paleolithic geese, 227
Steinfells, Peter, 239
Stella maris, 179
Stenton, F. M. , 33

Stevick, Robert D., 259
Stone, Merlin, 233, 240, 270n5, 274n18, 277n2, 278n7, 280n13
Straus, Barrie Ruth, 255n22
Structures, formal: maintained in translations, 250n5
Suicide: as preferable to rape, 24
Supreme Being, 232
Symbols of the Goddess: links between, and trees, 278n7

Tail-rhyme stanza: in *Emaré,* 52; in *Florence,* 93
Tale-type, 7; Apollonius, 27–28; Calumniated Wife, 7; Clementine, 27–28; Constance cycle, 7; Father-Incest, insufficient definition of, 29; Handless Maiden, 249n2
—Accused Queen, 7–8; source in *Lives of the Two Offas,* 32–33; variants of, 29
—Calumniated Queen, 43; insufficient definition, 29
Tannahill, Reay, 274n19
Theophany, 228
Thomas, Henry, 259
Thomas of Erceldoun, 9, 25, 250n5
Thompson, Janet, 281n14
Threat: of incest or male aggression, 7
Thryth (in *Beowulf*), 30 36, 182, 253–54n19, 254n20
Tiberius, 275n19
Tlecuauhtlacupeuh (goddess), 244, 282n18
Toews, John E., 235
Tonantzin (Aztec earth goddess), 278n9
Totemic banquet, 234
Totemism, 234
Townsend, Joan B., 228, 230–31, 239, 240, 277n5
Transcendence, 231, 232, 242, 247; as presented by Eliade, 278n6; valorized over chaotic flux, 229–30
Translation, philosophy of, 51, 250n5
Tree(s), 243; and other Goddess symbols, links between, 278n7

Trevet, Nicholas, 10, 251n7
Trial by ordeal, 268
Tristram and Isolde, 259
Turner, Edith, 270n1
Turner, Victor, 270n1
Typhon (god), 201

Unicorn Tapestry, 259
Universe, extension of, 281n16

Venus (goddess), 181
Venus (planet), 200
Venus Anadyomene, 198, 199
"Venus" figures, 211, 276n1
Verse form, 8
Vézelay: as location of Mary Magdalen's remains, 187–88
Via Ignatia (pilgrimage route), 190, 264
Vincent de Beauvais, 16
Violence: in Aphrodite's birth legend, 199; gendered and domestic, 23–27; sexual, in French pastourelles, 250n6
Virgin: Christian and pagan, 191; miracles of, distinct from Castaway Queen romance, 204
Virgin goddess of the Mediterranean (Isis), 199
Virginity: maintaining at all costs, 24; as protection against danger, 47; as status marker, 23
Virgin of Guadalupe, 244, 278–79n9, 282n18; as public art, 196; representations of, 195
Virgo (constellation), 191, 195, 200

Wailes, Bernard, 239
Wallensköld, A., 190, 263
Walsh, P. G., 202–3, 204–5
Warner, Marina, 184, 185, 191, 244, 270n5, 271n8, 273nn12, 15, 279n9
Wasserman, Julian N., 206
Wauquelin, Jean, 39
Wealhtheow (in *Beowulf*), 30
Weaver, Mary Jo, 231, 235

Weisl, Angela Jane, 251n11
Wentersdorf, Karl P., 255n22
Whitehouse, David, 218, 277n2
Whitehouse, Ruth, 218, 277n2
Wicca, 240
"Wife's Lament, The," 254–55n22
Wild, Robert A., 272n10, 274n16
Wilderness, 254n22; as refuge from threat, 7
Wilson, Evelyn Faye, 13, 251n10
Witchcraft, 241; practitioners of, 277n4
Witches, feminist, 240
Witt, Rex E., 206
Wogan-Browne, Jocelyn, 255–56n29
Woman adrift: in *Apollonius of Tyre*, 37, 175; as archetypal symbol, 21; in author's experience, 237; cast ashore at holy site, 207; in Castaway Queen tale-type, 40–41; with child, 28; and family dysfunction, 44; in Gower's *Constance*, 252–53n16; as helpless maiden, 214, 220; history of, 174; human protagonist, 247; as icon of female power, 173; as image of nonoppressive meeting of cultures, 246; incorporated into parentage stories of great men, 39, 180; in *Life of Aesop*, 207; in *Life of St. Kentigern*, 40; in *The Mill on the Floss*, 221; not fiction, 219–20; in Offa legend, 32, 254n22; omitted in Christine de Pisan's version of *Florence*, 92; oral vs. written tales of, 176; relation to Isis ritual, 210; in *Romola*, 221; "The Russian King's Daughter," 253n17; as soul, 45; as theme, 3–8, 10
Woman afloat: divine, 190; transcending cultures, 246
Woman in a boat, 216; divine, 181; in Iron Age rock carvings, 214; Sequanna statue, 189
Woman in the wheat, 245, 279n11
Woman's right to select own husband, 43

Woman's sea journey, 201
Women: as authors of own lives, 18; as
    protagonists of romance, 9, 17–23;
    as victims in romance, 17, 18; as
    victims of family violence, 21
World Tree, 232–33

Xenophon of Ephesus, 203
Xtabay (Yucatecan bird-goddess),
    228

Zimmerman, J. E., 187

MARIJANE OSBORN teaches poetry and medieval literature in the Department of English at the University of California, Davis, and is director of the UCD Medieval Studies Program. Author or co-author of five books—three on *Beowulf*, one on runes, and one on landscapes in medieval stories—she has also contributed to various other books, has published numerous poems, translations, and articles on a variety of subjects, and is currently working on a book about Chaucer and his astrolabe.